I0539013

RECLAMATION

HUGH A. FLOWERS

Copyright © 2015 Hugh A. Flowers
All rights reserved.

~~~~

No part of this book may be reproduced or transmitted or transferred in any
form or by any means, graphic, electronic, mechanical, including photocopying,
recording, taping or by any information storage retrieval system or device,
without the permission in writing by the author
Any resemblance to actual people and events is purely coincidental.
This is a work of fiction.

Paperback-Press
an imprint of A & S Publishing
A & S Holmes, Inc.

ISBN: 0692515259
ISBN-13: 978-0692515259

ACKNOWLEDGMENTS

I'd like to give a special thank you to Nathalie Kelley for once again painting the perfect cover art for this book. You did a wonderful job.

My thanks also goes out to Norma Eaton for her editing help. Your time is appreciated.

Sharon Kizziah-Holmes, thank you for everything. You and Paperback-Press made publishing this novel possible. You are a professional in every way.

CONTENTS

CHAPTER 1

John Bridges lay dazed in his car and tried to clear his head. He gradually realized he had been in a wreck and gingerly began moving his arms and legs trying to determine how badly he had been hurt. He soon realized he was hanging upside down from his seat harness. The car's engine was making a racket, as if the fan blades were striking metal, so he fumbled around in the dark until he shut off the engine, stopping the noise.

John couldn't see anything through the smashed windshield except a glow that told him his headlights were still working. He tried to move out of the car, but had forgotten that he was still in the seat belt harness. After what seemed an eternity, he found the release button and dropped to the roof of the car where he found the driver's door stuck. Uttering an oath, he then tried the passenger door which opened after he gave it a firm kick allowing him to crawl out of the vehicle.

John lay on the ground for a moment in an attempt to get his breath back and his mind functioning properly.

Eventually, he then sat up beside the car and again felt his body for any injures he might have missed before. He gave a sigh of relief when his only obvious injury was a small cut above his left eye, probably caused by the air bag inflating during the crash.

John had been on his way to St. Louis for a business meeting the following morning when he decided to stop for coffee, and was following another car on the exit ramp off of I-44 when there was an explosion of bright light just ahead of both vehicles, which he tried to avoid by braking hard.

Suddenly the bright light was gone and his headlights showed trees quickly approaching just ahead. Almost immediately he felt and heard the car striking the trees with a terrible thumping and screeching of tearing metal. The car started to tumble end-over-end while the air bag deployed in an explosion of white, followed by a severe crunch as the vehicle struck the ground and settled onto its top.

Using the car for support, he got to his feet and looked toward the front of the vehicle. Its remaining headlight revealed a stark outline of trees. He looked around, searching for any source of nearby help when he detected a faint glow through the trees behind his car.

The night was pitch black without even the moon's faint light to aid him, so John decided to crawl back into the car for a flashlight. He then started through the trees toward the glow of light. As he got closer to the glow he could hear a hum, which got louder as he approached.

His flashlight revealed a car with its nose down into the ground at about a 45-degree angle with its rear in the air, supported by tree branches. The engine was still running and steam was coming from under the hood, eerily lit by the car's headlights hitting the ground.

The vehicle was an older model Chrysler sedan, which seemed to have weathered the crash through the trees better than his lighter Toyota coupe. He pointed his flashlight up into the car where a motionless woman was lying against the steering wheel.

John opened the door and made the 5-foot climb up into the car where he managed to turn the engine off. The sudden silence was punctuated by the ticking of an overheated engine. He checked her for any obvious broken bones and other injuries before attempting to release her lap belt. He was considering the best way to get her out of the car when a flash of brown and white came up over the back seat and hit him in the chest, knocking him out of the car and sending him crashing onto the ground on his back.

John lay stunned for a moment trying to catch his breath when he was startled again by having his face licked by a very friendly beagle. After catching his breath and gathering his wits, he petted the dog while making sure it was uninjured before climbing back into the car. He cautiously began lowering the woman to the ground by slowly letting the woman's body slide down feet first while he pulled her into his arms.

This procedure worked without a hitch, except the dog made a pest of itself barking and jumping up at the woman as she was lowered. When he had her stretched out on the ground a safe distance from the vehicle, he then examined her as best he could. He found no broken bones; however, she may have received some cracked ribs. Her only apparent injury was a large bruise over her right eye that was starting to turn purple.

John couldn't help but notice that she was an attractive woman, but his thoughts were interrupted by a soft moan coming from the car, causing the dog to start barking again. He hurriedly climbed back into the Chrysler, where he found two other people in the back seat. After he had separated the individuals as best he could, he found that they were a girl and a smaller boy.

John lifted the boy out of the back seat and carefully lowered him out of the car. The boy was moaning when he laid him beside the woman, but John decided that before tending to him he should go back for the girl. She was heavier and more bulky than the boy, which made it harder to get her out of the car. However, he got her down safely and placed beside the other two.

After an examination of the boy and girl he found no evidence of broken bones and decided they must have struck their heads when the car left the road. He wearily sat down beside them with his back resting against a tree trunk, hoping they would soon regain consciousness.

John was looking around at his surroundings, which consisted of heavy forest growth, when he realized that there was no sound other than the gentle wind in the trees. It was late summer and there should have been lots of night insect noises. He then realized that he also couldn't hear any highway sounds.

He was thinking this is really weird when the small hairs on the back of his neck rose. When the dog started growling, John grabbed the flashlight and pointed its beam in the direction the dog was looking, where he caught a flash of movement through the trees. The dog immediately got to its feet and started barking in the direction of the movement. He quickly told the dog to stay and happily it obeyed. After what he had already experienced, he didn't want to go chasing a dog through the trees.

John briefly thought about looking for help, but he didn't want to leave the three he had just rescued. It was too dark and he might never find them again, and also there was the possible danger from the unknown presence he had just seen. He had heard that black bears had been spotted near here, so he decided he had better stay with them and see what dawn would bring. He leaned back against the tree, resting while he waited for them to wake up, but he was more exhausted than he realized because he soon fell asleep.

He awoke when he felt a gentle nudge and opened his eyes to find an angel with a blackened eye bending over him with a concerned expression on her face.

"What happened?" she whispered.

He looked at her in surprise, rubbing his eyes, before he realized it was the woman from the wreck. "How is your head? That bruise on your eye looks bad!"

She raised her hand to her eye and flinched. "Ooh, that's sore." She then felt around her head and body for other injuries.

While she was checking herself out he was admiring what he saw. He had previously noticed she was an attractive woman, but in the daylight she was really striking. She appeared to be in her mid 30's, with blond hair and a taut body that was evidently the result of a lot of exercise. She stood at almost six feet in height and the black eye did little to detract from her beauty.

He looked over at the children and asked, "Are they alright?"

"I woke them earlier and they appeared to be okay, so I decided to let them sleep," she whispered.

John smiled while holding out his hand. "We should introduce ourselves. I'm John Bridges and was on my way to St. Louis from my home in Springfield."

She grinned slightly and gripped his hand before answering, "I'm Sarah Lancaster and my children and I were returning home from a visit with my mother in St. James. That's Randy and Lillie. He turned nine last month, and Lillie is sixteen going on twenty," she added with a rueful smile.

Now that the sun was up he could see more of his surroundings, which appeared to be mostly mature pine trees with some larger hardwoods mixed in. There was little brush as the pine needles and the overhead tree canopy had smothered other growth.

Bridges rubbed his nose thoughtfully before asking. "What do you remember of the accident?"

Sarah considered a moment before answering. "I remember a blinding light, then a sense of falling and crashing sounds. The next thing I remember was waking up on the ground here."

"That's pretty much my impression of the crash too, except that I got you all out of the car with the help of the dog."

She chuckled at the thought. "I bet Patches was a lot of help."

He then told her what had occurred that night where he had seen the unknown presence. "Can you get the dog to stay with the kids while we look around and see if we can get some answers before they wake up?"

Sarah nodded her head and whispered, "Patches! Stay, with the kids!"

Patches immediately lay down beside the boy. John was looking up trying to determine how the car had arrived here. Apparently, the

Chrysler had first hit the branches about eighteen feet above the ground, and then the tree damage continued downward at an angle to where the car now rested.

Bridges looked at the evidence with unbelieving eyes. "This makes no sense at all! This can't happen! Your car looks like it appeared out of thin air and just crashed here." He shook his head slowly before continuing. "It's a good thing we were not going very fast when this happened."

He then snapped his fingers as a sudden thought occurred to him. He pointed at several nearby tall trees. "I'm going to try to climb one of these trees to get a better look at our surroundings and maybe I can tell where we're at."

He then picked a maple tree with low branches and began to climb until he got as high as the branches allowed. After slowly looking around in all directions, he climbed down and returned to Sarah.

John shook his head while looking at her in confusion. "Something's not right, I have no idea where we are. I've looked in all directions and there is no evidence of any roads, smoke, radio towers, or flashes of light... Nothing! Nothing but trees and rolling hills. It's like we're in Missouri but without any people or their works."

They were interrupted by a small voice. "I'm hungry. What are we doing here?"

Randy was sitting up and rubbing his eyes, as the dog started jumping and barking excitedly at the boy.

Lillie sat up then and stretched, but when she became aware of her surroundings, she looked at her mother and demanded, "Mom! What's happened?"

Sarah held out her hands to both her children who came to her. As she held her children to her, she turned to John who was standing nearby.

"This is John Bridges and both our cars were involved in an accident last night."

John smiled at the children as he asked, "How do you feel; any sore spots?"

Both of the children shook their heads, but then Lillie looked up at John with accusing eyes. "Did you hit us and cause the accident?"

Sarah hugged Lillie and explained, "No, Mr. Bridges had nothing to do with the accident. We really don't know what caused the wreck."

In confusion, Lillie looked at both her mother and John. He gave Sarah a questioning look, who then nodded for him to speak.

"We don't know what's happened and there's no sign of the highway anywhere."

Lillie and Randy both started to talk at once.

"What? You've got to be kidding! Mom! What's he saying?"

Sarah hugged them again and while looking into their eyes spoke earnestly, "Now listen to me! John and I did some exploring while you've been sleeping. There is just no evidence of anybody anywhere near here."

John thought he should get their minds on something else and suggested, "Hey, why don't we check out my car? Maybe it can tell us something."

Sarah smiled in understanding and nodded her head. "Come on kids, lets follow John and maybe we can learn something."

John cautioned everyone, "We better stay close as I've heard there may be bears near here."

When they reached his car they found the same kind of damage to the trees, except that his car had tumbled and had done more damage, both to the trees and to the vehicle.

John stared at the trees, trying to make sense of what he was seeing. He suddenly had a thought. "I'm going to try something."

John carefully crawled into the Toyota, avoiding the broken glass, and turned the radio on with the hope it still had power. The radio light came on, but when he tried the seek function for stations he had no luck. He then tried a manual scan for either an AM or FM station, but got nothing but dead air static. After turning off the radio, he crawled back out of the car and shook his head in frustration.

Sarah frowned in disappointment, but then had a thought. "What if others had this same thing happen to them? If so, then their vehicles should be nearby."

John hesitated a moment before he spoke. "I thank that's a good idea. Let's start a search pattern around the crash sites and see if we can find something."

They agreed, and following John's instructions they spread out within close sight of each other and returned through the trees in hopes of finding some trace of a highway or another vehicle. After about thirty minutes they gave up and started a circular sweep back in the direction they had just come. They had been walking about fifteen minutes when they encountered another wreck. John and the others stopped and stared at the vehicle with both hope and trepidation.

John then approached the wreckage and looked inside. He immediately recoiled and motioned the others away.

"Sarah keep the kids away, the driver's dead with a tree branch through his chest. He looks like he's been dead a long time as there's only a skeleton left." John considered a moment before adding... "The van's an older model, maybe an early '90's Ford truck, so he could have been dead for several years."

They tried the rear door which opened after a couple of hard pulls. Inside they found several boxes and crates which they immediately started opening. After John opened the first box, he turned to the family with a grin on his face. "It's an early Christmas! This must be an army surplus shipment as this box has military fatigue uniforms."

Besides the uniforms they found packs, canteens, web belts, shoes, and pup tents. They decided to leave everything as they found it until they completed their search pattern. However, they made a complete circle without finding anything else of interest and finally gave up the search.

After they returned to the Chrysler, John spoke. "Let's sit down and try to make sense of what we've found. As Dorothy said in the Wizard of Oz, 'we ain't in Kansas anymore', and we're certainly not in Missouri as we knew it. I know this is beyond anything we have ever experienced before, but we have to be open and ready for whatever comes our way. Sarah, what's your opinion?"

The family looked at him with stunned expressions. Both mother and daughter looked at each other with concerned expressions until Sarah finally sighed and gave John a frustrated look. "I'm in general agreement, what do you suggest?"

"We need to make a plan. I don't think help is anywhere near and we have to take charge and try to find our own way out of here. Let's get all our possessions together to see what we've got. I'll help you get your things out of your car and you can help me with mine."

CHAPTER 2

They started by removing everything from the Toyota, and brought what they had gathered back to the clearing next to the Chrysler. They then stripped that car of anything of value. Sarah suggested they segregate food items, clothing, and tools. She also noted a road atlas from John's car could be helpful in their travels.

John first looked at the food items. "We don't have much here, just some left over roast beef, brownies, a partial bag of chips, and almost a full liter bottle of coke." He looked at his watch and noted it was after noon. "I bet everyone's hungry, so let's sit down, relax, eat something, and get better acquainted."

Randy and Lillie both voiced their agreement as the mention of food made them aware they had eaten nothing since the previous day. Sarah then pointed to the roast. "This must be eaten first. John, why don't you drag that small log over here so we can sit together, and then after we eat a snack we can decide what we should do."

John smiled and then winked at Randy. "Come on Randy, help me move that log."

Later, after the group had finished their snack, John was helping Sarah dispose of their waste while the kids were playing with Patches. He attempted to become closer to her by asking some personal questions.

"I've never been married, but it must be nice to have children," and then before thinking, he blurted, "Where's their father?"

Sarah looked down and then set her jaw while looking him in the eyes. "He was killed almost two years ago in a training accident at Ft. Leonard Wood. It's been hard since Sam died, but he had enough insurance to take care of our needs."

John's ears were red with embarrassment as he apologized.

"I'm sorry about your husband, but even more, that I asked such a fool question." He then looked over at the two children. "However, you still have your kids."

Sarah slowly smiled as she looked at her children. "Yes, Randy reminds me more each day of Sam, and Lillie has been a help since he died."

They gathered around the possessions they had segregated. The only other nonfood items of value between the two cars were an old blanket from the Chrysler, and from John's Toyota they retrieved from his luggage the matchbooks and soap he had collected from the various hotels where he had stayed, a shaving kit that contained some antiseptics, and a sewing kit.

John looked at the others and realized that everyone was dressed for the summer weather, and he drew their attention to their attire. "We should decide which direction to take in our search for help. It's late summer now, and we only have about sixty days left of warm weather here, assuming that the climate is the same here as where we were before the crash. We're not dressed for cold weather, so I vote that we head south for warmer weather."

Sarah looked doubtfully at the endless forest. "How are we going to travel through that?"

John hesitated before answering. "The fastest and easiest method is by river raft, and if we're still in Missouri, then the Mississippi is less than 100 miles east of here."

Sarah looked at her two children and nodded her head. "Yes, I think you're right. If we don't find the river in a week or so, we should probably start south."

John nodded his head in agreement. "That should be enough time to decide if there's a Mississippi River here. However, before we leave I think we should go back to the truck and pick out things we need for our trip."

From the truck, they took what equipment and clothing they could carry and then returned to camp to pack everything they needed.

John looked at the variety of items that needed to fit inside the packs and shook his head in confusion. He turned to Sarah who was watching him with a smile on her face. "What! Is my inexperience that obvious?"

"Well, you do look a little lost," she said with a smile. "We've done this before. Remember we are an army family. Just watch us and then we'll help you if needed."

John watched as they placed items not immediately needed first into the pack, such as extra shoes and uniforms. Next were the other items and finally a half pup tent was rolled and fastened to the top of the pack.

He picked up Sarah's pack and checked its weight. "Wow, do you thank you can carry this? It must weigh thirty pounds."

Sarah nodded her head in agreement. "Yes, but I'm carrying Randy's extra shoes and uniforms and they're not light."

John then picked up Lillie's pack and compared the weight, noting that hers was lighter. "I'll take his extra shoes and one set of his uniforms. I'm bigger and should be able to handle the extra weight. If I can't we'll just divide it up again 'till we get it right."

The only person with extra shoes and two extra sets of uniforms was Randy, and he certainly couldn't carry the extra weight.

After John's pack was filled he raised it tentatively. "Well, it's not light, but I thank I can handle it." He then looked at his watch and checked the time. "It's getting late. Why not camp here tonight and get an early start tomorrow?"

Sarah nodded her head in agreement and then told Lillie and Randy to search for some wood for a campfire. They didn't need the fire for warmth, but it would give them a nightlight and might keep away any wild animals. Sarah started to prepare a fire pit and John began dragging small logs for seating near the fire.

That night they bedded down after a meager supper. John's stomach was protesting, but he put that aside as the rest of the party didn't complain. John had little survival skills, and he had only a few camping trips with his father to guide his actions. What was really worrying him was his sorry physical shape. His CPA accounting work had required little physical exertion and since he was not one to make time for exercise, he was about twenty-five pounds overweight. Sarah and her children looked in far better physical shape.

They decided to initially follow the ridgeline, as it appeared to be easier walking because of the heavy tree growth, and if needed they could pick a more direct line of travel eastward. John led the way, but Patches quickly roamed ahead of the group with her nose to the ground. He kept looking around, but couldn't detect any sign of what had caused the mysterious movement the first night. Even so, he still had an uneasy feeling of something or someone watching them.

After picking their way through the forest for about an hour, John called a rest stop. The boys went to one side of the ridge while the girls took the other. When they all returned to the ridgeline, Sarah came over to John and spoke softly, while handing him the liter of coke they were sharing until water was found.

"Have you given any thought to food when our supply runs out?"

"Yes, but all I can think of is roots and berries, and I'm not sure where to look or what's good to eat. How good a hunter is Patches?"

Sarah laughed, "She's a good rabbit dog, if there's any to catch, but we should have no trouble if the plant flora is not much different from where we left. My husband was a survival expert and he taught us much of what he knew on the many camping trips we took together." Then with a twinkle in her eyes she added, "However, we always brought along toilet tissue before."

John hugged Sarah and smiled. "Well, expert! Why didn't you speak up before now?"

She shook her head while giving him a rueful smile. "I wasn't sure how you would react and I didn't know how much experience you had, so I let things ride for a while. Besides, things were going pretty well with your leadership and the kids need a strong male influence."

They pushed on, taking breaks as needed until they came across a small stream where they decided to take a noon break for lunch and rest. It was shady and cool and looked like a good place to fill their empty canteens. They sat down and finished the remainder of the brownies, while Patches hunted downstream.

John looked at his surroundings with a satisfied grin, and sighed. "I'm really enjoying myself. No more pressure to meet deadlines and this has been a perfect day to hike through the woods."

He pulled the road atlas from his pack looking for any large streams or rivers in their path, when he was interrupted by the loud braying of a beagle on scent not far downstream from them. They all looked at each other with hopeful expressions as the sound continued and then abruptly stopped.

Randy jumped up and started running downstream. "She's got something, I bet she's got something for sure."

Randy wasn't gone very long before he and Patches returned with game. Sarah reached down and took the animal from Patches' mouth.

"It looks like a small rabbit, only the ears are too small," she said while looking at the others with a smile on her face as she held up the carcass.

"Well, at least now we know that there's game to eat in these woods," John said while affectingly rubbing Patches' ears. "Let's let her have this one and press on eastward, we need to make some more miles today."

The remainder of the day passed quickly and when they came upon a small river in the late afternoon they decided to camp for the night. The two children quickly started to make camp, gathering wood, and unpacking their tents to use as ground sheets, since there appeared to be no need for shelter tonight.

The dog immediately started hunting again and it wasn't long before he returned with two more of the rabbit like creatures. John gutted and skinned them out with his pocketknife, and then placed them on a spit over the campfire.

Sarah and her children searched the area for edible roots and berries, and by the time the meat was roasted to perfection they had returned with an assortment of tempting morsels. The family looked doubtfully at the roast meat, and then at John, as if asking why don't you go first?

He grinned and then picked up his share of the meat. "Okay, you ninnies. I'll go first."

The meat had a slightly sweet taste; different from his memory of rabbit he had eaten many years ago. The others wanted their share upon seeing the obvious enjoyment on John's face. However, whether it was rabbit or rat, the family group found the taste to their liking and finished the meal with gusto.

Patches returned to the camp by meals end and appeared to have satisfied her own hunger pangs. She lay down next to Randy where he was sitting on a log, which soon became her habit. They had arranged their bedding around the fire, but not too close as the nights were still fairly warm. The fire seemed to give them a sense of security without the hassle of flying bugs. The lack of night sounds still bothered John and the others, but it did have its advantages.

Sarah was thinking about John as she lay next to the fire awaiting sleep. He seemed to be a nice man and was wonderful with the children. Besides that, he was handsome, although a little overweight. It had been some time since she had thought about a man like this, not since her husband died, and she felt a little guilty.

John and the others were asleep only a short time when Patches' growling awakened them. John looked over to where she was standing with her hackles raised, looking off into the darkness. He grabbed for his flashlight and a hefty walking stick he had picked up that day, and moved over to where Patches was standing.

He reached down and placed his hand on her head and spoke softly, "What's out there girl? What do you see?"

He shined his flashlight beam in the direction where the dog was staring and moved the light around but saw no movement. By this time the entire camp was up and had moved behind John.

Sarah grabbed his arm and whispered, "What is it?"

"I don't know. Patches seems to think there's something out there but I haven't seen anything."

He finally shook his head and spoke to the others. "We might as well go back to sleep. If it comes back, Patches will let us know."

The new day came without further disturbance. John allowed everyone the use of his toothbrush and what little toothpaste he had. He rubbed his face, which now had three days of beard stubble, as he prepared to wash his face in the river water.

He looked over at Sarah as he finished. "This beard is starting to itch, but I might as well get used to it as my shaving cream wouldn't last long anyway. I've got a comb you 'all can use, but no hair brush."

Sarah smiled as she accepted the comb. "Thanks, my hair is getting tangled and feels like a rat's nest. If we don't find civilization fast, Lillie and I will have to cut our hair short to make it easier to care for."

They decided to only have one meal each day as it took too long gathering items to eat for three meals. After breaking camp and storing items in their packs, they started east again.

John groaned as they started hiking. "Boy, oh, boy, I'm sore in places I never knew I had muscles. You'd never know I'm only thirty the way I'm feeling now."

Sarah chuckled as she replied, "I'm hurting too, but mine is more from the beating I took in the car crash."

The kids echoed their mother's reply. They soon found themselves crossing several areas of grasslands as they followed a valley that generally led them eastward, but there still was no sign of habitation or other signs of civilization. They did cross several game trails along the valley floor, but caught no glimpses of what used them.

* * *

It was late afternoon of their fourth day when they came across an ideal camping spot at the end of a valley they had entered that day. A small waterfall was coming out of a hillside bluff and had formed a pool of water before continuing across the valley floor.

When the family caught sight of the still blue waters of the pool, they all whooped with glee and forgetting modesty, immediately removed their outer clothing and ran into the cool water. The pool was deep and they were able to swim within a few yards of the water's edge. Everyone was shouting their happiness as they played in the water, splashing each other, and forgetting there past discomforts as they soaked.

John was startled when Randy got out of the pool without any clothing and ran to play in the waterfall. He realized that they were almost naked in the water. He then looked over at Sarah and Lillie, who were both neck deep in the water.

"Look at Randy! Now what are we going to do?" he asked with a blush which extended to his ears.

Sarah and Lillie exchanged startled looks, and then swam together to shallower water where they could stand without exposing themselves. They whispered to each other while looking over at John from time to time. After several minutes they appeared to have come to a decision and turned to John.

Their faces were both red from embarrassment, but Sarah's voice was strong with resolve. "We agreed that you are now part of our family and, as such, an occasional glimpse of each other without clothes is unavoidable, especially in our situation. For safety's sake we may have to stay together, like now. We don't know yet what's out there and until we're sure, we have to take precautions."

The women then looked at each other, held hands, and with a determined look, walked out of the water dressed only in their bras and panties.

They stopped to pick up everyone's discarded clothing, but then hesitated, with Sarah looking at John. "We're going to wash our clothes. Could we use some of your soap?"

They then walked to the end of the pool spillway and began their task. John stood there dumbfounded for a few seconds, then left the water clad in only his boxer shorts, and after picking up a small bar of hotel soap from his pack, joined them.

John shared his soap with the women, and then shook his head. "This is a lot harder for me than you two. It might be easier if you both weren't so foxy looking," he said in obvious embarrassment. "However, I don't know why I'm making such a fuss. You're more dressed than if you were wearing a bikini."

Sarah and Lillie just looked at each other and shook their heads; although John thought he detected a smile on Sarah's face before she started scrubbing their clothes.

Later, Randy and Patches went hunting, while the others searched for edibles. It was well that their preferred campsites were also the best area to search for food. It wasn't long before they had gathered enough berries and roots for their supper, with enough left for a snack during their trek the next day.

Patches had found a new variety of game at this location that resembled a cross between a rabbit and a raccoon. It had the face of a raccoon, had fur and was the size of a large rabbit, but was tailless. Randy was excited as he detailed the fight the animal displayed as it was pursued by Patches. When roasted, the animal had the flavor more of a traditional rabbit, than what they had been eating before.

Randy suggested they start keeping the skins for later use. Since Randy had demonstrated his aptitude for hunting, the family agreed that he be their designated hunter and be responsible for the skins. Randy beamed with happiness at his family's recognition, especially when he was given the additional responsibility of caring for the only knife the group had.

That night as they sat around the campfire, they were voicing their joy at finding such a nice place. John looked over at Sarah. "Why not spend tomorrow here and rest up before continuing on? We've made good time and I think we can spare one more day."

The others immediately agreed and started to make plans for their small vacation from their journey. The next day, after a morning swim and a breakfast of berries, they started their planned tasks. John got his scissors out of his shaving kit and trimmed his beard, which didn't take long.

When Sarah saw what John was doing, she came over and inspected his work. "Not bad for not having a mirror, but you missed some spots."

John handed over the scissors and Sarah completed the trimming. When she handed the scissors back to John, she pointed to her hair. "Now you can cut my hair. It's too long and difficult to care for while we're camping out."

John frowned and shook his head. "But, I've never cut anyone's hair before. Why not let Lillie do it?"

Sarah smiled and then gave him a quick kiss on the cheek.

"I've thought of that, but I'm afraid of what she might do; besides I want you to do it. Lillie! Come over here and watch John cut my hair." When she came over, Sarah admonished. "You better make sure he does a good job, since he's going to cut your hair next."

John looked at Sarah's hair doubtfully. "Your hair is too beautiful for me to mess up. Are you sure you want me to do this?"

Sarah grabbed his shirt and pulled his face down to hers, looking into his eyes with her own blue eyes that held a hint of mischief, and said, "You better do a good job because you're the one who's going to have to look at it. Now do it right! I want it to be as short as yours."

John shook his head and decided that he wouldn't cut it that short and then looked at Lillie and silently mouthed no. He then tentatively started his cutting with the long hair in the back removed first. When the hair dropped off, Lillie groaned. However, she then shrugged her shoulders and made several suggestions as the cutting continued. Surprisingly, it wasn't long before he was finished. He and Lillie walked around Sarah several times, making some minute adjustments before they were both satisfied.

Sarah looked at them apprehensively. "How does it look?"

"Better than I thought it would when I started. Too bad we don't have a mirror so you can see how beautiful you look," John replied.

Lillie nodded her head at her mother. "It looks pretty and I want mine just like it," she said with a smile.

John groaned, but then with a forced smile he pointed to a place next to Sarah. "Sit down before I change my mind. At least now I have an example to guide me."

Lillie's hair was as dark as Sarah's was blond. She was also petite, while her mother was more Nordic. They just didn't seem to come from the same gene pool.

After he finished cutting Lillie's hair, Sarah looked it over carefully. "So this is how my hair looks. It's not as short as I asked for, but I like it better." She exclaimed with a smile.

"See, I knew you could do it with the right motivation." Then she threw her arms around him and gave him a long passionate kiss.

John finally pulled back from Sarah and looked at her with glazed eyes. "You continue to do that and I'll follow you anywhere."

Sarah slowly smiled, then wrapped her arms around him and placed her head on his shoulder. "No, we'll make this trip together, side by side."

They both turned when they heard Lillie sigh. With a smile on her face and tears in her eyes, she softly spoke, "Boy, that was a quick romance. You've only known him a week and already you've fallen in love."

Sarah held out her arms to Lillie and comforted her. "It's a lot easier when there are no distractions and we're together 24 hours a day. Besides, now that I know John I'm sure I would have eventually fallen in love with him if we had a longer courtship back home."

Lillie looked at her mother with tears streaming down her cheeks. "You've got your man, but what I am going to do? There doesn't appear to be anyone for me. In fact, the only two males I know of are John and Randy in this whole world."

Sarah looked over at John with a worried look on her face. "Yes, and we're the only two women!"

John tried to lighten the mood. "Let's don't jump to conclusions so soon. We haven't seen very much of the country yet and we may find others at any time."

He placed his arms around both women and gave them a hug and laughed. "When we do, you two just remember that I saw you first."

Lillie punched him in the ribs and smiled through her tears. "You dirty old man, you've already got yourself a woman."

CHAPTER 3

The following morning they continued their trek east, hopefully toward the great river that would take them south. Lillie continued the journey with a heavy heart, remembering her friends that she might never see again and uncertain of her future. She had just broken up with her last boyfriend the week before this adventure started, so she was not lonely for any particular male left behind. What concerned her was the uncertainty that she would find another man, compatible or not, in this new world.

Lillie watched her mother and John walking in front of the group. They were holding hands when the terrain allowed, and she realized that her mother hadn't been this happy since her father had died. There hadn't been any serious suitors since his death, although many had tried. Sarah just wasn't ready for a relationship until now. Lillie was only five when her real mother took off and abandoned her. Her father was in Germany at the time, so she was left with her grandparents until his return.

Her father was granted an early rotation back to a Stateside assignment so he could take care of her. She could only remember what her mother looked like from photos and had always considered Sarah her mother. Sarah had married her father eight months after his return and Randy was born about a year later.

Randy broke into her thoughts when he suddenly grabbed Lillie's arm and whispered, "What's wrong with Mom?"

She looked to where their mother was hip bumping John and then running ahead, laughing loudly. Lillie smiled down at Randy as she answered. "Mom's in love with John and sometimes you do goofy things when you're bitten by the love bug."

He snorted and shook his head. "She's sure acting crazy. I've never seen her do things like that before."

The day had started bright and sunny, but within minutes dark clouds had moved in and were now threatening rain. Suddenly, there was a nearby lightning strike and a loud explosion as the top of a tree disappeared. The group stood still in shock looking where the top of the tree had disappeared, when there was another lightning strike closer to them.

John shook himself out of his stupor and yelled for everyone to run towards a small clearing and lie down. While they lay on the ground the air was heavy with ozone as lightning strikes continued nearby, then gradually moved away as the storm continued on its way. They then heard a roar in the distance, increasing in volume as it approached them.

John jumped to his feet and yelled, "That's either heavy rain or hail, so we better find shelter fast! Let's run towards that bluff and hope we find something there."

The bluff was only about fifty yards away, but it seemed like 500, as the sound kept getting louder behind them. When they reached the bluff they didn't immediately find a cave, but there was a short ledge about seven feet off the ground that they all crowded under as the storm was suddenly upon them.

John yelled for everyone to put their backpacks over their heads for protection as the hail stones began falling, starting with pea size and quickly gaining in size until they were as big as soft balls. The sound was deafening.

John quickly picked Patches off the ground and held her close as the hail continued. She was trembling, but didn't panic as long as she was being held. They couldn't comfort each other by huddling together because the ledge was too narrow. The best they could do was stand close together, shoulder to shoulder, as the storm intensified.

After about ten minutes the hail lessened, then gradually stopped; however, the rain began and increased in volume as the hail quit. The rain and wind combined into a small monsoon, too heavy to see more than a few feet. Their shelter offered only slight protection from this onslaught and they were soon soaked to the skin. After another thirty minutes the rain and wind decreased and then suddenly stopped. They could hear the storm moving away into the distance until the only noise was the water coming off the bluff. The nearby trees were stripped of their foliage, and in some cases even their limbs were missing.

John looked at the others as they stepped out into the stark surroundings. "It's a good thing we found shelter. I don't think we would have survived that storm without it."

John dropped Patches and held out his hands to the other family members, who rushed into his arms, thanking God for their salvation.

They soon continued their journey, walking through the devastation until by late afternoon they had moved out of the storm's path. Looking back at what they had walked through it was hard to believe anything could have lived through the storm.

Later that night, the family was sitting around their campfire still in shock from their ordeal. John's arm was around Sarah as he contemplated their ordeal. "This storm was like none I ever experienced, nor read anything about. It must have been a small storm cell, yet it was of such intensity that it virtually eliminates anything in its path that is unprotected. In the future, we'll need to keep an eye out for approaching weather and when we see a similar storm approaching we must immediately seek shelter."

They decided that in the future when they camped, they would look for a site with a natural storm shelter, and if none was available they would construct a suitable shelter in case of another storm.

John was awakened from a sound sleep to find Sarah blowing softly in his ear. She put her index finger over her lips as a signal to be silent, then motioned for him to follow her. She led the way until they were just outside the view of the smoldering campfire, where she embraced John and initiated a passionate kiss.

She sighed as they came up for air, but while continuing their embrace. "I wish we could have some privacy away from the kids, but we can't leave them alone until we know what has been following us."

John chuckled as he nibbled at her ear. "I'm getting a little crazy too, and not being able to make love to you has started to leave me in a constant state of arousal. It's really kind of embarrassing trying to hide it from your kids, especially Lillie."

Sarah softly giggled, while holding him tighter against her body. "I've noticed and I'm pretty sure Lillie has too; maybe I can help you with your problem," she said as she lowered his pant zipper and knelt to her knees.

Suddenly, they heard Patches growling back at the campsite. John muttered an oath, while helping Sarah to her feet. They both ran back to the camp where they found Patches at its far side growling and looking into the darkness with her hackles raised.

John went to Patches' side and reached down to rub her neck. "What's out there girl? I wonder what it is that you see."

The dog looked up at John and wagged her tail, then turned back toward where she was looking before. She no longer growled and soon turned back to the family as if to say it's no longer there.

When John turned to the family, Lillie looked at him with a surprised expression, and then suppressed a giggle with her hand.

Sarah suddenly moved in front of John, shielding him from the others while whispering, "John, your pants are undone!"

Lillie snickered, "What were you two doing before Patches woke us up?"

Sarah gave her daughter a stern look. "Never you mind what we were doing!" Then in an apparent attempt to change the subject, she added, "John, we need to come up with a plan to find out what's been following us!"

John's face was still red, but he followed Sarah's lead. "Yes, I agree. Tomorrow while we're walking let's try to come up with a plan of action. Until then, we better try to get some sleep before dawn arrives."

The following morning found them in better sprits and they continued on their eastward trek. Randy suggested that they build some snares when they camp each night, which might catch what has been following them. John agreed, but they would have to make the materials they needed for the snares. That evening the Lancaster family taught John how to weave grass into a rope they could use for a snare.

After some trial and error, they soon got it right and had a finished product. They then had to determine the right snare to catch their stalker. Lillie said she could remember a trap her father had used, and then preceded to show them how it would work.

They decided they needed more grass rope to build at least three snares, so they agreed to stay at the campsite until they were finished. The following night they set four snares around the camp at about the distance they thought the stalker had approached in the past. They settled down around the fire as usual and prepared to go to sleep, when suddenly there was a crash from the direction of one of the snares, followed by a loud scream. They immediately ran toward the sound with a barking Patches in the lead.

Their snare had caught something as they could see movement in the trees ahead. John had the others stand back as he pointed the flashlight beam on their quarry, which had begun to make snarling sounds at their approach. Their prisoner was hanging upside down from a tree snare and was thrashing about, but it suddenly stopped all movement and sounds when the beam from the flashlight hit it.

The women gasped in surprise when they saw what they had captured. It appeared to be a human male dressed in animal skins. No one spoke for a moment, until he started to fight the rope again.

John quickly turned to the family as he exclaimed, "We had better restrain him until we find out what's going on!"

After they had tied him securely hand and foot, they lowered him to the ground. They then dragged him back to the camp where they put more wood onto the fire for enough light to see what they had captured. He appeared to be a young male, dark hair, not yet with a full beard, and while tall his body had not yet filled out. He was dressed in a single animal skin that covered his body front and back, which he had slipped over his head through a slit, and was tied at his waist to keep it in place. On his feet were skin shoes. But, what caught John's attention was the knife and scabbard attached to a modern belt at his waist.

John removed the knife, which appeared to be of army issue, and upon closer inspection had USA stamped on the blade near the handle. The knife had seen hard use, yet still held a fine edge. John tried talking to their captive, but he just stared back at them with a lost expression. He asked the others if they had any ideas, when Patches suddenly jumped onto the boy's chest and licked his face.

His look of surprise suddenly turned to joy as he muttered, "Good doggy".

The others looked at the boy with surprise, until they all started laughing and hugging each other. They had found another of their kind! The boy looked at the others with surprise at their jubilant antics, but finally started smiling as he realized they had accepted him. John used the boys' knife to free him, and then offered him what remained of their supper.

John tried again to communicate with the young man. He pointed to himself and said, "John". He then pointed back at the boy, who looked blank for a moment as if trying to remember, but then blurted, "Mickey", with a smile.

Everyone clapped their hands and repeated, "Mickey"! Then each of the family repeated their names to him, who repeated each name as if it was a treasure.

They spent several hours of the night adding to the vocabulary of their new found friend, but finally exhausted they all settled down to rest and tried to get some sleep before the dawn of a new day. When John awoke he looked around the camp and was alarmed when he found that Mickey was absent. He got the others awake and asked if they had seen Mickey leave, but apparently John was the first to notice his absence.

Randy suddenly exclaimed, "Patches is gone, too!" But, just then the missing pair walked into camp. Mickey had what looked like a small deer draped over his shoulder, and Patches was walking proudly beside him as if to say - 'look what we brought back.' The family gathered around Mickey to welcome him back, and then asked where and how he had killed the animal. John noticed that he now carried a small bow and three arrows, which he later examined. They were of crude construction, but apparently were sufficient to achieve their purpose. The animal did look mostly like a deer, except for its small size – about half the size of a deer that they were familiar with, yet according to Mickey it was full-grown.

John returned Mickey's knife, who with the help of Randy started cleaning the carcass while the others started preparing a cook fire and gathering roots and berries. That afternoon they had a feast and learned from Mickey how he had gotten here while they were roasting the deer.

He hesitated because his memory was vague, but he then started telling his story. "I remember that I was riding in a truck with my father when they suddenly left the highway because of a bright light in front of them and my father was killed. I've been alone every day since then living off the land. I was woke up by the sounds of your cars crashing nearby and have been watching you, trying to decide whether to approach you."

John hugged Mickey's shoulders as he asked, "How old were you when you arrived here?"

"I think I was thirteen."

"So, you've been here about how long?"

Mickey thought back before answering. "I think about four years. I've been through three cold winters since I've been here."

John told the family, "He must have been in that truck that we found with the army surplus supplies."

Mickey nodded his head as he replied. "I've not been back to the truck because my father's there."

Randy asked, "How did you get your knife?"

"My father gave it to me before we left."

They marveled that Mickey had survived so long on his own, especially for one so young.

Mickey nodded his head with a glum expression. "I kept fairly close to the crash site, but on my hunting trips I came across several more vehicles. Most were empty and looked like they had been there for years, but one car had the body of a man that hadn't been dead very long."

Sarah asked, "Mickey, do you remember your father's name?"

Mickey considered, concentrating hard, then said, "Jake", with a smile.

"How about your last name?" John asked.

Mickey tried but couldn't remember. "It begins with a L-a, and sounds like Laco something. Maybe it will come back to me."

John suddenly smiled as he excitedly said. "That truck had the name Lacobee on its side."

Whereupon, Mickey shouted, "That's it, that's my name."

John and Sarah conferred briefly, and then asked Mickey if he would like to travel with them in their search for civilization. Mickey's face brightened, and then he smiled as he accepted their invitation.

John asked, "How did you survive the recent storm?"

"I just crawled into a hollow log and waited for the storm to end."

The expanded family was only together another two days on their eastward journey, when while following a small creek, they encountered a large mound of rocks on a dry rock shelf. The mound of rocks was obviously man made, so they investigated.

John turned to Mickey. "Have you seen anything like this before?"

"No, nothing like that."

They walked around the mound trying to decide what it was or represented. John noticed at the top of the mound there was a cap rock, so he carefully lifted that rock where he found a small cavity that contained a piece of wood with markings.

When John turned to the others, they all gathered around to examine what he had found. The piece of wood had words scratched into it that, while faded, could still be read.

John slowly repeated the words for the others. "Party of 3 head E hoping to find a river flow S. It was signed Wm Harding, and dated 6/11."

Sarah gasped, "Why, that's only about three years ago."

John smiled at the family, "Well, at least we know that we're not alone, and others have the same idea about heading south. Let's put our own message back with this one and maybe someone else will find it."

The family moved on after returning the messages to the mound and the trek was uneventful until the afternoon of the 15th day, when they topped a ridge bluff and beheld a great river flowing south. John and the others stood and gazed unbelieving at the sight below.

Sarah, while squeezing John's hand and looking at the river, whispered, "This must be it - this must be the Mississippi."

CHAPTER 4

This news caused Lillie and Randy to shout with joy, and were soon joined by John, Sarah, and Mick, whose name they had shortened by common agreement. They all joined hands and laughing started to dance in a circle. After they had calmed down, John looked up and down the river for any signs of habitation. He had the others looking too, but they saw no movement, smoke, or other signs that would indicate people were nearby.

They then picked a way off the river bluff and made their way down to the river's edge. John was looking for a small inlet or slew that they could use to build their raft, but as they continued their walk south along the river, the shadows deepened until eventually they decided to find a camp location. They soon found a small stream coming through a break in the bluff into the river that looked good, so they decided to camp here for the night and continue their search tomorrow. Mick, Randy and Patches went hunting, while the remainder of the family looked for other edibles.

There was plenty of food for the taking and they soon returned to their campsite and started a fire while waiting for the hunters' return. They returned within the hour with four rabbit types, which along with the other items they had gathered provided a feast for their first night on the great river.

After the meal they sat close together around the fire, each lost in their own thoughts of past experiences and what may lie ahead of them.

John suddenly had a thought and turned to the others. "We can easily make it to the buff's top if we follow the stream and we might just see another campfire now that it's dark."

They excitedly agreed and were soon making their way up to the buff's edge. There was a partial moon out and they were able to approach the edge of the bluff without danger. The river was beautiful in the moonlight, but that was not their purpose as they searched both sides of the river for any light.

The family stayed on the bluff for at least an hour before Mick shouted, "Look! Downstream, where it bends to the left. That's a faint light, isn't it?"

They all looked where he was pointing, but they couldn't agree on whether it was a campfire or the moon's light on the water. John tried to fix landmarks in his mind so they could investigate that area later. The next morning they continued their journey south along the river looking for a place to build their raft. About mid-morning they found where a small river entered the Mississippi. John gave it some thought before telling the others that this may be what they were looking for, so the family picked their way through the brush with the hope that he was right.

In a short time they found an ideal spot on a gravel and sand bar next to a deep channel. Since none of the group had ever constructed a raft before and had no tools, they conferred on the best way to start. Since the raft was going to be too heavy to move, they decided to first construct a slide ramp upon which they would build their raft.

They set out to find and drag back to the site a variety of narrow logs found along the riverbank. Since they only had tree vines and long grasses to use for ties, they assigned Randy the task of gathering appropriate materials. After three days, they finally had enough materials to start the construction of the raft. While John and Mick worked setting up the skid framework, the others began to braid grasses into strong ropes. John found a short heavy log that he and Mick could use to pile drive the supporting posts for the skid rack.

They were lucky that the construction site was near a natural cave that could be used as a shelter in case of a storm. The work on the raft was hard and if it wasn't for their hunting skills, they wouldn't have had the strength to complete the task. Each night, after their one meal of the day, the family would gather around the fire pit to recap their activities of the day and plan for the next. Sleep was no problem, since they were usually exhausted each night.

John and Sarah had grown closer together as they worked to complete the raft. However, they never had the opportunity or the strength to consummate their romantic relationship. Finally, after almost eight days of hard work the family stood beside their completed raft.

Sarah looked at the makeshift raft doubtfully. "Are you sure this thing will come off the ramp, and if it does will it float?"

John thought a moment before answering. "Maybe if we put some mud on the skids it will make it easier to slide into the water."

Mick then held up a long vine. "We better attach this to the raft or it might get away from us."

Lillie laughed and then exclaimed. "Boy, that would be the berries if we lost it after spending all that work putting it together!"

After making all their preparations they were finally ready to put the raft into the water. John and Mick removed the wedges in front of the raft. As soon as the final wedge was removed, the raft started to move downward, slowly at first, and then faster until it slid into the water with a big splash. It bobbed up and started to float downstream until it was brought up short by the restraining vine.

They let the raft float downstream to the end of the gravel bar, where they tied it up. The family then loaded their possessions onto the raft and floated down the stream toward the "Mississippi".

They were on the river for about two hours when John became aware of the landmarks near the area where they had seen the suspected light over a week previously. Using large oar paddles he and Mick guided the raft toward quiet water where they eventually found a tree they could use to secure the raft. John tried to get his bearings by looking back toward the bluff from which they had first observed the light. The angle looked right, so he suggested that they begin their search from here. They spread out along a narrow level area that was protected by trees between the river and bluffs.

After about a fifteen-minute search, Randy called out, "Over here! I think I've found something."

The family ran toward his voice where they found him inside a shallow depression. Randy was standing next to an apparently well-used fire pit ringed with stones.

The area around the campfire was trampled, either from long use or by a recent large number of individuals. The remains of several fish skeletons were found in the fire pit.

John looked at the others with a worried expression as he commented, "Well, I don't think this was made by only our people. It's been used too much and we can now revise our thinking that there's no native people here. However, we don't know if they're friendly, so we better be careful with our campfires in the future."

Sarah's face went from joy to concern as John spoke. She then blurted, "You think they might be dangerous?"

John shook his head. "I don't know. Remember they built the fire pit in a depression, which might mean an attempt to avoid detection or it could be simply a windbreak. If they were trying to avoid detection that probably means that they fear something or someone. To be safe, let's try to observe them before making ourselves known." He hesitated a moment before continuing. "I think we should consider making some weapons for defense in case they turn out to be unfriendly."

The family looked at him blankly for a moment, then they nodded their acceptance of the potential danger. Mick raised his bow above his head for emphasis. John examined the fire pit in an attempt to determine how long ago it had been last used. It was obvious that it had rained on the coals and since it had last rained four days ago, meant that it was at least that long since these people had moved on. He was afraid to travel any further until they had some means of defending themselves. They decided to camp at this site until they could come up with something. In the meantime they looked for a cave in the bluff that they could use for a storm shelter.

The obvious types of weapons they could build were the bow, spear, sling, and club. John wanted something with more range than a spear or club. That meant a bow if they could come up with the proper materials. Mick's bow was too small for much range, so with his help they searched the surrounding area for the proper wood. They were lucky in that there were several different species of hard wood growing here, and it wasn't long before they had gathered several limbs that showed potential for a bow.

The North American Indians used the tendons from animals as bowstrings; however, the only animals large enough to provide what they needed were from the small deer. Mick had used braided skins for his bowstring, which had worked. While John was considering the string for a bow, he had the others gather materials for spears and clubs. It was well that Mick and Randy had been saving animal skins, as they could use strips to bind stones to forked branches to make clubs in addition to making bowstrings.

The spears were the easiest. They would find a long straight tree branch, then place the narrow end into the fire pit until it was charred. It was a simple task to rub the charred end on a rock until they got a hard point.

Randy asked about a throwing spear like the Australian aboriginals used. John tried to remember the design from his readings and TV shows that featured the weapon, and then tried to explain to Randy the theory of its use. Upon reflection, because of his small size, he thought Randy could probably use this type of spear easier than the other crude weapons they were building.

John thought that when they had enough tendons from their deer kills, they would try to braid them into a bowstring. In the meantime Mick was given the assignment of braiding bowstrings from the animal skins for two bows, while the others started looking for materials to make arrows. Sarah expressed an interest in a sling weapon and there was enough skins remaining to make one for her. Both Sarah and Randy practiced with their weapons of choice until nightfall.

Randy's weapon took longer to prepare, as the spears had to be fitted to the thrower. Once that was completed, the learning curve for its use was much faster than the sling. Randy's weapon had a range of almost that of the sling and was accurate at a greater distance.

After observing her mother and brother's efforts, Lillie decided that she also wanted to use a sling, so they agreed to construct another the next day. After posting a watch the family settled down next to the campfire. The depression kept the wind out and they were comfortable next to the fire as the cool night settled around them.

The following day, while the family was practicing with their weapons, John had finished carving the bow and was thinking of making a suitable arrow. It wouldn't be long before his weapon was complete. He remembered the fish bones they had discovered in the fire pit and wondered how they were caught. The obvious way was the use of a spear. He searched for a slender stick, and then looked for a shallow area where fish might be lurking. It wasn't long before he found a likely spot, but then he had to learn how to approach the fish without first spooking them.

The family returned to the camp when the wind brought them the aroma of fish being cooked. Sarah looked at the fish being roasted on sticks around the fire, and then hugged John as she excitedly asked, "How did you catch all those fish?"

"It's easy if you know how. I used that stick over there and just waited until the fish came to me. It took some practice, but it wasn't too hard to learn. I'm just glad no one saw me fall on my face while I was learning. You' all pick out your fish and turn it when you think it's ready."

The family all raved about how good the fish smelled as they tended their fish. This was their first fish since their journey started and they were ready for a change in their diet. Mick had forgotten how to eat fish, so the others had to caution him about bones.

Later, while the others were eating, John observed his adopted family with a smile. None of them resembled the party that had started this journey, especially himself. He had lost at least twenty pounds, had a full beard, and was in his best physical shape since high school. The women had lost what little excess weight they had, and with their hair cut short and in their loose uniforms, they looked much like solders on field duty. John had given Mick one of his spare uniforms, and Randy, while shorter than the women, didn't look too much out of place.

John, on reflection, was having the time of his life. He was experiencing the adventure of exploring this new world, and he had a family that looked to him for support and protection. Looking at Sarah, he realized that he was deeply in love with her and had become very protective of her and the children.

Lillie was hardly a child at this point in the journey. She had matured in both body and personality and was performing her share of the tasks. Randy had always looked at this journey as an adventure and had eagerly accepted all tasks he was given. He now regarded John as his father and tried to please him by tackling the tasks assigned with zest. Randy and Mick had bonded as brothers and they each taught the other what they knew of hunting; in addition, Patches had immediately accepted Mick as a hunting partner.

It was well that Sarah and her children had learned the survival skills taught by her deceased husband and their father. John shuddered as he thought of the problems they could have encountered without these skills learned by the family, especially since he had run out of matches to make fire. It was a bonus that they had Patches, and later Mick, to help them hunt for food. Patches had turned out to be a good watchdog as well. Yes, they were very lucky to be so well prepared for this adventure, even down to their clothing and shoes.

Sarah looked up at John and seeing his slight smile and reflective expression came over and sat next to him. "What are you thinking?"

He slowly smiled while giving her a hug. "I was just thinking how lucky we have been since we started this trip together. I love you and the kids very much and can't believe how lucky I am that circumstances brought us together."

Sarah sighed and laid her head on his shoulder. "I love you too honey, and it's us that are lucky to have found you."

He grinned and quickly kissed her cheek. "Then, we're all lucky to have found each other."

Randy's eyes filled with tears as he ran to John and hugged him. "I love you too, John." he said with a thick voice, then rubbed his eyes and smiled up at him.

Lillie and Mick were sitting together nearby, but they soon joined them and they all sat on the log hugging each other with tears of happiness in their eyes.

After they had recovered their composure, John looked at his family and spoke. "I think we can move on downstream tomorrow now that we have some protection. The raft is exposed, but if we stay offshore twenty yards or more, we should be safe. We will have to be alert for any movement on shore so we won't be ambushed later when we camp."

Sarah frowned and then asked, "What if we see something? Do we keep going until they are left too far behind before we camp for the night?"

"That, or move to the other side of the river to camp. Eventually, we are going to have to make a decision about these people, whether to attempt communication or to avoid them altogether."

The night had been noticeably cooler than what they had previously experienced and everyone huddled close to the fire pit for warmth. John awakened to find Sarah snuggled close to him and had wrapped an arm around his waist. She felt quite warm pressed against his backside, and it took some willpower to disengage and stir up the fire.

The next morning the family stored their new weapons on the raft and continued their way down the great river. The river looked beautiful with the mist rising from the water into the cool morning air and the day promised to be warm and sunny, yet it was clear that summer was almost over and the fall season was at hand. The rising sun soon warmed the family as they continued southward down the river. They kept a close watch on the shoreline for any sign of movement or smoke as the current took them downstream and were careful to keep their distance from shore.

John had been watching the bluffs and shoreline for any evidence of civilization. However, the only thing they found so far was that campsite. Until they determined where they were they could only guess what steps to take to better survive. He remembered from the road atlas that there was a large bridge network further south where I-57 crossed the Mississippi. If this was the future, there still might be some evidence of these bridges; otherwise they would have to wait until further evidence gave them a clue of where they were.

He suddenly felt the hairs on his neck raise, followed by Patches' growl as she looked toward the west shore. The family scanned the shore but couldn't see any movement. He still felt that someone was watching him, even after the raft continued its southward journey. Later, they left the bluffs behind and found the shoreline covered with tall pine trees. The growth was so dense that nothing could be seen more than ten feet from the forest's edge.

Sarah pointed at the dense growth. "I'm sure glad that we didn't have to blaze a path through that forest."

The others echoed her statement while John patted the raft thankfully. They decided to stop each afternoon around five p.m. to allow them sufficient time to set up camp and hunt for food. The only problem was finding a suitable spot to camp within that time frame. Since they were now making good time on the raft, John suggested they stop at the first good camping spot anytime after mid-afternoon.

However, it was almost six p.m. before the family found a suitable camping spot that day.

The forest continued until they finally found a clearing next to a small creek flowing into the river. There was even a sheltered spot to tie up the raft for the night.

They had just finished unloading the raft when Randy ran back to the family from his explorations and excitedly exclaimed, "We're not the first to use this as a campsite! There's a large fire pit over there next to that large rock, but it hasn't been used for a while."

The family immediately searched the area for anything left by the previous occupants when Lillie called out, "Hey everyone, I've found something over here!"

They immediately gathered where Lillie had discovered what appeared to be a burial site. A notch in the large rock boulders had been filled in with stones.

John hesitated a moment, then looking at the others he spoke uneasily, "I think we should uncover whatever is buried in there so we can have some idea of what or who these people are."

Sarah thought a moment and nodded her head in agreement. "Yes, we might discover something important here, so let's get started. Randy, I don't want you to see this and we need a lookout anyway, so you and Patches go back to the raft and guard our stuff."

Randy exclaimed, "Oh Mom!" He looked at his mother dejectedly; then hopefully at John who shook his head. Giving up, he called Patches and they started back toward the raft.

John and Mick started removing the stones until finally they had uncovered what was hidden. Apparently, the individual had not been buried there long, as decomposition was not advanced. She was naked and looked to be quite young. Apparently she died during childbirth, as a baby's foot could be seen protruding from her body. The young woman had human characteristics, but mutations were obvious. She had hair on her arms and legs much like a monkey from their own world. In addition, her eyes and ears were larger in proportion to her head than their own. She also was shorter and more muscular than what we consider normal for women.

When Lillie first saw the naked woman and the manner in which she had died, she immediately turned white and upchucked what little she had in her stomach. Sarah pulled her away from the scene and held her until she felt better.

John and Sarah both comforted Lillie until she could speak. "I forgot where I was until I saw how that poor woman died. We're really living in primitive times now aren't we?"

John nodded his head. "Yes, either the primitive past or future; however, she doesn't look like the pictures of primitive man. The bone structure of her head is all wrong for that, so I'm guessing we're in the far future with man on its long upward road again after some kind of near annihilation."

Sarah shuddered, and then looking up at John, spoke softly. "I don't think these people will ever be able to trust us to co-exist with them. We're just too different and I'm worried about both Randy's and Lillie's role in their society, even if they did accept us."

John studied Sarah's face for a moment, and then looked at Lillie who was still in her arms. "I'm thinking the same thing. Unless its unavoidable, we should give these people a wide berth."

They then began the task of replacing the stones on the woman's gravesite. That night the family was in a pensive mood. The day's discovery left them all with something to think about. However, Randy was the least affected. He thought only of the added excitement of the other people to avoid and the mystery they represented.

Lillie was still apprehensive about today's find and stayed close to camp. John caught Lillie staring at Mick several times; once he thought he saw a little smile as she watched Mick work at the cook fire. If anything, the find had brought the family even closer together.

John consulted with Sarah and Mick about posting a lookout, and they agreed to split the night watch with Mick taking the first three-hour shift. Sarah woke John at the appointed time, but stayed in his arms until he convinced her to get some sleep. He placed more wood on the fire and checked on the raft with nothing occurring the remainder of the night.

The morning brought a heavy fog on the river which had now become almost a daily occurrence. The mist hung low over the river and shoreline, making the fire's warmth a welcome greeting this morning as the family awoke to begin the new day. Sarah looked a little tired as she sat up and stretched her arms, but when she met John's eyes her face came alive and any sign of fatigue vanished. John sat down next to her and gave her a kiss, then while still embracing her they watched as the others broke camp with little wasted movements.

John spoke softly, "They are getting pretty good at this aren't they?"

Sarah smiled while watching her children work. "Yes, they've grown up these last few weeks, especially Lillie. You didn't know her before, but she was the typical teenager rebelling against parental authority. I don't know, but it might be your influence that has made the difference in her attitude."

At this point Lillie looked over at the two adults sitting on the ground in an embrace, and then shouted, "Hey, you two lovebirds, pick up your things so we can get this show on the road!"

She then reconsidered for a moment before walking towards them with a determined expression on her face. She stood before them for a moment, shaking her head as she fixed her mother and adopted father with a concerned expression.

"You two really take the cake. Why don't you go off by yourself and get it on? We can take care of ourselves until you get back; besides this sexual tension between you two is not doing anyone any good."

They both gaped at Lillie with open mouths, until Sarah finally composed herself. "Lillie, you're right of course. Why don't you three go down by the raft until John and I complete some long delayed personal business."

John finally found his voice. "Hold on, don't I have any say in this?"

Sarah gave him a long sultry stare, cutting off any further comment on his part. Lillie was already herding Mick and Randy towards the raft; who were complaining what was the big rush.

CHAPTER 5

Sarah looked into John's eyes and smiled. "Lillie has really grown up these last few weeks. She appears to accept you as the leader of our family and as my lover. The next question is how do you feel about this arrangement?"

John slowly smiled, and then kissed Sarah until they were both breathless. "Is that enough of an answer? I could say that circumstances have conspired to keep us apart until now, but that is only partially true. Part of my problem was that I have been troubled by a failed past relationship that ended only a few weeks before we met. I guess I've been afraid of another rejection."

Sarah sadly shook her head and then hugged him tightly.

"That woman must have been crazy. You are the most honest, considerate man I've ever met." Then while nibbling at his ear lobe she whispered, "Let's find out what kind of lover you are!"

In an frenzy they both proceeded to remove each other's clothing, until there was only skin between their bodies. Sarah pushed him away from her for a moment so that she could look at his body with an appreciative grin. "Wow, this trip has really brought out your muscles."

John's face turned red in embarrassment, but then he smiled as he replied. "All the better to satisfy you my dear. Besides, you've gotten even more beautiful than the first day we met." He said as he palmed her ample left breast and tweaked its nipple erect. Sarah sighed as she held his hand to her breast.

Suddenly, they were interrupted by Lillie's voice as she came running toward them. "Mother - John, come quick!" Lillie suddenly stopped as she came into sight of her mother and John.

"Ooh gosh! I'm sorry." She stared at the naked couple, looking slowly from her mother to John, and then with a slow smile exclaimed, "Wow!" She then shook her head with regret as she blurted, "I hate to break this up, but we have company!"

John and Sarah looked at her with open mouths for a second, but then hurriedly began to dress as Lillie watched with a slight smile still on her face.

John was dressing with his back to Lillie as he spoke. "What do you mean we have company?"

"Quick, if we hurry you can see for yourself."

Lillie's smile disappeared as John's bare behind was finally covered.

When they got back to the river John asked Mick, "Where are they?"

Pointing across the river he exclaimed, "You just missed them. They moved away from the river through that tall grass."

Lillie excitedly said, "When we got back to the raft, Mick noticed movement on the opposite shore, so we dropped to the ground and watched a group of about seven individuals moving south along the river bank."

John was holding Sarah tightly as he tensely asked, "Were there any women in the group?"

"I couldn't tell because of the distance, but I didn't see any kids," Lillie answered.

John pondered for a moment, then slowly shook his head.

"They must be a hunting party or the whole family would be with them. We had better stay here for a while longer before we get back on the river. I would just as soon not let them see us. Did they look like the body we found?"

"Yes, as best as I could tell from this distance," Lillie replied quickly.

"Were they carrying any weapons?"

She considered a moment before answering. "I could only see one club and two long spears, but they may have had other weapons."

"Maybe since they weren't all armed, it could mean that this is strictly a hunting party and one that doesn't expect trouble from anything dangerous - such as another tribe or someone like us," John said hopefully.

Sarah's face brightened as she realized that the danger wasn't as great as they first thought. Then giving John a knowing look, said, "Okay, since we're not going anywhere soon let's get back to what we were doing before we were so rudely interrupted by Lillie."

Sarah then gave her daughter a sharp look that clearly said that there had better not be any further interruptions.

As John and Sarah walked back to the clearing hand in hand, Lillie turned to Mick and Randy with a slight flush on her face. "Let's take Patches and see if we can find some game upriver a short distance."

Randy looked at the departing pair with a puzzled expression on his face, and then asked Lillie, "What are Mom and John going to do?"

Lillie placed her hands on his shoulders and smiled down at him. "They have decided to get married, which means John is going to be our father. What do you think about that?"

Randy looked at Lillie with a surprised expression on his face, but then suddenly jumped into the air with a loud whoop of joy. "Ooh boy, John's going to be my dad."

He then turned as if to go after them, but was stopped when Lillie grabbed his arm.

"No, let's let them have some time by themselves. It's been hard for them to be alone together."

She then nudged him upstream, while they both glanced backwards occasionally until her mom and John were out of sight. The "kids" later returned to the raft with another rabbit-like creature and three fish, which they had cleaned while waiting on their parents to return. After about an hour, John and Sarah approached the raft with dazed, but happy smiles on their faces.

Lillie ran to her mother and they happily embraced, while Randy ran to John and hugged him tightly. Sarah looked at Lillie with a question in her eyes as she nodded toward Randy, who was still hugging John.

Lillie blushed slightly as she spoke. "I told him you and John got married and he was our new father."

Sarah smiled slightly, and then looked into her daughter's eyes. "Well, how do you feel about us getting married?"

Lillie looked over at John with tears in her eyes. "I think I'm a little jealous because I love him too."

Sarah hugged her daughter as she looked at John, and then over at Mick, who was looking their way with a troubled expression. Sarah then smiled, as she felt that all would turn out all right after all.

They decided to stay the night and moved back behind the rocks to sit up camp as it offered the best screen for their campfire. The "kids" prepared their parents a delicious wedding dinner, but the newlyweds were oblivious to everything except each other. The next day the family scanned the opposite shore for any movement before they again proceeded south on the raft. They stayed near the west shoreline while maintaining a close watch on both sides of the river.

The day started cool and with a heavy mist as before, but quickly warmed under clear skies until they all thought it was mid-summer again. For a while, John enjoyed the unexpected good weather, but then he had a disturbing thought - this was undoubtedly the result of a low-pressure front which probably meant deteriorating conditions in a few days. He resolved to pay closer attention to any sudden weather changes and make sure they had adequate shelter each night.

The second day of clear skies and warm weather suddenly started to worsen about mid-day, beginning with high winds and the sky turning dark with ominous clouds. John started looking for a break in the trees on either shore. They were lucky as they soon saw where a small river merged with the Mississippi's west side. They pulled the raft onto the shore north of the merging river where they had sighted a line of bluffs and tied it down before looking for shelter. They then followed the bluffs, which were not far from shore, looking for a cave.

The high wind was particularly loud in the trees along the bluff with some limbs breaking off and falling to the ground with sudden crashes. John was beginning to doubt their chances of finding a cave, when suddenly in the bluff ahead he saw an opening. They hurried toward the opening, which was about six feet above the ground and had no handholds for climbing. John motioned Mick over and made a foothold with his cupped hands to provide him a boost up into the opening, where Mick disappeared for a few minutes.

Mick's grinning face soon reappeared. "It looks fine. It goes back quite a ways and its dry."

John helped Mick get back down so that he could help them look for materials to make a ladder. They piled tree branches up against the bluff until they had enough hand and footholds to reach the cave entrance. The family then went back to the raft to bring their possessions to the cave. Before leaving the raft they drew it into the small river and onto a sandbar where they double-secured it with their grass ropes and tree vines they found nearby.

It didn't take long to climb the makeshift ladder and place their belongings into the cave, but while they were working the wind intensified as the weather front was almost upon them, with loud thunder heard approaching fast. They were moving their possessions further into the cave when the storm struck.

Lightning strikes were so frequent that they were impossible to count, and the crashing sounds of thunder was so loud they couldn't think, let alone try to converse with one another. The family huddled together where they had placed their belongings as they prayed and comforted each other and hoped for the best.

Suddenly, John could smell a strong odor of ozone in the air and his body hair started to rise. For some reason the smell reminded him of the transformer for his old electric train set he had when he was a kid.

A bright greenish orange ball of light appeared at the entrance to their cave and then started to slowly enter. They watched the glowing ball's approach with incomprehension and awe at first, but then with fear as it forced them further back into the cave as it approached. They were all holding hands as they retreated; the only sounds they uttered were whimpering sounds of fear from Lillie and moans from Sarah. Randy carried Patches in his arms as it growled its warning at the approaching glowing ball of light.

The "Ball's" light bathed the cave with an eerie glow as the outside light faded in the background. They hadn't noticed it before, but suddenly there was the sound of an underground stream behind them. They stopped with their backs at the stream's edge, as they had nowhere else to go. Randy stumbled and almost fell into the rushing stream, but was steadied by Mick.

The "Ball" stopped its approach, but then continued toward John, where it hovered a few inches in front of his face. John studied the ball in almost a detached manner. It appeared to be about the size of a volleyball and was so bright that its edges were indistinct. He stayed frozen as the ball slowly dropped toward the ground then rose as it slowly circled his body. It returned to its original position in front of his face where it shot a small continuous bolt of lightning into John's head.

His body suddenly stiffened but remained standing as the "Ball" continued to shoot what looked like a strong static charge into his head. After what seemed ages to the rest of the family, but may have been only a minute, the "Ball" stopped its connection with John. He staggered until Sarah reached out to steady him, while the "Ball" moved back a few yards and slowly circled the family group until it returned to its original position. The "Ball's" glow suddenly increased intensity before it reversed its direction and left the cave, leaving behind a strong ozone smell.

The family was in sudden darkness with the "Ball's" departure. Sarah anxiously asked John, "Are you alright honey?"

He groaned while holding his head and then with a weak voice replied, "I think so. Is everyone else okay?"

The others responded almost together with a loud, "What was that thing?"

John answered with a slightly stronger voice, "I don't know, but let's get back to where there's some light."

He stepped forward a few steps away from the stream's edge and called out. "Everyone come toward my voice and let's join hands before we start back."

After the family gathered together, they followed John single file back toward the cave's entrance. They found that they had come over twenty yards before they finally reached their supplies. The lightning had ceased, but the wind was still blowing hard, and they could hear the sound of thunder decreasing in the distance as the storm moved away from them.

Sarah grabbed John's arm and turned his face to the outside light so that she could see if his head was burned.

"What was that thing? It looked almost like the description of ball lightning I've read about!"

John shook his head slowly. "Maybe, but this thing is intelligent. When it attached itself to me I could feel it probing my mind and then I could feel it make a judgment of some kind before it left me."

Sarah looked at John with disbelief. "You mean that thing can think?"

John nodded his head. "It's not like anything I've had any experience with before, but it obviously was curious about us and probed me for knowledge. But, most importantly, I got the impression that it was friendly, or at least benign."

Lillie interrupted, "What's that?" She then pointed outside. They all looked outside, then back at her with a questioning look. Then with a touch of impatience, she grabbed John's arm and pointed outside again. "There's no sound! The storm must have moved on."

They rushed to the cave entrance, where they observed a strange scene of destruction. Lightning strikes were apparent by the number of splintered trees with some still smoldering. However, the greatest amount of destruction was limited to an area about 200 feet away from the cave's entrance. It was as if their immediate area was shielded from further damage as the storm moved through.

As they looked at the scene in disbelief, Lillie whispered softly, "Do you think that thing had anything to do with sparing this area?"

John hesitated. "I think so. I was right when I said the object was friendly. This clearly shows it tried to help us." He turned to Mick. "Are you sure that you never encountered anything like this before?"

"No. I've seen big storms in the far distance, but my only other experience was when I was following you."

"Well, maybe the 'Ball' needs to live in the storm's environment to exist, and that may be the reason you never saw it before." John then looked up at the clearing sky. "It's getting late so we might as well stay here tonight. Let's go check out the raft, and then we need to make plans to either camp outside or stay in the cave tonight."

While Mick, Randy, and Patches went hunting, the others checked on the raft. They found it in good shape, with only a few repairs needed before they could continue their journey. The area of protection had continued all the way to the raft. However, the destruction resumed just across the small river from where the raft was tied. Trees were stripped of their foliage, and in many cases their branches were missing, stripped bare by large hail that still remained on the ground.

John shook his head and looked at Sarah. "I'll bet our hunters will find only dead game and fish. I don't see how anything could have survived unless it had shelter."

John and the two women repaired the raft, which didn't take long, and were returning to the cave when they smelled wood smoke and something cooking.

Lillie laughed. "That doesn't smell like fish to me."

John's surprised expression turned into a lopsided grin as he said, "Well, let's see what our hunters have brought us this time."

When they got to the camp they found Mick and Randy busy starting another fire and building racks to cook on. One fire was already roasting a small deer-like animal, which was the source of the aroma they had smelled. But, lying on the ground were at least a dozen large fish and another deer.

Mick looked up as they approached. "Hey you guys, pitch in and help clean those fish and the deer. We can go get more if you think we need to."

Randy pointed to Patches. "She found the dead deer not far from camp, and the fish were just floating in the river. We think lightning must have killed them."

John scratched his head as he appraised the number of fish and animals collected. "I think what you have here is more than enough. We'll have to spend another day here just to take care of this batch."

CHAPTER 6

That night they decided to sleep in the warmth of the cave as the hailstorm left the night cooler than normal. John took a torch from the fire and the canteens before going toward the cave stream for water. His previous trip back into the cave had been too fraught with excitement for him to observe very much of its contents and he was more than a little curious as to what was there.

The cave had only one tunnel until it reached the stream. However, across the water he could see what looked like two openings in the rock wall. The stream was cold and pure, and after taking a long drink John thought the water was the best thing he had ever tasted. He investigated the walls of the small chamber but didn't find any markings, so he returned to the others after filling the canteens.

That night the family discussed their experiences after the "Ball" entered the cave. Sarah and Lillie both thought they heard a low hum as it approached them, while Randy and Mick said they didn't remember any sound.

The family looked at John for his opinion; who shrugged his shoulders before answering.

"I was so scared that the only thing I remembered was the smell of ozone and the brightness of the object."

The other family members nodded their heads in agreement that they too had been frightened.

Lillie frowned in embarrassment as she confided, "I nearly wet my pants when that thing came after us, and I thought we were dead meat when it backed us up against the stream."

Sarah's face turned red with embarrassment as she exclaimed, "Lillie! Have you no shame? Watch your mouth!"

"Well I did. I was so scared that my knees were knocking so loud I thought I was part of a Latin band."

Randy started snickering, followed by the loud laughter of Mick, who received a sharp jab from Lillie's elbow. "That's not funny," she said while trying not to smile.

John smiled at Sarah's embarrassed silence as she glared at her daughter's improper response. "I think we can agree we were all frightened, but the experience didn't hurt any of us."

"Let's hope not. That electric-like connection it had with you still worries me," Sarah said as she looked at his forehead again where there was still a slight red mark showing.

John told the family about the cave openings on the other side of the stream and asked them if they should take time to explore them before moving on. Everyone agreed they needed a diversion and John suggested that after they finished preparing the food they would explore.

Later the next day John consulted with Mick about building a bridge across the stream. The stream was only about fourteen feet wide, but the current was swift and the water appeared too deep to wade across. They decided to tie several long, narrow tree branches together until the branches had enough strength to support their weight. The problem was going to be getting it to extend across the stream. Sarah overheard their discussion and suggested that working together they could raise it upright and let it fall across the stream.

John looked blank for a moment, and then smiled. "That's simple enough; however, I'm not sure the cave ceiling is high enough."

Sarah replied. "If it's not, we'll just have to find another way."

The next day the family made their way back to the stream where they found the cavern roof more than high enough for their purpose. The passage to the stream was sufficiently straight to get the pieces of their bridge through, so they returned to their camp to plan how to complete the bridge. John gave the family their individual assignments and they began the task of building the bridge. It turned out to be a bigger job than John had visualized, and it was early afternoon before they were ready to attempt placing it across the stream. They dug a hole to use as a stop when they raised the bridge to a vertical position. Randy held it in position while the others raised it up and then pushed it over the stream. The maneuver worked without any problems and then it was time to decide who would try the bridge first.

The bridge bottom was almost touching the water and would

probably sag some when the weight of their passage began. John suggested that they anchor their end and then send Randy across first to anchor the other side before anyone heavier tried the bridge.

Sarah set her mouth in a determined expression as she demanded, "Randy, you're not going across that rickety contraption first!"

Randy looked at his mother in disbelief and then in a whining tone replied, "Mom! It's perfectly safe and it's got to be me...I'm the lightest person here! Besides, even if I fall off into the water, they can pull me back."

Sarah looked to John for support, who nodded his head. "Randy, I'll go first but you'll all have to hold onto the safety line if I fall into the water."

Sarah then realized what the alternative was and after a moment said with a faint smile, "No. Randy you can go first, but you be careful or you'll get an early bath"

John tied the safety rope around Randy before letting him start. Randy started across slowly on hands and knees as he tested the bridge's strength, but with his slight weight there was no noticeable sag and he made it across without any trouble. He secured the other side of the bridge by standing on it and with a smile on his face that showed his pride in his accomplishment, said, "Who's next"?

Mick stepped forward and retrieved the safety line before placing it around himself. He picked up Patches, gave Lillie a confident smile, and then without any hesitation, stepped lightly across to the other side. The bridge sagged momentarily into the stream, but the weight was released too quickly to provide much drag.

Sarah claimed the next turn followed by Lillie who both crossed without any trouble. Now it was John's turn. He had been a little concerned since he weighed the most, but he crossed as Mick had without any problem.

They now were confronted by the two openings in the cave wall. One was about five feet high but very narrow. All but John could enter by sliding in sideways; who was just too tall to make this maneuver. The other opening was wider, but it was only three feet high. Mick volunteered to see where the taller opening went, while the others waited for his return.

Mick returned in about five minutes, reporting that this passage had ended abruptly without his finding anything of interest. John held his torch into the mouth of the smaller opening and observed a draft causing his torch to flicker and surge toward the opening.

He turned to the family and said, "This looks promising; let's all try this opening."

John then got down on his hands and knees and started into the passage with the others following holding onto the safety line. He soon found that the passage started upwards at about a twenty-degree angle and while the floor of the passage started as soft silt, this rapidly disappeared as they progressed onto rock which was hard on his knees. Soon, the passage leveled out and John entered a large chamber.

He stood and raised his torch above his head while the others slowly entered the dark chamber. What held their attention was a grimy rectangular object perched atop a stone base in the center of the chamber. The family slowly approached the object and John realized that it was slightly transparent. He used his shirt sleeve to try to wipe and remove what must have been the grime of countless years to better view its contents and then stepped back while uttering an explanation of disbelief at the body displayed. Everyone immediately took a step back when they realized what they were looking at and then voiced a variety of expressions.

Randy said, "Wow!"

Sarah and Lillie both grimaced while uttering, "Ooh gross!" They looked at each other in surprise and giggled.

John stepped back into Mick, which gave both an extra surprise and elicited "Shit" from John, and "Crap" from Mick.

At John's urging the others started helping him clean the sides of the coffin until they could get it as clear as possible. The body looked as if it had just been laid to rest, with no apparent deterioration. It was a man in a military dress uniform. On his shoulders gleamed five-star clusters and shoulder patches that depicted crossed missiles with a lightning bolt. His jacket had numerous battle ribbons and a nametag. John tried to clear the viewing area better, then made out the name - Kennedy. The uniform was somewhat similar to those used by the military from his experience, but still not quite right. Another disturbing factor was the condition of the body which indicated a breakthrough in preserving the dead.

John looked questioningly at Sarah. "Well, what do you make of this?"

"I know uniforms from my experience living with the military, and it's not quite what I've seen before. The style is only slightly different, but the patches and some of the battle ribbons are not familiar. However, the rank is of a five-star general which was as high as it got."

"I noticed that too." He then moved the torch to view the rest of the chamber. They had entered what appeared to be a burial chamber. Carved into the rock walls were openings for many bodies. John counted ten bottom openings and they were stacked three high.

Then, pointing at the empty burial openings, he commented, "The general's death must have been ages ago as all the other bodies left here have deteriorated to dust. Let's check them to see if any metal still remains."

The family immediately started looking for any remains left in the openings but found nothing. They then returned to the coffin and examined it for any additional clues. The base of the coffin was of a gray metal and the transparent material appeared to be some type of plastic. Upon closer examination John found stamped into the metal base an inscription. It was not clear at first, but after some cleaning they were finally able to read - UN/USA. He stared at the inscription for a moment before turning and staring at the others in almost shock.

"Well, I think this answers some of our questions. One of the possible places we are at is our far future. Now that I've seen this coffin and its contents, I'm sure. That body was not embalmed and still looks fresh. It must be in some sort of stasis field generated from the coffin's base."

Sarah and Lillie looked at the coffin in awe. Then Lillie blurted, "Then the other people are our descendants?"

He thought a moment before answering. "Maybe, but if so they apparently have mutated quite a bit since our time. It may have been caused by a nuclear or bacterial war, or maybe an accident could have happened that killed most of the people and animals off."

Sarah looked at John with tears in her eyes. "More than that, apparently all of the insects were killed off too. Plant life that relied upon insects for their reproduction had to adapt or die off as well. The earth as we knew it is gone."

Randy grabbed John's hand as he asked, "Wow! How long do you think it's been since this thing happened? Are we in any danger?"

"No. This must have happened long ago, maybe thousands of years. We aren't in any danger from that source. I wonder if our food source is sufficient to maintain us though."

Sarah smiled while pointing at Mick. "I think it's alright. Just look at Mick! He looks like he has done okay to me."

John started laughing too. "You're right, of course. But we still need greens and fruit in our diet. The best way to get this variety is to live in a climate warm enough to support their growth year around." John made another sweep of the chamber before he was satisfied. "Okay, let's finish our projects and continue our way south."

With that thought, they made their way back to the campsite; however, they did pull the bridge back into the river and set it adrift so that the other people would not disturb the coffin.

CHAPTER 7

The family had been on the river for four days without seeing anything of the mutants. However, John periodically got the feeling that they were being watched and they kept their raft beyond spear range of either shoreline. About mid-day they arrived at a convergence into the Mississippi of another large river. This river had a green tint, which extended far into the muddy Mississippi at the convergence point.

John stared at the new river with a thoughtful expression and then checked his atlas. "I bet that's the Ohio River, which means the old I-54 crossed near here! Let's keep a close watch on both shores for any sign of bridges."

Shortly, Sarah pointed to the west shore and exclaimed, "Is that concrete or a rock slab over there?"

John squinted his eyes and examined the area Sarah had pointed out. "It doesn't look natural..." He then looked at the opposite bank, but that side of the river was lowlands and nothing was apparent. "It could be, but it's been too many years for much of anything being recognizable. Well, let's assume that's the Ohio River. If I'm correct then we're approaching the Boot Hill of Missouri as shown in this atlas, and in about another 100 miles, give or take, we'll be in Arkansas or Tennessee, depending on which side of the Mississippi we camp. We should be getting into a warmer climate the further south we go from now on."

During their raft trip the family had to adopt several privacy procedures. When someone had need to use the "facility" that they had constructed, by common agreement, they would keep eyes away from that end of the raft until they said, "all clear". They also constructed a fire pit at the other end of the raft from mud and sand. When the fire was lit the raft could be turned to keep smoke away from the people on the raft. This change allowed them to cook a noon meal, assuming they could catch any fish or had some meat left over from the previous day.

Lillie and Mick were about the same age, but due to Mick's past isolation he was quite shy around her. He was quick to step in and help her with any chore she was performing, but he never initiated a personal conversation with her. Both Sarah and John noted that Lillie was getting concerned about his apparent lack of interest.

The tenth afternoon of their raft journey they stopped for the night and were preparing the camp. As usual they looked for a nearby cave for possible shelter in case of a storm, but none was found. Instead, they gathered large tree branches and constructed a lean-to against the bluff. The hunters then went in search of supper. In their absence John, Sarah, and Lillie completed their normal tasks in securing the raft and storing their gear in the shelter, and building a fire. After they finished their tasks, they usually performed needed personal jobs such as hair trims or washing clothes.

Today, John came back to the fire and found Sarah and Lillie in close conversation which immediately stopped when he walked up. "What's up, are you talking about me or just girl talk in general?"

Lillie turned red with embarrassment and looked questioningly at her mother who nodded her agreement. Sarah then replied, "We were trying to decide how to get Mick interested in Lillie."

He gave Sarah a lop-sided grin as he asked, "Are you sure you want to start that at their age?"

"John, Lillie's almost seventeen and Mick may even be older! Lillie is certainly older than Mick mentally and they're attracted to each other. It's just that he is so shy!"

He looked at Lillie considering, which made her embarrassment more apparent as her face got even redder. "Lillie, I think you're going to have to pick your time and then make the first move. His social development is severely limited, but he has shown much improvement since he joined us. Besides, there's no one else to peak his interest and I've caught him looking at you with a longing expression. He's got puppy love if nothing else."

Sarah hugged Lillie and then kissed her cheek. "It's just what I told you. He's a lot like John was, you have to make the first move and don't let him get away."

"Boy-oh-boy, we guys don't have a chance against you women."

"Honey, you're not complaining, are you?" She whispered as she nibbled on his ear lobe. Lillie grinned as she watched Sarah lavish him with love and affection. *So that's how it's done. Well, I should be able to do that,* she thought to herself.

Later that evening, after completing their meal, the family sat around the fire talking about their day and recalling past adventures. The temperature was mild and comfortable and best of all, there were no bugs like they had on old Earth to spoil their enjoyment of the evening. They eventually all turned in to sleep, with Patches acting as their watchdog.

It was early morning when they were awakened by her loud barking, and then she jumped on John and Sarah when they were slow to react because they had become entangled in each other's arms and their bedding. They eventually jumped up to see what was happening when they heard the loud rumblings of a storm fast approaching.

John shouted, "Quick, everyone grab your things and run for the shelter!"

The family acted without thinking and ran toward their prepared shelter. Lillie had her hands full and tripped, falling hard. Mick following behind hardly slowed as he picked her up in one arm and continued to the shelter. Lillie was still gasping for breath from the fall and his rough handling when Mick deposited her within the lean-to.

He hugged her tightly before asking, "Are you okay? Let me check you for cuts!" He implored.

Lillie smiled as Mick checked her for any abrasions and finding none asked her, "Can you breathe alright now?"

Lillie looked up at him and nodded, then grabbed his neck pulling him down to her and started kissing him. Mick was surprised and initially stiffened but gradually relaxed and started kissing her back.

When they broke from their embrace, Mick breathlessly exclaimed, "Wow, let's do that again!"

The storm broke around them at that moment with its usual violence of wind, lightning, and thunder. The family huddled together for comfort, hoping the shelter would hold together. Suddenly, the lean-to was luminous from the glow of a bright greenish orange ball of light! The "Ball" hovered just inside the shelter, then slowly approached John and hovered just inches from his face. It then continued through the lean-to and disappeared. The storm immediately seemed to split around their camping area and in a few minutes was gone, the sounds diminishing as it withdrew.

Sarah hugged John tightly. "Honey, you seem to have found a friend. Do you think it was the same "Ball" we saw earlier?"

He briefly considered her question. "It could be, or they have some means of communicating among themselves if there is more than one.

Whatever the case, I'm glad it's on our side."

Randy was huddled tightly to his mother and new father and whispered, "Me too!"

Sarah looked over at her daughter and Mick who were looking at each other in almost a stunned expression now that the storm had passed. Lillie pressed her finger softly against Mick's lips before pulling him into another loving embrace.

She whispered in John's ear, "It looks like Lillie has solved her problem."

They both laughed softly as they observed the pair looking at each other with love-struck eyes. They soon left the shelter to find little damage to the campsite and raft, so they returned to the camp to start the morning fire and prepared an early breakfast from the leftover supper meat. Randy and Patches went out to discover if they could pick up some fresh kill from the storm. Lillie and Mick looked at John and Sarah across the fire pit while holding their hands out towards its warmth. Lillie wore a happy expression while Mick appeared to be slightly embarrassed.

"Mick, it took you long enough to finally discover that you two were in love," Sarah said with a mock serious expression.

Mick shook his head ruefully. "Sometimes you have to hit me in the head to get my attention."

Lillie hugged him tightly and kissed his cheek. "Now you leave him alone. He's had little or no experience with girls before and this is all new for him. I thought he did pretty well myself," she said with a grin and a wink at her mother.

Randy and Patches ran into camp with Patches barking excitedly! "We found a camp of the Mutants and they were all killed by the storm."

"Hold on Randy, slow down and tell us what you found," John said slowly and softly.

Randy took a deep breath and said more calmly. "Patches and me..."

"Patches and I," corrected Sarah.

John smiled at Sarah and shook his head. "Go on Randy."

"Well, Patches and I went downstream to see if we could find some storm kill to bring back when we came across their camp about a half mile from us. They had camped under a bluff overhang which had come down on them during the storm."

John considered what Randy said, then asked, "They were all dead?"

"If any were left alive, they didn't hang around for me to find," Randy excitedly said.

John looked at Sarah with concern. "We had all better examine the camp. I don't want to leave anyone alone back here."

Sarah nodded her agreement and they all started downstream to the Mutants' campsite. They slowly approached the area of the campsite, carefully looking around to be sure that they were alone. They counted six bodies next to the bluff wall and it appeared that they had taken shelter under the overhang of rock when the storm approached.

John pointed to where the overhang had broken away. "That might have been caused by a lightning strike. I don't think thunder reverberations could have brought it down, but who knows."

They examined the weapons they could find, which consisted of two broken spears and a club. The spears were similar to what they had made but the club was a formidable looking weapon. It appeared to have been made from the fork of a tree. The club head was a knob where branches had sprouted and had been left sticking out to offer maximum injury to whomever or whatever was struck. It was made of hard wood and weighed close to eight pounds.

John picked it up and swung it trying to get a feel for the weapon. "Boy, I wouldn't want to be on the receiving end of this!"

John and Mick then examined the men more closely and discovered that they were all shorter than they were by at least six inches. They were more muscular in both arms and legs and their skin color was similar to the American Indian with dark hair. The facial features were similar to the female body they had found earlier, with larger eyes and ears than seemed right for their size head. Animal skins around their groin area were the only covering for their hairy bodies.

They decided on leaving the bodies as they found them, except that John kept the club. He told Randy that from now on he would do all his hunting with Mick and wouldn't go off alone. The risk was just too great with the Mutants as a possible threat. They did find one deer kill on their return trip to their campsite, which they took to cook on the raft while they continued their trek south.

The family spent another three days on the river without seeing anything of the Mutants; when suddenly Mick nudged John and quietly said, "Look there on the west bank!"

Lillie whispered, "It's a village!"

There appeared to be five teepee style huts constructed of tree limbs placed in a half circle with a common large fire pit in the center. Tending the fire were several females, with at least six children at the shoreline that were pointing at the raft and shouting back at the camp.

Sarah grabbed John's arm and asked, "Can you make out their language?"

"No, but I get their meaning! Let's see how they react to our presence."

Suddenly, three men ran into camp and then down to the shore. They were carrying spears, which they now brandished, shaking them angrily, while shouting toward the raft.

Lillie, while holding onto Mick's arm, whispered, "What's got their shorts in such a twist?"

"Do you think they've had experiences from people on rafts before?" John wondered out-loud.

"I hope it was from our people and not some more advanced Mutants," Sarah exclaimed.

It wasn't long before they left the village behind, but the three men followed them along the shoreline for almost a mile before giving up. It was now mid-afternoon and they would normally be searching for a campsite.

John pointed to the east shore. "Let's try that side for our camp tonight."

The other members of the family quickly nodded their agreement while steering their way across the river. Generally, the east side of the river was flat lands, but not along this stretch which had medium to high bluffs along both banks. They finally found a likely spot about two hours before dusk and made camp. The hunters went in search of game, while the women and John hunted for a nearby cave. They soon found an opening in the bluff which John approached with care as the two women backed him up with spears at the ready.

The opening went deep into the bluff and John needed to use his flashlight. He was thankful its battery still had a charge as he walked into the darkness of the cave. He had purposely used it only in emergencies. The cave went back about fifteen yards and appeared to have been used for shelter before. There was evidence of a fire near the opening and dry grass and leaves were left in the rear. He returned to the opening and told the women this cave should work out fine.

CHAPTER 8

The women went to a nearby clearing and started the fire pit while John explored the surrounding area. He started from the cave and went south along the bluff face looking for something unnatural. He was not expecting a Kilroy was here type of writing, but when he saw the scratches on the bluff wall he was both surprised and alarmed. He ran back to the campsite and brought the women to see what he had found. Sarah and Lillie stared at the writing in surprise and then with fear.

Sarah turned to John and asked, "What's this mean?"

"We were smart that we didn't stop at that Mutant village! These people were lucky they got away from them after they found out they eat their enemies. If they hadn't had a rifle they may not have made it. Even so, they lost one of their party."

Sarah looked at the writing again and traced it with her fingers. "This says three continuing south and is dated June 2012. That's not that long ago!"

"Yes, it looks like more people from our time have passed this way on their way south. I wonder when and where we're going to find them."

After the hunters returned with their bounty, they were told of their find. After their evening meal, John started a discussion of what steps they should take now that they knew the Mutants were unfriendly. He suggested that they practice daily with their weapons so that they would become proficient in their use.

Mick added, "We should only hunt upstream in the future, because at least we would have had a look at where we've been."

John nodded his head in agreement. "That's a good idea, but I think we should place a limit on the distance the hunters travel from camp."

The consensus the family agreed upon was a half-mile limit. Later that night as Sarah and John cuddled together next to the fire, she whispered, "Have you noticed a change in Patches?"

"What do you mean?"

She smiled, and then replied, "She's pregnant you dope!"

"How can you tell?"

She hugged him, speaking softly. "We women always know these things."

He smiled, but then looked into her eyes with concern. "You're not pregnant, are you?"

She laughed before answering. "No, but I wouldn't mind if I was."

"Well, hold off until we get where we're going if you don't mind," he said. Then he smiled and gave her a passionate kiss.

Sarah gave his ear an affectionate nip before breaking apart. She then considered Patches for a moment. "She must have gotten pregnant when we were visiting Mother who has a male beagle. How long have we been on this trip?"

"I haven't kept track of the time, but it's got to be about two months. What's the gestation period for a dog?"

"I think it's been about that long, so she must be due any time now."

That morning John suggested they begin practicing with their weapons an hour each day before they resumed their raft trip south. After they started their practice, it became obvious that they should have been doing this all along. However, at the end of their first practice session they didn't look near as bad as they had at the beginning.

John was pleased with their efforts and decided to give them some positive feedback. "Well done. You all look good, especially Lillie! I didn't think anyone could be that accurate with a sling."

Randy grimaced. "That's because she's been practicing more than me."

"Maybe so, but I think it's because she has more muscle to use with the sling. Besides, you did quite well with the throwing stick. Maybe we should practice more with our individual strengths and cross train with other weapons when we have the time."

They all congratulated each other on their strengths and John realized that as a group they possessed a formidable defense against anything but an ambush.

John lent his voice to his thoughts as he explained, "You have done well, but we have to know how to use our weapons without conscious thought in case of an ambush, especially for our hunters."

Mick considered the ambush possibility for a moment, but then smiled. "I think we have a secret weapon in Patches. She will let us know if any of the Mutants are near."

Sarah then remembered that she hadn't told Randy about Patches and pulled him aside. "Randy, Patches is almost due to have puppies, so you will have to watch her closely. She might try to go off somewhere to have them."

Randy watched his mother closely as she explained about Patches, then loudly yelled, "Yahoo! We're going to have puppies!"

The family all stared at Patches and they now could see her teats were starting to bulge with milk and she had obviously gained weight.

Lillie laughed with glee, pointing at the dog. "Patches is going to be a mother!"

Patches seemed to grin at them as if to say, what's the big deal. They soon continued their trek south on the river. They left the bluffs behind as the river twisted and turned in its southern journey. They noticed that the trees had started to change colors brought on by the early fall season's cool nights.

John and Sarah were sitting together on the raft observing the beautiful colors along the shoreline. "It's well we're this far south already as winter is not far behind this color change. We should be far enough south when winter does arrives to not feel its bite," he commented.

Randy excitedly exclaimed, "Look! Patches is having her pups!" Patches had been lying on their store of animal skins and was now delivering her brood. One was already out and another was on the way. When she was done, she had four whimpering puppies that she was cleaning up with her tongue, and then all was quiet as they found her milk. She had delivered two males and two females.

John observed, "Well, this is going to slow Patches down. Mick, you and Randy will have to do without Patches for a while. That means while you're hunting you need to be extra careful to avoid ambushes."

Sarah whispered to John, "I've been thinking. The reason we're going south is because we think it will be easier to survive in a warmer climate. Using that reasoning, won't there be more of the Mutants in the south as well?"

"Yes, it's possible... Maybe even probable that there are more of them. But, apparently they wage war on each other's tribes or villages, so that may keep their numbers down."

"That's not a pleasant thought. We may have to do battle with them too!" she said with dread.

"Yes, it's very likely, but we'll try to avoid them if possible. In the meantime we had better practice with our weapons until they become second nature to us."

The family continued south another two days with only one sighting of a small band of Mutants on the east shore. They were obviously seen because the party stopped and shook their spears at them.

"This is bad. Either this group has had past dealings with our people or they view all others as their enemy," John said as he shook his head.

They decided to pick a campsite on the opposite side of the river from the group sighted. It happened that this shore was the bluff side which they favored because of the possibility of a cave shelter.

The family soon found a likely spot to tie up the raft and the hunters left shortly after they were sure they were alone. John again cautioned the hunters to be careful before they departed. Lillie used a sack made from the skins Mick and Randy had fashioned to bring the pups ashore and then fixed a spot for Patches and the pups near the campsite. When they were searching for a likely cave John became uncomfortable as a strange feeling came over him.

After they found a shelter he asked the women, "Do you feel something odd about this place?"

Sarah looked at Lillie and shuddered. "It gives me the creeps," she said in a shaky voice.

"Me too! I hope we don't have to stay here tonight," Lillie added.

The mother and daughter huddled close together and gave each other a big hug before returning to camp. They walked back into camp to find a large German Shepherd dog between Patches and the pups, and themselves. The dog had its hackles raised and started growling in a threatening manner.

"Whoops, what have we here!" John said, while holding the women back with his outstretched hands. They slowly backed away from the dogs and conferred.

Sarah whispered, "What's it doing here and how do we get our dogs back?"

"I don't know, but let's try to make friends. You both stay back here and don't do anything unless it tries to eat me," he said with a smile, whereupon Sarah punched his shoulder.

"You be careful!"

John slowly approached the growling dog whose aggressiveness increased as he got closer. He stopped about fifteen feet from the dog and tried to coach him into a better mood. Now that he was closer he could see that the dog had a collar which meant that he wasn't dealing with a wild animal. He slowly reached into his pocket and withdrew a small piece of dried meat.

He showed the meat to the dog and tried to get him to come get it. When that failed, he threw it in front of the dog which stopped growling and stepped back while looking at the meat. The dog then slowly approached the meat and smelled it while watching John. It then picked it up and started eating it while watching John with raised ears.

John called to Sarah, "Do you have any more dried meat?"

She called back, "Catch it!"

He retrieved the meat and offered it to the dog again. This time the dog slowly approached John and took the meat from his hand without hesitation.

John called to Patches, "Here Patches, come here girl," and the dog came to John. While he was petting Patches, the German Shepherd brushed up against him wanting some of the same treatment. As he was petting both dogs and rubbing their ears, he called for the women to approach slowly. Patches immediately went to Sarah and Lillie who made over the dog as John had done. The German Shepherd watched the women closely as they approached and then went to Lillie and smelled her scent. He then whimpered and jumped up on Lillie while licking her face.

John grinned. "It looks like Lillie's got herself a dog whether she wants one or not."

Lillie had quieted the dog down and was looking at its collar. "This says his name is Rocky," she said, while petting the dog and examining him for any injuries.

She found an ugly healed scar on its right rear leg. "It looks like someone or something caused this," she told the others.

John thought about the situation and then replied, "Obviously, Rocky didn't get here by himself. My guess is the party he was with was attacked near here by the Mutants and he was probably the only survivor."

The women stiffened and turned white, while looking around the area. John quickly tried to put them at ease.

"Relax, there's nobody near here or the dogs would let us know. Especially Rocky who's sure to let us know since his last encounter with the Mutants was not friendly."

The women relaxed and smiled with relief at John. "You'll let me know if anyone is near won't you," Lillie whispered to Rocky while rubbing his ears as he looked at her with soulful eyes. He then jerked in her arms and started growling, looking upriver.

John urged Lillie to hold him tight because this may be Mick and Randy returning from the hunt. When the hunters walked into the camp they were stopped by the sound of a growling dog.

Lillie spoke softly to Rocky, "It's okay boy, they're friends." She kept repeating this until his growling stopped, but he remained stiff and alert in her arms as he watched the newcomers. She called for Mick and Randy to slowly approach her and Rocky so that they could become acquainted with the newest member of their family. It wasn't long before they were friends with Rocky. When Lillie hugged and kissed Mick, Rocky tried to nudge him aside so he could get some of that treatment.

That night after they were full of roasted deer, they sat together discussing Rocky and what might have happened to his owners. Rocky was lying on the ground next to Lillie, while Randy was playing with Patches and the puppies. John theorized that Rocky's owner must have been a young woman similar in appearance to Lillie.

"I'm just glad he survived so he could join us," Lillie said as she rubbed the dog's ears.

Sarah leaned against John while holding him tightly. "John, how long ago do you think this attack happened?"

"I'd guess not more than a year. That scar on his flank, while healed, still has a little pink tissue around it."

Sarah shuddered. "I wonder how many of our people have suffered a similar fate?"

The family had now grown to two men, two women, a young boy, and six dogs as they continued their journey south. Rocky took to rafting as if he had done it before, which he probably had with his prior family. The pups roaming quickly became a problem keeping them on the raft. Mick and Randy wove an enclosure from small tree branches that seemed to do the job, at least until the pups got bigger.

It had been almost a week since Rocky joined their family and he now joined the hunters when they left camp as if this had been his duty previously. This relieved both John and the two women as this gave the hunters some protection from an ambush. They had seen groups of the Mutants more frequently now along the banks of the river as they traveled south. This seemed to agree with their conclusion that more of them would live in the southern part of the country.

The river had flowed through flatlands for the past three days when suddenly they entered the edge of a large circular lake that was at least 300 yards in diameter.

John puzzled about the lake as they slowly drifted across it with the current. "This looks like a crater lake, maybe a bomb crater. If I'm correct, this is about where Memphis should be."

The women looked at him with their mouths open, then Sarah grabbed John's arm. "You think this used to be Memphis!"

When he nodded, she anxiously whispered, "So this is what caused our civilization to end."

They fell silent as the raft slowly crossed the lake and left it behind. The flatlands continued as they floated south. The banks of both shores were heavily wooded with only occasional breaks in the wilderness. This at first worried John since he thought that the Mutants would use these breaks as well. But, as the wilderness continued he began to suspect that these breaks could only be reached from the river, and he had not yet seen any Mutants on the river.

It was late afternoon of their third month anniversary of their trek when they found a break in the wilderness to make camp on the east shore. They had an added bonus as it included a small clear stream flowing into the river.

After securing the raft Sarah pointed to the stream and excitedly said to Lillie, "We've got clean water to wash clothes and take a bath tonight!"

John chuckled and held his shirt out from his body.

"I don't know about you, but I'm getting tired of smelling like river mud."

Sarah wrinkled her nose at him. "Are you saying I smell like that too?"

"We all smell like that."

Sarah grabbed his arm and pulled him toward a deep hole in the stream and started stripping them of their clothes. They then started washing each other with sand until their skin turned pink. Sarah sighed and then moaned with happiness as John gave her neck and back muscles a vigorous massage, then she playfully returned the favor.

They suddenly became aware that they were not alone in the water. Mick and Lillie were emulating their activity, with Lillie now rubbing Mick's back muscles. She looked over at Sarah and winked while continuing to rub her man's back.

Randy was in the water too, giving Patches and Rocky baths. John gave Sarah a questioning look to see if she had any objections, but she warily smiled and shook her head.

"I guess we're comfortable with each other and our relationships, so who am I to object."

The women busied themselves with washing clothes after the hunters left the meadow heading up the small stream while John prepared a fire pit and gathered limbs for a shelter. The pups were now weaned from Patches who was now free to join the other hunters. The pups amused themselves around the clearing while everyone else was working.

That evening the family relaxed after their meal enjoying the sunset across the river and later watching the antics of the pups around the campfire. The pups loved to engage in horseplay, fighting mock battles and chasing each other until finally even they collapsed next to Patches.

Sarah snuggled up against John and whispered in his ear, "Let's go soak in the stream."

He looked at her with questioning eyes, and she nodded with a smile. Sarah told the others they were going swimming and then pointedly told Lillie that they wished to be alone, who responded with a wink at her mother while she cuddled up to Mick with a secret smile on her face as her parents left the campsite.

The family decided to spend another day at this location and rest. The raft also needed some repairs and the little meadow with the clear stream was just too good to leave. The dogs appreciated the break in travel as well and were having a good time romping around the meadow.

Lillie washed the hunters' clothes they wore yesterday, while they wore clean clothes. She noted that Mick's clothes were getting thin as they saw more use while hunting. Randy had already outgrown his first set of clothes, so she called Sarah over and proposed they use them to repair all their clothes as the need arose.

Sarah held up Randy's outgrown clothes as she commented, "It's a good thing John suggested we pack several sizes for Randy. He's grown like a weed these last few months. You know, I think you're right, if we use patches to reinforce Mick's clothes it should keep them from wearing through."

Lillie looked down at her own army fatigues. "What are we going to do when these wear out?"

Sarah shook her head in frustration. "I guess we go native and wear grass skirts. Seriously, until we figure out how to weave cloth, we'll have to use whatever is handy."

Lillie touched her mother's shoulder and with a serious expression said, "Mother, Mick and I have decided to make it official and get married. I want some words said before witnesses for my marriage. I know you and John just went and did it, but I want something more. Do you think John would officiate as head of the family?"

She took Lillie's face in her hands with tears of happiness in her eyes. "I know you realize you're young to get married, at least by our old standards; but I agree if you both feel it's time to make it official, I'll consent to your wedding. I'll get together with John and we'll do it this afternoon or tonight."

The two then put their heads together and started planning the upcoming nuptials. She hesitantly asked her mother's advice on matters involving marital bliss and wedding night jitters. Sarah gave her advice based upon her own two marriages and told her not to worry about her wedding night. Just go with her feelings.

Later that evening, the wedding party gathered under a hastily constructed arbor of wild flowers. The bride's head was adorned with a crown of wild flowers and she carried a bridal bouquet of wild roses.

The flowers they gathered for the crown were a slightly different variant of old earth daisies. Instead of a yellow center, these were pink centered. The roses used in the bouquet were without thorns or scent and had a larger bud than wild roses they had been familiar with.

In a simple ceremony the two said their vows of love and commitment and then John pronounced them man and wife before God and her family.

John and Sarah hugged and kissed the bride, while John took Mick aside and gave him some fatherly advice. Randy ran into Lillie's arms with tears in his eyes. She consoled him by telling him that she was still his sister, even if she was now married. It was a joyful and tearful gathering that evening around the fire as they had their last meal at Lillie and Mick's wedding site.

They made an attempt to make this wedding meal special and had gathered as many different edible berries and roots they could find to go with roasted deer. After the meal they entertained themselves as best their circumstances allowed. John took Sarah into his arms and danced to music only they heard, while Lillie and Mick watched in awe. Finally, Lillie pulled Mick to his feet and they danced along with John and Sarah.

The new married couple eventually left the camp and made their way to their prepared nuptial bed. They were both excited and apprehensive as they approached the bed's isolated location. The only light was from a quarter moon which cast an eerie glow on their pale bodies as they disrobed each other. They slowly embraced, then explored each other's bodies until they had worked themselves into a fever pitch. The couple then started making love gently, then more feverish as their passion grew.

Later as their passions were sated, they lay in each other's arms until they felt their hearts slowly settle down from their fearful pounding. The young couple held each other tightly while expressing their love for each other. Lillie thanked God for providing this loving and kind man for her husband.

CHAPTER 9

The next morning the couple approached camp with a light heart and somewhat sore muscles. Sarah saw their approach and elbowed John. "Here comes Lillie and Mick. They walk just like a newly married couple." Then she softly laughed into his shoulder.

John smiled at the approaching couple. "They seem happy, don't they? Now, don't embarrass Mick! He's new at this and even after being exposed to this rowdy bunch, he's still basically a shy young man."

Lillie went to her mother and hugged her while whispering in her ear. "Mick was great! Now I know why you drag John off into the bushes so often." Then she joyfully laughed.

Mick turned brick red as Lillie and Sarah laughed. John pulled him aside away from the women. "Don't worry. They're not laughing at you, but in the joy you provided your new wife."

Mick slowly smiled. "Maybe, but she has me wrapped around her little finger."

John placed his arm around Mick and laughed. "Welcome to the club, my boy."

The family continued their trek south with another three days passing since the wedding. Sarah and John were sitting together watching Lillie and Mick fawning over each other. She leaned over and whispered in his ear, "Why don't you do that anymore?"

John responded by grabbing and kissing her passionately. When they both came up for air, Sarah sighed. "You need to do that more often. It's not up to the kids to set a good example."

John kissed the end of her nose and meekly said, "Yes dear."

They entered an area of bluffs again and soon passed by another Mutant village. These people gave no reaction other than point at their raft as they passed. This village was a little larger, with ten huts that were constructed differently. Instead of a teepee type, these were more rounded and constructed of sticks and mud.

John pointed at the dwellings as he commented. "Those huts look more like permanent construction. There must be a ample food source to justify that."

They then passed a cultivated area, as Sarah excitedly explained, "That looks like corn and squash being grown there!"

"You know, this group of Mutants seem more advanced. They may not have to compete for hunting lands like their northern brothers. Maybe these people aren't as hostile. Oh well, we can always hope. Let's not let our guards down though. Tonight we'll camp on the opposite shore," John said as he looked back at the village.

They now had daily sightings of Mutants on each side of the river. They also saw several more of the farming villages, which appeared to be getting larger as they traveled south. After a week of experiencing this increased activity they found it more difficult to find isolated campsites. They changed their routine in selecting campsites by waiting until dusk before heading into shore in the hopes of avoiding hunting parties. Also, this late in the afternoon they should be able to see camp fires or smell smoke if any were nearby.

This particular evening, they entered a bluff area that sloped almost immediately into the river, but they found a small flat wooded area against the bluff that looked promising as they guided the raft into shore. John, Mick, and the two larger dogs left the raft first to search the area while leaving the others there until they were sure the area was safe. The dogs were heard barking, and then Mick started shouting excitedly. They then heard someone running in their direction, so the women and Randy prepared to defend themselves.

Suddenly, John appeared through the trees. "It's okay, we're alone."

Lillie tensely asked, "What was all that noise about?"

He chuckled. "Mick almost got run over by a deer the dogs flushed. But, he killed it before it could get away. Randy, Mick needs your help with the skinning!"

Randy's face lit up and he hurried toward the sounds of the dogs, followed by the pups. John helped the women secure the raft and establish a campsite within the trees to hopefully hide the fire's glow. They found a small clearing in the trees, perfect for their purposes. Even better, it didn't appear to have been used as a campsite before. He returned to the raft for their packs while the women prepared the fire pit.

That night they dined without fear of discovery. The married couples had started alternating sleeping near or on the raft. This gave them some security protection for the raft as well as privacy away from the rest of the family. Tonight was John and Sarah's turn at the raft.

Sarah fixed their bedding near the raft while John inspected the raft's lines. He called to her, "Let's go in for a swim and get some sweat off us."

She immediately stripped off her clothes and yelled, "Last one in is a rotten egg!"

They enjoyed themselves until the cold water forced them back to the shore, shivering from the night's cool air on their wet bodies. They ran for their bedding where they wrapped themselves together and later made sweet passionate love.

Sometime later, Sarah wistfully remarked, "Togetherness is nice, but we need these breaks so we can renew ourselves. I'm glad you thought of it, dear."

"I had to do something. The sexual tension was getting so bad that even Randy and the dogs were starting to notice," John said and then chuckled as he moved to softly nibble her ear lobe before kissing her passionately.

The morning brought a promise of bad weather. The wind brought in heavy dark clouds that raced across the sky. John met with the family and they all agreed that they should stay where they were until the weather settled down. The wind increased to gale force and they all helped in pulling the raft on shore to avoid its breaking loose. They then tried to waterproof their shelter as best they could and settled down to wait out the storm.

The rain arrived first in an increasing volume until a deluge was falling. The wind drove the rain almost horizontally with such force that their shelter gave little protection from the wet even though they had some windbreak inside the trees. Everyone was soon soaked even through their animal skin coverings. John, Sarah, and Randy wrapped their skins tighter around the three of them and hoped that their body heat would keep them warm. Lillie and Mick followed their lead and soon she was giggling beneath their covering.

John grinned at Sarah and whispered, "That's one way of increasing your body heat." He started massaging Sarah's body which she reciprocated until they were all toasty. The wind and rain lessened and suddenly stopped. There was an eerie silence for a few minutes until, with a roar the storm was upon them again. This time there was hail and lightning in addition to the wind and rain.

John said, "Oh boy, I hope that 'Ball' comes to our rescue and calls off the hail and lightning!"

As if answering his call, a glowing ball appeared outside their shelter; hesitated briefly, then moved slowly inside until it stopped before John who had raised himself. The "Ball" hovered before John's face for a few seconds, then a small lightning charge flashed between it and John's head. The connection lasted for almost a minute before stopping, whereupon the "Ball" left the shelter.

John wavered and would have fallen back except for Sarah grabbing him as she urgently called to him, "John...John! Are you alright? Can you hear me?"

She then shook him when there was no response. The others gathered around offering their support when John finally faintly moaned, and then while holding his head, moaned again louder.

Sarah was frantic as she held him and sobbed. "Honey, tell me you're alright! You've got to be okay!"

He looked up at her face and in a weak voice said, "The pain is going away now. But, it was a bear for a while. It felt like a spike in my brain."

Sarah smiled through her tears. "Next time don't wish for that dammed "Ball" to come and save us!"

He smiled at her and pulled her down for a kiss. "I'm feeling better now. I think the reason it affected me so strongly this time was because it communicated with me."

They all looked at him with surprised stares. He gave them a quirky smile as he continued. "I know it sounds crazy, but the 'Ball' really did speak to me. You didn't hear anything?"

They all shook their heads no. Sarah then shook him gently. "Honey, don't you remember. The 'Ball' shot lightning at you, just like before."

"Well, it wasn't like before because this time it hurt! The 'Ball' wanted me to know that in two more days of travel down the river we need to leave the raft and head east."

They looked at him with surprise and then each started asking questions at once. John held up his hand until there was silence. "It said the river ends soon and we'll eventually find others like us. It also said that we will know where to leave the river because of the loud noise from the water ahead."

Lillie softly repeated, "Loud noise from the water ahead."

John gave her a lopsided grin. "Have you ever heard the sound from a large waterfall?"

"Yes, I think it would be a good time to leave the river if it means going over falls," she said with a smile.

They all became aware that the storm had moved on so they broke camp and resumed their southern journey.

That evening they decided to camp on a good-sized island in the middle of the river. The island was far enough from either shore to offer protection from the Mutants. It was heavily wooded and had a sandy beach on the downstream side where they pulled their raft high enough to prevent it from drifting away. In addition, there was a grounded tree trunk nearby which they used for a tie down.

Since they were on an island, it was not likely there were any Mutants here but to be sure, the hunters did a quick check for any other inhabitants. Soon they were back with the all-clear news before leaving again to hunt for dinner. The pups, while still growing, were not yet of the size to keep up with the hunters. They stayed with the campsite group, checking out their site selection, and generally following the family around while they were doing their tasks.

Dusk was falling when the hunters returned with their game. Mick and Randy excitedly related their experiences while on the hunt. It seems deer and other animals either swam or were carried to the island by floods and were trapped here. In any case, they had a large selection to choose from and had brought back enough for them to sundry for their coming overland trip.

John put his arm around Mick's shoulders and praised him for his foresightedness. "We'll need several days to prepare the meat on racks. In the meantime, we need to prepare ourselves for the trip. Let's practice with our weapons and make sure the packs are in good shape for our coming hike."

Randy had become quite good with both the throwing stick and sling, while the others excelled in at least one of their chosen weapons. The bow was still their most accurate weapon, with which Mick and John continuously practiced. Mick was deadly at up to thirty yards while John's range was almost as good. His accuracy was increasing as he practiced and he hoped to equal Mick's expertise soon.

Those who used the sling had each made themselves a small bag for carrying good stones. If they got into a fight while traveling, they wouldn't have time to look for stones. Along those same lines, Mick and John made themselves extra arrows, and the throwing stick users made several short spears. By the time the meat was ready, the family had everything else in order for their overland trek.

Their last day on the river was stressful as they eagerly waited for the noise they had been told to expect. They were traveling fairly close to the east shore of the river in case they had to come ashore quickly.

Listening for the noise and watching the shore for the Mutants had put everyone on edge.

It was early afternoon when they first heard a muted roar ahead on the river. They edged the raft closer to the east shore as the roar got louder until finally they could see water spray arising from the river about a mile ahead. It was here where they saw several rafts beached ahead. John pointed to the rafts and motioned to Mick to help pull their raft alongside the others.

The hunters left the raft first and did a fast survey for any enemy before returning for the others. They all collected their belongings, making sure nothing of value was left behind, and then followed John along the bank toward the falls, with Mick bringing up the rear. John was following a narrow trail between the river and the forest as he set an easy pace so that the pups could keep up. The forest consisted of mostly old growth mixed trees with little underbrush where it was unlikely any Mutants could hide for an ambush. It wasn't long before they couldn't hear each other talking because of the extreme noise from the falls now less than a quarter mile away.

As they neared the falls, mist blowing up drenched everything, including the family as they walked towards the edge. The banks were now bare rock with the river flowing over the edge with such volume that the roar was painful to their ears. The rising mist was so heavy they couldn't see the bottom of the falls, nor much of anything beyond the cliff edge. John pointed east along the cliff edge as the direction they should continue. As they made their way further from the falls they eventually came to a clear overlook.

At the overlook they could see that the cliff face extended in almost a straight-line east as far as they could see. They could now see the bottom which was at least 1,000 feet below, and looking south they could see a large body of water on the horizon.

Sarah gripped John's arm tightly and spoke loudly so he could hear. "What happened here? The Gulf of Mexico shouldn't be this close!"

John shook his head and yelled that they should get further away from the falls. When they had gotten far enough away from the falls so they could converse easily, he called a halt. They all sat down near John so they could more easily hear what he had to say.

He looked at them with a lop-sided grin as he began speaking. "This is as new to me as you. That has got to be the granddaddy of all waterfalls. The cliff face may have been the result of tectonic plates shifting causing severe earthquakes and this section to drop."

Lillie interrupted. "You might be right, but this has got to be the biggest change we've come across yet!"

John nodded his head and then pointed back at the falls. "That more than anything else we've seen points to a great deal of time passing since our own time."

He hesitated a moment before continuing. "As for the Gulf being this close, that could be caused by a combination of the land dropping and there being more water now in the oceans. We don't know all that's happened since our time, but this is another probable example of the result of such occurrences. My bet is the great kill-off from whatever reason resulted in heavy rains and/or the melting of the ice caps. The ice caps were starting to melt even in our own time so that theory might be more likely."

Sarah looked at him for a moment with concern evident on her face before speaking. "Honey, since we don't really know what caused this, your theory sounds pretty good to me."

He looked at Lillie who nodded her head in agreement. The family, after a few minutes of reflection, started their trek east following a worn path between the forest and a long drop off.

They had traveled about three hours when approaching dusk forced them to seek a campsite. The thunder of the falls was only a faint murmur when they found a clearing suitable for their purposes. It was soon evident that they were not the first to camp here. A well-used fire pit was ready for their use with a supply of firewood stacked close at hand. Nearby was a mound of rocks with a capstone similar to what they had found earlier on their trek.

He looked under the capstone and found a folded animal skin. The other family members gathered around as he unfolded the skin carefully and held it up to the fading light. Written in charcoal was a message dated 9/12 which said, "Party of 3 heading east." Signed Wm Harding. Added at various dates were messages from six other parties with the most recent being 7/14, a party of four. The seven different entries reflected a total of twenty-one people. John picked up a piece of charcoal from the fire pit and added their party to the list before replacing the message where he found it.

John turned to the others as he finished his task. "Well, that last group is not too far ahead of us and we all seem to be going in the same direction so maybe we'll meet up eventually."

This thought seemed to perk up the family's morale as they prepared their camp. That evening, John and Sarah were standing near the edge of the drop off, looking out toward the Gulf. He had his arm around her shoulders and she was leaning her head against him. The lowlands were in darkness as the moon had not yet risen. That darkness was broken sporadically by points of light from campfires.

John pointed to the lights. "Those must be camps of the Mutants, as I'm sure if it were our people there would be one big settlement."

Sarah sighed. "You're right. We would need to stay together for protection."

Mick and Lillie joined them at the overlook and echoed Sarah's comments. The two couples sat and watched the moon rise over the strange vista until it was high enough to make the Gulf glisten. John turned to his mate and kissed her passionately.

Sarah cuddled closer to John and sighed. "It is a romantic sight, isn't it?" She softly whispered.

The other couple must have had similar thoughts, as they were gripped in a passionate embrace. John pulled Sarah to her feet and they went in search of a more private place to continue their lovemaking with Sarah leading the way.

* * *

The family had been following the trail next to the cliff edge for two weeks. Sometimes the trail left the cliff as it bypassed a ravine or some other natural obstruction, but eventually it always returned to the cliff edge. They were now walking between a heavy forest growth and the cliff.

The pups were now a fully functional part of the family. They allowed two young dogs to go with the hunters and kept two at the campsite each afternoon. Randy had named the two young male dogs "Trouble and Hunter," while Lillie named the females "Princess and Brownie." The names fit the dogs personalities, except for Brownie who was named after her predominate color.

The young beagles were all good hunters, but Hunter was the best of the lot. He even surpassed Patches in the nose department. All the dogs were trained to follow voice commands, especially the command to stay silent. This command could prove life saving if they had to hide from a group of Mutants. While on the hunt the beagles' normal braying was a natural for flushing game.

They had been on the trail for only an hour when John saw movement ahead. He turned to the others and motioned them to take cover in the woods while softly commanding the dogs to remain silent. Lillie had her hand on Rocky's collar seeking to calm the dog. She could feel him trembling with anticipation as a group of four Mutant hunters approached. They were laden with game and were not paying close attention to the trail, which was good news for the family.

The enemy party passed them without even a glance in their

direction. John waited until they were out of sight and then silently motioned the family back onto the trail heading east. It was almost twenty minutes before he called a halt and congratulated everyone on their behavior. They gave him a nervous smile before they continued their trek.

CHAPTER 10

The afternoon of their fourth week on the trail they were surprised to see the cliff face take a noticeable southern turn. John stopped and pulled out his atlas and considered where they might be.

"I think we may be in Alabama, but we haven't come across any large rivers yet and we need to cross two before we reach mid-point across Alabama." He let the others see where he was pointing on the map.

Mick pointed ahead at the far cliff face. "Isn't that a waterfall over there?"

They all looked and Lillie acknowledged that she could see one but that it was a long way off. John and Sarah shook their heads and looked at each other ruefully.

"It's hell when you get old and can't see as well as you could when you were their age," John said, with Sarah nodding her head in silent agreement.

They continued on for another hour before making camp. After the hunters left and the campsite established, John conferred with the two women. "These two rivers we have to cross look wide on the map, so we may have to build rafts to cross them. Of course we might be further north than I thought, in which case we may only have one large river to cross."

Sarah grinned at her husband. "Honey, you worry too much. We'll handle whatever we come across, just like we've done before. Besides, I've got every confidence in your ability to take care of us."

Lillie grinned at her parents and shook her head. "Mother's judgment may be clouded by her love for you but she's right about one thing. We would have been up the creek without you. You have made us self-sufficient and together we can handle anything."

John gave Lillie a lopsided grin and held out his arms to the two women who came into his arms hugging each other, all with tears in their eyes.

The family stayed on the main trail which continued to follow the cliff face as it curved further south. They eventually came to the waterfall Mick and Lillie had seen from a distance. Its source was a small river which according to the atlas might be the Tombigbee River in Alabama. They followed it upriver about two miles where the banks were sandy and the current not too swift.

John called a meeting and suggested they stop near here for a few days to rest, clean clothes, and make general repairs. The others met that suggestion with wide smiles and loud jubilance. They then decided to find a crossing upstream and establish a campsite on the opposite shore. They crossed about a mile further upstream and followed a trail downstream a short distance where they found an established campsite.

The women started washing their clothes while the hunters searched the area downstream for any sign of Mutants. Mick and Randy returned in about two hours and reported no signs, at least back to the cliff. They then took all the dogs except Rocky to hunt for game. The pups were now fully-grown and followed Hunter as the lead dog, including Patches, their mother. They made quite a hunting pack and it wasn't long before they returned to camp with game.

It was now late afternoon and a deer was roasting over the fire. The women had finished their washing and John had fixed a drying rack so that the wash could dry overnight. Lillie asked John for the pants he had worn at the original crash site so she could have Mick wear them while she washed all his clothes. He told her to keep them as Mick needed them more than he did. He then stripped to his shorts and asked her to wash his clothes as well.

Sarah took them from Lillie and shook her head at John.

"You need to have those shorts washed too. As soon as your other pair of pants gets dry then those shorts get washed."

He grinned at her and quipped. "Be gentle, they're all I've got."

At dusk they all went into the river for a long needed bath, leaving the dogs to guard the camp. The couples washed each other while Randy played with whichever dog he could get into the water. Sarah was rubbing John's back with sand until he complained of her harsh treatment. She replied, "We have worn those clothes until they could

71

stand alone and it's taking some effort to get this dirt and grime off of you."

When she was finished, he said with a roguish grin, "Now it's my turn!"

But, before he started he gave her a passionate kiss. Then with a handful of sand he began taking the grime off her skin until it glowed. Lillie and Mick were still washing each other when John and Sarah left the water in search of a private place to make love. They both had become quite aroused during their washing exercises and only stopped long enough to pick up their bedding.

Later that night they returned to the fire, sated from their lovemaking. Lillie and Mick returned soon after but their soft laughter didn't disturb the other sleepers. It was well that they had the dogs to watch over them because they were all in a deep sleep minutes after settling into their bedding.

The next morning the refreshed family members continued their eastward walk along the cliff. They were still in a heavily forested area, following a path along a narrow open space near the cliff edge. The cliff continued to slowly turn south, which gave them a good view of the trail ahead.

They were on the trail for almost four hours when suddenly John saw movement ahead. He immediately waved the others into the woods. After they were all under cover and the dogs cautioned to be quiet, John and Mick checked what was ahead on the trail.

It was well that they had moved quickly, because a hunting party of Mutants was leaving the forest onto the trail only fifty yards ahead of them. The Mutants waited until their party was together, then departed along the trail away from the family. It was a large hunting party, six adults and four younger members. They all carried spears which two of the younger hunters put to use carrying game between themselves.

After they were out of hearing range, John told his family they should wait here until they were out of sight. Since they were in a forced rest period, they might as well use it to their advantage. The women passed around some leftover roasted deer while the men tended to the dogs. The dogs were initially tense, but soon relaxed as the family settled down where they were.

John periodically watched the Mutants as they followed the trail ahead. After almost an hour when he next looked down the trail, they were gone. He watched for another fifteen minutes but they never reappeared.

John turned to the others and roused the ones taking a nap. "I think they left the trail up ahead about an hour's walk from here. So, as we get near I'm going to have you all wait while I scout ahead."

Sarah looked at him with a worried expression. "Honey, you take Mick and Rocky with you. If something happens you'll have better protection and we can provide backup if needed. We'll be alright by ourselves, the beagles will let us know if there's any of the enemy nearby."

He looked at the others and after they nodded their agreement, he nodded his head in acceptance. When they got close to where he thought he had lost sight of the Mutants, he stopped and had the family move into the woods. Then he, Mick, and Rocky proceeded slowly along the trail.

Eventually, they came across a side trail that dropped into a ravine as it moved away from the main trail. Rocky didn't seem concerned about any nearby Mutants, so he had Mick return for the rest of the family.

When they returned John pointed out that they now had two trails and must decide which to follow. They had encountered side trails before and had in the past stayed on the main trail. He indicated that the Mutants went on the trail away from the bluff, but that his vote was to continue on the cliff trail so that they might avoid contact with them. Sarah and the others agreed without any further discussion.

They noted that the height of the cliff face they were following had sharply declined and was now only half its former distance above the coastal plain. They soon crossed a large river, which according to his road atlas was probably the Alabama River. They followed along the trail for another week before the cliff ended abruptly; however, the trail continued in a southeasterly direction through a thick forest of tall pines and hardwoods.

They found several more side trails but elected to stay on the main trail until they encountered a sign of some kind. John was hoping for another mound of rocks with a message.

The hunters had no problem getting game and streams were plentiful for their needs. After another five days the trail ended at another large river they were not able to ford without building a small raft for their packs and dogs. The atlas indicated that it was probably the Chattahoochee River separating Alabama from Georgia. They held onto the raft and swam with it to the other side without incident.

They found three similar rafts beached on the shore where they picked up the trail again. Their spirits lifted when they realized they were still on the same trail as the other people from their time. John called a rest while they changed into dry clothing. Before they started again he showed the others the atlas and pointed out that the next big obstruction ahead was the Atlantic Ocean and unless they changed direction, their journey should be about over.

Their pace along the trail seemed easier with the knowledge that their travels may soon be over and they might soon encounter others of their kind. That night they camped beside a small lake. The weather had remained mild during the day but was cool at night. However, the fur bedding and the couples snuggling kept them warm. Randy made do by sleeping close to the fire inside his fur bedding and surrounded by his dogs.

The family was huddled close to the fire and watching the night sky flickering occasionally with lightning flashes and distant thunder. They hadn't encountered any storms since they left the Mississippi, but had seen several distant storms pass at night. Sarah shuddered when a particularly loud thunder boomer was heard.

John tightened his grip around her shoulders and softly spoke, "Babe, it's a long way off and moving away from us so don't worry about it."

She leaned into him more tightly and looked up at him.

"I know honey, but I keep thinking of the last time that 'Ball' zapped you and how it affected you. It just gives me the shakes!"

"I know it's scary, but remember it was trying to help us and didn't intend to do me any harm." Her only response was to hug him more tightly.

* * *

The girl saw the campfire as soon as she left the woods. It was like a beacon drawing her closer, yet it held danger for her too. She had spent the day hunting for food, whatever was edible – berries, roots. Once she had caught a rabbit thing, but it didn't taste good raw and she threw-up what she had swallowed.

She began to crawl closer to the fire, hoping these people were not like the others who had killed her family. She could now make out several figures moving around the campfire and they looked like they were all dressed alike. She thought they looked like soldiers, except for one who looked too small, maybe about her size. They had dogs! The others didn't have dogs and they didn't dress like these people. The others didn't hardly wear anything, just some skins around their middle part.

She hoped these people were friendly. Can I take a chance and let them know I'm here? She thought some more, but fear won out and she decided to wait until morning to make that decision. She watched the figures until they lay down around the campfire to sleep, and although she had found little to eat that day which caused her stomach to ache, she too fell into an exhausted sleep.

* * *

The family was awakened at daybreak by Rocky's loud barking then the braying of the beagles. Everyone quickly grabbed their weapons and looked toward the woods where the dogs were pointing. They spread out and readied their various weapons in case of an enemy charge. John quietly urged everyone not to attack anyone until he gave the word as they may be friendly.

He told the dogs to be quiet but urged them to be alert. Rocky edged closer to Lillie but maintained a low growling sound while watching the woods.

After about five minutes without any movement, John turned to the family. "You all stay in place and take your lead from me."

He then walked slowly forward until he was about halfway to the woods where he stopped. He dropped his bow and waited a few minutes.

After no response, he tried speaking. "Hey out there! We come in peace and wish you no harm."

Almost immediately, there was movement and a young grimy faced girl stood up and looked at him hesitantly before smiling broadly and began to run towards him. John was surprised for a moment, but didn't hesitate to stoop and accept her when she ran into his arms.

He asked her softly, "Are you all alone?"

She nodded then buried her head in his chest and started crying. Sarah hurried up to them and looked questioningly at John, who shook his head while trying to comfort the girl. They returned to camp with Sarah carrying his bow; however, John had Mick and the dogs kept close watch for any Mutants.

The girl appeared to be about ten years of age and was very dirty with her dress almost in tatters. She appeared to be in good health except for being very thin. Sarah and Lillie fussed over her until she quieted down and finally smiled at the women. They offered her food which she ate as if starved.

Mick returned to camp and reported that the dogs detected no Mutants near the camp. Princess came up to the little girl and nuzzled her while she was eating. She petted its head and murmured "good doggy" before continuing her meal.

When the girl finished eating, John tried to find out how she got here. He asked her if she could speak, and she nodded her head shyly. He asked, "What's your name?"

"Jenny," she replied softly.

"Jenny, what's your last name?"

"Ellsworth," she said with a slightly stronger voice.

"Where are your parents?"

She stared at him a moment, looking like she was about to start crying again, but with a little shudder regained control of herself and spoke softly. "They're dead, everyone's dead."

Then with a stronger voice she continued, "They killed Mom, Dad, Joey, and baby Katie!"

"How did you get away?"

"I was picking berries on the other side of the lake when they started killing everybody. When I saw them hit Mom with a club, I think I fainted. When I woke up everyone was gone. Nothing was left but blood... Lots of blood."

She then turned white and started to throw up her recent meal. The women attended to her while John consulted with Mick and Randy.

"Mick, you and Randy have to be very careful in your hunts! I know I've stressed this before, but this just brings it home more than ever. The Mutants have to be considered our mortal enemy and are to be avoided at all costs. If we come across a small party, we can't let them escape to tell anyone about us! Do you understand me on this?"

They both grimaced, but then nodded their heads in agreement, remembering Jenny's horrific story. The women had taken Jenny to the lake to clean her up, and then gave her one of Randy's outgrown uniforms. She looked like a different person now, especially after she had eaten something to replace what she had lost earlier. Her cheeks had some color and her eyes were clear again. What they had thought was dark hair, was actually a strawberry blond color after it had been washed.

Sarah told the others what Jenny had related to her and Lillie of her attempt to stay alive for the last month by eating berries, roots, and other things she could find in the forest. Her description of the people who killed her family matched the Mutants. She had seen our campfire last night, but was not sure we were friendly. So, she had tried to get closer this morning to watch us when the dogs got her scent. She was too afraid to show herself until John came closer and said something.

Randy sat down next to Jenny and tentatively smiled. She shyly smiled back at him. He then held out his hand which she took and shook as he said shyly, "Hi, I'm Randy. You've said yours was Jenny, is that short for something?"

She nodded her head and smiled tentatively. "Jennifer... But everyone calls me Jenny."

"You look about my age, I'm almost ten."

She grinned and nodded her head. "I turned ten about six months ago."

"I thought so. You're less than a year older than me, so we can have some fun together. I've been all by myself without anyone to play with except the dogs."

He pointed to Lillie. "She's my sister, but since she got married to Mick she's not much fun to be with. Where did you come from?"

"You mean before we got stuck in this place?"

He nodded his head.

"I'm from Jackson, Mississippi, and we were heading home from New Orleans when I woke up here. I was asleep in the back seat and thought we'd been in a wreck. I don't know how we got here. When we got out of the car we were close to this huge cliff. There was this path we started following and we didn't have any food except some snacks. Dad made a spear when we saw a small deer run across our path, but he didn't get one very often."

Randy pointed to his family. "We're all from Missouri and we rafted down the Mississippi just like Tom Sawyer and Huck Finn until we got to the cliff. Then we followed it like you did. We've got hunting dogs and Mick and me; I mean Mick and I are the hunters for the family," He said proudly with a wide grin on his face.

She said with a mischievous smile, "I bet you're the best hunter in the world."

He puffed out his chest and smiled back at her. "You wait and see, you've already ate some of what we brought back."

The other family members grinned at the exchange between the two kids and wished they hadn't met under these conditions. John asked Sarah if she thought Jenny was strong enough to continue and she reluctantly nodded her head. He then had everyone prepare to continue the journey.

CHAPTER 11

John and Sarah were sitting together the next night watching the others interact with Jenny around the campfire. The hunters had returned with their usual game which impressed Jenny because her father had not been a successful hunter.

Sarah whispered to John, "Honey, her arrival is a godsend for Randy. I've been worrying myself for most of this journey about his chances of finding someone when he grows up. It looks like the Lord does provide."

"Babe, I've been thinking along those lines myself. It seems like every time we needed some help or guidance, it's been taken care of."

He slowly shook his head. "We're pretty good, but we've needed lots of help to get this far."

Sarah hugged him tightly. "Like I said before, the Lord provides."

The next afternoon they stopped early to refresh their skills with their various weapons. Randy showed Jenny the throwing stick and the sling, both of which he had developed substantial proficiency. After his demonstration of each weapon, she tried the throwing stick first but even after several tries she couldn't get the hang of it. She then tried the sling and was immediately more successful. He gave her some additional instructions in technique and watched her practice until she was hitting the target tree four out of five times from a distance of twenty yards.

That night Randy was bragging about Jenny's ability with the sling, saying she was a natural and it wouldn't be long until she was as good as he was.

Jenny blushed with happiness from his praise. "I don't have near the distance Randy does, but I'm improving."

John came over and hugged her. "You're doing great. We all had to learn how to use the weapons we use and it wasn't easy. It takes lots of practice to be good and we're going to have to be very good if we're going to beat the Mutants in a fight."

Jenny looked up at him with a grim expression. "Don't worry, I'm going to practice until I'm the best with a sling that there ever was."

"It looks like we're going to have to practice more if we don't want to look bad against Jenny," Lillie told Randy with a smile.

They were three more days on the trail without seeing any of the enemy. Shortly after the mid-day break on the fourth day as they were rounding a bend in the trail, they came face to face with a group of four Mutants. They just stood and looked at each other in surprise for a moment before John suddenly shouted to his family.

"Spread out and prepare to attack!"

The Mutants immediately started running at them from only a scant thirty yards distance, screaming loudly and with their spears down in attack position.

The first to attack the Mutants was Randy with his throwing stick. At this close range he hit the lead male in the stomach, knocking him back into those following and forcing them to move around him as he lay screaming his life away. The slight delay gave the family time to use their own weapons, which dropped two others with multiple hits. The remaining male continued to run screaming toward them when Jenny hit him squarely in the head with a stone from her sling just as Rocky sprang at his throat.

They stood in stunned silence looking at the bodies lying on the ground until John spoke, "Mick, make sure that they're dead! The rest of us will retrieve our spears and arrows, then we'll drag their bodies off the trail and cover them with brush."

He assigned these tasks, in part, to get their minds off the killing. It was well they didn't have time to think when the attack started; they had all acted on instinct from practice with their weapons. When they finished their tasks, John called them together for a group hug and a hearty well done. Sarah and Lillie looked like they were in shock at what they had done.

John spoke quietly, "I know you haven't killed anyone before. But, remember that it was either kill or be killed by these people. I'm sure you wouldn't want to be grieving over one of us lying dead here instead of them."

Both Sarah and Lillie nodded their heads in agreement and gave

John a tentative smile.

"Now take a deep breath and try to put this episode behind us and think positive. We are alive and we must be ready to kill those we meet again if we want to stay that way."

They then continued on for another four hours until they found a suitable campsite.

Later that evening after they finished their meal he called them close around the fire and did a recap of their battle. "We were good and very lucky. If the Mutants had been closer when the attack started, we might not all be here now. More important, Jenny's accuracy at the end may have saved someone from injury."

He grinned at Jenny, while the others hugged her. Jenny blushed at their praise but wanted to fair, so she spoke hesitantly, "I can't get full credit for that last enemy I hit; Rocky should get credit too!"

John chuckled and put his arm around her as he said, "Jenny, if we're ever in a similar situation, you and Rocky are our backup. We've been bloodied and now know what to expect."

Two days later they came to a clearing with a large spring. It was early afternoon and they usually wouldn't stop for another two or three hours, but this was just too good a spot to pass up. John stood guard while the others stripped and gingerly stepped into the cold water. Jenny held back until coaxed by the women to strip and join them. She seemed shy about taking her clothes off in front of Randy, but relented when he turned his back to her while she got into the water.

After everyone else had finished their bath, John had his turn. It was well that the day was warm because it was doubtful they could have tolerated the cold spring water in the coolness of night.

Sarah was cutting Jenny's hair to match the other women's style when John finished his bath. He stood watching them for a few moments before asking his wife if she would trim his beard when she got done. When Sarah finished with Jenny's hair, John walked slowly around her critically examining the haircut. Jenny looked up at him apprehensively until John slowly gave her a smile.

"Jenny, you look like one of the family now."

Sarah winked at her husband then said to Jenny, "Well, as one of the family you get to help wash clothes."

Sarah led Jenny off to the springs overflow to help Lillie with that task. John saw the hunters off while he and Rocky guarded the camp.

When the hunters returned with their bounty, Sarah was trimming John's beard while Lillie and Jenny were picking berries nearby. After the meat was put on a spit over the fire, Mick and Randy stripped and put on their spare pants so that the women could wash their dirty clothes. It didn't take long before the women were back quizzing the hunters about the hunt and if they had seen any signs of the Mutants.

Sarah was looking at her new daughter who had been assimilated into their family group. The clothing problem had become more acute with her addition and Sarah decided that Mick would be their first project. Using their accumulated animal skins they came up with a pants and vest that looked quite good on him. They designed the clothes so they could adjust for some expansion in size. Mick's body had filled out since he joined the family and was now heavily muscled in both the leg and chest areas.

They then decided to design a dress for Jenny whose design they could adapt for their own use. After consideration they decided on a wrap design with ties at the side and the length down to below her knees so that it would continue to fit as she grew.

When the garment was finished, Jenny modeled her new dress before her family.

"It fits fine and there's enough room for me to move and even run without it binding me." She shyly smiled at Randy and asked him, "What do you think, does it look okay?"

His face got red as he answered, "Yeah, you look like a girl now instead of another boy."

She smiled at him, then ran over and kissed him on the cheek.

"Cripes! Why did you do that?" He exclaimed as he rubbed his cheek. The rest of the family laughed at his discomfort while Jenny just smiled as Randy left the group and sat with the dogs.

It wasn't long before every family member had a new set of animal skin garments. John suggested they try to put together some kind of footwear as their shoes would not last forever. The women came up with Indian style moccasin's that seemed to work all right as long as they didn't have to walk over sharp rocks. They decided to pack their shoes for later use and began using the new footwear.

Sarah looked at her family in their new attire and started giggling. They looked at her questionably until she relented.

"Oh, I was just thinking what people back home would think if they could see us now."

"Well, we're the fashion setters here. All I need is a coonskin hat and my wardrobe would be complete," John said jokingly.

They all laughed as they visualized him wearing such a hat. Randy, however, took that suggestion seriously and began to secretly gather furs from the raccoon type animals. He got together with Lillie and figured out how to make them into a hat. The biggest problem was determining John's hat size. Lillie solved this problem when she next cut his hair; she used a piece of lacing to get his size.

After the hat was finished, they waited until after the next evening meal to make the presentation. Sarah was aware something was in the works but didn't know what. She watched as Randy edged over to John with his hand behind his back hiding something.

"Dad... Ahh Dad, Lillie and I have made you something you've been wanting. So here, I hope you like it."

He then placed the hat on John's head. John's surprised expression turned to joy as he realized what the present was after he took it off and turned it over in his hands looking at its craftsmanship.

"How did you make the tail?"

"Well, since these Raccoons don't have tails, I folded and stuffed its skin to make it look like a tail."

John rubbed his fingers around the simulated tail and smiled. "It looks real." He then placed it back on his head while asking, "How's it look?"

Randy beamed at him. "You look just like Daniel Boone! I'm going to make one for me and Mick too."

Lillie and Sarah looked at each other and smiling shook their heads in mock disbelief.

The family continued their easterly trek following the main trail. John estimated they were at least midway across Georgia, but wasn't sure how far south they had come. A few days later, that concern was made moot.

John heard something ahead and called a halt. He and Sarah listened to the sound which seemed to come and go. Suddenly Sarah smiled and shouted, "That sounds like surf! We must be close to the ocean."

He shook his head in disbelief as he answered, "We can't be at the coast yet! It should be at least another fifty to one-hundred miles from here."

Another ten-minute walk found them on a sandy ridge overlooking the beach. The trail split north and south and sitting at the cross trail was another rock pile. Before John looked for a message in the pile, he looked along the coastline. To the north the coast seemed to angle eastward slightly while to the south it looked more westward.

He pointed to the north. "Up there would be South Carolina and south would be towards Florida. Let's see which way our people decided to go."

He lifted the capstone and removed a piece of driftwood. The terse writing said, "Went N - think Fla under water."

John handed the message to the other family members, and while they were reading he was thinking about the writer's conclusions. Sarah handed the message back to him, which he returned to the rock pile.

"I think they're right. The oceans have risen substantially and most or all of Florida must be under water. Our best bet is to go north; I hope not too far. I would think we would need good land to farm and hunt, which means we'll need to go inland at least twenty miles. Let's see where this trail takes us."

That night they camped in the forest next to the beach. The breeze off the ocean was quite chilly, so while the hunters were gone John constructed a windbreak between the ocean and the campfire. The hunters took a little longer to find game, but returned with a small deer for their supper. They huddled together behind the break enjoying the heat of the fire while waiting on their meal to cook.

Sarah snuggled up against John, each sharing the others warmth. "Honey, I don't think I want to live next to the ocean. It just gets too cold at night!"

He hugged her closer and laughed. "Yes, but it does have some good fringe benefits."

She looked up at him, grimaced, and then dug into his ribs with her finger.

Mick seeing their interaction laughed also. "John, I go along with that too."

Lillie's answer was to snuggle closer to her man. Randy and Jenny were each wrapped up in furs as well with the dogs lying as close to the fire as possible.

Two days later, the trail forked again with a fainter trail heading left in a slightly northwest direction. To the left of this trail was another mound of stones. There was no message but John took it as a sign to follow this side trail.

The trail led back into the forest and within fifteen minutes they could no longer hear the surf. By late afternoon they came into a part of the forest that had Spanish moss hanging from the trees. Randy commented on how spooky it looked as they were walking under it.

Jenny giggled as she replied, "It's just moss."

He gave her a little shove, and then with a mischievous smile said, "Maybe, but it looks really weird, almost like fingers reaching down to get you."

Jenny stopped and looked up at the moss and shivered then looked around to see if anyone had seen her. She had fallen a little behind the others so she ran up beside Randy and took his hand.

They camped next to a small river that night. It was much warmer away from the ocean and the family had taken turns soaking in the stream. Randy was taking his turn with John and Sarah while the others were tending to the camp after their swim.

Sarah was rubbing John's neck and back muscles as they sat in the water. "Honey, wouldn't it be nice to be able to soak like this every night?"

He sighed as her hands worked the tightness from his muscles and replied, "This is about as close to heaven as there is."

"Okay, it's my turn for a little of that heaven."

The next morning as they crossed the stream, John noticed a small mound of rocks on the other side. In it was another message that said follow the stream west. There was no trail, so the Mutants didn't normally travel in this direction. When they left the trail they were careful not to leave evidence of their passing.

CHAPTER 12

The family followed the stream for three days before coming upon an encampment. Their first indication was the smell of wood smoke and Rocky's growl. They halted their advance and sought shelter deeper into the forest. John told them to stay hidden while he, Mick, and Rocky found out what's ahead. Sarah and Lillie's faces showed their concern as their men left them. In the meantime they readied their weapons in case of need.

John suggested that they move away from the stream and approach the camp from a different direction in case sentries on the stream approaches. They slowly approached the camp and finally were able to see some structures through the trees. As they got closer they could see what appeared to be a typical log house from early America. As they moved around the perimeter of the camp they saw movement and three other log houses. It wasn't long before they could see into the center of the camp.

John and Mick looked at each other then smiled as several men and women from apparently their own time period were working on drying racks for skins and meat. They couldn't hear what they were saying until one of the men yelled to someone out of their sight. "Hey Jacob, bring that knife over here."

John slowly smiled as he became sure who these people were. He told Mick to unstring his bow as he demonstrated with his own before walking to the edge of camp and announcing their presence.

"Hello the camp! May we enter?"

The people of the camp immediately dropped whatever they were doing and grabbed their weapons. John and Mick didn't move while the people looked at them. An older white haired black man pushed his way through the people until he was standing in front of the group. He looked like he was approaching seventy years of age but was still a bear of a man who held a long spear with a wicked point at the end.

"Who might you be?" He bellowed.

John smiled at him as he replied, "I'm John Bridges and we've been trailing you since Missouri, that is if you're William Harding."

The man smiled and motioned him forward. "Let's talk. I imagine we've both got stories to tell."

John walked up to him and said, "William Harding, I presume."

The man nodded his head and shook John's hand. "You gave us a start when you got past our sentries."

"We smelled your smoke, but wasn't sure who you might be - so we scouted the camp before revealing ourselves. I've got the rest of my family downstream. Is it alright if I bring them into camp?"

Harding looked surprised, then hastily replied, "Surely, bring them all in. How many do you have?"

"Our wives, two kids, and five more dogs."

John had noted that there were no dogs in camp when they entered and had observed Harding's delighted looks at Rocky.

Harding broke into a loud laugh. "Great, we need another established family and the dogs are a wonderful bonus. I'll go with you while you retrieve your family."

As they were walking back toward his family, John asked, "Have you had any trouble with the Mutants?" When he got a blank look, he hastily added. "I meant the natives of this time frame."

Harding slowly smiled at him. "So you've figured that out! No, not since we've settled here. I think we're far enough from the trail so only a stray hunting party will find us."

John stopped and with a concerned expression said. "About two weeks ago we unexpectedly came upon a four man hunting party which immediately attacked us. If we hadn't been training almost every day with our weapons we might not be here today."

Harding's face showed concern as John related his story. "Were any of your people hurt?"

"No, it's a strange thing...we acted on instinct and killed all of them before they could get close to us. Each of us was responsible for at least a combined kill. My nine year-old son made the first kill and his ten year-old sister combined with Rocky got the last one."

Harding shook his head in wonder but then hopefully asked, "Are your other dogs like Rocky?"

"No, just Patches and her four off-spring - all full blood Beagles and great hunters for this type of game."

John's face grew grave, "I should tell you that in two instances we picked up the lone survivors from Mutant raids. We got Rocky while we were still on the Mississippi, and then we found my ten year-old daughter who had watched her family being slaughtered. Have you or the other people in your group had any problems with them?"

Harding considered for a moment and then slowly spoke, "Two families were attacked on the Mississippi when they got too close to shore but no one was hurt; and we had another family that was attacked twice, once on the Mississippi where they lost one member and again since the great waterfall. They were ready this time and were able to dispose of that small hunting party with only a minor injury to one of their family."

John shook his head sadly. "We may eventually have to build fortifications for this settlement, either that or move to a better defendable position. Where are your sentries placed?"

Harding pointed ahead. "Jackson is just ahead and Peterson is about 100 yards west of camp."

John shook his head in concern. "We're going to have to talk later about this."

They continued on past the sentry who expressed surprise when Harding told him about John's move around him to get into the settlement. They continued on until they reached the area where his family had taken shelter. They joyfully ran out to greet them and John made the introductions. When they returned to the settlement, the local people came forward eagerly to greet them.

There were twenty-one people in the welcoming group of mixed races which included men, women, and children. John did a quick count and with the addition of his family and the guards; the settlement population increased to nine men, twelve women, and six children. Randy was only the second male child. The settlement was definitely top heavy on women. He also noted that three of the women were heavy with child.

That evening John and Harding were discussing the settlement and its future. He asked Harding how many of the men and women were couples and he replied, "Six are married, not including your people, and two of the men are over sixty years of age. The single women range from 28 to 45 years-of-age."

John's face revealed a troubled expression as he replied, "How are the single women getting along? Is there sharing of the food?"

Harding snorted and laughed. "Better not let Mary hear you suggesting that the women don't carry their weight. She's one of the settlement's best hunters and we share and share alike on all food."

John's face relaxed as he smiled at Harding. "This whole trip I've treated everyone as members of a close family, and I see the settlement is still small enough to continue that policy."

He then pointedly asked Harding if he was married, who sadly shook his head. "I lost my Betty Ann on the trip. She couldn't take the thought of leaving her children and then the hardships of the trip finally did her in. We picked up another couple while on the trip and traveled together."

John told Harding how he had started the journey with Sarah and her family, their survival skills taught by her deceased husband and finding Mick and Jenny.

"I tell you now, if it wasn't for my family I don't know what I might have done."

Harding chuckled. "Yes, family keeps a man going."

John looked hard into Harding's eyes trying to judge his response before making a decision to speak.

"I have to know something. Did you or any of the other parties have experiences with an intelligent life form that had the appearance of ball-lightning?"

Harding looked at him strangely, then slowly smiled. "Apparently you and I are the only ones. Did it actually speak to you?"

John nodded his head excitedly. "The first time it seemed to just read me, but the second time it warned me about the approaching falls on the Mississippi. That time its effect about did me in."

Harding placed his hands on John's shoulders, squeezing hard. "Boy, you must be important to it, or them. I never could tell if there was more than one. My experience was similar to yours but my instructions were to leave markers along the trail and finally to place the encampment here."

"Did it give you any reason why it wanted us here?"

Harding rubbed his chin whiskers thoughtfully. "Not really, I just assumed that would come later."

"I wonder how many more of our people are going to show up here," John said thoughtfully.

The family had been in the settlement for a week and had already started to merge into its daily life. With the help of the other men, the family constructed for themselves a log house similar to other houses in the settlement using stone axes. The only difference was that they needed a larger house to accommodate the size of their family. The floor plan was different as well and included two enclosed bedrooms, one on each side of the house for the married couples. Above the bedrooms in the loft area were two more bedrooms for the kids. The remainder of the floor space was a common area that included a large fireplace, dining area, and seating for the family.

Both Sarah and Lillie insisted on privacy in the bedrooms since that had been most lacking since their marriage. This arrangement also separated the kids' sleeping area now that they were getting older.

The family's hunters proved their worth to the settlement by the game they provided. Mary Diggens, the settlement's best hunter until the family arrived, conceded their ability and joined their hunting party. Mary's hunting ability had been hampered because her only weapon was the spear. The family's use of the bow and throwing stick, plus the hunting dogs greatly increased the amount of game taken.

Mary's husband had been killed by the Mutants before her arrival at the settlement. She just turned 28 and was a very attractive brunette of Asian descent on her mother's side. She had given John a close appraisal when he first arrived until she found out he was already married. Mary was slightly younger than the three other single women and it appeared that the first single man to join the settlement would be the cause of stiff competition for his affections. The sixteen year-old single male already in camp was just too young to get the women's attention, but that might change after he got a little older if no one else became available.

Sarah and Lillie quickly became aware of these women's problem and kept their husbands on a close rein when they were around. Lillie was becoming a little jealous and uneasy about Mary being with Mick on their daily hunts.

William Harding, while still single, seemed to have an arrangement with Janet Muny, the oldest single woman. Janet had traveled with Harding soon after they arrived in this world. Her husband had died during the trip due to a heart attack. Harding obviously had affection for Janet but still mourned for his deceased wife.

John had discussed security arrangements with Harding, who was the settlement's founder and leader by common agreement. He and Harding agreed that their best defense was the Mutants' lack of knowledge of their existence. John suggested that their sentries be placed further out from the settlement. He remembered that his first hint of the encampment was the smell of wood smoke so he suggested that they should be placed beyond that distance.

Since they had never encountered the Mutants' movement after dark they saw no reason to post guards after dusk. They didn't have the men to guard against approaches other than along the small river which was the most likely in any case.

John suggested, and Harding agreed, that the guards should be armed with bows or other long distance weapons. Almost all the men who served on guard duty, when given their choice, had selected the bow because of its range and ease in learning. After a week of practice with their new weapons they had become quite proficient in their use.

John also developed an early warning system, a horn made of bark strengthened with tree sap. When John first tried the horn, the settlement stood still in shock.

Harding came over with a smile on his face. "John, you scared the crap out of everyone with that thing!"

John looked at him in surprise and then blew the horn again. The eerie sound caused the people of the settlement to shudder until the sound ended.

John grinned at Harding. "I built this horn as a warning device, but I bet it would scare the 'Bejabbers' out of any members of the Mutants who heard it. Maybe enough that they might turn around and leave the area."

The townspeople experimented with the distance it could be heard and found they didn't need to move the sentries in any closer to town. Even from that distance the sound was haunting.

John, with Harding's blessing, had Sarah and Lillie train the women with weapons of their choice. Since the majority of the settlement were women, it made sense they be trained in its defense. After watching their instructors' demonstration of the various weapons, the majority picked the sling and the remainder decided on the bow. The sling presented the advantage of being able to be carried with the individual unlike the bow because of its size.

This close relationship with the other women soon bonded the married and single women together. The single women assured those married that they wouldn't poach on their husbands, but hoped they realized their desperate status, especially the three single women of childbearing age. The eight married women had husbands ranging in ages from seventeen to fifty-six and four had children. Three of these four women were pregnant again. Sarah shared her husband's forebodings that if more single men didn't show up soon, something drastic would have to be done.

After another week of training, the women seemed to be ready to help defend the settlement. John and Harding watched their training progress and were delighted with the results. Mary Diggens already traded her spear for the bow and was now an even match with Mick when hunting. They now needed extra people to carry the game back to camp and less time was needed hunting to fulfill their needs. John suggested to Mick and Mary that they not concentrate their hunting in any one area, that they range further out in the future to save the close-in game for emergencies.

John was afraid that as the settlement grew they would eventually run out of game. In any case, what they needed was another source of food. He asked Sarah if she thought she might recognize plants they could use and she was ecstatic at the thought of something besides meat to eat. After some thought, she and John prepared pouches and water containers to bring back their finds.

They departed the next morning as part of the regular hunting party who decided to follow the stream westerly for three miles before starting their hunt. In the meantime, John and Sarah searched for edible plants. That afternoon they walked back into camp with success from both hunts.

Sarah called the women together and showed them the plants she had brought back and asked for volunteers to help put in a garden. They all wanted to help and luckily they had women with gardening experience who volunteered their knowledge on how best to do it. By nightfall, with the help of both women and men volunteers, they had established a garden alongside the stream.

The following day they started building an irrigation system to keep the plants watered. Since the water source was so near, it wasn't difficult to build. Sarah had found samples of wild squash, several other kinds of gourds, strawberries, corn, and spinach.

She hoped they would find other varieties to add to their garden and asked the hunters to bring back anything that looked like it might be edible. Corn was Sarah's best find and they planned to use most of their first crop for seed in their next planting.

John and Sarah were standing together watching how the irrigation system was working when they heard the warning horn from downstream. He yelled to the others to grab their weapons and follow him. They heard two more horn blasts as they hurried downstream in anticipation of a fight.

John was beginning to worry when he didn't encounter their sentry who should be retreating towards them. When they finally reached the guard post they found Jack Peterson grinning at them. He held up the warning horn and started laughing.

When he finally got control of himself, he said, "There were three of them coming my way when I gave a blast from the horn! You should have seen them. They jumped in the air and started shaking, and then when I gave them another blast of the horn they started backing away until they turned and ran away, leaving their weapons and game behind. I gave them a final blast of the horn as they were leaving, but I don't think they could have run any faster."

John grinned as he slapped Peterson on the back. "This horn might be the best weapon we have against the Mutants."

He then turned to other members of the defending force while considering their next move. "Joe, you and Jacob go with Jack and chase after them for about a mile, and be sure to blow that horn every once in awhile to keep them moving away from here."

The men laughed and joked with Jack as they followed after the enemy. When the defending party walked into camp, the settlement excitedly began asking questions about what happened. When Peterson's story was retold, they looked on with awe and then started laughing until many had tears running down their faces.

Harding patted John on the back as he exclaimed. "That horn of yours may turn out to be our savior. This is wonderful news."

CHAPTER 13

Sarah, who had been part of the defending force, hugged John. She then called to the group to get their attention. "I've tried to keep track of the days since we started our journey, and unless I've made a mistake... Christmas is next Saturday. Let's get a tree and decorate it. I think John just gave us all the best Christmas present of all! What do you think?"

There was stunned silence for a moment, someone cheered and then the townspeople shouted their agreement. After some initial confusion, the settlement became busy making plans for the Christmas celebration. John and Mick volunteered to find a suitable tree, while Harding pointed to the center of the open area as the best place for its placement. He then accompanied them in their hunt for the perfect tree.

It was well that Harding accompanied John and Mick, because the tree they brought back into the settlement needed three people to carry. They dug a supporting hole, and then with some additional help raised the tree. After the townspeople admired their work, the women started decorating the tree with the help of the children.

Christmas morning the settlement gathered around the tree to celebrate Christ's rise from the dead. Harding led the townspeople in the Lord's Prayer, and then said a short Prayer of thanksgiving. He told the gathering that he hoped the New Year would bring more of their people into the settlement. They eventually broke apart into family groups for their own private celebrations.

Sarah noticed that the single women joined together into their own group after wistfully watching the families gathering together. She went to the individual families and suggested they each take in one of the women for the celebration. When the wife of each family walked toward the single women, they watched their approach with hope and a little apprehension. Upon hearing their invitations they all gleefully accepted.

Sarah returned to her family with Mary Diggens at her side. They all welcomed her into their home with happy cheer and then exchanged presents. This Christmas was like none they had ever experienced before. The gifts were handmade and were all of a practical nature. Before her announcement to the townspeople, Sarah had previously told her family that Christmas was near and they had been making preparations. John went back to the workshop and returned with a crib he had been working on for a week.

When he presented it to Sarah, Lillie ran to her mother with happy tears in her eyes as she cried, "Why didn't you tell me?"

Sarah smiled through her own tears. "I wanted to be sure before I told you, but John jumped the gun and went ahead and made the crib. I guess he wants this baby as much as I do."

Sarah's children hugged her and wished her happiness. Mary, with tears in her eyes, came over and hugged her as well.

"You're a lucky woman to have such a loving family," she whispered in Sarah's ear.

Sarah blinked back her own tears as she hugged her back. She and Lillie presented their husbands with an animal skin shirt to replace the vest in cooler weather. Mary, who was dressed in a combination of skins and worn out clothing asked the women to help her make a dress like their own. She said that she and the other women of the town had been admiring their attire since they arrived.

Sarah and Lillie smiled at each other knowingly and then gave Mary an appraising eye. Sarah nodded her head finally and took Mary's hand as they walked back to her bedroom. They returned shortly with Mary now wearing a dress of skins.

She beamed at the family and proudly said, "Look what Sarah gave me. She said this was the first dress she had made for herself. But wow! This is so much better than what I was wearing." She hugged Sarah again and then with tears in her eyes, said, "I've got nothing to give to you."

"Sure you do, your happiness and thankfulness is all the present I could wish for."

Randy and Jenny had also exchanged presents. He gave her a braided skin belt, and she gave him a quiver for his throwing stick spears, which had a long strap to carry it over his shoulder. They each gave the other a hug and Jenny kissed Randy on the cheek. His face turned red, but he didn't object as he had the previous time she kissed him.

Mick gave Lillie several beautiful fur pelts that she had been wanting for trim on her dress. She held the pelts up for the others to admire then gave him a passionate kiss.

The settlement gathered later that morning to sing Christmas Carols while the hunters made a quick hunting trip for their Christmas Dinner.

The following morning, John and Sarah just awakened but were reluctant to leave their warm bed. She snuggled closer to John and one thing led to another until they were in the throes of passionate lovemaking. Afterwards, John was on his back trying to get his breath while Sarah was gazing at him like a Cheshire cat licking her chops. She then snuggled back against him and purred. Sarah ran her tongue across his chest and then smiled at him and whispered, "I told you we could make love while I'm pregnant, at least until the last trimester."

"Yes, but I thought we needed to be a little more gentle while we made love."

"That will come later. Right now I want some more of my favorite husband's loving."

When they finally got up and entered the common room, they found the kids had already left the house, but Lillie and Mick were still in their bedroom. From the muffled sounds coming from within, they were in the process of making love. Sarah smothered a giggle and hurriedly pulled John outside.

He asked Sarah, "I wonder if the kids left because of the sounds of our lovemaking?"

"Probably, but it's a natural thing and I don't think we did them any harm. They both are aware of where babies come from. However, when they get older and their hormones become active, we'll have to be sure they're not around when we make love."

* * *

A month later, another family group found the settlement. They consisted of a single man of about 30, and his three daughters ranging in age from six to ten. Also in the group were sixteen year-old identical twin brothers, George and Greg Anderson.

Kit Campbell said he found the boys on the trail and that they were the only survivors of their family. Campbell said they were all from Alabama and had no idea of what was going on.

George Anderson told their story as he began, "About a month ago we were away hunting when our family was attacked. We returned after the attackers had left, but found only blood at our campsite. We decided to continue following the trail until they found Kit's camp the following night. He offered to let us join his family for mutual protection, which we gladly accepted."

Harding welcomed the new group and introduced each family group to the new members. The following day they helped Campbell start building his log house. The Anderson twins elected to stay with the Campbell family for the time being. This arrangement seemed to work best for the settlement as all children found by families along the trail were adopted within that family.

Sarah, who had been a sixth grade teacher before her marriage, consulted with Harding about starting a school for the younger children. He called a meeting of the settlement which agreed that starting a school was a wonderful idea. They selected the Bridges' house because of its large size and floor plan. Classes were to be held each weekday morning.

The settlement men built two long tables with bench seats for the students and a desk and chair for Sarah. Since she had no school materials, she had to make do with what she could make herself.

Sarah's first class had seven students with two from her own family. The settlement members found a large piece of slate which John placed on an easel he had built. Chalk was harder to find, but they found a soft stone they used as a substitute. She had the older children refresh their own memories by showing the younger students how to solve problems in arithmetic and spelling. The studies seemed to be working well and still left the afternoon for work and play in the settlement.

* * *

The family had just celebrated their third Christmas at the settlement. Sarah had given birth to twins, Sadie and John Jr., with Sadie named after Sarah's mother. In addition, Mick and Lillie were expecting their second child in three months. Their first, Prudence, was born six months after Sarah's twins. The two older children were kept busy babysitting the three toddlers when their parents were occupied with settlement business. Jenny, to her delight, had to do most of this duty because of Randy's periodic hunting duties.

Both Randy and Jenny had grown, both physically and emotionally, in the past three years. Jenny, now almost fourteen, had blossomed into an attractive young lady. Randy, who had just turned thirteen, was already taller than his mother and his body was starting to fill out. The other young girls in the settlement were competing for his affections, but Randy didn't seem interested. All Jenny had to do to get his attention was blink her green eyes at him and he would come running.

Kit Campbell had married one of the single women, Rachel Walker, after a year's courtship and was now expecting their first child. There had been no other arrivals in the settlement since the Campbell family and no one now expected any future additions from this source. There had been only one more contact with the Mutants and this too had come from the east. They had retreated in fear, just as the first encounter, when the sentry blew the warning horn.

John was watching his wife talking with several other women of the settlement and was thinking how beautiful she looked even after the trials of the journey and giving birth to their twins. He still couldn't believe his good luck in finding such a women who could love him. She looked in his direction and smiled, then winked at him before continuing her conversation.

There were now three unattached single women remaining in the settlement, two of childbearing age, and there were no single males within twenty years of their age. John and Harding had discussed this problem on and off for the last six months. Eventually, Harding called a meeting of the settlement, placing the problem before them. He suggested the married couples discuss the possibility of any who would accept another wife in their family. He announced that he and Janet Muny were getting married and they had already agreed to accept another wife into their family. This created much discussion among the various families, some of it quite heated before they broke up to make their decisions.

In the Bridges household, John was initially adamant against adding another wife. Sarah just shook her head and smiled at him as she continued to try to change his mind.

"Honey, just think about these poor women. They're without a husband and they all want children just like every other woman in the settlement. I don't want to share you either, but it will be in everyone's interest if we get this problem settled. Our children are going to be in this same situation, at least until a more favorable male population is established."

John shook his head again but then in resignation asked, "Babe, are you really sure you want to do this?"

She nodded her head as she hugged him tightly. Lillie was happy that she and Mick didn't have to make such a decision. The single women had already ruled Mick out as a potential husband because of his young age.

A week later Harding called for a list of those families willing to take another wife. This verbal list was given to the single women and included two other families besides the Harding and Bridges family.

They must decide among themselves which husband they preferred, then it would go back to the families to see if they would accept the applicant. This arrangement seemed fair and was accepted by all parties.

The Bridges, Harding, and Campbell families each received a bid. After discussion within the families, John and Sarah accepted the bid of Mary Diggens, the Campbell family accepted the bid of June Decker, and the Harding family accepted the bid of Jill Copeland. All parties agreed upon a trial period where either party had three months to back out of the arrangement, and no consummation was to be made until after the trial period and actual marriage.

The Bridges family knew Mary quite well by this time. She and Sarah had become best friends and John had already thought of her as an attractive, friendly woman who knew her own mind and was not afraid to let others know her opinions.

Lillie liked her as well and wasn't threatened by her presence as Mick had eyes only for her. Besides, Mick and Randy knew her well from their hunting trips and already considered her one of the family.

The day after the bidding was finished, Mary moved into the Bridges' house. Sarah realized the house had become crowded with the new children and now another wife. She pulled John aside for his thoughts on the matter.

"Honey, we need an addition to our home. We need another bedroom for Mary and at least two more for the babies."

He looked surprised for a moment and then nodded his head. "Babe, I didn't see this coming. I must be getting old. Let's get together with Lillie and Mick and come up with a plan."

They used the material from the single women's house to rebuild their home. First they removed the roof and added another floor to the house, giving them almost twice their original space. They made space for six bedrooms upstairs and four large bedrooms downstairs, which should give them enough room for the foreseeable future.

The other families wishing to expand their homes used the remaining building material. John and Mick helped, along with others in the settlement, make improvements to these houses. Lillie and Mick had already made plans to move into their own house after their next baby was born, but with the bigger house they decided to stay on a little longer.

Mary assumed some of the household duties of her new family in addition to her hunting duties which she still elected to fulfill. Sarah also welcomed her help with the three toddlers. Mary loved the children and spent much of her free time playing with them.

John and Mary were shy with each other initially, but they soon grew closer as they became comfortable with the two wives situation. John soon became used to having two women fuss over him, and Mary seemed happy with Sarah being considered the senior wife and the head of running the household.

After two months into the trial period it became clear that Mary had fallen deeply in love with John. While John loved both women, his deepest affection was still for Sarah. Both women knew this without being told, yet it didn't change Mary's love for John or her friendship with Sarah.

CHAPTER 14

The expanded families were now past the trial period which both parties agreed to make final in all three cases. Sarah and Mary both wanted this marriage to be formalized by a ceremony witnessed by the entire settlement. Sarah also wanted to be part of the ceremony since they had not formerly exchanged vows.

Harding agreed to perform the wedding ceremony for the new brides who had all finalized their marriage agreements. Harding's own new wives being included in the ceremony presented a problem at first, but that was solved by John and Harding switching places, performing for each other that part of the vows.

It was quite a celebration for the settlement having so many weddings at once. The first wives of John and Harding were married first, followed by the vows of the three second wives. When they finished the ceremony, each expanded family hugged and kissed each other, followed by the settlement's congratulations.

That evening the settlement had a feast to celebrate the occasion. The settlement's garden now was producing a greater variety of produce and included corn, spinach, squash, beets, a mutated form of potatoes, and barley. Meat was still the main dish, but the produce ensured that they were getting their needed vitamins and minerals.

Harding held up his hands to get everyone's attention and then spoke to the settlement, "We've been struggling for over five years to get this settlement established. But until John Bridges and his family arrived I didn't think we were going to make it. You all are aware of the changes they have brought to the settlement. We are eating some of that tonight. His hunting dogs have helped too. He brought five with him, which have now expanded to over twenty. In addition, the German Shepherd mix has produced a new breed useful in guarding the camp. But more important is our children are being schooled in reading, writing and arithmetic. Complicated social problems have been resolved due to their influence and help and we should give them a loud thank you."

He then waved the Bridges family forward while the settlement gave them a wild applause. Harding then held up his hands again for quiet. "We should set this day aside as our annual Thanksgiving. We have truly got much to be thankful for."

He paused as the settlement gave a loud positive applause to the resolution. Harding then proclaimed that every June 1st hereafter would be celebrated as their Thanksgiving.

John then held his hands up for attention. "Our settlement needs a name and since William Harding started and headed our settlement I thank it only appropriate that it be named after him. If everyone agrees, let's call this place the town of 'Harding'."

The settlement screamed their acceptance, and yelled "Harding", over and over again. Finally, Harding held his hands up for quiet.

His face was dark with embarrassment as he said, "Okay, we do need a name. But once you call it a town we need to take official action towards a local government. We don't need much now, but we need to formally elect a mayor who will be responsible for running the town. I've been doing this unofficially for much too long and I'm tired of the aggravation. I believe a younger man or woman should be elected to fulfill those duties and I nominate John Bridges!"

There was shocked silence from the settlement after Harding's statement. Then Kit Campbell shouted, "I second the nomination for Bridges for Mayor!"

The settlement started to applaud their agreement until Harding held up his hands again. "If there are no other nominations, I suggest we vote by a show of hands."

The settlement raised their hands in approval for John as the first official mayor of Harding. After much shouting and celebration after the vote, settlement members pushed John forward to speak.

He stood before the townspeople looking slightly dazed until he raised his hands for quiet. When the assembly finally grew silent, he decided that he should go ahead with his idea for a town council.

"Friends, I'm happy to continue in the footsteps of William Harding, our founder. But as your new leader, I'm going to need help and I would like to appoint four council members to make the large decisions for the town. If anyone has business before the council meeting, place it before me at least one day before the meeting next Tuesday. I want to thank everyone for their vote of confidence and I hope I live up to your expectations."

After his speech, John was surrounded by the townspeople wishing him well. John hugged both his wives and placed his arms around them as they slowly walked back toward their home with his children following close behind. He was already thinking about whom to appoint to the first town council of Harding.

Sarah, as the head wife, made the determination for the wives sleeping arrangement with their husband. She thought Mary should have the first month after her marriage with John. After that, they would alternate every week with him.

When hearing of this arrangement, Mary happily hugged Sarah but then hesitantly asked, "Are you sure - a whole month?"

"You'll need that month to become comfortable with each other in bed, besides I'll try to get him alone during the day," she said with a wink and a sly smile.

"Two can play that game then." Mary giggled. "Poor John is going to be worn out trying to satisfy two randy wives."

The next day John was out trying to find willing council members to serve. His first pick was Rachel Walker Campbell, who had previously been an attorney. He needed her to be sure they did things correctly. In addition, she was one of the second wives and he wanted their representation on the council.

He then asked the twins, George and Greg Anderson, if one of them would be interested. Greg agreed after consultation with his brother. John now had a young single member on the council.

He tried several of the married couples before Jack Peterson agreed to serve. His final member he saved for last as he knew he might have trouble talking him into serving. He wanted the other members in place as a bargaining tool before he was approached.

When he arrived at the house, Harding's first wife Janet came to the door with a smile on her face.

"John, I've been expecting you, come on in. Bill is out back doing some chores - I'll call him in."

Harding, after washing his hands outside, came inside and shook John's hand. "Well, have you got the council together?" Harding said with a smile.

John grinned and gave him the names of those individuals he had selected and why. Harding frowned.

"But, that's only three, you need one more."

John slapped Harding on the back. "Bill, we can't put you out to pasture just yet. We need you on the council for the town to feel comfortable, and remember it's for only a short time."

Harding frowned at him as he bristled. "Where have I heard that load of bull before?" He then looked at Janet for approval. She came over and kissed his cheek.

"Bill, you're still needed here, so quit hedging and say yes to John!"

Harding smiled at her and kissed her forehead lovingly, but then asked, "What about Jill?"

"You never mind about Jill, we've already talked about this and she agrees with me."

Harding then smiled at John and shook his hand. "I guess you've got me too."

The first council meeting was attended by most of the townspeople. Since they had no way of keeping minutes the meeting was open to the settlement. The only matters before the council were the term limits of four years for Mayor and two years for the Town Council. John placed before the council his initial proposal for term limits on both the Mayor and Council members. After some discussion among the council members, the resolution passed with no dissenting vote. The council then voted to meet the first Tuesday of each month hereafter.

After his first week as Mayor, John wanted to resign. He didn't realize the number of petty grievances a small community could dream up, from the smell of an outhouse to the crying of babies.

Sarah just shook her head. "You have to take the bad with the good and you have to solve the small problems as well as the large ones."

"The large problems are handled by the council; I'm stuck with the gripes that don't amount to a hill of beans!" He complained.

"Then they should be easy to take care of, isn't that right honey?"

His only response was a meek "yes dear."

The hunting party was now being rotated instead of only having permanent members. This was started because of school classes for Randy; then as new members got a taste of the hunt more people wanted their chance in the rotation. At the beginning, there was at least one member of the original hunters on each hunt until enough people became skilled in hunting with dogs and knew what areas to hunt. This rotation let the original hunters spend more time with their families and gave them more time for housekeeping chores.

The town's first disaster occurred the second week of John's term as Mayor. Mick had led a party of four hunters and six dogs that morning. Randy was attending school and Mary's turn in the rotation wasn't for another week. Their first indication of trouble was shouting as Kit

Campbell, a member of the hunting party, ran into camp and stopped for a moment in indecision – then continued on to John's house. John met him at the door and tried to calm Campbell until he could get his breath back.

Kit finally gasped that a party of six Mutants had ambushed them about four miles northwest of the settlement. He needed to bring back help as Mick and Jacob were hurt and would need to be carried back to the settlement. He said they drove off the ambush party, killing all but one who appeared to be injured. Sarah was holding onto Lillie as they heard the news, but when Mick's name was heard as one of the injured, she cried out and fainted. Luckily, Randy was there to help Sarah place his sister in bed.

John sent for Janet Harding, who was a nurse, before beginning to arrange a rescue party with Mary as the leader. Janet Harding arrived and upon hearing how far away the injured people were, told John to go ahead and start their return and she would meet them along the way. She knew she couldn't keep up and thought she would get to them faster this way.

John informed Harding of the problem and had him take charge of the town's defense while his twelve members left to bring back the injured. Mary and Campbell led the way, with four of their guard dogs to make sure they didn't run into another ambush.

When they got to the site of the attack, they found George Anderson tending to the two injured men. Mick had taken a spear into his chest and was bleeding heavily while Jacob's injury was to his thigh. He asked George how badly injured he thought the escaped Mutant was, who angrily replied, "He had an arrow in his chest and stumbled that way." He pointed north.

John considered for a moment before speaking. "Kit, take four men with bows and two dogs to make sure he's dead. Be sure to bring back the arrow, because we don't want to leave any evidence of how he was killed if they find his body. When you finish, try to catch up with us as we head back to Harding."

They rigged two stretchers to carry the injured and retrieved all weapons from both parties before starting back. They had traveled only a third of the way back toward town when Campbell's party rejoined them.

Campbell informed John, "We found the dead enemy only 120 yards from where he was hit, so we buried him and the other bodies in the underbrush before returning toward Harding."

John gloomily clapped Campbell on the back and told his party well done before they turned and hurried to catch up with the main group which had stopped ahead upon Janet's arrival.

They finally arrived back into town to meet the stricken faces of friends and family. Sarah had them bring both injured men into her house and place them on the school desks so they could work on their injuries. Sarah had already dismissed class and sent the students home. John and Janet Harding comforted Sarah who was gripping the limp arm of Mick, realizing that he was dead as he lay on the table.

John placed his arms around his wife as she broke down and started crying, while Janet left them to attend to Jacob's wound. Janet had tried to revive Mick when she arrived on the trail, but soon realized that he had bled out from his severe chest wound. She had finally given up - sobbing.

She checked Jacob's flesh wound again and the bleeding seemed to have stopped. Some of the older women had knowledge of plants with medicinal properties and had prepared a paste in case of an emergency such as this. Janet placed a liberal amount of the paste on the wound and then gave Jacob a stick to clinch between his teeth before she started closing the wound with needle and thread. She then placed more paste on the closed wound and told him to keep it covered with a clean cloth and she would check on it tomorrow for another treatment.

Lillie was still in her bedroom being tended to by several of the townswomen until Sarah and Mary relieved them. She looked into Sarah's eyes with hope until she saw the glum expression on her face. They both gathered her into their arms as they all cried while holding and comforting each other in their mutual loss. John, Randy and Jenny couldn't get into the bedroom with the women but were holding each other with tears in their own eyes as they stood in the bedroom doorway giving each other support as they all grieved.

John had all future hunts composed of at least six men and women and at least two guard dogs for an early warning of any future ambushes by the Mutants. He had consulted with Harding and they both agreed that the ambush party must have been a fluke and unless they had other sightings of the enemy, this precaution should be sufficient.

The next day a funeral service was held for Mick attended by all the townspeople with John giving the eulogy. There was not a dry eye by any at its conclusion. He was the first to be buried in the Harding Cemetery near the small river that was named in honor of Mick's death, the *Mick*.

Sarah and Mary were afraid that Lillie would lose her unborn child so they and the rest of the family were careful to make her as comfortable as they could. Janet Harding came over and checked on Lillie every day until she was sure that the immediate danger was past. Lillie's depression was of concern by the family. However, Prudence, her three year-old daughter, wouldn't let her brood. She demanded her mother's attention until Lillie had no choice but to think of her instead of her own grief. Two weeks later Lillie was almost back to her old self but she continued to make daily visits to Mick's graveside, bringing fresh flowers.

CHAPTER 15

Almost two months later, Lillie gave birth to a healthy boy whom she named Michael. While John and Randy loved the children, they had to escape from the house after a few hours of listening to the racket three toddlers and a new baby make. However, the children had four enthusiastic women to watch over them who delighted in their noise.

Mary suspected she was pregnant as she was three weeks overdue with her period and had informed Sarah who congratulated and then playfully kidded her.

"Be prepared for twins if I'm any example of John's work."

Mary smiled wistfully as she spoke, "If it is, I hope they're boys. This town needs more men."

Two months after Michael's birth, the first young man came courting Lillie. There were three young townsmen who had no other marriageable women to court. All the other single females were too young. That only left Lillie, who had two small children. That situation would have put off a normal young man hunting a wife but here she was a prize. They had been waiting a decent interval since Mick's death to begin courting her.

George Anderson was the bravest of the three and came knocking on the Bishop's door to ask John, as head of the family, if he could court Lillie. John gave him a surprised look but then grinned as he comprehended what was happening. He told him to wait outside as he consulted with Lillie. Instead, he went to Sarah and told her what was going on. She covered her laugh with both her hands and then told him to follow her back to Lillie's room where she was breast-feeding little Mick.

John knocked on the doorframe and then he and Sarah entered. Lillie looked at them questioningly but just as John started to speak, Sarah excitedly interrupted. "Young George Anderson is outside wanting to court you."

Lillie looked at them with her mouth open for a moment, and then quirking her mouth and eyebrow asked, "Are you serious?"

Sarah excitedly smiled at her daughter and replied, "Yes he's out there, and I bet two others are going to be on his heels beating a path to your door."

Lillie gave them a pained expression, but then told John, "You go keep him company outside while I make myself look decent and then I'll talk to him. I don't want him inside here with all these kids running around; not yet anyway."

John and George were sitting outside the house on a bench when Lillie appeared at the door about an hour later. John excused himself and left the two alone. George quickly stood up and shoved a bouquet of wildflowers at her. She jumped a little in surprise as the flowers were thrust into her hands.

She smiled at George and softly said, "John said that you wished to court me!"

His face reddened, then squaring his shoulders with resolution, firmly replied, "Lillie I've always thought you were a beautiful women and I was a little jealous of Mick. I don't want to rush you so soon after his death, but I thought I had better put myself first if I'm going to have any chance with you."

He continued to look her in the eye as he awaited her response.

Lillie was impressed with his courage and he was a fine looking man. She took his arm and told him to walk with her so they could get acquainted. She already knew his family history but let him repeat it as they walked.

She asked, "You know about my two children?"

He nodded his head and replied, "I like children."

He gradually loosened up as they walked and he started talking about his hopes for the town. "I want to be part of the effort to make this community a success. I know that we live in a dangerous place but that just makes it more of a challenge. My brother and I are good hunters and we both participate in tending the town garden. All I'm missing is a family."

After he finished speaking he gave her an expectant smile, but Lillie only gave him a smile as they continued walking. When they got back to her house, Lillie had decided on a plan.

"George, I've heard that you are not alone in wishing to court me so I'm counting on you to inform the others, if they are interested, to be here tomorrow afternoon after supper so I can work out a courting schedule with all of you."

She then kissed him on the cheek before entering the house.

All three suitors showed up at the appointed time and Lillie had them sit down in the common room while she stood and just looked at them for a moment before speaking.

"I'm going to allow each of you four dates on an alternate basis after which time I'll eliminate one from the competition. I'll then court the remaining two until I'm sure of whom I'd prefer or I might decide against both of those remaining."

The young men initially appeared shocked at her attitude but then they could see her point. Why waste everyone's time if she didn't like one of them at the beginning.

The townspeople were amused at the courting procedure dictated by Lillie and fondly observed the evening walks she had with her beaus. After the first designated four dates, Jack Bates was the first person rejected. He accepted defeat gracefully but knew after the second date that he would not make the cut.

The Anderson twins remained and Lillie liked both of them. She was having a hard time deciding and not because they were identical twins. Their personalities seemed to slip back and forth between the two. When she was dating Greg, sometimes she would swear he was George. George was always more outgoing and had a great sense of humor. But, Greg sometimes exhibited these same features when he normally was a quiet, morose individual. She eventually began to suspect that it was George playing both brothers.

They were two months into the courtship between the two brothers when Lillie decided to test her theory. At her next date with George, she "accidentally" scratched his ear as she gave him a good night kiss. When Greg showed up for his date the next evening, his ear had the same scratch she had given George.

When she saw the scratch on his ear, Lillie rubbed it gently then pulled his ear hard until she brought his face down to where he was looking into her angry eyes.

"What game are you pulling here George? I've suspected something wasn't right for some time now."

He looked at her with a startled expression and then started to deny everything. However, judging from her angry expression he decided that the truth was his best course of action.

"Would you let go of my ear, please?" He meekly requested.

She released his ear but then stepped back a step with her hands on her hips in a furious stance.

"After our first meeting I told Greg that I loved you and he agreed to step aside. You never had a date with Greg, it was always me trying to make Greg's persona less attractive to you," He said with pain and anxiety in his voice.

Lillie kicked him in the leg hard enough that he almost fell. She then grabbed his ear again and pulled him into the house. They made quite a scene as she dragged him into the common room. John and his wives were working at one of the tables when they burst through the door. She stopped before them, still holding George's ear, and then angrily demanded of Sarah, "What do you do with a man who has lied and deceived you? Who has made a fool of you before the whole town?"

John spoke up, "Well, we could hang him up by his thumbs outside your door, or we could horse whip him before the whole town, or..."

Sarah punched him on the shoulder and said, "Honey, be still. This is serious."

She looked at Lillie's furious expression and at the cowed young man in her grip. She put on a serious expression in an extreme effort not to smile.

"Lillie, what did he do to you?" She softly asked.

With fire still in her eyes she related how George had deceived her. George just stood there leaning over anchored to Lillie's hand by his ear, with the expression of a doomed man.

Sarah shook her head at George who then looked even more pathetic, if that was possible.

"Lillie, let go of his ear and come upstairs so we can talk."

She then pointed at the bench seat next to John. "George, sit down and don't move until we come back."

John sadly shook his head at him. "George, you idiot! You should have known that you couldn't pull off that deception forever. What were you thinking?"

George just shook his head in misery as he looked upstairs where Lillie was deciding his fate.

When they got upstairs to one of the empty bedrooms, they sat down facing each other. Lillie was still furious, so when Sarah smiled she heatedly asked, "What do you think is so funny?"

"This one is it then?" Sarah asked, now with a serious expression.

Lillie's anger abruptly ended as she considered what her mother had said. Sarah smiled as she saw the expression change on her daughter's face from anger to doubt to finally wonder and happiness.

Lillie sadly smiled at her mother and shook her head. "What am I going to do with that dunce?"

"Well, you did the right thing in confronting him in his lie and making sure he was sorry he ever thought of the deception. I would go a step further and impress upon him that you're smarter than he is and that he can't hope to lie to you and get away with it."

Lillie slowly smiled and then softly said, "He is such a lovable dunce though, isn't he?"

The following week George and Lillie were married before the entire townspeople, officiated by John as the Mayor. After the ceremony and feast, George moved into the Bridges household. Having a ready-made family didn't faze him even when he realized he had to deal with Lillie's whole extended family. Everyone had to make some adjustments to George's addition to the family but they soon settled down to the new routine.

CHAPTER 16

Mary was definitely pregnant and at six months she was as large as Sarah was at that time with her twins. All three of the second wives were in various stages of pregnancy and Harding was prancing around as proud as a peacock. John was as solicitous with Mary during her pregnancy as he had been with Sarah and was looking forward to more children.

George had fit into the household as if he had always been there. He now loved Prudence and Mick almost as much as he did their mother. Lillie watched them play with each other with a smile on her face, thanking God for sending her another good man.

Sarah was glad that they had expanded their home as it looked like it would soon be full of children and was wondering when Lillie or herself would add to the family again. She shook her head in wonder. Before this upheaval in her life, she would never have dreamed of the changes in her life she had before her. All in all, she had a good life here with John and her family and if she had a choice, she would keep what she had here.

John had discussed this same thought with her recently and his attitude was that he had not begun to live until his arrival in this time era. His family was now his whole world and nothing would get him to go back to his old life.

John and the town council met several times trading ideas on how to improve their living conditions. The consensus of opinion was that they needed some method of making metal. Before they could do that they needed to find a mineral source such as copper or iron ore. Deep mining was out of the question without tools so they needed to find a source at or close to the surface.

Jacob Bell, who had recovered from his leg wound, told the council that he could recognize most minerals from his previous profession as a college chemistry and geology professor. He suggested that the hunters bring back any rock samples they find, especially any from a rock outcropping from a hillside that has a black or yellow color.

There were several hills near the town so the hunters started bringing back rocks for him to identify. Most of what they brought back were of no use, but several looked promising. He eventually arranged a special party of men to help him survey the sites where these samples came from.

John had been getting cabin fever, so he and Sarah volunteered themselves along on the trip. The party consisted of eight men and women, all armed in case of contact with the Mutants. Randy was leading the group because he was the man who found the promising samples and knew where to find the location again. They reached their first location after a three-hour walk. While Jacob was looking for minerals, the rest of the party took a break and enjoyed the scenery.

After an hour, Jacob came back to the party with a smile on his face. "Well, this looks like a good site for iron ore. However, we don't know how extensive it is. Let's go on to the other two sites and check them out before we head back."

The next site was reached in less than an hour. It was located in a steep valley with rock outcroppings along both sides. When Jacob first saw the valley he stood still and slowly scanned its sides.

He finally turned to the others and quietly said, "I'll need more time at this site, so let's find a place to camp until I'm through here."

Randy pointed down near the center of the valley. "There's a small spring down there that should provide a good camping spot."

He and two others then went hunting while John and the rest of the party proceeded to the spring. Once the camp was established, Jacob and the others proceeded to search for minerals. They returned at dusk to the smell of roasted meat. Randy welcomed them back and wanted to know if they had found anything.

Jacob nodded his head excitedly. "I think this is going to be a good location. I've found several different kinds of minerals useful in smelting and refining iron ore, and I've even found evidence of copper and iron ore here. I'm going to need at least another day to finish up here."

When the party finally returned to Harding after another two days at the site, they had good news for its citizens.

At a town meeting held the next day Jacob outlined what they had discovered. In addition to the minerals they were seeking, they had found coal which was needed in the processing of the ore. He told them that the recovery of the ore from the hillside plus it's processing was going to be very labor intensive. He thought that they should establish another camp in the valley and rotate men from the village since the valley was over a three-hour walk.

There was much excitement at the news and a little apprehension from the wives who would miss their husbands and worry about their safety. John met with the town council on how best to proceed. They agreed with Jacob's plan for a separate camp for the ore processing and asked him how many men were needed at that site.

Jacob said, "I could use all the men, but I realize that's impossible. With Mick's death, there are only twelve men. Obviously, we have to use some of the women for light work, hunting, and guard duty."

They finally settled on two men to remain in town to help the remaining women and children guard it against the enemy. They would rotate two men and two women between the town and ore site on a weekly basis. The older children that could blow the horn would act as lookouts for both locations.

They eventually settled on eight men and four women at the ore site; two men and two women on the ore camp hunting party, one of the town men and three women for their hunting party, and a total of four older children as lookouts for both sites. The two lookouts at the ore camp would also rotate back to town on a weekly basis. This spread out the townspeople more than John liked but there was no help for it.

What was doubly difficult about mining the minerals was the lack of adequate tools. All they had were stone axes and sharp sticks to dig out the ore from the hillside. They would have to weave stick baskets to carry the ore where they needed it. It was going to be a very slow backbreaking effort as they started the process of making metal.

When the ore camp was established Jacob Bell started construction of the smelting equipment they were to use. As soon as sufficient ore was accumulated they began to mine the coal outcropping which was to be the heating element of the process. Bell was not an expert in this process as he only knew the basics and had to improvise many of the elements of the process.

They were working for almost three months before they achieved their first success in smelting iron. Now they had to figure out how to convert this into metal tools. On their first attempt they dug a form in the clay earth for a pick head then poured the molten metal into the form. After it cooled, they tried it out digging ore and found that their first try was a success. They refined the process and soon were turning out various tools helpful in their work.

When Bell decided they had enough raw iron, he suggested they could now move on to the next step of making steel. He decided their best chance of success was to build a crude blast furnace of stacked limestone. After experimenting with coal and charcoal as the heating element, supplemented by the use of a bellows to increase the temperature, they eventually got the results they wanted.

They worked at producing bar steel until they could move the operation back to Harding. It took another two months before they had what they considered a sufficient supply of steel. After building two four-wheeled wooden carts, it took several backbreaking trips to move the steel bars and tools they had made back to town. The normal three-hour walk took nine hours of pulling and pushing the carts along the trail and another day between trips to rest up.

When they got the last cartload to Harding, John decided to call for a week of vacation from their labors to the delight of the townspeople. During this week of relaxation, John and the council members must decide how they were going to use the steel and iron they had brought back with them. Obviously, they needed metal arrow and spear points for defense of the town, but that would take only a small part of their supply.

John suggested axe heads, knife blades, scrapers, and other wood working tools, door hinges and latches, and nails. Other members suggested hand plows for expanding their garden. John finally decided they should hold a town meeting and bring these suggestions before the townspeople and ask for additional input from them.

At the town meeting the council members also decided where to place the workshop. They decided that since the shop was going to be the center of activity, it should be placed in the town's center. Since there was a danger of fire from the furnace they decided against enclosing it in a building, but instead they would work in the open air with only a thatched covering for shade from the sun.

Mary had given birth to twin boys three months prior to the ore camp being shut down. By chance, John was home during his normal rotation and was able to help Janet Harding and Sarah with the delivery.

When the twins were born he gave each a kiss on their forehead before handing them to Mary. She held the two boys in her arms with a blissful expression.

"John, what are we going to name them?"

He thought a moment before answering. "Why not name them after our fathers."

Mary looked at them proudly as she replied, "James and Robert it shall be. James will be the blond headed baby as he most favors my father."

His wives had now produced two sets of twins which along with Lillie's other children brought the total up to six small children in the household.

With the townspeople all back in Harding, it made for easier living in the Bridges household. With three mothers sharing the workload, and with the help of Jenny they were all able to take some needed quiet time for themselves.

Janet Harding, being the only trained nurse in town, decided to start a nursing school. She went to the various family homes and talked with the older girls to see who might be interested. She found four who expressed an interest, including Jenny. They decided to use the Harding house for the school, as Jill, Harding's second wife, was overdue in her delivery. The girls were soon going to get some practical experience as a midwife.

The girls followed Janet around on her rounds, observing as she tended to the sick, injured, and new mothers. Jenny seemed to express the most interest, and through her questions and willing participation, soon became Janet's best pupil. Janet was hoping to get a cadre of nurses available in case a medical disaster should happen to the town. However, after two weeks only Jenny and another student remained. The other two girls didn't have sufficient interest to get past the blood and child birth trauma.

Janet was happy to have her two best pupils remain, because there was plenty of practical experience for the two students to learn from. The steel making process provided them patients with burns, scrapes and cuts, and other injuries; but assisting in the child birthing process was the most rewarding for them.

One afternoon, after six months of nurses training, Jenny returned home to hear the joyful news that both Sarah and Lillie were pregnant. She eagerly hugged both women while excitedly congratulating them. However, Sarah gave her a melancholy smile.

"I was hoping to have more children before I got any older, but this may be my last pregnancy and I'm a little sad because of that."

Jenny hugged her in encouragement and said eagerly, "Janet said that women have successfully given birth well into their forties, and I wouldn't give up hope yet. Besides, if you have twins again you'll have your hands full until you're a grandmother and then you'll have grandkids to look after."

Sarah shook her head at the thought, but then smiled happily. "Twins, I wonder if I can be so lucky again."

Lillie laughed as she pointed at her own belly. "Look at me. I'm bigger now than I was with the other two this early. I think this house makes twins!"

Jenny giggled, then said, "I don't think that's how it works!"

They both laughed as her face turned red with embarrassment, causing her to laugh too. The next night Jenny was called into service as a solo midwife for the first time. Janet was busy with another delivery so Jenny had to fill in. She was excited and a little apprehensive as she arrived at the Campbell house to help deliver Rachel's first child. Rachel had begun to think she was barren, but was now excitedly hoping for a son.

When Jenny arrived, Rachel was disappointed and apprehensive because she was expecting Janet, the experienced midwife who had already successfully delivered ten babies in Harding. Jenny, while experienced, looked too young at almost fifteen to be performing this duty.

Jenny knew she had a problem when she saw the frightened expression on Rachel's face. She immediately went to Rachel and held her hand, talking softly. "Don't worry, I've assisted Janet as a midwife five times and never had a bit of trouble. If there are any problems, Janet is only minutes away."

Rachel finally calmed down and then forgot their conversation as her labor pains resumed. June, Campbell's second wife, already had a baby girl and now helped Jenny in the birthing process. After another two hours of labor, Rachel gave birth to a healthy girl. However, she was not finished and a few minutes later she gave birth to a boy. Her first solo midwife duty and she had delivered twins! She was ecstatic with joy as she gave the twins to the new mother to hold while Kit Campbell looked on in awe.

Rachel looked at her babies with tears of joy in her eyes. She smiled at Jenny and thanked her for her services.

"If anyone asks me, you're the equal to Janet as a midwife."

Janet Harding soon arrived to check on Rachel and when she saw the twins she exclaimed, "What have we here! Jenny, it looks like you had your hands full."

She then checked the twins' status with Jenny's help. Finding no problem with the twins or their mother, Janet gave them back to Rachel where they immediately started feeding. Janet had delivered a healthy baby girl and both mother and baby were doing fine. After Janet and Jenny exchanged information about the deliveries it was well after midnight before Jenny returned home.

Sarah had waited up for her and asked how the birthing went. Jenny, while tired, was still excited about her experience. "I delivered twins, a girl and boy, both loudly proclaiming their entry into this world. Janet delivered a healthy little girl."

Sarah smiled at Jenny's enthusiasm as she related her experience with the delivery. Although she thought she knew the answer, she asked Jenny what the sexes were of the new births since they had arrived in town.

Jenny thought a moment before answering. "Of thirteen babies, four were boys and nine were girls. Why do you ask?"

Sarah shook her head sadly as she answered, "The birth rate is still running more girls than boys. If this continues for any length of time it will mean, out of necessity, the practice of men taking second wives will become common. I wonder if our genes have a built-in emergency response when the species is threatened."

Jenny looked at her with a puzzled expression for a moment, but then her face cleared as she realized what Sarah said had a direct bearing on her.

"You mean in a few years when the other girls and I are old enough for marriage, there's not going to be enough men for each of us?"

"Yes, the younger married men will need to take care of the women who don't have husbands."

"You mean like John taking Mary as his second wife," Jenny said with a quiver in her voice?

Sarah hugged her tightly and whispered, "I know it's hard to think of sharing your husband with another woman but look how well it's worked for us. The trick I think is for the first wife to be comfortable with her love for her husband and to first become close friends with the prospective second wife."

Jenny stubbornly argued, "But, Mick or George didn't take a second wife!"

"There was no need after the three single women married. In fact, right now there's a shortage of women for the two single men in town, but soon that will change again."

Jenny, with fire in her eyes angrily replied, "When Randy and I get married, I won't let him take a second wife!"

Sarah shook her head and regarded her sadly. "Jenny you might think that now but after watching those poor single women without a husband, your heart can't help but soften toward their plight. Now let's go to bed, this is enough talk about something that you may never have to worry about."

CHAPTER 17

The next day Sarah decided that her students should learn about steel making, so she arranged with Jacob to explain the process from ore to finished product. Then he would show the class what was happening in the workshop as they made tools. Since the workshop was the town's only industry, it was important that everyone understand how it operates.

The class was a success and a great change of pace for the students. She conferred with Jacob about teaching advanced courses for her brighter students, so that his knowledge could be passed down and would not be lost with his death. He agreed as soon as the workshop could run without his hands-on attention.

John found that he had to rework the arrows he was using once he added the metal tips. They were top heavy but worked better once he lengthened the shaft and added leather feathering for better control. He surprised even himself at how well the finished product performed. It increased his effective range by at least fifteen yards and if he had a stronger bow he suspected that the arrow would perform even better.

John consulted with the other men on how to get a greater pull on the bow and the consensus was that it had to be lengthened. Now that they had metal axes, they could cut their bows from the tree with a built-in curve for added strength. After some trial and error, they eventually produced a longbow with about a forty-five pound pull. Using the new arrows they found that they had almost doubled their effective range from their old weapons.

John was named the town's Armorer by the town council based

upon his experiments with the longbow. He decided to make it a family affair and added Randy and George to his team. They soon became experienced in the art of making the new longbows and arrows. Mary tried the new bow, but had difficulty with the stronger pull. However, using her old bow and the new arrows brought a smile to her face. The new arrows flew straight and further than she had previously experienced.

Both Sarah and Lillie were late into their pregnancy and according to Janet Harding, they should each expect twins. Sarah greeted the news with joy but Lillie, while happy, was also apprehensive about giving birth to twins. The women's great size prevented them from doing most of the household duties; however, Mary and Jenny took up the slack as much as they could. While Jenny was busy on a nursing assignment other townswomen volunteered their help.

While returning late from a midwife assignment with Jenny, Janet pointed up at the moon.

"It's almost full. I bet Sarah and Lillie will both deliver before this time tomorrow."

Jenny smiled at her mentor and then laughed. "Is that an old wives tale, or is it because they're both overdue?"

"You just wait, then we'll see if it's an old wives tale."

The next afternoon Sarah began to have labor pains followed an hour later by Lillie. Jenny had John go after Janet and Jessica Campbell, the other nurse trainee, as she was going to need all the help she could get. Janet arrived first and double-checked both mothers who were doing fine. She had Jenny try to calm George and then John when he returned with Jessica. The fathers went to their wives' bedsides to hold their hands and offer moral support when the labor pains hit.

George held up his hand in surprise after Lillie's labor pain had eased. "I think she broke it. I don't have any feeling left in it."

Jenny looked at him doubtfully. "Let me see your hand! Now wiggle your fingers. It's okay; she just cut off circulation in your hand for a while. Next time use the other one."

Lillie smiled at Jenny as she teased her husband. "He's alright, it's just that this is his first baby and it's a little overwhelming."

"It's not only my first baby, but twins! What a way to start," George complained.

Lillie may have started her labor last, but she was the first in delivering a baby girl. When Sarah heard the baby's cry it started her delivery of a baby boy, and they almost tied in delivering their second babies. They each had identical twins. Janet delivered the Anderson twins, while Jenny delivered the Bridges' twins. Jessica and Mary were kept busy with the newborn babies as they were delivered.

Both John and George were distraught when the babies started being born so close together and they each tried to get a glimpse of their new babies as the midwives cleared their airways and wiped them off. Eventually, they got to hold their new children before giving them to their mothers.

Sarah looked over at Lillie and smiled. "We won't have to worry about mixing these twins up, will we?"

John kissed her on the forehead and lightly touched his new sons. "I'm out of name ideas, what do you think?"

She considered for a moment before answering. "We could name them after Mr. Harding and Jacob Bell. They're two of the leading citizens of Harding."

"So its William and Jacob. But, how are we going to tell them apart?"

"It's easy Honey, I'll just tie a leather strap around William's ankle."

Lillie smiled at her mother and said, "I think I've got mine named too. George, what do you think about naming these two Gracie and Sarah?"

"After my mother and yours? That's nice, but which one is Gracie?"

"You pick and I'll put a strap around her ankle too."

The next day John told the other two men in the family about his plans to expand their home. He drew an outline in the dirt showing the house and then a one-story addition at each side. These additions would each contain two large bedrooms leaving the six upstairs bedrooms for the children.

The main floor of the original house would become a larger common room for work and socializing.

Randy was looking at the floor plan with a puzzled expression, then blurted, "There's only four bedrooms downstairs and we have seven adults."

John looked at him with a blank expression for a moment, then smiled. "Randy, think a moment here. I'll take one with either Sarah or Mary, the alternate wife will take one, George and Lillie will take another, and the last one is for Jenny. You'll have an upstairs room until you and Jenny get married."

Randy face became red with shocked embarrassment before replying, "How did you know we're going to get married?"

Both John and George laughed as Randy's face got even redder, if possible. John finally put his arm around him and said, "Boy, you must have been the last to know. From the first week after Jenny joined our family, it was obvious she had set her cap for you. Besides, since we've been in Harding you haven't even looked at another girl. Have you two decided when you're going to get married?"

"No, Jenny said we should wait another year or two until we grow up some more."

"Jenny's a wise women. You'll be a lucky man to have her as a wife."

* * *

Two months later, the townspeople were startled by the sound of their east sentry's horn blowing as he ran into town screaming that the Mutants were coming. The town's emergency plan immediately went into effect. All young children, and babies with their mothers were to take shelter in the Bridges home, the town's largest house. They were to be guarded by three men and four guard dogs including Rocky. The rest of the townspeople armed themselves to meet the threat.

John led his squad with longbows to cover the east approach to Harding, while a mixed squad with slings and throwing spears acted as backup and covered the other approaches. Each squad also had at least two guard dogs for additional support.

The east sentry reported to John. "I saw at least six enemy men and they're not far behind me. These Mutants weren't frightened away at the sound of the horn but instead started running toward me."

John had ten men and women positioned about three feet apart, shoulder-to-shoulder, when the Mutants ran out of the woods. They stopped when they saw the townspeople facing them with what they thought was nothing but a long stick as a weapon. Their leader spoke to the others in his band, whose eight members spread out on either side of him.

The Mutant leader then began a loud chant waving his spear at the townspeople, quickly imitated by his followers. John told his people to attack on his command at the man directly opposite them with their far right archer to take care of any that are missed. The Mutant leader started his charge and John gave the order to attack. The first nine archers fired almost as one at a distance of thirty yards with every arrow striking a target. However, one of the Mutants was not targeted and continued his charge for another five paces before the tenth archer's arrow hit his chest.

John called to the other squad to see if they saw any activity from their direction but apparently the nine who attacked from the east were all that there was. The leader had taken two arrows both almost dead center in his chest. After checking the fallen Mutants, they found that their wounds were all fatal, from either chest or gut wounds, except for one Mutant who was struck in his side. The arrow that hit the last enemy went completely through his body. John was very pleased with his longbow creation's accuracy and power.

The wounded enemy was screaming in agony from his injury but wouldn't let anyone near him. Anytime anyone would get close he would swipe at him with his club while growling like an animal. Finally, John shot an arrow into his chest to finish the problem before any townsmen got hurt.

He called his squad together. "I want to congratulate all of you on your outstanding performance and for your long hours of practice with the longbow which has paid off with the successful defense of Harding without any injuries to the townspeople."

By this time the other townspeople had gathered to congratulate the archers and examine the dead enemy. Mary, who was one of his archers, stood next to her husband with a satisfied expression on her face as if a debt had been repaid for Lillie's slain Mick.

Most of the townspeople had seen Mutants before but for many people this was their first opportunity for a close examination. All the Mutants had long black hair that came down to their shoulders. However, some had headbands to keep it away from their faces. They were heavily muscled in the shoulders and legs but the tallest was only about five foot six inches. The vile smell that arose from the bodies stopped many of the townspeople in their tracks. Several women fled with their hands over their mouths trying to keep from puking.

John assembled a scout party of ten men and women to retrace the Mutants' path to see if more were near. He then had to deal with another problem. He needed extra sentries to cover the east and west paths into Harding. The background noise of the workshop had been too loud for anyone to hear the warning horn, so rather than move the sentries closer to town; he decided to add another to each post to relay the warning.

The next day, with the workshop back in operation he did a test to see if the relay system worked. The nearest horn could plainly be heard above the sounds of the workshop. After discussion with the council, because of the manpower shortage, they decided to use in the nearest relay the older girls who had provided sentry duty while the ore camp was in operation.

The scouting party returned to town without encountering any more of the enemy. John then called a special town council meeting to discuss whether or not to plan a punitive attack on any nearby Mutant settlements they should find. His thought was to clear at least a twenty-mile safe zone around Harding to avoid accidental discovery by Mutant hunting parties.

The council invited all townspeople to the meeting for their comments which resulted in passage of the mayor's resolution. They also added that semi-annual scouting parties would search the boundary of the twenty-mile zone to ensure that no new enemy settlements encroached, with the first search to begin no later than the following week.

Mary spoke up, "I think that since the last attack came from the east, we should start in that direction."

John replied, "I hope that the last attack was the extent of that Mutant tribe's manpower and they have moved away from Harding."

"Yes, that's possible but we have to start somewhere," Mary replied.

John nodded his head in agreement, then added, "A twenty-mile sweep east would take about three days, then we can have another team depart until all four points on the compass are covered. The search should be finished in two weeks if they didn't encounter any problems."

Mary was the leader of the first scouting team which returned as scheduled the afternoon of the third day. She met with the council and reported.

"We found a deserted Mutant camp about twelve miles east along the *Mick*. Based upon the condition of the campfire coals they had been gone at least two days. Their trail led further east along the *Mick*. We encountered no other signs of the enemy in our sweep back toward Harding."

Mary was happy to be back home and when she entered the Bridges home with John, her twins and the rest of the household greeted her eagerly. She picked up her twins with tears of happiness in her eyes as she accepted their joy in her safe return. The family wanted to hear all about her trip and what she had seen at the Mutants camp.

Later that evening after things had quieted down in the household, Mary took John's hand and whispered to him that she needed a bath and coyly asked if he wanted to join her. They slipped out of the house and then walked east along the *Mick* until they reached the family's favorite deep bathing hole. They were sufficiently far enough from Harding to ensure their privacy. They both stripped and jumped into the stream with shouts of glee and then groans as they entered the icy spring water.

After some playful water activity, she passionately kissed her husband and then demanded that he scrub her back and shoulders. He did better than that as he massaged her body, releasing the tension in her tight muscles and then by applying light pressure to her most sensitive areas soon had her trembling with passionate excitement. She finally had all this titillation she could stand and urged John to move to the stream bank where they made passionate love.

After the heat of their passion cooled as they lay in each other's arms, she asked about Sarah and their newest set of twins. He responded by giving her all the news of the household since she had been gone.

She poked him in the ribs and said, "That's not what I mean! Have you been giving her the loving she needs from you since she had the twins?"

"You two are more like sisters than competing wives. You're always looking out for each other making sure that the other is being treated fairly. To answer your question, she seems quite happy with our love life, especially after last night."

Mary responded by roughly pushing him over on his back while giving him another passionate kiss.

"Would you have us any other way?" She slyly questioned.

"I've got to be the luckiest man alive with two lovely passionate wives who like each other and compete to make me happy."

Mary laughed and then playfully nipped at his earlobe. "You better believe it you big lug."

Sarah and Lillie's newest sets of twins were receiving lots of attention in the Bridges household. Between the six older children, the three mothers, and Jenny, they never lacked for company. All the older children had rooms upstairs, two to a room. This left one room for Randy and two rooms for play and future expansion for the two new sets of twins.

The expanded common room made it much easier to care for the babies and toddlers. There were always at least two women on hand to care for the children which sometimes became quite hectic. However, the men helped out when it became too much for the women to handle. All the children loved John who delighted in telling them stories about his past life and the trip to Harding through the wilderness.

The mothers were happy when John distracted the children with his stories but laughed when he put a funny spin on some occurrences that had actually been quite scary. Then there were other stories he told that were pure fiction. When this happened, Sarah and Lillie would look at each other questioningly and then just smiled as they shook their heads.

The children would delight in asking John to repeat a certain story and then protest when he didn't get it just right in the retelling. In one instance he had tried three times before giving up and asking the children how the story went, much to their delight.

The scouting teams eventually completed their search without finding any other signs of the Mutants. This relieved the townspeople greatly. John, after consultation with the town council, decided that they should start having Sunday as a day of rest with services at night so that the sentries could attend.

They had two days until the first Sunday service to find a lay preacher to lead them in prayer. No one claimed to have any such experience so John met with the council again and suggested that each of the council members take their turn then let the townspeople select which one they liked the best. The council at first rejected this idea until he placed a two-month time limit for anyone selected.

John, while quite nervous, thought that since this was his idea he should be the first to lead the services. The Sunday night service was held in the town center with torches lit creating an almost festive atmosphere. The townspeople brought their own seats while John's pulpit was an upright log.

The cool summer evening was pleasant for their first open-air church service. He tried to make himself and the congregation comfortable by telling them of his lack of experience but of his own faith in God. After relating his own experiences from the start of his journey until reaching Harding, he credited his survival to his faith and God's help. He then pointed out how the attacks on them by the Mutants had brought them together against a common enemy and how they should now give thanks to God for their very survival.

The congregation shouted its amen to John who then asked them to sing some songs before they retired from the service. There was dead silence for almost a minute before Mary started singing "Amazing Grace" in a beautiful soprano voice. Her voice was so heart rendering that she was almost half way through the song before others followed her lead. She led the townspeople in three more songs before John called the Sunday Service to an end.

After the service the townspeople congratulated John on his sermon but the greatest kudu's were for Mary and her great singing voice. When they got home the whole family again made over Mary's singing.

John kissed her and jokingly said, "If it hadn't been for your singing, our first Sunday Service would have been a bust."

Sarah hugged her and then with a wink stated, "The next time we can't get the babies asleep you can sang them a lullaby."

The workshop activity slowed with only tool making continuing. Most of the towns needs had been filled, with only specialized items being made now. This left the townspeople more free time to do repair work and/or additions on their homes and improvements to the town's garden. The garden was in continual production because of the mild climate and had been expanded to the point that meat was only a supplement to their diet. This reduced their hunting requirements and took some of the pressure off the declining deer population.

The hunting parties had ranged further out to get their meat letting the close-in deer population recover. This also allowed them to check for any Mutant sign. Because of this, the hunting parties were increased to eight members for their own protection.

CHAPTER 18

About two months after their first twenty-mile sweep around Harding, a hunting party came across new Mutant sign. The hunting party led by Jack Peterson was operating fifteen miles southwest of Harding when their guard dogs came across a recent trail of a large Mutant hunting party.

Jack decided to follow them and see if they had a camp close by. He left two men behind with the beagles, while the rest followed the trail. They hadn't gone four miles when they smelled smoke. He told the main party to stay put while he checked the camp out. As he cautiously moved toward the camp he encountered no guards as he moved through the heavy growth of trees to within twenty yards of the clearing.

The camp consisted of twelve adult men, fifteen females, and about twenty children. The men and some of the older male children were celebrating their successful hunt while the women were preparing the meat. Considering the shelters constructed and the large bone pile, they had to have been here at least six weeks.

Jack returned to his party and informed them of what he had seen. They then headed back to Harding to give the townspeople the bad news. Along the way they killed two deer, so when they entered Harding no one paid their arrival too much attention. Jack soon sought out John and relayed the discovery of the Mutants' camp.

John immediately called a council meeting to discuss the enemy's sighting. He suggested that they surround the camp on three sides and then try to scare them away from the area by sounding the horns.

Hopefully, the eerie sounds would drive them toward the unprotected east side. If not, they could always use force. The council voted to adopt John's strategy and they would send all their able-bodied men and women, with him as the leader.

John did a survey of the women with babies and the men and women over sixty. He was left with ten men and nine women. The older children and adults would be left with six guard dogs to protect the mothers and children of the town.

John and his squad of eighteen men and women, supplemented by eight guard dogs, started the following mid-day for the Mutant camp with the plan to arrive three hours before sunset. He wanted to be sure their hunting party had returned before they attempted their scare tactic. Jack Peterson acted as their scout leading the way towards the enemy's camp.

They reached the camp about an hour sooner than their planed arrival and John sent Peterson to scout the camp to see if everyone was there. He soon returned and reported that the camp was intact. John then dispersed his squad according to the plan with instructions of when to start blowing the horns.

After about fifteen minutes the north horn started its eerie bleating, followed in five seconds by the west horn, then in another five seconds by the south horn. At the first sound of the horn the Mutants appeared startled then apprehensive when the second horn started. When the third horn started it's bleating, the leader shouted to his followers who started gathering their belongings and then hurriedly moved east away from the camp.

John had the horn blowers spread out and follow them for at least ten miles to ensure they left the town's twenty-mile restricted zone. His squad followed to make sure that they didn't turn back against the horn blowers and proceeded at a slow walk to ensure that the women and children of the Mutants could stay ahead of them. They reached what they thought was the twenty-mile limit about an hour before sunset where John called a halt. He had the horns sound for another fifteen minutes before they turned back.

The team returned to the abandoned Mutant camp and stayed for the night. They helped themselves to the meat left behind and searched the camp for anything else of value. John had the dogs set out to guard against the return of the enemy while they slept. The next morning they burned the shelters before starting home.

When they arrived back into Harding, John was relieved to find the town safe while the townspeople were jubilant at their safe return. He called a council meeting and informed them that the Mutants had been scared off without any loss of life on either side. He cautioned them that the area would have to be checked again in about six weeks to ensure they didn't return. The council received the news with a cheer and then surrounded him while slapping his back and congratulating him on his successful plan of action.

Later, after the celebration for the successful trip ended, John and his family returned to their home still carrying the glow from the town's gratitude. His wives and the older children in the household fussed over him with respect and honor.

After he was settled into a comfortable seat, the children started climbing into his lap until he was overwhelmed. The mothers had to pull the children off him scolding them about their behavior.

Sadie, one of John's first born and the apple of his eye, shyly asked, "Daddy, could I sit in your lap while you tell us about your experiences against the Mutants?"

He smiled at her as he picked her up onto his lap. The other children gathered around him on the floor.

He asked them where he should start and Sadie excitedly whispered, "When you got to their camp, daddy!"

He smiled down at her and then when he looked questionably at the other children, they excitedly exclaimed, "Yes!"

As he related his experiences to the children, his wives and Lillie soon lost themselves in the story the same as the children. When he got to the part about Mary leading one of the horn blowing sections, the children smiled at her with pride while she blushed at their admiration. After he finished the story, the children excitedly wanted him to repeat it again.

When John started to tell the story again, Sarah and Lillie wistfully exclaimed that they had missed all the excitement. Randy and Jenny, who had guarded the town with the older children, also said they wished they could have gone with John. However, Jenny as one of the two young nurse's was needed in town because Janet Harding had been one of the members of John's squad.

When John finished telling his story for the third time, the mothers got the children upstairs for naptime. When they returned downstairs, both of his wives made over him again as Lillie and Jenny watched with smiles on their faces. Lillie proudly said, "We're glad that a battle was not needed and nobody from town was hurt."

John nodded his head in agreement. "Yes, if they have a superstitious fear of this place, we are better protected than having a group of people out for vengeance because we killed members of their clan."

Lillie and George then informed the family that they thought it was time they had their own house now that their own family had grown to six people. Sarah looked stricken at the news of their planned move out of her house. Lillie rushed to her side when she saw the tears and tragic look on her mother's face.

Holding Sarah tightly, Lillie tried to console her. However, Sarah soon recovered as she realized that her daughter's departure from her home had to happen eventually. John and the other family members said they understood, but would miss having them in the household. The next day the men of Harding helped cut the needed trees and move the logs to the location of the new Anderson house.

Lillie and George decided on the same floor plan as the original Bridges home. Their new home location was only two houses from the Bridges, so they wouldn't be moving very far away. The new metal axes made the task of house building much easier than their former old stone axes, and the new home was completed in less than two weeks by the Bridges and Anderson men working together.

On the day of completion, George carried Lillie across the threshold of their new home. Later, Sarah and the rest of the Bridges household helped them move their belongings into the house and make it livable. That night the Bridges household felt a large empty place without Lillie and her family and was generally depressed as its members missed their presence. John held Sarah while sitting together trying to comfort her loss of a daughter leaving home.

"Babe, she's just moved a few feet away and you'll see her every day. Why, I bet she and the kids are over here every day just like always."

Sarah shook her head with tears in her eyes. "No, she's got her own family now just as she should. It's just hard for me to adjust my thinking to the fact that she's an adult now and must make her own decisions for her family. But you're right, they'll be over here most of the time."

* * *

The town of Harding was in its eighth year of existence before experiencing its first storm. When John left his house in the early morning he sensed something in the air. The air seemed charged with energy much as it had prior to the approaching storms on the trip to Harding. He quickly made his morning visit to the outhouse, then alerted the household to prepare for a severe storm.

While his family started their preparations, John alerted the remainder of the town. While he was gone shutters were placed on windows and loose items were secured in anticipation of the expected storm. John was looking at the workshop's sunshade roof of loose tree branches with a worried expression but then shook his head. There was nothing that they could do to protect it from a strong wind.

Within a half-hour, dark heavy clouds began to form. John soon saw lightning and heard the thunder approaching the town. William Harding stopped by John's house and they shared a knowing look. They were probably going to be visited by a ball lightning messenger who usually seemed to travel in these severe storms. Sarah was also concerned and came to John in fear of what might soon occur. He tried to calm her fears but still remembered his last painful experience with the *Messenger* and he couldn't hide his own anxiety from her. Harding tightly gripped his shoulder in understanding and then wished him luck before returning to his own home and family.

The wind increased in volume and a sudden gust blew dust into the air causing John to look toward the workshop just as the loose roof blew away. He gave one last look at the darkening sky before entering his home with Sarah still clinging to him tightly. He sat down in the common room and asked all the other family members to seek shelter in the far downstairs bedrooms. His wives refused to leave him alone and asked Randy and Jenny to watch over their children in the bedrooms while they stayed with John.

The storm arrived with full force. Lightning was striking the ground around the town with such a frequency that the thunder's deafening sounds almost smothered the sounds of the wind screaming around the house. At each loud crash of thunder the large log house vibrated. This caused Sarah and Mary, who were sitting on either side of John, to hold him so tightly with their faces pressed against his chest that he had trouble breathing.

John purposely left the outside door open in case the ball lightning messenger should visit him. He was watching the door with apprehension when a glowing light approached through the darkness of the storm. The *Messenger* was suddenly at the doorway, its glow illuminating the common room and bringing with it the strong smell of ozone. Both Sarah and Mary raised their heads to look at the source of the light and then moaned as they pressed their faces back against John's chest.

The *Messenger* slowly entered the room and approached John and his wives. John felt strangely calm now that the entity was before him. Maybe it was the support of his wives who also were now calmly watching its approach, or maybe the entity itself had this effect.

This glowing ball was larger, about the size of a basketball and stopped about a foot before his face and hovered, repeating a glowing alternating green, orange, and blue color. It must have repeated the cycle of colors five times as if trying to decide how to proceed when suddenly a thin continuous electrical spark shot from it to John's head. The connection continued for almost five minutes but to Sarah and Mary it seemed much longer.

The connection broke with an audible crack, then John slumped against his wives. They all fell to the floor in a dead faint. The *Messenger* departed through the door, leaving the room in darkness. The storm soon began to recede and within minutes was gone leaving the area in a dead calm except for the fading sounds of its departure.

William Harding came running up to the doorway then came inside to help revive John and his wives. The rest of John's family silently gathered around to offer their support. Randy had informed them of John's past history with the entity they dubbed, *The Messenger*. Jenny placed a cool wet cloth on John's forehead which brought him awake with a start. After a brief moment of confusion, he slowly grinned at his dazed wives who were now awake too.

"Well, it looks like we survived another meeting with *The Messenger*," he said while gently rubbing his forehead.

Sarah touched his forehead tenderly and spoke softly, "Honey, how do you feel?"

He held up his fingers and wiggled them then did the same to his toes. "I think I'm okay."

He then hugged his wives and asked them if they were okay. When they nodded their heads, he held up his hands to Harding and asked him to help him up. When he was standing, he took several tentative steps and then while using Harding for support he turned and sat at the long table. Harding then helped Sarah and Mary to their feet; whereupon, Sarah hurried to give John water to drink while Mary lit a lamp to brighten up the room.

John rubbed his forehead. "I feel pretty good except I feel weak and I have this sore spot here."

Mary brought the lamp close to John's head to examine his skin. "You have a red mark there but it doesn't appear to be a burn."

She turned to Jenny and asked her to examine the mark. After her examination, Jenny agreed that it didn't appear to be a burn.

Harding asked Sarah, "How did John get the mark?"

"That's the scary part. The ball lightning that we call *The Messenger* shot a continuous thin spark of energy into John's head!"

Harding looked into John's eyes, then said, "Your eyes look clear. Do you remember anything about the experience?"

John replied eagerly, "It was just like the last time it talked to me except this time there was not as much pain. It wants us to do something! There's another human settlement about a two-week's walk north of here that is under attack by our enemy, the Mutants. It wants us to get them to join us here before they're all killed!"

Sarah broke in excitedly, "Honey, I got that message too!"

Mary interrupted. "I received that same message! It must have come through you while we were holding onto you."

Harding's face showed great concern, then asked, "Do you know how to find the settlement?"

"*The Messenger* gave me general directions but also a warning. It said that the Mutants in that area are numerous and will attack us on sight - as if we didn't already know that."

Harding rubbed his chin in thought. "We need to call a council meeting about this as soon as the storm damage is repaired."

That evening the council met. There was so much interest that the entire population of Harding also attended. They had heard about *The Messengers'* visit with John and were anxious to hear the details. John first told the townspeople of his and Harding's past dealings with the entity and what they guessed its motives were. He then related his most recent experience with the entity and what it had asked them to do. He asked the council to consider whether they should risk its members to help this other settlement. He reminded them that these other people would make them a stronger and more diverse community and would make their own survival more certain.

Jack Peterson spoke up, "How critical is the time factor. If it takes us two weeks to get there, do we have enough time to reach them before they're all killed?"

John considered the question for a moment, then answered, "You have a point, but I don't think *The Messenger* would send us there if there was no hope of reaching them in time."

The council asked for a show of hands from the townspeople for helping the other settlement. The response was unanimous to aid the other settlement.

John smiled his support for their decision and then asked, "I need volunteers for the rescue mission. This mission is going to be very dangerous as we can expect to have battles with the Mutants. It's even possible that some of you might not come back."

By the time the meeting had broken up, John had more volunteers than he could take and still leave the town protected. Since the trip north had to be made quickly, he needed the strongest men and women available. He also needed medical experience, but Janet was too old for a journey this long. He decided to take Jenny as her trained replacement. He knew that with Jenny going, Randy wouldn't rest until he was part of the team as well.

His final selection was about the same size as the last team they had assembled but was comprised of younger members. His greatest concern was how Sarah would react to both Randy and Jenny being part of his team. The Bridges' household had four members, including Mary, on the team of ten men and eleven women, plus ten guard dogs. John hoped that their new weapons and the dogs would give them a big advantage against the enemy.

John made a quick trip home to tell Sarah of his plans. He gave her a kiss and a hug before setting her down on a chair. "Babe, the rescue party is going to include Mary, Randy, and Lillie."

Sarah's face went white with apprehension as she looked into her husband's eyes. She then whispered, "Oh my!" She then rushed into his arms with tears of concern not only for her children but for John and Mary as well.

That evening when all the family members were present, she counseled them to watch out for each other and come back home.

Later, she pulled Mary aside. "Mary, you've been around John long enough to know that he sometimes takes chances he shouldn't. Look after him and make sure he doesn't get hurt."

The next day was spent preparing weapons and supplies for the trip north. They planned to return in four or five weeks if all went well. John, after consideration, decided to take two horns along for signaling and as a means to throw fear into the Mutants.

The rescue team assembled early the following morning in the town center, surrounded by relatives who came to see them off and wish them success and safe return on their journey. John had a three-man and two-dog advance scouting party leave fifteen minutes before the main party. He hoped the small advance party would make less noise than the main party yet be large enough to handle any hunting parties they might meet. He then led the way as they left single file out of town into the forest following the *Mick* east. They would turn north when they reached the main north-south trail.

He had the team set a fast pace for the first twenty-mile stretch, the safest part of their journey. His instruction to the scouting party was to follow the main trail north for about 200 miles, at which time they would turn inland. The trail was mostly through forestland with only occasional clearings. That evening they caught up with the scouting party who were preparing the overnight camp for the main party. John estimated they had traveled about thirty miles for the first day.

At the end of the third day they hadn't yet encountered any Mutants but had seen fresh sign several times, mainly their campsites.

The next morning John consulted with Kit Campbell, the lead scout. "Kit, I think you may need extra people in your party. Who would you want?"

Kit considered for a moment before answering. "I think you're right about increasing my scouting party. Mary is about the best person beside myself - if you can spare her," he added with a smile.

John grinned back at him. "I'll be all right. Besides Mary will be back with me each night."

CHAPTER 19

About mid-day on the fifth day, the main party was met by Mary. She hugged John when they met before saying, "The other scouts are following a large hunting party of Mutants and you should proceed with caution until they meet you at the inland fork in the trail."

John nodded his head. "That can't be much further. Do you want to stay with us or return to the scouts?"

Mary considered and then replied, "I'd better return. Who knows, they might have need of me." She then gave him a kiss before leaving at a fast jog back toward the other scouts.

They followed the trail for another two hours until they reached the fork where the scouts were waiting.

Kit Campbell and John met to be sure that this was the correct fork to take inland.

John nodded his head. "Yes I'm sure this is the correct trail inland. Kit, you better move more slowly from this point on as the Mutants are supposed to be more numerous in this area. I'm guessing that we have another short week before we reach the settlement."

The scouts then moved ahead on the inland trail which the main group followed after a short delay. They were two days on the inland trail when they had their first encounter with the Mutants. Kit and Mary had been trading back and forth as the lead scout. Mary was leading when she literally came face to face with the Mutants before either knew they were there.

Mary reacted first by yelling, "Spread out!"

The other three members of the scouting party immediately came up beside her as they faced a larger Mutant hunting party of five men not more than thirty-five feet ahead of them. The leader of the Mutant hunting party screamed something at them while brandishing a long pointed spear. They were just starting to move toward them with threatening spears when Kit ordered the scouts to attack. When the arrows were in the air, the two dogs ran toward the enemy. The arrows found three targets while the dogs attacked the remaining two Mutants. The two who were attacked by the dogs had no idea of their danger until the dogs leaped onto their chests, tearing at their throats.

The scouts stayed at the scene until the main group arrived. Kit had a satisfied look on his face as he reported to John. "We were surprised on the trail but even so our volley of arrows all hit a Mutant." He grimaced as he pointed at one of the bodies with two arrows in his chest. "We do need to better target our enemies based upon their positions, but the dogs took care of those the arrows missed."

John nodded his head. "Don't be too hard on yourself. The scouts did a great job and didn't get even a scratch. You can't get any better than that."

John had the bodies moved off the trail and covered with brush before they continued as before. However, John added two more people and another dog to the scouts before they left.

Twice more the scouts came upon small parties of Mutants on the trail but they were similarly disposed of before they reached the main party. Later, the main rescue party smelled smoke and the sickening smell of cooked human flesh before they heard the sounds of battle ahead of them.

Kit Campbell soon returned from his forward scouts and joined John for a meeting.

Kit's expression was grim as he spoke. "The settlement is being attacked by a large party of Mutants and they've set a fire at the main gate of the stockade."

John asked, "How many of them are attacking the settlement?"

Kit turned his head away from John as he struggled with his emotions before answering. "I made a quick count of at least thirty men. However, I didn't see any lookouts and all their attention is on the stockade. I bet if our team attacked their rear we could kill most of them."

Kit then added with his anger showing in his expression and voice, "John, they have a settler being roasted over a fire outside the stockade!"

John's face was like stone as he and Kit quickly conferred plotting the deployment of his team and the best use of the horns. When they were both satisfied, Kit started giving the team their assignments. John then instructed the two horn blowers to make their sound when he gave the signal to attack.

The Mutants were bunched together trying to storm a burning narrow gate that led into the fortified settlement. The rescuers were shocked to find the smell of burning flesh was a human being roasted over a fire outside the stockade, but none broke position as they regarded the Mutants with renewed hate.

The horns began to blow their eerie sound causing the Mutants to pause and look around. The archers first wave of arrows felled at least fifteen of the enemy. The unwary survivors turned in shock to meet this new threat when another wave of arrows hit them killing all who remained standing.

John split his force to check the area for any stray enemy and help put out the fire at the stockade. When the fire was out he and his family approached the stockade's door. He stood outside the gate and yelled for permission to enter. There were two men and three women already at the gate checking to be sure the fire was out. They looked in shock at the number of Mutant bodies lying on the ground between the gate and their rescuers.

An older white haired black man came to the front and exclaimed, "Thank God you're here!"

John stepped forward and spoke, "I'm John Bridges from the town of Harding on a rescue mission here. If you have any wounded, we have a nurse with us."

The settlement's leader slowly smiled then shouted for help in moving the bodies away from the gate. His face turned grim when he saw the body of one of his own had been removed from the cook fire by the Harding rescuers and was now lying on the ground. As this was being accomplished, he came up to John and vigorously shook his hand. He then lost control of his emotions, laughing one moment and then crying on John's shoulder the next. An older black woman, who appeared to be his wife, approached them and took the man by the arm and led him away while talking softly to him.

A young woman then came up to John and introduced herself as Candice McCune the daughter of their leader, Ralph McCune, who was now being attended by her mother. She asked about their nurse as they had injured in need of attention inside.

John introduced his daughter Jenny as the nurse. Candice looked at Jenny with surprise then smiled and called over a woman to show Jenny the way to the injured. Candice gave John a appraising look as he was an impressive sight dressed in animal skins and coonskin hat while leaning against his long bow.

She smiled as she pointed to his clothes. "I like your duds. How long have your people been living here?"

John removed his hat. "You like it? My son Randy over there made it for me as a birthday present several years ago." At her nod of appreciation, he continued, "Most of us have been at Harding for over eight years. How about you?"

"Almost two years! Two years of hell where we've lost almost half our people!"

John looked at his own family then asked, "How many do you have left?"

"We have six men, two of which are injured, eleven women, and six children."

John shook his head. "You must have suffered terribly." He then placed his arm around Mary and introduced her to Candice as his second wife.

Candice's mouth gaped open. "You have two wives!"

Mary looked at her sadly and then defiantly replied, "These are difficult times and men are in short supply. Just look at your own situation, six men and eleven women. Our case is even more difficult, and with the birth rate of over two to one women over men, there was no hope in sight."

Candice looked at Mary thoughtfully then ruefully said, "I guess you people had longer to assess the situation and came up with the obvious solution." She turned to John with a smile. "I guess you came to take us back with you. Let's go see how many of the injured can walk."

Kit came back to report there was no further sign of Mutants and the wounded had been disposed of. John had him set up sentries around the settlement. The remainder of his people began to help the settlement members get ready for possible travel the next day.

As they walked into the stockade, Candice remarked, "You call those animals...Mutants?"

John frowned. "Yes. They are what remain of humans after the big kill-off. What did you call them?"

"Animals! That's what they act like so the name fits." Candice then shuddered and pushed her hands forward as if pushing the thought away before continuing. "I can't believe that you have dogs. None of us had any when we arrived here."

John nodded his head. "Yes, they've been a big help. My first wife had a dog and we picked up another on the trip to Harding."

He then checked with Jenny and found that the injured could all walk. He asked Candice if her people could be ready to move in the morning.

She excitedly nodded her head. "We want out of here as soon as possible!"

The next morning Kit Campbell left with five scouts fifteen minutes before the main party which then proceeded at a slow walk toward Harding. Candice began questioning John about how he knew about their situation here and the town they were heading toward.

John hesitated a moment before asking, "Have you been visited by an entity that has the appearance of ball lightning that travels in severe storms?"

Candice looked at him in surprise. "No. Are you pulling my leg?"

John shook his head while looking at her steadily. "How about severe storms that approached your stockade before veering off without causing much damage?"

Candice suddenly realized that he was serious and thought back to when storms threatened them. "Yes. I can think of two times when that happened. The last was only about two weeks ago."

John nodded his head in understanding. "Well, about two weeks ago I was visited by the entity I described to you. We call it *The Messenger* and it wanted our town to come rescue you and bring everyone to Harding before your people were all killed by the Mutants."

Candice looked at John with her mouth open in amazement for a moment before replying, "You've got to be kidding me!"

John shook his head and then frowned before answering, "Okay, how do you think we knew you were here then?"

Candice looked at him really for the first time. He appeared to honestly believe what he was saying so maybe it did happen just as he described. She had to trust him because he appeared to know what he was doing.

She had one more question to ask though. "How long did it take you to get here?"

John slowly smiled before answering. "About two weeks."

"Okay, I believe you, but your story is still amazing. How about Harding, what kind of place is it?"

John's face brightened as he recalled his happy times there with his family. "Well, it's located next to a small river named the *Mick* after Harding's first death by a Mutant attack. The townspeople have established a vegetable garden to supplement their diet and they have added new varieties periodically as they are found in the wild. We have also started a steel making plant that is presently used for tools and weapons production, and we have log houses whose construction is now much easier with steel axes."

She then asked about the Mutants at that location. John smiled slightly as he responded. "The town was only attacked once and they were all killed. The Mutants for the most part have been scared off by the horns."

Candice looked at him questioningly. "Horns? Oh, you must mean that strange sound I heard when you attacked them?"

"Yes, what did you think of them?"

She smiled slightly as she responded, "Well, to be truthful I was more concerned about the Animals trying to get inside the stockade than the horns but it did raise goose bumps on my arms."

The rescue party was just two days on their return trip when the Mutants launched a series of small suicidal attacks. They were no match for the humans' weapons and superior numbers. Nevertheless they might have been able to kill some of the townspeople if not for the dogs who gave ample warning of the enemy's presence. For six days the rescue party endured at least one attack daily.

The seventh day started normally except John had both the scouts and the rear guard stay closer to the main party in case of an ambush. Their dogs warned the six-member scout party that Mutants were near and their horn blower sounded a warning. Almost immediately the rear guards warning horn was heard as well. The Mutants seemed to be in a frenzy as they attacked both the scouts and the rear guard. The main party split and came to their aid swarming the attackers with superior weapons and numbers. The relief party was uninjured except for a minor flesh wound suffered by one of the dogs. The enemy seemed to disappear after this last attack.

The rescue party arrived back into Harding a little over five weeks after leaving the settlement. The rescued McCune Settlement people were in awe as they entered Harding with the townspeople welcoming everyone as they arrived. There was much joy and jubilation as the townspeople joined their husbands and wives in the rescue party. The Harding children ran to welcome and become acquainted with the six children from the rescued settlement.

John was almost knocked to the ground when Sarah ran into his arms sobbing with joy. He hugged and kissed her for several minutes before waving Mary over into a group hug that included both his wives. His children then crowded close to welcome back their father and one of their mothers. Randy and Jenny crowded close as well to share in the homecoming.

After things had settled down he took Sarah's hand and approached Candice. After introducing Sarah as his first wife, he pointed out his large family who were nearby watching him expectedly with almost unbridled anticipation.

He laughed when Candice asked about their excited expressions. "They're excited because they want me to tell them stories about the rescue trip."

Sarah hid her laughter with a hand before speaking. "John tells the best stories. The kids make him tell them several times at a sitting, and later when he retells it and he leaves something out of the original tale, they complain until he gets it right."

William Harding came up to them and was introduced to Candice by John. He and John conferred a moment about the disposition of the new people and then John turned to Candice. "Until your people can build your own houses, we will split your people up among our townspeople. I've got the most room and can handle your family, another couple, and up to four kids."

He then pointed out his house and had his wives help Candice make the distribution of her people among the local townspeople. That night the expanded townspeople had a celebration meal as they became acquainted. The Bridges household had to do a little room shuffling to accommodate the extra people that night but eventually everyone had a place to sleep.

The parents of the six children seemed happy with the sleeping arrangement after checking out the rooms then went to their other assigned quarters. The Henderson family staying in one of the Bridges downstairs bedrooms had a young daughter upstairs that was included as one of the six McCune Settlement children, plus a seventeen year-old daughter in their own room.

The next morning the townspeople helped the new people fell trees and transport logs to their building sites. They would construct seven houses, six for the new families and one for the four unmarried women of the settlement. Sandra Henderson, one of the single women, had decided to continue to live with her parents.

To speed up the construction, the men concentrated their efforts on one house until the roof was raised, then moved on to the next one. After seven weeks, all houses were occupied and were completed except for some inside finishing touches. The unmarried women's house was the last to be finished. However, under Candice McCune's leadership and donations from the other families it was soon livable.

The town's two young bachelor men, Jack Bates and Greg Anderson, at twenty-two and nineteen years, were soon courting the three youngest of the unmarried women. Sandra was the youngest at only seventeen, followed by Diane Wilson at twenty, and Sheila Grant at twenty-three. The men decided to date the women much the same as

Lillie's courtship by George and Greg Anderson except in this case there was an extra woman.

After a month of courting it became clear that Diane Wilson had lost out. Jack Bates and Sandra Henderson, and Greg Anderson and Sheila Grant had paired off. Both couples courted for another two months before they decided they wished to get married and petitioned John, as the Mayor, to marry them in a joint ceremony.

John asked them to wait until a house for Jack Bates could be built as he was still living with his parents. They agreed and two weeks later John conducted a double ceremony that was attended by the entire town. Entertainment for the townspeople was scarce and any diversion from the norm was welcome. Storytelling by the adults to the children was almost as popular as TV was to children in the old world.

After the joint wedding a meal was prepared in their honor with the celebration lasting well into the night. Sometime during the celebration the newlyweds disappeared into their respective homes, not disturbed in the least by the noise of the party givers.

CHAPTER 20

The people from the North Settlement was assimilated into the social and working schedule of Harding within three months of their arrival. Candice McCune approached John with a request. "Mary Lou, Diane, and I want to start the bidding process for a husband."

John nodded his head, but then frowned in thought before speaking. "I understand your desire but I'm not sure there are three families ready to accept another wife."

Candice looked at him in disappointment before replying, "I know it's going to be tough. Just do the best you can."

The next day John called a town meeting and gave them notice of the single women's desire to become junior wives and requested that any family who would be willing to accept another wife into their family should leave their name with him within a week's time.

That evening the Bridges household discussed the possibilities of the three single women finding a suitable husband. John pointed out that there were now eighteen families for them to choose from.

Sarah shook her head at him sadly. "Honey you're not thinking clearly. Six of those men are over sixty, including Harding, who already has a second wife. Two were recently married and are not likely to want another wife in the family which leaves only ten possibilities. Four of these men are from the Northern Settlement who haven't yet become comfortable with the idea of a second wife which brings the possibilities down to six men."

Mary thoughtfully added, "Of these six, John and Kit Campbell already have second wives. Unless some men from their old settlement show an interest, it looks like slim pickings to me."

John looked worried and shook his head sadly. "Yes, and remember Lillie's attitude against another wife in her family. It really does look bad for the single women!"

By the end of the week only the Jacob Bell family had submitted their name for the bidding process. John conferred with Candice about the possibility of getting some more families from her old settlement interested in accepting another wife.

"I've already tried, and their wives wouldn't even consider such an idea yet." She then looked at him with speculation before asking. "How about the men who have already accepted second wives. Maybe some might be interested in taking another?"

He shook his head, but then agreed to ask each of them to reconsider. John then consulted with the William Harding and Kit Campbell households and relayed the appeal from the single women. After a lengthy consultation among themselves they each responded that they would add their names if John would do the same.

John reluctantly returned home to give his wives the news. They listened without comment to his efforts on behalf of the single women and then the response. His wives looked at each other silently for a moment, then at Sarah's nod they went to another room to discuss the proposal.

Mary hugged Sarah, then sadly shook her head. "I can't find it in my heart to deny these women a chance to be a wife and mother but you'll have to make this decision as first wife. Do you think John can love three women as well as the two of us, and even more important can we get along with another wife?"

Sarah, with tears in her eyes, nodded her head slowly.

"John's heart is big enough for six wives. That's not the problem; it's whether or not we can accept another woman sharing his affections?"

Mary hugged Sarah tightly while nodding her head in agreement. "We know the three bidding women and they all seem like nice enough people. Candice and Mary Lou were both previously married and are about our ages. Diane is much younger and would probably want a younger husband."

"So you think that if we get a bid it will be between those two," Sarah said as she considered the possibilities. "I think Candice already has a thing for John, so she will probably place a bid here."

They conferred some more and finally reached their decision. The women joined John in the common room where Sarah gave him their answer.

"We agreed that you could place our family name up for bidding," she said with a weak smile.

John looked at them with pride and hugged them both, but then asked, "You're sure about this?" When they nodded, he said, "Okay, but if we don't think we are a good fit we can always decline the marriage."

Candice brought the three bids to John after only two days of discussion among the women. Candice apprehensively watched John's face as she slowly told him how each woman voted. John had gotten a bid from both Candice and Mary Lou Graham, while Diane Wilson had bid for Kit Campbell.

John looked at Candice questioningly as he asked, "You and Mary Lou know that I can only pick one of you for the probationary period."

She nodded her head while looking him in the eyes. "We know, but we both think you're the best for us! We have a second choice picked out, but we needed to give you the first opportunity to accept us."

John slowly smiled at Candice's bravado and the honesty of her answer. "I'll bring your bids to the families and you'll soon know if they are accepted."

John met with his wives to consider the bids for their family. "Well, guess what? We got a bid from both Candice and Mary Lou. I prefer Candice based upon her personality and ability to get along with others. What do you two think?"

Sarah and Mary looked at each other a moment before Sarah turned to John and said with a slight grin, "We had already decided that it would probably be both Candice and Mary Lou bidding for our family and agreed to accept Candice. John, we don't want to consider any others for a wife candidate, at least not at this time."

He looked at them in surprise for a moment before shaking his head. "I never get over being surprised at how my wives can figure out what's going to happen before I even have a clue. Well, I hope this is going to work out because I don't want my wives unhappy with each other or at me."

Kit Campbell's family accepted Diane Wilson's bid and after the Bridges family accepted Candice, Mary Lou Graham bid for the Jacob Bell family which accepted. The ninety day probationary period would start for the three women the following Monday.

The three families each helped move the candidate wives into their new homes and get settled. When Candice was shown her room in the Bridges home, she entered it with surprise at how it had been decorated with not only her few things, but with objects taken from other family members' rooms to make it more comfortable. She turned to Sarah and Mary with tears of happiness in her eyes and started to thank them when they suddenly embraced her as she cried in their arms.

The three talked about Candice's duties during the probationary period outlining what each woman's responsibilities were. She was told that as first wife, Sarah was to have final say in any disputes and that any attempt to get her way through John would result in her rejection from the family.

Candice shook her head at Sarah. "I'd never do anything behind your backs. If I had a problem, we would get it resolved among ourselves. However, I've never been in a situation that I couldn't get resolved to everyone's satisfaction."

Sarah smiled at Candice but then became serious. "We're breaking new ground here, so bear with us as we try to establish a personal relationship with each other that isn't strained by any jealousy between wives over who gets more of John's attention."

Candice shyly asked, "How do you split your nights with John?"

Sarah hesitated a moment considering before answering.

"We have been sharing his bed every other week but every third week is going to be too long for us to wait our turn. I'm thinking of changing it to three nights' each so we each can get back to him in seven days." She then pouted her lips with some anxiety. "So far he's been able to take care of our needs but with three wives...I don't know."

Mary smiled dreamingly. "He's a great lover, but you should be aware that we've had nothing but twins from him. We need lots of help taking care of all the children."

"I love kids but my George and I never had any before he was killed. I would love to have my own children."

Sarah hugged her and whispered in her ear. "Don't be too concerned. We like you and John seems taken with you. If we work this right I'm sure everything will turn out fine."

John's first four-year term as Mayor came to a close and he was re-elected without anyone running in opposition. The town council members had changed once during his first term, but the original members were also re-elected along with John. He was happy to deal with a familiar group of individuals.

The probationary period soon passed for the single women and both they and their families agreed that the marriages should proceed. This would be the third wife for both the Campbell and Bridges family, but the adjustment period seemed to go easier for them than their second wives'. Perhaps having two wives already in place to fix problems they had previously encountered helped.

John usually did the marriages as the Mayor of Harding, but since he was one of those being married he asked William Harding to perform the ceremony. The entire town attended the triple marriage ceremony which was held at dusk so that all the townspeople could attend.

The brides wore fresh flower garlands on their heads and carried the traditional bouquet which was thrown to the young women of the town after the ceremony. The brides' deerskin dresses had been individually accessorized and they looked quite beautiful considering the lack of materials they had to work with.

After the ceremony the townspeople celebrated with the traditional feast which lasted well into the night; however, the new married couples soon slipped away to their respective prepared honeymoon site.

John and Candice had come to love each other during their ninety-day period of living together. They each learned much about each other during this period; however their building passion had remained untapped until now. He selected a cool grassy site next to a deep swimming hole on the *Mick* about a half-mile from Harding as their wedding night romantic escape. His other wives had prepared it for them so when they arrived they found their bedding set and ready for use.

John held Candice close as he gave her their first passionate kiss. The kiss soon turned into a frantic flurry of activity as they each tried to pull the other's clothing off. Candice was the more aggressive as she finished removing John's clothing first and then helped him finish removing her last garment.

They stood for a moment just looking at each other with passion filled eyes. John slowly caressed her high ebony breasts when suddenly she jumped into his arms wrapping her long legs around his body as they fell to the ground in a passionate embrace. Their pent-up passions exploded as they made urgent physical love until they both found their release.

They made love twice more that night before they cooled off in the nearby stream. Later, they lay together holding hands until he pulled her to him and kissed her first on the mouth then her neck as he worked his way down her body, lingering for a moment at her breasts then down past her navel until his lips finally met the center of her sexual passion. After a few minutes of stimulation Candice arched her back, moaning his name as she reached yet another orgasm.

She pulled him up into her arms, whispering, "Uncle, I've had all I can stand!"

He hugged her tightly, kissing her earlobe, then both fell asleep in each other's arms where they spent the remainder of the night. They returned to Harding late the next morning walking close together holding hands. When they entered the Bridges house they were greeted by his other smiling wives who took their bedding from John and had the two newlyweds sit down at the table while they prepared them a meal.

Sarah observed they both appeared happy but exhausted from their night of lovemaking. Candice caught her eye, then soundlessly formed the word "Wow" with her mouth while pointing at John whose attention was on his children.

The senior wives had agreed to give Candice two weeks with John before they started the sharing schedule. Sarah didn't want John to become too attached to Candice before his old wives had a chance to reestablish themselves.

The next day Sarah noticed that Candice seemed unusually tired and didn't get up early for her scheduled chores as usual. She seemed to limp around the house slowly as if in pain. Finally, after almost a week into Candice's marriage, Sarah asked her if she had a problem.

Candice grimaced as she slowly lowered herself into a chair. "Sarah, is John always this aggressive in his lovemaking? We must have made love five times on our wedding night and morning and at least two times every night this week. I'm so sore that I have trouble walking. My first husband was lucky to perform twice a week."

Sarah put her arm around her shoulders and smiled while biting her lower lip to keep from laughing. "Yes, we're very lucky to have such a great lover and husband." She considered Candice's condition as she eagerly volunteered, "If you want we can start the sharing schedule early. That is, if you need some rest?"

"I never thought I'd ever say I've had too much loving but I do need a break from John."

"Okay, I'll take my three nights beginning tonight and your turn will come up again in seven nights. I've really missed my husband's loving but come to think of it, I believe that his sexual appetite has increased since he's taken more wives. I just thought it was because we were familiar with each other's sexual desires." Sarah thought to herself, *I'll have to check with Kit Campbell's senior wife, Rachel, if she'd noted a similar change in her husband's libido. I hope because of our demands John doesn't have an early sexual burnout.*

The household soon settled into its new pattern with each wife sharing John's bed without any further problems. Candice's love for children helped in the care of the family's six children. They returned her obvious love for them and soon were treating her as another mother in the family. The children never lacked for supervision and love from all the available women in the household.

Jenny was still performing her duties as a nurse but she had plenty of time to help with her sister and brothers. Sadie, who was six, and the only other girl child in the family, didn't have any problems with her brothers. She seemed to have a certain power over them as they joined together to protect her from any harm. She in turn showed her affection for them by showering them with love and favors.

Jenny was Sadie's idol and offered to help her in her household duties as she followed her around the house. She returned the child's affection and happily shared some of the easier chores with her. Whenever her brothers found her struggling with a bucket of water or other heavy task, they would immediately help her finish the job. At first Sadie was annoyed that they finished a task she was doing for Jenny but then she realized this left her more time to be with Jenny.

Jenny and Randy's romance was still active; however, she had convinced him that they were still too young for marriage. To placate him and in an attempt to keep the other young women from trying to steal Randy from her, she agreed to set a tentative marriage date in ten months, the eighth year anniversary of their arrival in Harding.

The years had brought great changes to these young people both physically and mentally. Randy had grown into a tall muscular young man and according to Sarah strongly resembled his natural father. His hunting prowess was unequaled in the town and he had designed several better defensive weapons for the townspeople.

Jenny's body had changed from a tall skinny girl into a voluptuous young woman who caused admiring stares from all the adult men much to the dismay of a jealous Randy. However, it was her nursing abilities that earned her the town's respect and standing.

Sarah was at first concerned about her son's and Jenny's romance but soon realized that Jenny's was the dominate personality and would guide the relationship around any of Randy's sexual advances. Her smile was enough to get him to do anything she wished.

CHAPTER 21

John's thoughts recently had returned to *The Messenger* and its purpose on this world. Even more important to him was how and why it chose to help humans from another time and place. They still weren't sure if there was a purpose in their being here in this time and location.

None of his discussions with William Harding or Sarah had resulted in a clear understanding of their present situation. It was quite clear that *The Messenger* had guided their journey to this location and their rescue of the other settlement. There was even some evidence that it was responsible for the deaths of a Mutant hunting party found near one of their campsites.

Whether or not the entity was directly responsible for their departure from their time had not yet been proven, although was strongly suspected. The very fact that they all had come from approximately the same time period pointed to an outside source being responsible. He had begun to suspect that *The Messenger* was an intelligent entity created by whatever apocalyptic disaster happened in their now far past.

His daughter Sadie interrupted his musings when she asked to sit in his lap. She looked into his eyes with a concerned expression as she asked, "What's wrong Daddy?"

He ruffled her hair as he considered how to answer her question. "Well Sugar, I was just thinking about how we all got here and what it all means."

She considered his answer for a moment and then smiled as she replied, "Daddy, that's easy. *The Messenger* wanted us here because it wanted us to start over again to have a new beginning."

She then hugged his neck, kissed his cheek, and ran outside the house to play with her brothers. John slowly smiled as he considered her words and thought, well, it could be as simple as that. We were the beginning of a new mankind, a reclamation of Earth.

He decided to check with his wives and see if they wanted to go on a picnic with him without the kids as a distraction. He walked up behind Sarah and put his arms around her as he kissed her neck. She leaned back against him and sighed as she smiled.

He softly spoke into her ear. "How about you and your sister wives come with me on a picnic. Are you ready for a vacation away from the kids?"

Her face brightened as she quickly considered who was available to baby-sit their children, before turning around and hugging him. "That's a great idea. We need to get away from the house and kids for a short break."

John and his wives only walked a short distance east along the *Mick* to their favorite swimming hole which had a nice grassy area next to the stream and was shaded by a tall tree. They were between the two sentries so they felt safe here during the day. However, they still carried their weapons with them and had brought along Rocky.

The women busied themselves setting up the ground cover and food while John walked to the stream's edge and looked at the cool inviting water. On an impulse he quickly removed his clothing and jumped into the water. His wives looked up at the sound of his loud splash and then with playful giggles quickly stripped and followed him into the water.

His wives dunked his head under the water, which he reciprocated when he could catch up to one of them. They played together for about a half hour when they decided to help wash each other. This was the first time they had all been together without the children and were really enjoying themselves.

After everyone was squeaky clean, they lay together on the picnic cover. John smiled as he looked up at the sky and thought, *we have got to do this more often.*

Sarah leaned over him and looked into his eyes. "Honey, let's do this again sometime soon."

They were interrupted by the eerie sound of the horn sounding the alert. There was no time to dress as they reached for their weapons to meet the nearby threat. They had just got set with his wives looking at him for instructions on whether to flee toward town or prepare to attack when the sentry was seen running toward them.

Jack Bates stopped when he reached them and reported that six

Mutants were following close behind him. John had them spread out to meet the threat with the instruction to wait until he gave the word to attack.

The Mutants suddenly came into view about thirty yards from the defenders. They came to a stop when they saw the five men and women awaiting them. All but Sarah had bows, who continued to use the sling. The Mutants wolfishly smiled at the women defenders then suddenly attacked giving a wild yell as they ran forward.

John gave the order to fire as soon as they moved toward them which also was Rockys' signal to attack. The four bows twanged almost as one as their arrows went true into four of the enemy. Less than a second later a stone from Sarah's sling caught another in the head while Rocky took out the last enemy by ripping out his throat.

Bates turned to John for instructions when he first became aware that they were all naked. His face turned red but he kept his eyes on John's face as he pulled his knife and asked, "Should I make sure they're all dead?"

John started to nod his head in agreement, but instead said, "Sarah, why don't y'all gather our clothing before the townspeople show up." He then turned to Bates. "I'll back you up in case you need help."

Sarah brought his and her clothing which they hurriedly donned. John and his wives had just finished dressing when the first townspeople came running into the clearing.

Harding was puffing a little but smiled when he realized only the Mutants were hurt. Randy was also in the group as he knew his family was out here. Harding asked John, "What happened here?"

John looked at his wives and slowly shook his head in disappointment. "We couldn't even have a picnic without having Mutants spoil it."

Bates excitedly told the others about how John, his wives, and he had stopped the approaching enemy in their tracks. He laughed then added; "The Mutants thought they had an easy kill when they saw that three of the five defenders were women."

The townspeople smiled at the thought knowing how deadly the townswomen were with their weapons.

John took charge and had six men and three guard dogs scout back east for five miles to make sure there were no other Mutants in the area. The other townspeople returned to Harding excitedly talking about the recent attack.

John and his wives returned to their picnic area where they waited until the sounds of the townspeople had faded before he drew them into a group hug. His eyes were shinning with unshed tears as he said, "I thank

God that no one was harmed in this attack."

His wives gave him confident smiles as Sarah kissed him and said, "Honey, we had complete confidence in your ability to get us through that attack and anything else we might find."

He gave them a tentative grin as he responded. "Your confidence is what got us through that attack." He hugged Sarah and then complimented her. "Babe, I didn't realize that you were that good with the sling!"

"Well, don't tell anyone else, but I was aiming at the man the dog killed. I'm going to have to do more practicing with the sling before it gets me into trouble."

Mary and Candice grinned while John just looked up at the sky thanking God for small favors. He then gave them another group hug and asked if they wanted to finish their picnic which received an enthusiastic "Yes" before they pushed him down on the ground cover. They then uncovered the food and took turns playfully hand feeding their husband while nibbling at the food themselves.

When they returned to Harding the people they met gave them congratulations for a job well done along with amused smiles.

After the second smile and almost laugh from a townsman, John looked at his wives and sighed. "Bates must have told everyone in town how we fought that battle naked!"

The Bridges women looked at each other and then started laughing. He snorted in surprise and asked, "What's so funny?"

Candice snickered. "It was the look on Jack Bates' face when he finally realized we didn't have any clothes on. It was priceless as he tried to act as if it was natural to do battle in the all-together."

Sarah's smile turned to a grimace as she thought of something. "Oh my... I bet our children are going to tease us when we get home!"

As they approached their house, they could hear one of their children hollering that they were home, and then they all came running out to meet their parents. They were soon surrounded by their children who welcomed them back and then started to demand that John tell them all about the battle.

John held up his hands in surrender and told them to follow him into the cool shade and he would relate how their mothers saved the town of Harding. The children looked at their mothers in awe as they followed him into the shade.

John had their mothers sit with him before he began his story. While they were getting settled, other children and some adults of the town came running when they saw John was going to tell his story about the battle.

John waited until everyone was settled and then related the *Battle on the Mick*. When he got to the part of them rushing into the battle naked, there was much good-natured laughing from his audience and smiles of embarrassment from his wives. He then told of the Mutants' overconfidence when they saw that most of the defenders were women and how each of their mothers had killed one of the enemies. He then concluded that since they had killed the majority of the attacking force, then they were responsible for saving the town of Harding.

There was silence for a moment from the audience, but then they all cheered for the women heroes of Harding. The Bridges women looked at him in shock at first then embarrassment as everyone proclaimed them as heroes.

Sarah poked him in the ribs as she whispered, "Honey, we'll get you for that."

He laughed at his wives' shocked expressions. "You were worried about being kidded that you fought the battle naked. Now that part of the story is what made you all heroes."

Mary frowned. "I don't know this is any better. Now we have to live up to our reputations. I bet everyone will now want us to strip down before a fight."

"Maybe, but not because it would confound the enemy," he said jokingly.

That comment caused his wives to jump on him and pummel him in a mock attack while the townspeople cheered them on. His wives eventually let John up after he apologized to them and he was properly chastised. The children then started asking him for a retelling of his story while his wives returned to the house to look after their babies. Soon Randy and Jenny, who had been babysitting, joined the audience to hear the story retold.

That afternoon John consulted with Harding about the possibility that the Mutants had followed them south from the other settlement. They finally agreed they couldn't wait for another attack but should send out a scouting party to see where this last hunting party came from.

That night a special council meeting was held with all the townspeople in attendance. John put before the council his concerns about the Mutants and requested a scouting party be sent out in search of their camp. The Council voted in favor of John's proposal and left it up to him to make arrangements for the expedition. The next morning Kit Campbell led a party of six young townspeople and four guard dogs out of Harding.

John had told the townspeople at the Council Meeting they should keep their weapons close by in case of an attack and not to rely entirely on their early warning system. The citizens of Harding seemed to think this was good advice as many were carrying weapons as they watched Campbell and his scouts leave.

Sarah decided to practice with the bow as it seemed to be more accurate, especially when a screaming enemy was charging at you. John gave her a forty-pound pull longbow that he had made especially for women. She looked at the bow doubtfully because it was as tall as she was. He pointed to a nearby tree where he had marked a man-sized head and chest for better targeting purposes.

He grinned at her as she gingerly tried the bow's pull tension. Sarah nodded to herself as she accepted that she could handle the tension and then with a determined look she notched an arrow into place and aimed at the target tree twenty yards away. Remembering her past instructions, she allowed for distance and slowly relaxed her fingers on the string.

The arrow hit slightly high of her aim in the chest area but would still have been a killing hit in the neck. Sarah smiled slightly as she notched another arrow then made a slight sighting adjustment before shooting again at the target, this time hitting dead center in the chest area.

John chuckled as he gave Sarah a hug. "That's much better and either one of those shots would have downed your man."

"These new longbows are great!" She said as she shook the bow and then excitedly asked, "Can I keep this bow?"

When he nodded she quickly notched another arrow to continue her practice session.

The scouting party returned late the next afternoon just before dusk. Campbell hurriedly reported his findings to John.

When he arrived at John's house his expression was glum as he reported. "There is a large encampment of at least twenty men and forty women and children about fifteen miles east of Harding on the *Mick*. They hadn't been there long or we would have seen a hunting party before yesterday. They seemed to be working themselves into a frenzy over something, probably the missing hunting party. My guess is that they're going to send a large party our way the first thing in the morning."

John nodded his head in agreement then placed his hand on Campbell's shoulders. "Well done, but now we have to get the town ready for an attack."

John called for another town Council Meeting immediately. It wasn't long before the entire population gathered at the town's center. He hurriedly related Campbell's findings and conclusions and suggested they take immediate defensive action. The Council agreed with his assessment and asked what he had in mind.

John hesitated a moment gathering his thoughts, then with a firm solution in mind, he said. "There's a long draw that they need to pass though about five miles east of here. Kit, do you think this would be a good place to ambush them?"

Kit thought a moment then with a flush of excitement answered, "You bet! That would be a perfect place to hit them from all sides!"

John smiled as he confidently said, "Okay, that's the plan. We send out a sentry tonight in case they move before morning, while we get our weapons together and make final plans. We leave three hours before dawn so we can get into position."

The townspeople were in position at the ambush site an hour before dawn. The only people left in Harding were mothers with small children under twelve years of age and people too weak to make the trip. That left them with 38 men and women to spring the trap.

The draw in which they hoped to spring the ambush was a little less than 100 yards long with twenty-foot sides rising above the floor of the draw. The plan was to place townspeople on each side and when the horn was sounded, they would attack. When the archers began to fire from the sides, other townspeople would attack from each end trapping the attacking force within the draw.

CHAPTER 22

Dawn came and there was no sign of the enemy. John checked with Kit and asked, "Where are they?"

"Well, if they didn't leave their camp until dawn it would take them almost two hours to get here. So, I still think they're coming."

John then passed the word to the waiting townspeople along both sides of the draw. John fidgeted as the waiting started to take its toll. It had been over an hour since dawn and still no sign of the enemy. Suddenly John could see movement, then the attacking force appeared jogging toward him, while his small party remained hidden at the east end of the draw. He waited until the Mutants all entered the draw before he gave the signal for the horn to be blown.

The eerie sound of the horn stopped the attacking force of twenty-five in their tracks, but when the townspeople rose into position on either side of them the Mutants turned to meet this new threat. The way the enemy was strung out along the path made them easy targets for the townspeople. There were six archers along each side of this section of the draw and their first volley of arrows took out ten of the enemy.

The enemy flinched from this demonstration of firepower but instead of running away they tried to climb the sides of the draw. They hadn't gotten more than eight feet up the sides before the second volley hit them. Eight more of the enemy fell and with only seven of their attacking force left, they tried to escape down both ends of the draw.

John's force could see four of the enemy heading toward them, but waited until they were within twenty yards before his six archers let loose their volley, killing them all.

The remaining three Mutants didn't make it to the other end of the draw. They died as they ran the gauntlet of townspeople arrows. None of the townspeople had been injured in the attack.

John had his force make sure of the enemy dead and saw to their disposal. He then sent ten of his force back to Harding to strengthen its defense while the remainder started towards the enemy camp. He thought he would try the horn scare again, hopefully driving the old men, women, and children out of the area.

When they reached the enemy encampment they spread out as before and started blowing their horns. The Mutants immediately gathered their belongings and started moving quickly away from the sound of the horns. As before, the townspeople set a slow pace so that the weak could stay up with the group leaving.

After pushing them eastward about twelve miles he stopped his force and consulted with Kit. "Kit, I think the enemy should be pushed east until at least the main trail, but keep it at a slow pace and let them rest at night."

Kit nodded his head in agreement before replying, "It's going to take at least another two days before we get to the main trail, but I don't need this many people to do the job."

John thought a moment before asking, "Do you think fourteen people and six dogs would be enough protection if you meet another group of the enemy?"

Kit gave him a wolfish grin and nodded his head. John then told him to send a runner to Harding if he needed help, otherwise he would expect him back in town in about five days.

John then led his part of the force back toward Harding. They stopped at the enemy camp long enough to set it on fire before continuing west. They arrived in Harding early the following day where the townspeople all came to meet them as they walked into town. Their cheering welcome quickly dissipated the defending forces fatigue as their families greeted them. Sarah, Mary and his children ran to meet John, Candice, Randy and Jenny who were at the head of the column.

Their clan, who were shouting, "welcome home", quickly surrounded the four Bridges. John hugged his two wives, who had tears of happiness in their eyes that all members of their family had returned safely. He then gathered the three family members who had been with him into a group hug as he complimented them on a job well done.

Candice had been with him when they met the four Mutants who were trying to escape, and had been responsible for one of the kills. Randy had been in charge of the party at the other end of the draw and wasn't involved in any of the fighting. Jenny had stayed behind John's force until after the fighting was over but had hurried to see if Randy was alright before checking to see if anyone else had been hurt. Luckily her services were not needed by anyone.

After the homecoming celebration was over the family returned home. Later that evening John asked the family if they wanted to go bathe in the *Mick*. He felt especially grimy and was sure that the other family members in his force felt the same.

To his surprise his entire family went with him to their favorite bathing spot. They all stripped and got into the water together, including Jenny who had long since lost her modesty around family members. The cool water was refreshing to John and the others as he relaxed sitting on the bottom with his back against the bank.

His wives came over and pulled him into deeper water so they could wash his body. He was enjoying their efforts as they rubbed the soreness and dirt from his body. Finally, he offered to return the favor to Sarah while Mary and Candice worked on each other.

Jenny and Randy were washing the children who were enjoying playing in the water. Finally done with them, Jenny asked Randy to scrub her back and she would return the favor.

Jenny arched her back in joy as his finger massage drew the tension from her body. Randy finished up by rubbing the dirt from her back down to her buttocks where he stopped. Randy was so tall that she had him walk to the bank, where she had him sit in the shallow water with his back to her while she stood so that she would have enough leverage to return the favor of the massage. He was surprised at the strength of her fingers as she dug into his muscles pulling the tension from his body. She then had him move back into the stream so she could finish washing his back.

When she was done, she turned him around and pulled his face down to hers and gave him a passionate kiss. She then led a dazed Randy over to John and Sarah.

While still holding his hand, Jenny said, "Randy and I want to get married."

John and Sarah both slowly smiled as Sarah replied, "So you think you're both now ready for marriage?"

Jenny nodded her head. "Yes, we know we're young, but we've both grown emotionally and physically in the past year and I feel that we're ready."

John looked at Randy questionably, who without hesitation said, "I've been ready for some time and have just been waiting until Jenny said the word."

"You've got a steady head on your shoulders and Sarah and I have observed how well you have managed your relationship with Randy. Not many young women could have held up to the temptation of hot young love," John confided as he hugged Jenny.

Jenny blushed and then spoke softly, "Sometimes it was hard, but I kept myself under a tight rein when we started to get too hot. But, I think what really made up my mind was this last attack by the Mutants. I realized that we don't know how long we have in this life and I want to enjoy it to the fullest while I can."

The wedding of Randy and Jenny was set for the following Saturday just six days away. Jenny's mothers had combined their efforts to ensure that everything would be ready on time.

Randy had gone to the workshop and with help from Jacob made rings for both Jenny and himself. When he showed the rings to John, he was so impressed that he immediately went to the workshop and designed a set of rings for his own wives and himself.

Randy's rings were of polished steel while John decided on something different. His ring was three tiered; two polished steel rings with a raised gold ring in the center. Sarah would receive a gold ring while Mary and Candice would each receive a polished steel ring.

He had told his wives he was getting them wedding rings and obtained their ring sizes so it was no surprise when he gathered them together for the presentation. He first showed them his three-tiered ring with the raised center of gold. The wives were fascinated that he could work gold into the metal and thought it was beautiful.

John then presented the gold ring to Sarah as the first and senior wife and passionately kissed her after placing it on her finger. Her eyes started to tear as she held her hand up to the light.

"It's just beautiful and for some reason I feel complete now."

Mary and Candice crowded around her admiring the ring until he asked Mary to accept her ring. He placed her polished steel ring on her finger and then gave her a fervent kiss. She then raised the ring in admiration for both Sarah and Candice to see. Candice then hurried to him to receive her ring. After the ring was placed on her finger she excitedly jumped into John's arms and gave him a heartfelt kiss.

The three wives held their ring fingers together admiring their beauty and workmanship. They then gratefully hugged him for his kindness and thoughtfulness and wanted to see his ring alongside theirs.

Sarah grinned at her sister wives. "The other families with multiple wives are really going to be envious."

Candice snickered. "Not only them, but most of the newly married couples don't have metal rings."

John chuckled as he looked at his ring. "It was Randy's idea to make the polished steel rings for Jenny and himself. I just took the idea a step forward."

Sarah smiled at John and gave him a hug. "Regardless, at their wedding day when the other wives see these rings, there is going to be a lot of work done at the workshop trying to duplicate these pretty things," She said as she held up her ring finger.

The Campbell force arrived back into town on Friday afternoon, the day before the scheduled big wedding. Campbell reported to John that the enemy was pushed to the main trail, where they continued south. They had seen no sign of any other enemy parties during their trip.

The much anticipated Saturday evening wedding finally came with all the townspeople present. John, as Mayor, presided as the Bride and Groom stood before him. The Bride was beautiful in her simple deerskin dress accented by fur trim at the neck and hem. She wore flowers weaved into her hair and carried a bouquet of mixed wildflowers. The Groom looked handsome and impressive in his best deerskin pants and decorated vest made by his bride-to-be. He had found a small-mutated white iris that looked somewhat like an orchid that he pinned to the breast of his vest. It matched those weaved into his bride's hair.

As they stood before John waiting for his words to finalize their marriage, he thought back to the time he had first met the bride and groom and the adventures they had together on their long journey to Harding and the experiences that followed.

With unshed tears in his eyes he began the wedding ceremony. After both parties said their vows and rings were exchanged, John pronounced them man and wife. There was a great cheer from the crowd as both the bride and groom were well liked and respected. The newlyweds headed a greeting line before the wedding feast. The newly married women of the town were anxious to see the rings that were exchanged as they each asked Jenny to hold it up for them to see. Following the Bride and Groom in the reception line, stood all members of the large Bridges clan.

The envious townswomen really slowed the receiving line down, especially when they got to see John's and his wives' rings. At the end of the line the townswomen could be seen talking to their husbands and pointing at their bare fingers.

The Bridges women had prepared the town's first wedding cake from flour made from the first wheat crop. They hadn't yet been able to make icing but instead decorated it with edible fresh flowers. When the townspeople caught sight of the cake they all wanted a piece so a long line started to form.

The Bride and Groom sliced the first piece and found a place to sit down. The Bridges wives then started serving the cake but soon ran out which caused groans of disappointment from those still in the waiting line; but that changed to cheers when they brought another cake out to be cut. Eventually everyone had a piece of wedding cake and then the real feast began.

There were three deer being roasted over an open fire and dishes of fresh vegetables and bread to choose from. This was the first white bread the town had seen as well. Before, all they had was cornbread and the townspeople were really enjoying themselves with this addition.

Another surprise they hadn't expected was a solo performance by Mary Bridges. She started singing and her beautiful voice stopped all conversation as they all tried to get closer to hear her performance. She sang three popular songs from their past and when she stopped for a drink of water; the townspeople began asking her to sing more of their favorites. They managed to persuade her into singing several more songs and joined in with a resounding applause when she finished her performance.

Jenny and Randy both gave Mary a hug of thanks for making their wedding one that the townspeople wouldn't soon forget. The newlyweds soon left the festivities while the townspeople continued their celebration.

The newlyweds took their parents lead in selecting a spot on the *Mick* east of Harding. Both were still virgins and as they reached the spot prepared by their parents they stood over their bedding just looking at each other trembling with excitement and anticipation. Randy tenderly pulled his wife to him in a passionate embrace while smelling the flowers in her hair.

He then placed his finger under her chin raising her head slightly so that he could look into her eyes. "Jenny, I didn't think this day would ever come. I've loved you so much that sometimes it hurt just looking at you."

She smiled at him with tears of happiness in her eyes as she whispered, "I think I've wanted you for my husband since the first time I saw you when we were just children. I've also come to love you so deeply that it's been a real challenge not to give in to my emotions."

He then kissed her, at first a chaste tender touch on her lips that soon became a fiery passionate kiss for them both. When they finally broke apart they each had to gasp for breath then each frantically started removing their clothing. When they were both nude they just stood and admired each other's bodies that were bathed in soft moonlight.

Jenny moved closer to Randy and moved her hands tenderly over his chest muscles and down his sides until she came to his manhood which she tenderly held as it came urgently alive. Randy pulled her into another passionate kiss until they both dropped onto their bedding where they made love for the first of several times that night.

During that night they learned many things about each other's bodies including what each most enjoyed in their lovemaking and just how deep their passion for each other was. After their third bout of lovemaking they lay together resting in the afterglow of passion fulfilled. She had her head resting on his chest, her fingers moving tenderly through his chest hairs feeling as content and at peace than at any other time in her memory.

When they regained enough energy to move again, Randy pulled Jenny up from their bedding and into the cool water. The shock of the water brought them both alert again as they held each other. They just stood together in the water for a few minutes enjoying their closeness. He then playfully fell backwards into the water taking her with him as she screamed as the water covered them both.

They played in the water for some time until they realized how tired they were. Randy helped Jenny out of the water and back onto the bedding where they lay together in each other's arms until they fell into a peaceful sleep.

CHAPTER 23

The next morning they returned to the Bridges home where the newlyweds had decided to continue to stay. When they entered the household everyone greeted them and wished them well, especially the children who really didn't understand the change in their status yet.

Sadie, who was now seven, still considered Jenny her mentor and best friend, ran to her when they first arrived and tried to jump into her arms in greeting. Jenny, who was accustomed to this greeting was not prepared for the pain caused by the soreness in her muscles and they both fell to the floor.

Sadie was frightened as she lay on Jenny's chest looking into her eyes that were tight with pain. Sarah ran to help her children up from the floor, asking them if they were all right.

Jenny looked flustered for a moment but then carefully moved her arms and legs. "I didn't know I was so sore and weak until Sadie jumped on me but I'm okay now."

She smiled at Sadie as she playfully wagged her finger at her. "Just don't do that again for awhile until I get my strength back. Do you want to help me move Randy's stuff down to my room?"

Sadie nodded her head. "Oh yes. Does this mean that we have an extra room upstairs now?" She said as they slowly climbed the stairs.

Jenny chuckled. "Yes, do you have plans for it already?"

"It will make an extra play room until the first twins need it."

Randy had looked a little tired when they entered, but now was sitting at the table asking if there was anything to eat. When Jenny came

166

down with an armload of his things and heard him, she came over and playfully rapped her knuckles against the back of his head. "Hey! Get off your duff and help move your things and then I'll get us something to eat."

Sarah smiled as she watched Jenny take over her wifely duties of keeping her husband in line and tending to his needs. She then watched as Randy moved out of his upstairs room, thinking that it wouldn't be long before they would have need of that room as they had more births in the family and when the twins got older.

Sarah's prophecy was proven when only a month later Candice told her sister wives that she might be pregnant. Candice was excited as she brought the good news to Sarah and Mary. Her face glowed with happiness as she asked their advice about her pregnancy. Sarah asked her how did she know for sure she was pregnant.

"I suspected that I was when I missed my first period, but after missing the second one and this morning's nausea, I'm now pretty certain."

Sarah nodded her head agreeing with her assessment and then took her into her arms congratulating her as Candice wept with happiness. Candice had previously confided to her sister wives that she feared she might be barren because she hadn't conceived during her first marriage.

Sarah called Jenny into her room and told her that Candice was probably two or three months pregnant and would she check her over and give her any needed advice or suggestions.

Jenny suddenly smiled at Candice and hugged her tightly. "Great! I know how badly you've wanted children of your own and now you're going to get your wish. Why don't you relax and let me examine you."

After Jenny examined Candice she agreed that Candice was pregnant and then explained the symptoms she should watch out for. Sarah put her arm around Candice and ensured her that they all would take care of her.

John had been thinking about making rifles for defensive purposes. He had consulted with Jacob Bell about the formula for making gunpowder and was now considering where to find the raw materials. Bell said he had seen traces of sulfur and saltpeter at the old mining area and would go with him to see if they could find enough for their needs.

John and Jacob joined the next hunting party so they could act as protection while they searched for the needed minerals. The two carried a pick and several skin sacks in case they found what they needed. Upon arrival in the old mining valley the party stayed together until they were sure no Mutants were present. When they were certain they were alone in the valley, John had one of the hunters stay with them for protection while the others continued the hunt.

Jacob Bell soon found where there was an outcropping of sulfur that was fairly easy to recover. They soon filled three sacks and moved on in search of saltpeter. Bell stood for a few minutes looking at the rock outcroppings nearby and across the valley. He finally pointed at a particular area across the valley which later turned out to have the saltpeter they needed.

John then asked him about lead that he would need for shot. Bell and he searched further along the outcropping where eventually they found the needed lead. It was well that they didn't need very much as its weight was easily twice the same volume of the other items.

While they were waiting for the return of the hunters, Bell, who now had two wives, asked John about his living with three wives.

John slowly smiled as he recalled fond memories. "Well, Jacob it's like having two - only better. My wives get along great and share the workload, and with all my kids that's saying a lot. The sex is great too. It's almost as if they're trying to outdo each other. How about you, are your wives getting along?"

"I was concerned initially, with Mary Lou being ten years younger than Judy and me. However, she fit right in and like you said the sex is great. Judy and I had gotten into a rut sexually but when Mary Lou arrived that all changed. Now that Mary Lou is about due with our first child, Judy feels like a mother too. We never had any children of our own and this child is a godsend."

Later that afternoon the hunters returned to the rendezvous spot and helped carry the bags of ore back to Harding where they arrived tired and ready for some family comfort. John decided to stack the ore sacks inside the workshop before heading home but his wives met him there anxious to see that he was all right and his trip was successful. John greeted them warmly and gave them each a kiss and a hug. As they walked back toward their home they brought him up to date on what had happened while he had been gone.

Sarah smiled as she said, "Randy and Jenny had their first fight. I knew she had a temper but she really gave him what for when Randy wouldn't pick up after himself. I guess I did spoil him a little. In any case, she made a believer out of him and he promised to change his ways. When we came out to meet you they were back to being two lovebirds again."

John chuckled. "It sounds like Jenny runs a tight ship."

Sarah stuck a finger in his ribs, then while giving him a wicked grin said, "Let's go down to our swimming hole tonight after supper. Just the four of us and no kids; what do you say?"

He grinned as he saw the eager anticipation on his wives' faces. "That sounds good, but you'll have to give me a good rub down when we get there," he said as he moaned and faked stiffness in his back.

Candice pinched his behind as she giggled. "We'll all give you a rub down, you faker." Causing all of them to laugh.

Later that evening they finally reached their favorite spot on the *Mick* after much anticipation. They all stripped and went into the cool water, playing their customary water games with each other before just sitting together in the water and relaxing in each other's company.

Sarah finally pulled John up onto shore where she had him lie face down on some spread animal skins. She then proceeded to massage his neck and back muscles, digging in with her fingers until she felt the tightness leave. His groans turned to sighs as she worked the tightness out of his muscles.

She then patted his buttocks and said it was his turn to do her. He turned over and looked at Sarah as she sat on her knees next to him. She was still a beautiful woman and had maintained her tight trim figure even though she had given birth to five children. He pulled her down on top of him and passionately kissed her.

His other two wives came up and broke them apart, giggling as Mary complained, "We can't let you start that or we'll have an orgy in nothing flat. Come on, get up and give Sarah her massage while I do Candice and then you can finish up by giving me one. I've been dreaming of getting a massage from you since Sarah suggested this little outing."

John and Sarah each groaned their disappointment as they followed her instructions. Both Sarah and Candice echoed each other's moans and sighs as they received their massages. Finally Mary had the others make room for her as she lay down for her eagerly awaited turn. The other wives smiled as they watched the expression of bliss on Mary's face as John worked the knots out of her muscles with his skillful fingers.

The next day John started mixing a small batch of gunpowder to see if he had the formula correct. He ground up some charcoal and combined the sulfur and saltpeter in the proper portions. Then he placed the mixture into a sack and cautiously shook it up until it was thoroughly mixed together.

John placed a small portion of the gunpowder in a small gourd and took it outside the workshop and placed it on the ground. He used a long lighted stick to ignite the powder, causing the gourd to blow apart with a satisfying loud explosion.

John was smiling to himself as he wiped bits of the gourd from himself when the townspeople came running to see what had happened.

He explained that he was all right and that his experiment in making gunpowder was obviously successful.

His next problem was learning how to make the gun barrel and deciding how big to make the bore. After some discussions with Randy and George it was finally decided to make an iron cast in two pieces so that it could be removed easily after the steel was poured.

They thought long and hard about how to make a hole for the flash powder that would ignite the gunpowder in the barrel. John decided to use a wood sliver that would form a hole before it was burned up by the hot steel.

They eventually assembled the parts of the cast and then poured the hot steel into the casting. They then dunked the whole casting into a water tank for about five minutes before removing the casting from the water, breaking it apart and reinserting the barrel into the tank of water. They ended up with a barrel five feet long and after reaming out the flash powder hole and the barrel, they were ready for testing.

John decided for their first test that they place a light load of gunpowder and wadding into the gun barrel and firmly secure it on a workbench. He then primed the flash powder hole and was ready for the first test firing. He had everyone at the workshop take cover in case the barrel exploded; while he stood behind a makeshift wooden shield as he carefully edged a long burning stick toward the powder.

When the firebrand touched the gunpowder there was a flash and then an explosion as the weapon fired. The first test was a success so the next step was to make ball shot for the rifle. Randy constructed a small casting to make the ball shot and then poured the hot lead into the molds. They now had shot to experiment with to help them determine the right powder load.

John used the same powder load he had used previously before he rammed home the ball shot and wadding. After aiming the rifle barrel at a target sixty yards away, he secured the barrel for firing as before. John than rechecked the aim of barrel to make sure it hadn't moved when it was secured. He didn't have to warn the townspeople this time to take cover as most were observing his progress from a distance.

John again took precautions in firing the weapon and the townspeople were holding their ears as he placed the firebrand against the flash hole. It again fired without incident and Randy ran to the target marking where the shot hit. John thought he needed to use slightly more powder as the shot had hit about three inches low of his aim.

The next shot was on target so they now needed to figure out a self-measuring container for the gunpowder. Randy and George had been helping him with the casts and now put their efforts to designing the powder container while John designed a stock and firing assembly.

A week later they were ready to demonstrate to the townspeople their version of a flintlock rifle. The three men drew straws as to who would have the honor of the first demonstration shot. John smiled as he drew the short straw.

He then demonstrated the loading procedure to the townspeople using a deerskin pouch with a stopper that doubled as the correct measure for the gunpowder. He carefully poured the gunpowder down the barrel, added the shot and wadding, and tapped it home with a ramrod. Then after priming the flash hole, he aimed at the target.

George and Randy managed to add sights to the barrel which made aiming easier. John took a deep breath and thought, *I hope I don't burn off my eyebrows,* just before he squeezed the trigger. The rifle fired as before with a loud flash-bang sound and while he expected the rifle to kick as it fired, he didn't expect the mule kick he got as the butt of the rifle slammed into his shoulder. He rubbed his shoulder ruefully as the onlookers laughed. Randy marked the target where the shot had hit and everyone shouted their glee as it had hit within an inch of the center of the target.

Randy and George each took their turn and all did well but both complained about its kick. John then tried using a little less powder to dampen the powerful kick and got similar targeting results without as severe a kick as before. They now had a powerful new weapon they could use against the enemy.

While Randy and George worked on constructing more rifles of similar design, John started work on a shotgun to be used as a short-range weapon. The bore would be larger to hold a large number of small shot and hopefully would make its shot coverage at least five feet wide.

In a month of hard work the three armorer's finished four rifles and two shotguns. John thought they would need twice this number for an effective defense. When a rifle or shotgun was finished, volunteers were asked to learn its operation and practice firing the weapon until they were proficient in its use. There was no shortage of volunteers as every adult male in the town wanted to learn how to use one of these new guns.

CHAPTER 24

The scouting parties continued their sweep around Harding and they increasingly encountered larger hunting parties of Mutants. John's fears were finally realized when the last scouting party returned to town and reported they had met a large enemy hunting party of ten where two of its members had escaped. The town's scouting party of eight had suffered two minor wounds. Jack Peterson, the leader of the scouts, reported that if it hadn't been for their guard dogs it might have been much worse.

John called a council meeting to report the scouting parties' encounters. "I've been dreading the time when the enemy finally escapes to report who we are and the weapons we use. This has now happened and the encounter occurred about twelve miles east of Harding along the *Mick*. I suspect that there must be a large encampment of the Mutants nearby to support the large numbers of hunters we have been finding. All of the recent encounters had been from a general easterly direction, but this one has been the closest to Harding. I suggest we send out two scouting parties to try to find the enemy encampment, with instructions not to engage any stray hunting parties they might encounter but instead try to follow them back to their camp. Once a camp is spotted they should immediately return to Harding and report their findings."

The council called for a vote of the townspeople who wholeheartedly agreed with John's plan. After seeking Kit Campbell's advice on the size of the scouting parties, they agreed a small scouting party of only three or four men with two dogs would be easier to avoid detection by the enemy. That decided, the two scouting parties left early the following morning.

John and his two fellow weapon makers took stock of the firearms they had produced. They each had a rifle and a shotgun which they kept loaded and ready for action. In addition, another six rifles and three shotguns were in the hands of the townspeople. Besides the firearms, the townspeople maintained their proficiency with the longbow and other weapons. John was now confident they could handle almost any kind of attack by the enemy.

Three days later Kit Campbell's patrol returned about mid-afternoon looking exhausted. Kit reported to John while his men warily returned to their homes. John welcomed Kit into his home and had him sit at their table while Sarah provided him with fresh water to drink.

Kit took a drink and breathed a sigh of relief. "I decided that the best way to stay hidden and be able to follow any hunting party was to find a spot close to the *Mick* until one showed up. We were in position about sixteen miles east of Harding when we saw a large enemy party of twelve heading east with their game. We let them get a little ahead of us and then followed them back to their encampment which was only another five miles east along the river. I snuck in close to see how many people were there and counted forty men and another seventy women and children. There may have been more hunting parties out but I doubt it as it was almost dark."

John whistled softly. "That's the biggest encampment we've seen yet and this one is close to Harding!"

Kit nodded his head sadly. "I take it that Jack Peterson's scouting party hasn't returned yet?"

John shook his head. "I'll give him another two days. In the meantime I'll call a council meeting tonight to tell them of your findings but I'll recommend that we wait until Jack returns before we do anything."

After Kit left, Sarah sat down next to John and placed her arm around his shoulders. "Honey, are we going to have to push these Mutants out of the area too?"

He kissed her cheek softly and looked into her eyes. "We have to keep them away from us if we're going to survive. This size of an encampment presents real problems for us. I just hope Jack doesn't bring back more bad news."

The next afternoon Jack Peterson's scouting party arrived in town. Jack and his party looked even more exhausted than Kit's party had looked. John met him at the workshop as the scouting party walked into town. Kit Campbell hurried over when he saw them arriving and waited with John while Jack and his party refreshed themselves with cool water.

Jack gave them a wan smile and then gave his report. "I decided to head northeast of where the last attack had occurred until we found a game path that appeared to have more than normal traffic. We waited under cover for almost a day before a large hunting party appeared heading east with their kill. We then followed them until they returned to their encampment. I would guess that it's at least thirty to thirty-five miles northeast of Harding and contained thirty men and about fifty women and children."

John shook his head sadly before asking, "Did their huts look like a permanent settlement or temporary?"

"I think they've been there awhile. They're outside our sweep and we wouldn't have picked up on them unless we encountered one of their hunting parties."

John looked questioningly at Kit who shook his head.

"The encampment I found looked recent with only temporary shelters in place."

John told Jack about the larger encampment Kit's party found and then asked them about their thoughts in how to get rid of both these camps. Later that night a town meeting was called to report on the scouts' encounters.

John reported to the council with all the townspeople present to hear the news first hand. "I'm bringing you grave news. The scouts have found two enemy encampments. Kit's camp of forty men and Jack's of thirty; however the larger encampment is the greater threat at this time because of its closer proximity to Harding and should be dealt with first. I suggest we time our arrival at the camp at nightfall for a dawn attack. We should be able to avoid its hunting parties by arriving late in the day and at dawn they all should still be in camp. If we try using the horns on all sides of the camp except east maybe they'll be confused enough to leave that way without a fight."

Jack Peterson laughed before shouting was heard from the crowd of townspeople. "That tactic worked for us before with good results!"

John chuckled as well but then spoke loudly so everyone could hear. "I have a bad feeling about this group so we'll be prepared to fight at the first indication they're not going to cooperate."

John then asked for the same people that were at the ambush battle except for those men now injured and women pregnant or with small children. His party of volunteers was almost the same size as before, 36 men and women, and ten guard dogs. Mary replaced Candice, who had been with him previously; and Randy, Jenny, and George rounded out the Bishop clan's contribution.

When Mary told John she was coming with him, he initially was against the idea. However, Sarah told him that she and Candice could handle their kids and she wanted one of his wives looking after him. With that kind of logic he knew he was beat. Besides, Mary was as good with a longbow as any townsman.

John decided to take the six shotguns with his party as backup. He thought the risk to Harding was slight but with the nine rifles and extra manpower he had left behind they should have adequate protection.

The next day was spent getting ready for their departure the following morning. It also gave the scouting parties time to rest before they set out again. Sarah cautioned Mary to look after their husband and to not let him take any unwarranted chances.

Sarah would give almost anything to be able to join her husband but she knew her duty was to keep the household safe for his return. Candice's pregnancy was going well but she couldn't have kept up the fast pace required to go with them. Her duty was to stay with Sarah and help safeguard the children.

The next morning the attack party left following the scouting team who had left before them. They caught up with the scouts at the site of the last encounter. It was early afternoon and since it was only about ten miles further to the enemy encampment, John decided to wait here for two hours before moving forward. He had the scouts move ahead and behind the main party about two hundred yards in case any enemy hunters approached their position.

At the appointed time he started the main party moving again towards the enemy encampment. At dusk, John at the head of the column was met by one of the scouts who reported the encampment was just 200 yards ahead. He went ahead with the scout to confer with Kit Campbell, the lead scout.

The encampment was indeed large and the townspeople were outnumbered almost three to one. However, the adult enemy males outnumbered their party by only about eighteen people. John hoped that their surprise attack and better weapons would give them the edge.

John's original plan to move against them from three sides still seemed viable so he left the scouts to observe the encampment while he and Kit returned to his forces to make the final plans. He had Jack Peterson lead twelve men and women with two shotguns to cover the north side while Kit Campbell would lead a similar contingent to cover the south side of the *Mick*. The remainder would stay with him with the attack to start at dawn when his horn sounded followed by the horns from the north and south.

John told the horn bearers to blow their horns until they get a response from the encampment. The townspeople were instructed not to attack unless it was obvious that the Mutants were not going to move out and the shotguns were not to be used unless the enemy rushed their positions. The townspeople wouldn't move into position until one hour before sunrise. John told those not on guard duty to try to get what rest they could before they attacked.

Mary and John cuddled together, neither able to sleep, but each taking comfort in the other's nearness. Randy and Jenny were lying nearby with each trying to sleep until Jenny finally moved into his arms seeking his comfort from her fears about the coming battle.

At the appointed time everyone who had managed to sleep was awakened and the various groups moved into their planned positions. The townspeople moved slowly trying their best to avoid any sound that might awaken the enemy encampment.

As the eastern sky started to glow with the approaching dawn, the townspeople became increasingly tense. Slowly the encampment came to life with the women leaving their shelters to start the morning campfires. No men had yet awakened; however, there was sufficient light now to see, so John gave the order to blow the first horn.

As the eerie sound of the horn began followed by the horns from the north and south, the women began screaming, causing the men to erupt from their shelters. They milled around the clearing confused by the eerie sounds from three sides. Finally, a large brute of a man who was apparently their leader started shouting orders to gather his men together for a fight.

John quickly ordered his best archer to kill the leader. The leader was just about to give his first order when arrows from three directions hit him. He stood for a moment with a surprised look on his face until finally dropping dead before his men. Apparently the leaders of the other two bracketing groups had also given the order to fire.

The Mutants started screaming with fear and began running toward their families apparently urging them to pick up their belongings so they could leave. Some just grabbed their women and children and started running east out of the camp.

John had the horns keep up their eerie sound as the enemy left heading east along the *Mick*. He had the north and south groups keep pace with them to make sure they stayed along the *Mick* while his group pushed them forward.

John and three others in his group stayed behind to search the camp for anything of value and then to set the shelters on fire. After they had set fire to the shelters John noticed something unusual in a bone pile. Looking closer he found human bones mixed in with animal bones. He felt slightly sick as he realized that this group of Mutants probably ate this person. This was additional proof that they were cannibals. Acting on impulse he grabbed an animal skin bag left behind by the enemy and put a skull and two leg bones in it before running to join the main party.

About two hours into the forced march, three family groups tried to leave the eastern course by heading north but when the lead male was killed they moved back into line hurrying along even faster. They moved the enemy along for two days, stopping their push only at nightfall. When they reached the main north/south trail, the enemy after a small hesitation turned south. John's force followed them for another ten miles before stopping and returning to the *Mick*.

John congratulated everyone for their fast thinking that prevented a full-scale battle. He then asked Jack Peterson where the next enemy settlement was located from here.

"I believe the other encampment would be northwest of our present location but I think we should follow the north trail for a few miles where we'll probably find a direct trail west to the enemy camp."

John nodded his head in agreement but had everyone take a short rest before they resumed their march.

John and the rest of the Bridges clan were sitting together eating some deer jerky they had brought with them when he remembered the bones he had picked up back at the Mutants encampment. He showed the others the bones and what he planned to do with them. Mary looked shocked at first but then her expression turned into a wicked grin as the others voiced their agreement.

As the main party marched north they were surprised and then amused as they spotted the Skull and Crossbones guarding the *Mick* trail west. John didn't know if this symbol carried the same meaning here but if it didn't, any trespassers would find out the hard way.

The group marched another five miles before encountering a side trail leading in a westerly direction. John patted Peterson on the back for his insight as they turned toward where they thought the next encampment would be.

It took them almost two days before the scouts returned to warn the main party that the enemy camp was only three miles ahead and since it was only late afternoon, they decided to wait another two hours before making their approach.

When they arrived near the encampment, it was almost dark with just enough remaining light so that the attacking force could disperse without making noise through the trees. John and his two scout leaders then approached the camp perimeter to better observe its activity. This camp was slightly smaller than the one they had just moved out but they still outnumbered the townspeople.

John motioned to his men and they retreated back toward the main group. He conferred with them and they all agreed that the last strategy worked so well they should try it again here. He had his scout leaders head the two flanking groups as before while his group would act as the pushers, assuming this encampment didn't decide to fight. His horns would again announce the beginning of the attack at dawn.

The townspeople received their instructions for the coming attack and they then tried to get some rest. The long march had dulled their natural apprehension before a battle and many immediately fell asleep. John worried about the next day's attack and tried to remember if he had forgotten something in case a fight developed.

He was worried, as all good commanders were, if his people were properly prepared if the plan should fall apart.

He was lying next to Mary, frustrated that he couldn't sleep because he couldn't keep these fears out of his mind. She pulled him close and slowly kissed him until his only thoughts were of her and his prior worries were forgotten.

At the appointed hour everyone was awakened and the three groups moved slowly into position. The morning was overcast and daylight was slow to appear. The women of the enemy encampment appeared first just as before and started making the morning cook fires. They looked up at the dark sky and hugged themselves as if feeling bad forebodings.

The day had finally gotten light enough so that the column could see properly so John gave the signal to blow his horn. As the first horn sounded its eerie blast, the other two echoed its eerie sounds on all sides except east. The women, as before, started screaming their fright as the horns began. The combined sounds of the horns and screams of the women brought out the men with spears raised, who then milled about in confusion looking around the clearing for any approaching threat.

One of the enemy saw movement in the trees to the camps north and grabbed two of his tribe, pointing where he thought the intruders were. They then started running toward that side screaming for the others to follow them. The three running men had taken no more than five steps before arrows felled them. The others who had just started to follow them suddenly stopped short at this unexpected weapon.

One of the townspeople started screaming a wolf's howl in cadence with the eerie horn sounds, the volume increasing as more townspeople joined in starting on the south side and moving around to the north. The Mutants were completely scared out of their wits by these developments and first one and then the others began to make preparations to leave.

They left heading east with the townspeople keeping pace. John stayed behind again with two others to burn the camp. He hunted for their bone pile where he found more human bones which he took with him.

They harried this bunch of Mutants much as they had the others, letting them rest at night and then at dawn pushing them further east. When they reached the north/south trail this bunch turned south as had the others. John stayed behind and planted another Skull and Crossbones at the west trail's entrance before catching up with the column.

When the Mutants reached the *Mick* trail and saw the warning Skull and Crossbones guarding it, they shied away from it and continued to hurry further south. After another ten miles John stopped the push and the column started their return to Harding.

When they returned to the river, John called a halt and sent out hunters for a celebration feast. They spent the night getting a needed rest after a hot meal of roasted deer. Three days later they walked back into Harding to a reunion with loved ones and a celebration of their safe homecoming.

CHAPTER 25

John was happy and relieved to find that the town of Harding had survived their long absence. His family was waiting to give him and the other members of the Bridges Clan a hero's welcome. Sarah and Candice both hugged him tightly with tears of happiness in their eyes as they kissed him in turn. They then hugged and kissed their sister wife, Mary. The other members of the Bridges Clan, Randy, Jenny, and George also received a big welcome. Then the children pushed their way through the crowd and gathered around their father as they competed for his attention.

As usual, Sadie got their father's attention first. He picked her up and gave her a kiss on the cheek then sat her down and gave each of his kids a hug and a kiss. As they walked toward home, Sarah held his hand tightly but then looking up at him she held her nose and told him he needed a bath.

She then added, "We're going to have a family swimming party later tonight."

After sitting down to have a refreshing cool drink of water and catching up on household and Harding news, he cleaned up before the big feast that evening. He then conferred with the town council who decided that he should give his report on the attacking forces activities at that evenings homecoming feast.

That evening when the townspeople had gathered, John stood before them and called for his two scout leaders to join him. "I want you all to be aware that these men's efforts contributed greatly to our success in driving out the Mutants."

John explained each of their contributions as he told the story of the attacking parties' success in running the enemy out of their area; best of all without any injuries to the townspeople and with little loss of life to the enemy.

"I also tried to put some fear into any Mutants who would try to approach Harding by placing a Skull and Crossbones at the two trails leading here from the east. The last group of Mutants certainly shied away when they first saw it."

There was some satisfied clapping from the townspeople upon hearing this news. Everyone hoped that maybe this warning notice would keep the enemy away from Harding. He then called for any questions from the townspeople about this or any future plans for the defense of Harding. After answering several questions, he said the celebration should begin.

Later that evening the Bridges family made the trip to their favorite swimming hole on the *Mick*. The family members who had been part of the attacking party were ready for a bath and were the first ones into the water followed soon after by the rest of the clan. The children were especially joyful in their water play but the adults soon joined into the horseplay.

After the usual massages that John and his wives received from each other, Sarah called an end to the party. The women than got the children out of the water and dressed before starting back home.

The next day John met with the town council to discuss strategy. He told them that for some reason the Mutants seemed to be pushing further south in great numbers. None of those driven out had elected to return north. They discussed various reasons for their movement south, but the one they feared most was a strong menace that the Mutants were fleeing from.

John suggested they keep a watch on the north/south trail as it crossed the *Mick* to determine the numbers traveling south and possibly who or what was driving them. He suggested the four-man and three-dog scout party rotate every week. After some debate they all agreed they needed some advance warning from this new threat.

They worked out a schedule the next day with Jack Peterson and Kit Campbell leading the initial two scout parties. As the men gained more experience, they would relieve the scout leaders with other qualified people. John was guessing they might have to keep this watch going for some time.

Two months later, the watch patrols had observed over 300 enemies traveling south. These numbers seemed to be increasing based upon the last scout report. Jack Peterson led the scouting party that had left two days ago to relieve the party already in place and John was anxiously awaiting their report.

Two days later, a scout from Peterson's party came running into Harding about mid-day. He immediately reported to John who was working on a new rifle at the workshop. Seeing the runner coming John had a sudden premonition of something disastrous.

The man looked exhausted so before he let him begin John had him sit down and drink some fresh water. While he was catching his breath John sent runners to fetch the other Council Members. They soon arrived and the scout had recovered sufficiently to tell his story.

His flushed face slowly turned white as he recounted what they had discovered when they arrived to relieve the other scouting party. "We found their four heads mounted on stakes next to our own Skull and Crossbones sign. There was initially no sign of the guard dogs, but after searching the area we found where two of them had been butchered. The third dog returned badly wounded and died soon after. Peterson sent me back with the warning while his party would remain to try to find out who had killed our scouts."

John and the Council Members were stunned as they listened to the scout's story. When he finished his report, John slammed his fist against the table he was standing next to, startling everyone. His face was a mask of fury as he started pacing back and forth. Finally, he turned to the council members with a cold smile on his face and proposed a plan of action.

They listened in silence as he talked, occasionally looking at each other and then back at him in fascination. When he finished he asked for their input. They looked at each other for a few moments but then all nodded their heads in agreement.

William Harding stood up and came over to shake his hand and then placed his arm around his shoulder. "Boy, I don't know if it will work but we're going to shoot our wad on this one. If it doesn't work there's going to be nothing left to stop them."

That evening, John as Mayor told the townspeople of the massacre of the scouts and then placed the Council's decision of their planned response before the people as well as the high price of failure. They asked for comments and any alternate suggestions before they called for a vote.

The townspeople had been shocked to hear of the deaths of four of their members. Greg Anderson, the scout leader, Jack Bates, George Tucker, and Ralph Bigalow, who all had now become the town's heroes. However, the townspeople realized that their future depended upon the success of John's plan of action and they responded as they had in the past with their affirmative vote.

Anderson and Bates were original members of Harding, while Tucker and Bigalow were from the north settlement whose members had again suffered a tragic loss. Everyone was thirsty for revenge and if his plan worked they would recover a terrible price against their killers.

John consulted with Kit Campbell on the details of his plan and its timing until they were both satisfied with the results. The next morning Kit left Harding leading ten men to support Peterson and his men. In the meantime, John prepared the townspeople for the coming battle.

All the able townspeople would join in this battle. The older children would be responsible for taking care of the younger ones. Their mothers would care for babies but all others would carry weapons into battle. John's force totaled twenty-six plus the advance scouting party of fourteen for a total of forty men and women.

He intended to use all twenty of the flintlock rifles and shotguns. He hoped these weapons would make a difference in the battle against whatever force he met. Sarah and Mary were reluctant to leave their children but realized that there was no other choice.

They needed all able-bodied people at the battle line. Candice was four months pregnant but felt strong enough to join them. Lillie would stand beside her husband seeking vengeance against her brother-in-law's killers.

John's column left at mid-day heading east along the *Mick*. They reached their destination early the second day, traveling slower than normal because of their older and pregnant members. The column had reached a draw similar to the one where they previously ambushed Mutant attackers. John's plan was to use the scout party as bait and draw the enemy into this trap.

He decided they needed some advance notice before the Mutants entered the draw so he sent two men about two hundred yards east of the draw so they could give the townspeople advance warning of the approaching scouts.

John guessed the enemy had placed the heads where they did as a means of informing them if someone from Harding had found them. If the heads were removed then the Mutants knew to be wary of an attack from the townspeople.

John's plan was to leave the heads in place and let the enemy feel easy about following the *Mick* west toward Harding. When they eventually encountered the scouts, who were going to be stationed about an hour's run east of the ambush site, they should think they were just a relief party for those already killed.

If all went well they should chase the scouts through this draw and not suspect a trap. The problem now was when would the enemy attack? John had taken a chance in delaying his march as long as he had but there was really no other choice. He had needed the extra time to prepare and then to reach this spot.

Not knowing how much advance time he had, he dispersed his people evenly on each side of the draw. Each group also evenly shared the firearms. He did suggest they save the shotguns for when the enemy tried to scale the sides of the draw. The signal to start firing would be the sound of a horn.

The adults gave the younger members of their party advice on how to stay alert and how to aim at their targets. Not knowing what to expect from their enemy caused some concern from the townspeople but they had complete confidence in their ability to overcome whatever came at them.

Nightfall came but John didn't relax his vigilance and called for no campfires. He also instructed Kit to be watchful at night as these people might not be averse to attacking during this time. That may have been why Anderson's party was taken by surprise.

The next morning he sent replacements for the two advance runners and then toured both sides of the draw, evaluating the townspeople's morale and offering support where he could. At mid-day he sat with his wives sharing some deer jerky and speculating on whether or not the enemy would even show up.

Sarah hugged him and suggested he take his own advice and be patient. He smiled at her and shrugged his shoulders. "I'm just worried about the scouts. Did I set them to engage the enemy too far away where they could be overrun before they got back here?"

"Kit helped you work that distance out so he should know how fast he and his men can get back here. So stop worrying about something you can't change."

John nodded his head in agreement but continued to have a worried expression on his face.

Randy and Jenny walked up and Jenny asked, "How are y'all holding up?"

Candice pointed at John and shook her head. "You should know how John is. He'll worry about things right up to when the battle starts."

They all smiled but like John they hoped the wait would soon be over. All three of the nurses were on the battle line with only Janet to be kept in reserve because of her valuable medical skills. John looked at the people he was responsible for and hoped that they didn't lose very many in this fight. They had been lucky in their battles up until now.

Suddenly, both of their runners came back yelling, "The scouts are no more than three minutes behind us."

The two groups immediately dropped into cover and waited for the scouts to appear. They soon came through the draw running like the devil was chasing them.

John had only time to note that all the scouts appeared to have made it when suddenly their pursuers appeared. They didn't slow as they entered the draw two abreast. There must have been sixty plus men screaming after the scouts' blood. John waited until they were all in the draw before signaling for the horn. When its eerie sound was heard, the screaming horde suddenly stopped their mad dash as they realized they were in a trap.

They didn't have time to make plans because the townspeople immediately opened up with both rifles and longbows. The first volley killed or wounded nearly half their force. Before they could mount a charge up the sides of the draw the scouts let fly with their own volley killing ten more of their number. The enemy force staggered under the successive blows from the townspeople, but then they split their remaining force and started up the sides of the draw throwing spears as they came only to be cut down by the shotguns and longbows.

This enemy force had been especially fierce and their size was bigger than the Mutants they had met before; however, other than their larger size they appeared to be the same general breed and hadn't developed any better weapons.

Later, Kit related that the Mutants had come down the trail with forward scouts, which his party eliminated. However, when the main party found their bodies they had come after them with blood in their eyes. It was well they didn't have any further to go when they got to the draw as they were about done in.

John checked for any casualties among the townspeople and was distressed to find two dead and three wounded. The nurses were busy with the wounded while he checked to see who had been killed. Ralph McCune, Candice's father, and June Campbell, Kit's second wife were lying close together with spears in their chests. With tears in his eyes he found Candice and told her the bad news.

She looked at him with a shocked expression and then collapsed into his arms sobbing while Sarah and Mary immediately came over to offer their support. Kit Campbell and Jack Peterson came toward John to report when they saw the Bishop family holding each other in their grief.

When John saw Kit approaching, he reluctantly turned to meet him. Kit saw the tears in John's eyes and his grief stricken expression, and asked what had happened. John wrapped his arm around Kit's shoulder and told him of the death of Candice's father and then of June's death.

They both stood together with John's arm around his shoulder both weeping for their losses. He told Kit to wait then gathered Candice in his arms and asked if she wanted to go to her father. When she nodded her head he gestured to Kit to follow him as they went to the fallen heroes.

He later consulted with Jack Peterson about manpower needs who agreed with John's idea to send ten townspeople to help carry the dead and injured, along with the Bishop wives and the Campbell family back to Harding. The remainder of the column would dispose of the bodies of the enemy and return to the north/south trail to leave another grisly warning to trespassers.

CHAPTER 26

The townspeople arrived back at the main north/south trail where they removed the heads of their four slain scouts that would be returned to Harding for burial with honor. In their place they hung thirty-two heads of the slain Mutants.

Everyone not on guard duty, without hesitation, performed this gruesome task with much distaste. The group then went north to the next west trailhead and hung another thirty-three heads next to the Skull and Crossbones.

They could only hope this would be enough deterrence to keep these bloodthirsty Mutants away from these trails. They then returned to the *Mick* trailhead heading west toward home.

Three days later the townspeople warily walked into Harding much to the delight of those who had remained in town. It was a happy reunion between parents and children but the celebration was spoiled by the deaths and injuries of the men and women who fought for the people of Harding.

That evening they had a mass funeral for those slain. Another six graves joined Mick in the town's graveyard. John gave the eulogy for those slain, ending with the hope that those slain in the defense of Harding would never be forgotten by future generations. He then asked family members to speak for their loved ones.

When it came time for Candice to speak for her father she told of his struggle to keep the north settlement safe from the enemy and of their eventual salvation by the people from Harding. She said her father had many times expressed a debt he owed the townspeople which now had been repaid.

When the Bridges returned home that night, he waited until Candice was settled in her room before calling Sarah and Mary together for a conference. "I think we should offer Candice's mother the option of moving in with us at least until she felt able to take care of herself. Do any of you have any objections?"

Sarah looked at Mary with a slight smile and then they both came over and hugged him. "We've already talked about that possibility but haven't asked Candice yet if she wants to do that. We weren't sure you would want a mother-in-law in the same household," Sarah said with a twinkle in her eyes.

"I should have known my wives would have already thought this through. I've got no objections to her living here and if she becomes a problem we can always move her back to her home."

The next day they asked Candice whether or not she wanted her mother to come live with them for a while. She responded with a big smile and tears of happiness before replying, "Oh yes! That would be wonderful." She then hugged and kissed her husband and her sister wives.

As it turned out, Joyce McCune seemed anxious to move into the Bridges household and was looking forward to be near her daughter and all the children. His wives helped move her belongings into Randy's vacated upstairs room which she liked mainly because this was where all the children were.

The children hadn't had a grandmother before Candice married into the family and were a little shy with her at first. However, her love of children soon made her the center of their attention.

They especially loved her storytelling about the old days where they had those strange animals in a faraway place called Africa. When she told about her first trip in an airplane and how high in the air it got they were spellbound.

John Jr. and Sadie asked their father if Grandma was fibbing or did she really fly across the sky like she said. Sadie looked at John questioningly as she asked, "She said she flew just like a bird. What's a bird Daddy?"

He looked surprised for a moment and then chuckled. "It was a small creature that had wings and could fly through the air." John held out his arms and flapped them as he swooped around the room and then picked her up in his arms.

Sadie giggled and hugged his neck not sure if he was kidding her or not. She was wise enough to know that her Daddy sometimes added things to his stories to make them more interesting. She was thinking that maybe as you get older you do that more often and since Grandma was really old maybe she did it all the time. Well, true or not it still was a good story and she wanted to hear more.

The wives were very happy that Joyce McCune had joined their household. Not only was she a godsend as a babysitter, she was a kind and gentle person who made everyone feel better when she was around them. John and Joyce got along great which somewhat surprised him as people from the north settlement generally didn't agree with the idea of multiple wives.

John's curiosity got the better of him and one day when they were alone he asked her what she thought of his having three wives.

She looked at him with a surprised expression for a moment but then shyly smiled. "Why John, until we arrived in Harding I didn't give it a thought. However, I now see the need and as long as they involve a loving relationship such as in this household, I'm all for it. Candice loves you very much and is looking forward to having your children." With a mischievous grin she added, "She's even hoping to have twins like your other wives."

"Yes, Candice and I love each other very much but I love my other wives too; especially Sarah, my first wife. When we married I thought she was the only one for me but things happen and now look at me."

He shook his head remembering the circumstances leading to his taking a second and third wife. "I would never have taken another wife without Sarah's approval. She's the one with the big heart. The one who was willing to share her husband with another women."

Joyce smiled at him and placed her arm around his waist as she replied, "Yes, they all are wonderful women to be able to share their husband but the husband has to have that something that makes it possible to keep them all happy."

Candice walked into the room and spotted her husband and Mother talking together with her arm around his waist. She smothered a giggle as they looked up at her approach.

"Mother, you're not campaigning to be another wife, are you?" She said as she looked at her mother with a mock stern expression.

Not to be outdone by her daughter, Joyce kissed John on the cheek and gave him a hug. "I asked if he was interested, but he said his other wives would object to having such an experienced lover join them."

John joined in on the joke by giving her a long kiss and then looked at Candice as he replied, "I can see where you get your spunk and your mother does bring up an interesting point. Maybe she can give you girls some pointers with all the experience she has."

Candice's mouth dropped open in surprise and then realizing how hard her leg was being pulled she started laughing, with the others joining in. She snickered as she realized what a combination her mother would make to the marriage. She was really happy that her mother and John got along so well but she didn't want them to get along too well as she laughed again at the thought.

The deaths of the scouts left four young widows, one with a baby. They all would eventually wish to remarry since they were young and probably still wanted to have children. Their problem was again the lack of single men. John shook his head as he hoped the problem would resolve itself without his direct involvement.

John was thinking how the wolf sounds along with the horn had contributed to the north encampment's decision to leave without a fight. He was also considering if a drum beat cadence might be more effective when used with the horn. He discussed the idea with Randy and George who thought it would be worth a try. They would need at least six drums and probably eight for it to work properly.

Randy and George built a drum and experimented until they found the right sound before building seven more. They recruited eight older children and showed them what sound they wanted and the cadence to use and then left them to practice.

When they started their practice drumbeats the other children and adults came over to watch. After they seemed to have it down pat John started blowing the horn to supplement the drums. They began to improvise the drumbeat until they had a cadence that worked better. Kit and Jack came over to John as they were practicing. Noticing their arrival he asked them what they thought.

Kit nodded his head while he grinned. "I thought the horn was scary, but with the drums it should scare anything away!"

Jack laughed and voiced his approval as well. The kids, who were the drum bearers, were evenly divided between girls and boys between the ages of twelve to fourteen.

John nodded his head at the drum bearers. "If we take them with us they will have to receive training in the longbow."

Kit nodded his head, and then he voiced an idea. "How hard would it be to make crossbows for them. They could carry them easier and learning how to fire them should be easy."

John looked at him in amazement, "Why didn't I think of that? I'll have Randy and George start working on them. This would work for some of the smaller women as well. However, I think they will need some help with the crossbows as they're busy with the rifles and shotguns. Do you know of any townspeople who might want to help?"

"Why not us? Jack and I both would like to try our hand at making the crossbows," Kit said with enthusiasm.

He nodded his head in acceptance and they went to the workshop. John explained to Randy and George that they wanted to make crossbows and asked if they had any ideas. Everyone then put their heads together for a design which eventually included a built-in lever for drawing the bowstring. It made drawing a fifty-pound bow a snap even for a young girl. The shafts for the crossbow were easier to make as well since they were so short.

After they had constructed the first three crossbows, he had the boys and girls start practicing with them until they could build enough for everyone. The children didn't have any problem with them and soon were as good or better than their best archer. Carrying the crossbow in a sling over their back was a must as they also had to carry their drum.

In three weeks every drum bearer had a crossbow and was proficient in its use. John had done a survey of the women regarding whether they would prefer a crossbow rather than what they were presently using? The women had been observing their use by the drum bearers and six said that they wished to try the crossbow.

It only took another two weeks to fill this order and John now felt that the town was better protected with the addition of this new weapon. Even an eight year-old was able to use the crossbow and they were to receive training in case of need.

The town slowly resumed its normal routine except for the larger and increased frequency of the scouting trips around Harding. The scouts made two trips east for every trip west because of the threat from the north/south trail east of Harding. After another two months the scouts hadn't discovered any new sign of the Mutants and they were beginning to think placing the heads at the trailheads had done its job.

Candice's pregnancy was in the last trimester and it appeared that she too was going to give birth to twins. She and her mother were both ecstatic about the coming births; however, Candice spent a lot of her time sitting because it was difficult to move around due to her large size.

The children were now used to one of their mothers being pregnant and knew to treat her with loving care. Sometimes they would ask to feel her stomach or hold their ears close to hear the babies' heartbeats. Sadie seemed to be more compassionate and went out of her way to fetch things Candice needed and would stay close and talk with her about things that interested her. Sadie was a refreshing change from the male dominated children of the Bridges household.

A little over two months later Candice delivered the expected twins with both Jenny and Janet in attendance. She was well cared for with all the adults of the household trying to offer help. In the end the births were without problems with both the mother and babies doing well.

Candice got her wish for a girl and a boy. John was all smiles as he held the little girl in his arms and then the boy.

John asked, "Do you have any names in mind for the babies."

She smiled at the babies for a moment. "How about Ralph for my Dad. You can name the girl."

John smiled at the little girl. "Sadie is named after Sarah's mother, so let's name her Grace after my mother."

Candice looked lovingly at her children. "Ralph and Grace. Those are wonderful names for two beautiful babies."

The rest of the family crowded around the babies, each wanting to see the new additions to the clan. Later, when most of the family had left the room, Joyce picked up her grandchildren and kissed them both on the forehead before placing them back into their mother's arms.

Candice asked her mother, "How does it feel to be a grandmother?"

"I've already got six grandchildren but these two will be my favorites," she responded with a smile. Joyce looked at little Ralph with tears in her eyes. "If only Ralph could see his namesake, he would be so proud."

Candice looked at her mother with tears in her own eyes. "I'm sure that he's looking down at him right now and he's the proudest grandfather ever."

CHAPTER 27

John made another trip with the hunters to the mining valley for additional gunpowder ingredients and lead a month after Candice had given birth. They now had twenty rifles and fifteen shotguns and had almost used up their initial supply of gunpowder. He saw no need to make any additional firearms as they had enough for every adult male with several spares left over.

They found they had to make additional crossbows as most of the women now preferred them to the longbow and firearms. John and his two scout leaders thought they now were in a good position to defend themselves with their present weapon mix. However, they all were uncomfortable with the lack of enemy activity and felt something was building against them.

The next evening the Bridges family were taking their bath together at their favorite spot on the *Mick* when they could hear a storm approaching in the far distance. John had everyone get out of the water and hurry toward home. From past experience he knew they probably had just enough time before the storm would be upon them.

When they entered Harding the townspeople were trying to batten down all loose items. They did the same around their house while Candice and Joyce took care of the children. When the lightning strikes started to get close everyone ran for cover. John felt he was about to get another visit from *The Messenger*. His wives shared this same thought and had moved everyone else to the downstairs bedrooms while they stood with their husband.   They didn't have long to wait as the storm was suddenly upon them.

The vibrations and thunder from the lightning strikes shook the house and deafened its inhabitants. John and his wives were holding each other tightly trying to comfort each other, when the familiar glowing ball appeared at their doorway. *The Messenger* slowly entered the house and stopped in front of them carrying with it a familiar strong smell of ozone.

It's glow intensified to a bright white light before the static charge connection was made to John's forehead. He and his wives all stiffened as the charge connected and they didn't move until the connection was broken several minutes later with a loud pop. They then collapsed together in a heap on the floor. Jenny and the other family members rushed to their side as *The Messenger* left through the doorway.

John's wives recovered first and they were trying to help Jenny revive him when he seemed to catch his breath and then opened his eyes. He soon sat up and rubbed his sore forehead until Jenny placed a wet compress on the red spot, but she didn't think he had a burn.

John looked at his wives and asked them, "Did y'all receive the message too?" They all nodded their heads and then sat next to him with their arms around his shoulders. John looked out through the doorway and noted that the storm had passed but its sounds could still be heard as it moved away.

His family helped him to stand and then sit at the common table while they waited to hear what the entity had to say. John and his wives helped themselves to some fresh water as they all tried to gather their thoughts. He looked at Sarah for a moment and when she nodded her head he began telling what they had learned from their visitor.

"*The Messenger* said that we were in great danger from a large gathering of the fierce Mutants from the north. They intend to search for us and then destroy everyone they found. We don't have much time as their scouts are out searching for us right now!"

John looked at his wives for confirmation hoping he had gotten the message wrong but when they nodded their agreement, his facial expression became one of resolution. They had fought battles before and they would win this one as well. John had the men of the family run to tell of an immediate town meeting as he and his wives gathered their strength for the coming battle.

It wasn't long before everyone had gathered to hear from John what *The Messenger* had said. When John, supported by his wives, had retold the entity's message, there was shocked silence from the townspeople.

John then continued. "This news was not unexpected as Kit, Jack, and I had anticipated something like this and have been preparing the first draw near Harding for another ambush. Since the northern trail that branched west didn't lead directly to Harding, we expect them to approach along the *Mick*. We also anticipate that the attack will be at night."

The stunned silence of the townspeople was broken by questions of how they were going to know they were coming and how they were going to be able to see them to fight from a distance.

John held up his hands for silence. "I had hoped the fight would come during the day, but a night fight would aid us as much as the enemy if we prepare for it."

He then brought Kit Campbell and Jack Peterson up before them and had them tell the townspeople what preparations had been made. When they were done, the townspeople's faces had all assumed a wolfish grin of anticipation for the coming battle.

John gave instructions to the sentries to move their posts away from the *Mick* trail, but remain close enough to observe any movements and not to sound the alarm unless a large number of Mutants approach Harding. He wanted to know if the enemy had found Harding but didn't want them to be aware we had observed their movements.

Two days later the east sentry came running into town with the news that a three-man Mutant scouting party had discovered Harding's location and then returned back east. John notified his scout leaders that phase two of their plan was now in effect.

Scouts were sent out to deliver an early warning for the town while the townspeople were given specific assignments in the coming battle. Like the previous attack all the able townspeople would join in this battle. Mothers with young babies, children younger than ten, and townspeople older than seventy were exempt. The seniors and older children would protect those staying in town. That evening the defenders left Harding, knowing that some of their people might not survive the expected engagement that night.

The draw had been prepared with dry grass and brush lining its sides from east to west. In addition, bramble bushes had been formed into barrier at both the east and west ends of the draw. The east barrier was left open to funnel any Mutants from the sides of the trail to the center of the draw.

John relieved the scouts sent further east with fresh men to bring word of any approaching attack force of the enemy. The townspeople were instructed to get into their assigned positions along each side of the draw and then they waited for the expected enemy to appear. Their wait depended on where the enemy's main force was waiting for word from their scouts. It could be hours or days before they arrived at this location. However, John and his scout leaders were betting on an attack tonight.

About two A.M. the scouts returned yelling, "There's a large bunch of Mutants only minutes behind us!"

They then took their assigned posts. The Mutants had sent three of their scouts about a minute ahead of the main group showing them the way. John had anticipated this and had assigned four men to eliminate them when they reached the west end of the barricaded draw.

They could hear the approaching enemy before they became visible in the moonless night. The enemy scouts passed first and in less than a minute the main party appeared. They didn't hesitate as they entered the draw following their scouts who unknown to them had already been killed by silent arrows.

The Mutants entered the draw three abreast which was as wide as the trail allowed and were strung out for over fifty yards. John estimated that there must be over 120 men in this group.

When the last of the enemy had entered the draw, the scouts who had been hiding behind the bramble barriers used long poles to move the barriers across the east entrance of the draw blocking any retreat by the Mutants. The horn was sounded to signal the townspeople to attack and start phase three of the plan.

The townspeople threw flaming torches down into the draw to catch ablaze the tender they had provided for this purpose. The enemy immediately tried to scale the walls of the draw but was repulsed by deadly fire from its sides by both rifles and arrows. The townspeople had the advantage of having their enemy backlit by the fires while they were in darkness. Suddenly, withering fire from the shotguns tore their ranks apart not giving them a chance to mount a serious charge against the townspeople.

Without warning the small fires exploded into a firestorm causing the townspeople to withdraw from the draws' sides or be burned along with the remaining Mutants who were screaming their agony as the fire consumed them. Those of the enemy who made it up the sides were aflame and were immediately killed by the townspeople who looked on in horror at what their plan had achieved.

Later, as dawn revealed the extent of their victory they counted 128 bodies of the Mutants. The townspeople had only suffered two wounded who were able to return to Harding on their own. In their last two battles they had killed over 190 of these fierce people. They resolved to place these heads beside the others at the *Mick* trailhead to discourage any further attacks.

John stood with his scout leaders as they viewed the burned wasteland with horrified expressions while the stink of burned flesh intensified their disgust.

"They can't have many more warriors to send against us, can they?" John asked.

Kit Campbell shook his head sadly. "I wouldn't think so. They had to wait almost four months to gather this group. I would think they would avoid us in the future but who knows how these people think!"

John and Jack both nodded their heads in agreement and then the leaders began giving orders to remove the bodies and place the heads in a pile for later transport to the trailhead. The women and older children were released to return to Harding while the men would finish this distasteful task.

John noted that shafts from crossbows killed many of the enemy proving their worth in the first battle. The scout leaders told him that the crossbow users had gotten off at least three volleys before the firestorm engulfed the enemy. The longbows had only gotten off four. The rifles and shotguns were only fired once during the battle but were a key element in repelling the enemy from the sides of the draw.

The remaining ten men began their walk to the trailhead to deliver their trophies while the two scouts lead the way in case of more enemy along the trail. They reached the trailhead without incidence and added the additional heads and reposted those that had been knocked down by the enemy. Apparently this attack force had traveled here without bringing their families.

When they arrived back into Harding it was to a subdued celebration. They had eventually acknowledged that the fire probably had saved many of their lives but the memory of the screams and smell of burning flesh would remain with them for some time.

The men were exhausted, especially John and his two Captains, Kit and Jack. They had planned this battle for some time and were happy that it had resulted in another victory for the town without any deaths on their side.

John's wives met him as he walked into town and immediately shied away holding their noses. They told him they were taking him to their swimming hole to get cleaned up. He realized that he was still covered by soot from the fire and must smell terrible. Sarah and Mary placed their arms around him as they steered him toward the *Mick* while Candice walked ahead of them carrying a change of clothing for him.

When they got to the swimming hole they stripped him of clothing then removed their own before helping him into the water. Sarah and Mary used their own homemade soap to cleanse him while Candice washed his clothes. The two women working on John started to giggle as it became clear that he had recovered at least some of his strength as he started to rub their bodies as well.

Candice looked up from her task of washing clothes when she heard Sarah and Mary laughing in enjoyment and then sighing in passion as he returned their favors. She threw the garments onto shore and went to join the fun, yelling "No fair" at her sister wives.

They eventually all lay together on shore counting their blessings and grateful that the family had survived another battle. The wives lay against their husband trying to get as close to him as possible each expressing their love for him by their actions.

When they returned home late that afternoon their children met them at the door welcoming them back and asking John to tell them the story of the battle. While he got them settled around him in preparation for his storytelling, Candice went to check on her twins.

She found them in her room where her mother was tending them. Ralph and Grace had outgrown their baby cribs and now were sleeping together on a short child's bed brought down from upstairs. She softly asked if they had been crying for her milk when her mother shook her head and motioned for them to leave the room.

Joyce placed her hand on Candice's arm and smiled. "They are just the best behaved babies I've ever seen. You were a real pill when you were that age crying for the nipple all the time. It was much easier when I put you on the bottle as it gave me some time for myself."

"Mama, it's no problem for me since I've got plenty of milk for both of them. Although, Ralph makes a pig of himself sometimes."

They walked into the common room where they noticed Randy and Jenny seemed excited about something as they fidgeted and looked at each other expectantly. When Candice and her mother sat at the table all of the adults were then present in the room.

Randy cleared his throat nervously and then opened his mouth to speak but nothing came out but a squeak.

Jenny grinned as she shook her head at Randy. "What Randy was trying to say is that we're expecting a child sometime around Christmas."

John and Sarah blinked at each other in surprise for a moment then jumped up to congratulate the happy couple.

Randy beamed at them as he finally found his voice and exclaimed, "You're going to be grandparents again!"

The other adults in the room rushed over to add their congratulations as well giving the two expectant parents the limelight.

Later, Jenny pulled Candice aside and asked with a worried expression, "Do you think it's possible I'll have twins like y'all did?"

Candice started to grin at her then decided to respond seriously because she seemed to be sincerely concerned. "Well, we all are John's wives and while Randy is John's son he was adopted like yourself. So, his genes aren't passed on to Randy. However, Lillie has given birth to twins so Randy might have these genes from his mother's or father's side of the family."

"I guess it would be okay to have twins but I was hoping to ease into motherhood with only one baby to care for," Jenny said wistfully.

Candice put her arms around Jenny and chuckled. "That's what I thought but I wouldn't change those twins for anything now."

She hefted one of Jenny's breasts gently and grinned at her. "Besides, it looks like you have the equipment to handle twins if they do arrive."

Jenny's face colored slightly as she placed both her hands under her breasts and compared them to Candice's milk filled breasts. "I don't think I'm near as big as you in that department, and yours have gotten even bigger."

"Yours will too even if you don't have twins." Candice giggled briefly and then stiffened as she heard a baby cry. "Well, duty calls. Do you want to observe my twins in action?"

Jenny grinned as she nodded her head and followed Candice into the room where both babies were now crying.

John observed while Randy was proud of being an expectant father he was also a little afraid of the dangers of childbirth for Jenny. He put his arm around the broad shoulders of Randy and tried to put him at ease.

"Randy, my wives, including your mother, had no problems with childbirth and they were all twins since we arrived here. Jenny is about the same age and body size of Lillie when she had her first child and she didn't have any problems during childbirth."

Randy nodded his head at what John had said, but with tears in his eyes, blurted, "I know all this, but I'm still scared for her even with Janet as a skilled nurse present."

"It's the nature of men to worry about their women during childbirth. It's a natural process but sometimes things go wrong and that's what we worry about," John said thoughtfully.

George nodded his head in agreement. "I was really worried about Lillie when she had our twins because of the lack of a doctor if something went wrong but everything went smoothly. I'm sure you're worrying about nothing."

Lillie and her children arrived at the house wanting to know what the big discussion was about. When Randy told her Jenny was expecting, she beamed at him and gave him a hug before leaving to find Jenny. She found her with Candice who was feeding the twins and congratulated her on being an expectant mother. She then asked if she was getting pointers on how to nurse twins.

Jenny flushed and then laughed. "Gosh, I hope I'm not going to have twins. I was just asking Candice about the odds of me having twins and she said it's possible but there was no telling for sure."

Lillie laughed and then jokingly said, "You're not using your head. Look at the twins in this family. It's like we're predestined to have them."

Candice laughed too then shook her head. "Don't listen to her because she's just trying to pull your leg. You know that the odds favor a single birth...But then she does have a point," she added with a wicked gleam in her eyes as she smiled at her twins.

Sarah had been watching this conversation and decided that enough was enough. "Jenny, you should know better than to listen to these two. Why, they have no idea at all of your chances of having twins. Now you come with me and get your mind off twins or you're going to have them for sure."

They all laughed at that as Sarah dragged her out of the room. Jenny felt like one of them now that she was pregnant. Before, she was just another kid trying to act like a grownup. She eagerly followed Sarah back into the common room with Lillie trailing behind.

Jenny immediately noticed the glum face of her husband and hurried to his side asking what was the problem. When he refused to answer her she looked at John questioningly.

"Ooh, he's just getting worried about you."

Jenny jabbed Randy in the ribs with a sharp finger getting his attention. "Is that true, sugar bear?"

When he nodded, she snuggled up to him and kissed him on the cheek. Come with me as I've got just the thing to make you feel better. Randy's face suddenly turned an embarrassed red as he followed her to their room and shut the door.

John smiled at Sarah as he whispered into her ear, "I don't know about him, but that certainly would cheer me up."

She jerked her head around to look into his eyes. "Why you randy old rooster! You're always ready for that but so am I." She grinned at him as she grabbed his arm leading him toward their bedroom.

Lillie shyly smiled at Mary as she started pulling George toward the door. "Come on honey, I've got something to show you at home."

After they left, Mary slowly shook her head as she muttered, "Well, that sure cleared the room fast."

CHAPTER 28

The next day Jacob mentioned to John they needed to mine some more ore before too long as their bar steel was running low. John suggested they try to do all the refining in Harding this time because of the threat from the Mutants. He didn't want to split his force any more than was necessary and decided to bring back what he needed for more gunpowder as well.

John decided that he could spare twelve men as miners with two of the older girls and six guard dogs acting as their sentries. With the women and the older men defending the town with crossbows and shotguns he hoped that the town would be safe in their absence.

They left Harding with some feelings of apprehension about the trip but mostly about leaving their loved ones behind. It took a little longer arriving at the mining area since they had to pull the ore carts along a trail designed for foot traffic. They arrived in late afternoon and decided to spend the remainder of the day fixing up their camp, posting sentries, and sending a hunting team out.

The townspeople spent four days mining enough ore to fill their two carts; however, they found that the use of steel tools made mining much easier on this trip. They decided to separate the material in the carts by the use of removable dividers. This should make it easier to keep the ore separate during the trip back to town.

Finally, the mining party was ready for the return trip. The girls and the dogs were given the job of guarding them as the men were busy moving the carts along the trail. They soon discovered that even with wide wheels the carts sometimes sank into the ground making it difficult to move. They eventually developed a method of placing short branches under the wheels when they encountered soft areas.

When they arrived in Harding the townspeople ran forward to help them get the carts next to the workshop. The members of the mining party were exhausted and decided to wait until the next day to begin work on refining the ore.

The wives of the men immediately made plans to clean them up before letting them into their homes. After feeding them a hot meal they all made their way toward their favorite swimming areas on the *Mick*.

Lillie's family joined the Bridges for a joint outing. When they arrived at their spot everyone immediately stripped for a plunge into the cool water. After soaking for a time enjoying being with their families again the three men each received a thorough washing from their wives. The men had missed having their daily baths and enjoyed having the women fuss over them.

The next day the townsmen started building a new blast furnace next to the workplace. Using the knowledge gained from the furnace constructed at the mining area, they built what they hoped would be an improved version.

Once the blast furnace was finished they started the process of smelting the iron ore. The children hadn't seen this process before and were interested observers but were kept at a distance because of the danger of burns. This was the town's main industry so they needed to become knowledgeable of both the theory and the actual workings of the steel making process.

The men took turns staying with the audience answering the children's questions and explaining why they did things to achieve the results they were after. Surprisingly, there were almost as many girls as boys in the audience.

Within a month, the process resulted in the first production of steel from this batch of raw ore. Their experience resulted in a faster, better grade of steel for the town's use.

Fall weather in Harding brought cooler nights and more rain. As long as they didn't have a heavy frost this winter the town's garden should flourish as it had in the past.

Scouting parties brought no news of any Mutant sightings; however, foot traffic on the north/south trail was still heavy based upon the trail's trampled condition. The enemy heads were still posted at the trailheads so it was possible they had achieved their goal.

Life in Harding continued in its established pattern except for the four young widows. They still lived alone in their houses except for

Sandra Bates who had moved back into her parents home. Sheila Anderson visited the Bridges household seeking John's advice and counsel on the widows seeking approval as junior wives.

John discussed the possibilities with her and pointed out that there were now four families with multiple wives which left nine families with only one wife. However, because of the advanced ages of some of these men only six were young enough to be attractive to these young women. Due to other problems that number was further reduced to four possible men.

Sheila nodded her head in understanding and resolved to try to educate those families not already of a mind to accept several wives in their family. She said they needed as big a choice as possible when it came time to make their bids.

John's wives were present during this discussion and they suggested that the women visit those households they were interested in and try the direct approach.

Sarah placed her arm around Sheila's shoulder and pulled her aside. "The one you need to convince is the wife. Without her approval you don't have a chance."

Sheila slowly smiled at Sarah in understanding and promised to pass the word to her other sister widows. She then met with them to plan their strategy. They each already had specific men in mind so they helped each other design the best approach to convince a specific wife to accept another wife in the family.

After several days of planning they each began their planned attack. Sheila knew she would have problems with her pick but was determined to succeed. She met Lillie at the *Mick* gathering water and was soon in friendly conversation with her. They were already friends since each had been married to one of the Anderson twins.

Sheila was asking about her children, especially the new twins born from her marriage with George Anderson. They continued the conversation as they returned to their adjacent homes with Lillie inviting her over to see the twins.

She cultivated this genuine friendship for about a month until she felt that maybe Lillie was able to at least listen to her argument. She was at Lillie's house visiting, talking about how well the multiple wife families were getting along. Especially, how well her mother's family had adjusted to where they had even accepted Candice's mother into their home.

Lillie was no fool and had known for some time that Sheila was interested in becoming a junior wife to her husband. The way the conversation was heading today she felt sure that Sheila was finally going to put the question to her.

Sheila was so intent on gathering her courage to say her prepared argument that she missed the small smile on Lillie's face. When she began to speak, Lillie placed her hand on her arm causing Sheila to stop and look at her smiling face. Lillie then drew her into her arms and kissed her on the cheek.

"I know you want to become a junior wife in our family and I've already discussed this possibility with George who has agreed."

Sheila's eyes filled with tears as she hugged her friend. "Ooh, you just don't know how happy you've made me. Since Greg died I've been without direction or purpose with not even a child to care for."

Lillie smiled as she pointed to her children. "You can practice with mine until you have your own."

"I'll consider all the children ours just like the other wives do," Sheila said while wiping tears of joy from eyes.

The other three widows had similar success with their picks and they decided to start the formal bidding process. Since the women had already made informal agreements with the families the process didn't take long. The families agreed to the ninety-day trial period that hopefully would result in final marriages for all four women.

John and Sarah were pleasantly surprised when they heard that Lillie had agreed to accept another wife in her family because while she had been married to Mick she had been adamantly opposed to the idea of a second wife. Maybe the experiences of the other families with multiple wives had influenced her decision. But, whatever her reasons, the results were in the best interests of Harding.

Jenny gave birth to an eight-pound girl on December 16th of the new calendar, year 9 N.B. (New Beginning), since the start of the Harding settlement. Both parents adored their daughter, Alice, named after Jenny's mother. John and Sarah now had another grandchild living with them and lavished their love on her. The other wives considered her their grandchild as well and she never lacked for someone to love and cuddle her.

The New Year brought junior wives into three new families now making six families with multiple wives out of a total of thirteen families. Sandra Bates had been accepted into the Kit Campbell family as his third wife. She filled an empty spot in their family caused by the death of June who was killed in battle.

The new wives preferred to be married in a joint ceremony. These women had joined together in a tight bond created by the common deaths of their husbands and wanted their new lives to start together. John, as Mayor, had the couples say their vows together and then pronounced them married under the laws of man and God.

This was the biggest wedding held to date and the celebration was its match. The townspeople ate the rarely prepared cake, this time with icing made from sugar cane they had discovered and were now growing. Sugar was a real treat for the townspeople, especially the children. However, the parents began to worry about the effect of sugar on their children's teeth.

The women had found several kinds of plant leaves that when brewed made an excellent tea. The sugar greatly added to its flavor and made a popular drink by both sexes. In addition to the cake and tea served, they had the usual deer and vegetables. The new brides soon left with their husbands to their prepared honeymoon sites.

The townspeople now had more leisure time and some of the families had begun to play card games in the evening. The people had brought three decks of playing cards with them from old Earth and since they were so popular they were now trying to duplicate more of them from materials now available.

This effort led to the production of metal shears, steel rollers for thin flat steel, and metal impression stamps to make the card designations. The effort used in making these playing cards was substantial considering that it was for a leisure item. However, these production tools were later used for the manufacture of essential tools and equipment.

The first items produced were cooking pots, metal grills and spits for broiling meat, and better gardening tools. Later, they produced lighter arrowheads and better feathering for the shafts of arrows for the longbows and crossbows increasing their effective range.

John was now trying to produce a cartridge case for a new single shot rifle. With a fast reloading rifle the townspeople could better defend themselves. He and his armorers finally developed a punch press that formed the bullet casing he needed for the rifle. They then developed the powder igniter to fire the bullet and a bullet mold to fit the casing.

The casing was sized to fit the present bore of the flintlock rifles so they could use its barrel castings. They just needed to modify it to include a hinge at the bottom of the barrel. John's idea was for the barrel to break away from the stock at the breech for easy reloading.

However, it was going to take some more thought to get it to work properly. They needed to cast a new breech plate and hinge to closely fit together with the barrel. Then they had to design an easy locking device to hold the two pieces together tight enough to withstand the pressure created by firing the rifle. They eventually had the rifle assembly ready for a test firing with the new bullet.

Using the same caution they had used when testing the flintlock rifle, they tied the new weapon down to a bench which was aimed at a nearby target. Using a shield and a long string to pull the trigger, John fired the weapon.

The loud cracking sound was different from the muzzle-loading flintlock. The bullet striking the target made a different hard-hitting sound as well. They rushed to the rifle to examine it for any damage. The barrel lock held together during the firing and the rifle assembly appeared undamaged. They took it apart to make sure no internal damage was done before test firing several more rounds through the rifle.

The accuracy would have to be tested later when they added its stock and sights. One of the townsmen had previously had a hobby of woodworking and volunteered to make the stock for the new rifle. While he was working on the stock, the armorers began work on a two-barreled shotgun of a similar design as the new rifle.

The new shotgun's two barrels would be forged together and would be of a shorter length and bigger bore than those of the flintlocks. Modern shotgun shells had a soft non-metal sleeve holding the shot. Theirs would be all metal with a thin lead covering to hold the shot and powder within the casing.

About a week later, Peter Haskins had the rifle stock finished and installed on the rifle. He held it out for them to admire. John took it from him and turned it around admiring the craftsmanship. He placed the butt of the rifle against his shoulder testing the fit and balance.

He finally turned to Peter and shook his hand for a job well done. He gave the weapon to Randy and George for their comments while he asked Peter how he had gotten so close a fit. Peter smiled slyly at him.

"Well, I'm an antique gun collector as well as a woodworker and I've made reconditioned stocks for some of my rifles."

"Why didn't you let us know? We would have had you helping us in the design!" He said in confusion.

"I started to, but then thought you might come up with an innovative design from those of the past. I had no idea of how to make shells for the rifle and your ideas for the flintlock worked just fine. If you couldn't think of how to make this rifle assembly I was all set to make suggestions but I wasn't needed."

Peter then proceeded to make some suggestions for cosmetic changes to the rifle assembly that would make for a cleaner design and easier function. He also said that when John was ready for a bolt-action rifle he had some suggestions.

"Well, since you're such an expert on guns look at our plans for a new double-barreled shotgun." He walked toward the workbench.

CHAPTER 29

While the weapon makers were busy with the new guns, Jacob Bell had been busy planning a small steam engine. He had been thinking of one ever since they returned from the mines with more iron ore. The town council had authorized Jacob's project as it would have far reaching effects for the community. The steam engine could power a variety of endeavors including a sawmill.

Jacob decided to build the engine away from the town's structures for safety and noise reduction. He and his fellow workers cut a clearing in the forest about 300 yards northwest of the town center so that the surrounding trees would act as a noise buffer when the steam engine was operating. Jacob didn't have the equipment to make a pressure gauge so he would have to rely upon a safety valve to keep the engine from exploding from too much steam pressure.

The townspeople came to watch the construction of such a large project and helped the workers whenever possible. The first finished pieces of the boiler were placed on the mining carts and transported to the building site to be completed later.

Eventually, the engine parts were all completed and moved to the construction site. They first built a log platform to support the weight of the engine and then construction began. As the engine construction started to come together the people became more excited. After working on the project for three months they were finally going to see if it would work.

They had diverted water from the *Mick* through a trough system to a newly constructed water tank near the steam engine. When they had selected the site for the engine they made sure it was lower than the river so that the trough would gravity feed the river water to the tank. Using a portable trough from the tank they filled the water reservoir of the boiler. They then used the wood scrap from cutting the clearing to start a fire in the boiler to build steam pressure.

Jacob let the pressure build until they could see steam escaping from the control levers. He crossed his fingers before turning the control valve letting steam pressure into the pistons. At first there wasn't any effect but slowly the pistons started to turn faster and faster until he turned the steam off and released the pressure from the engine in a great whoosh of sound and heat.

The townspeople all clapped their hands and shouted their joy at another accomplishment for the town. Jacob went back to the workshop to work on the sawmill equipment now that they had a working engine to power it.

Making the circular saw blade itself was fairly easy but cutting the edge into the blade was more difficult. They had to make the cuts even all around the blade to keep it in balance when it was running. They finally developed a pattern that repeated itself on the blade's edge.

When they attached the sawmill equipment to the engine they were ready for a real test of its ability. Jacob waited as before until he judged sufficient pressure had built up then turned the control valve letting steam into the pistons which started to turn. When he judged enough power had been transferred he engaged the sawmill blade which began turning faster and faster.

The men then ran a log through to test the cutting edge of the blade. The noise was horrendous between the sounds of the steam engine and the saw blade cutting through the log. People were holding their ears in pain as they continued to watch the operation and they all breathed a sigh of relief when Jacob shut the sawmill down and dumped the steam out of the engine.

"It's a good thing we thought of the noise factor before we built this project," Jacob said warily but then grinned after being congratulated at the success of the sawmill by John and others.

John asked, "Do you think the workers need to wear some kind of ear protection?"

Jacob grinned back at him and pointing to his ears acting as if he couldn't hear what was asked.

John then asked him how difficult would it be to add electric power to the system. Jacob shook his head at him and ruefully smiled. "I'm good, but I need copper wire to make a generator. Even if we find copper ore the procedure to make wire is beyond me."

John looked wistfully at the engine but then shook his head and grinned at Jacob. "I guess that will have to wait until someone comes up with an idea on how to solve the problem."

John then had a sudden thought, how far did the sawmill sound carry? He walked east to the furthest sentry and asked him had he heard the sound of the sawmill?

The sentry nodded his head. "Yes, I heard a faint noise but it didn't last long. Was that the new sawmill?"

John decided that the sound was a problem but not enough to make any changes at this time.

The town soon became accustomed to the sounds of the steam engine and sawmill. One of the first benefits from the sawmill was wood floors for all the houses. John decided that his house needed additional improvements as well so he set aside beams and other building materials to air-dry before he would start construction.

He had his wives think about a complete redesign of their home and offer suggestions before he started construction in another six to nine months. After consideration, they decided they would need four bedrooms for the adults and a minimum of six bedrooms for the children since they now had nine children and more coming.

Mary had given the family the good news that she was pregnant again. Although it much too early to tell, she was expecting twins based upon the past birthing experiences of the Bridges household.

The Kit Campbell and George Anderson households were going to expand as well and had also decided to rebuild their homes to add extra rooms. Both Sandra Campbell and Sheila Anderson were pregnant which was the deciding factor in their decisions. This was the first pregnancy for both new wives but the senior wives in their families were making sure they were properly taken care of.

George Anderson decided to tear down his brother's old house and use its materials in the expansion of his home. His family had a combined total of four children and now with Sheila expecting they needed the extra room. They decided to build according to the present floor plan of John's home which would give them plenty of room to expand.

John and Randy were helping George in this project with their wives helping Lillie and Sheila move items so that construction could begin.

In less than a month the Andersons had a newly remodeled home that should meet their needs for the foreseeable future. Lillie gave her family even more good news that she was pregnant again and was expected to give birth only weeks apart from Sheila, her sister wife.

However, George was a little overwhelmed at the news for while happy to have conceived more children, he now had two wives pregnant at the same time. He asked John for advice on how to handle the situation.

John chuckled when George first approached him with his problem. "Boy, I feel sorry for you. When they both get too big to do anything, whose going to take care of them plus you and the kids?"

George's face turned white as he grimaced, just now fully realizing the trouble he was facing.

John placed his arms around his shoulders and gave him a reassuring hug. "Don't worry, you're family and we'll lend a hand when you need help."

George gave him a weak smile and a sigh of relief as he shook John's hand.

Sarah had overheard the conversation and now came over to give George a hug and a smile of sympathy. "I'll stop by from time to time to make sure everything's okay, and I'm sure Jenny and Janet will check on them too. So don't worry about them, they'll be well taken care of."

"Boy, oh, boy, I got the new house ready just in time. I'm really going to need the extra room even sooner than I expected," George said with relief.

Like the Andersons, the Kit Campbell family had decided to use his third wife's old house for building materials because of his own family's growth. He had arrived with three daughters and his new wives had produced three more children with another now on the way.

About a month later, the townspeople were awakened from a sound sleep by a sharp earth tremor. John, at first, didn't know what was happening. Then it came to him they were experiencing an earthquake and he immediately started getting everyone out of the house.

The quake lasted for three minutes but seemed much longer. After the quake subsided, the townspeople went back into their homes for bedding to spend the rest of the night outdoors. They were afraid of aftershocks that were almost sure to occur, and before morning there were three more quakes, each almost as severe as the first shock.

The next day they saw a dark smoke flume reaching far into the sky to the northwest of Harding.

Sarah and her sister wives were flanking John with their arms around one another when Sarah asked, "Is that a volcano and how far away is it?"

John answered, "It looks like one but the distance is hard to tell. It appears to be a long way off, maybe as much as eighty miles."

John and the Town Council met to consider how the suspected volcano would affect the town. The wind was presently blowing almost due east which would carry the ash cloud north of Harding. Also of concern was how the ash and earthquakes might affect their water supply.

The townspeople checked their houses for damage but the worst damage they could find was with some mud caulking between the logs. They continued to receive aftershocks but they had been diminishing in intensity. The ash cloud was getting larger but so far the wind was still carrying it away from Harding.

The glow from the eruption could be seen clearly at night and was frightening to some of the townspeople; however, the children were fascinated. The third day of the volcano eruption brought an end to the quakes and the ash cloud now seemed to be abating. In another week, the only sign of the volcano was a wispy cloud above its peak. None of the townspeople had any previous experiences with volcanoes so they didn't know if this was the end of the activity or only a prelude to greater activity.

The wind had shifted slightly so they now received a rotten egg sulfur smell from the volcano. John sent scout parties to the west and east to the north/south trail to monitor any increased traffic from the Mutants fleeing from the volcano. The scouts returned after six days to report seeing about 200 Mutants heading south on the main north/south trail but no activity was noted to the west of Harding.

John discussed the enemy movements with the scout leaders and they all agreed that maybe the ash forced those Mutants to the north of Harding to move south away from this area. According to the scouts, the enemy showed no desire to enter the *Mick* trail when they caught sight of the grisly warning skulls. They had continued on south without stopping.

John, after considering their movements, thought it was even possible the people of Harding had earned a taboo label from these primitive people and the volcano eruption had only reinforced their belief.

John asked Jacob Bell, "Why would a volcano develop where no previous activity was known?"

Jacob just shook his head in wonder before answering. "From my recollections volcanoes were caused by shifts in the underlying tectonic plates and that since there were no other signs of past or recent volcano activity, he was at a loss to explain this eruption."

CHAPTER 30

Later that night John was relating to the family his conversations about the Mutants southern movement and Jacob's lack of understanding of why this sudden eruption occurred here when Sarah slowly smiled at him as she said, "Honey, why not put it down to divine intervention. Stranger things have happened to us since we arrived at this place."

He gave his wives a troubled look. "I'd never been a real religious person before we arrived here but there definitely has been intervention, whether it's by God or some other source. You know, God probably had a hand in making *The Messenger* when the cataclysm that wiped out most life on earth occurred."

Little Sadie frowned at her parents. "I told you before that the reason we're here was to start over."

John and Sarah looked at her in surprise before asking in unison, "How do you know this, Sadie?"

Sadie blinked her eyes at her parents then shyly smiled. "*The Messenger* told me the first time it visited us here. It said that we are to start over and repopulate this world in God's image. What does it mean, in God's image?"

The family looked at her in shock for a moment until Sarah hugged her tightly and answered, "It means that God wants people like us to repopulate the world. I think God also hopes we don't make the same mistakes our people did before."

John looked at Sadie for a moment before reaching a decision and then asked. "Has *The Messenger* talked to you before or since he gave you this message?"

"The last time it was here it told me that it would drive the bad people away so we could have peace. What's peace, Daddy?"

"It means no more wars with the Mutants, honey. How did it talk to you?"

"I heard it here," she said as she pointed at her head. She then stiffened and angrily looked at her father. "I'm not either making up this story!" She said defiantly as she pouted at him.

John looked at her in surprise as he knew he hadn't spoken those words of doubt. He tried thinking a question at her testing her ability to read his thoughts.

Sadie's face cleared as she smiled at him. "Yes, I can hear you, but you have to be close to me. I can hear *The Messenger's* thoughts from further off."

He then thought to her to try to talk to him without words. She looked surprised at the question, but then with comprehension at what her father was asking her to do, she tried to do a task she had never tried with him before. They just looked at each other in extreme concentration until finally John smiled at her and gave her his silent confirmation that her message was received.

Sarah had been watching this silent byplay between her husband and daughter with concern until John finally turned to her and announced that Sadie was a telepath.

She looked at him in astonishment, then blurted, "What do you mean, a telepath?"

"I know this sounds crazy but Sadie can hear what we're thinking. At least she can hear what some people are thinking."

He turned to Sadie and asked her if she can hear what everyone is thinking?

"No, I can hear what my brothers think most of the time and I could hear your thoughts after the last visit from *The Messenger*, but I've really not tried to hear anyone else. Oh, I just remembered I can talk to Ann Harding."

The boys were upstairs playing so he tried calling them downstairs silently. Getting no results he asked Sadie to try calling them downstairs without using her voice. Almost immediately the five boys came running downstairs wanting to know what she wanted.

John called them over to him and told them he wanted to play a game with them. He then asked John Jr. to think something to his brothers and see if they could hear the message.

He gave his father a surprised look and replied, "We can all talk to each other that way except Sadie can do it from further away. We can even soothe Ralph and Grace when they get cranky and we can hear their thoughts when they get hungry or want company."

"How about me, can you hear my thoughts?"

"Not very well, only when we're close like now."

His wives looked at their children in shock until Sarah asked, "Why didn't you ever tell us that you could do this?"

Sadie shook her head and answered, "We thought all brothers and sisters could do this and didn't think to ask the other kids if they could talk to each other without words. By the way, Grace's mind voice is really loud and she could be even stronger than me."

Candice gasped. "But she's only a baby. How can she talk to anyone?"

John pondered what had just been revealed and tried to seek a common cause. He turned to Sarah and asked, "How old is Jill Harding's child?"

She considered a moment. "She's about six years old, why?"

Sadie smiled at her father. "Do you want me to call to her?"

John gave her a relieved smile as he replied. "Not just yet. I think *The Messenger* is somehow responsible. Both William Harding and I have had direct contact with that entity and I believe it has changed our gene makeup so that our children have this gift. Both Mary and Candice had contact at our last meetings with *The Messenger* before they conceived their twins. Maybe that's why Grace seems to be a stronger telepath than Sadie."

Mary patted her stomach and smiled. "You mean these kids may turn out to be an even stronger telepath?"

"They might but it appears that the girls are stronger than the boys for some reason. When our kids start having their own children, eventually everyone may become a telepath. Just think, no one will be able to lie to each other and they'll be able to communicate with each other without speaking."

John turned to Sadie and started to ask her to talk to her friend Ann Harding when she smiled and said, "I already did and William Harding is now on his way over here with Ann."

When Harding arrived with his daughter he was confused and looked a little scared. John related what he had just learned about their children, including Ann, and then asked his input on what they should do about informing the rest of the townspeople. Harding still appeared dazed as he looked at the smiling children who looked as normal as any other child in the town.

He finally shook his head and looked into John's eyes. "I don't think the people are ready to hear this news yet. I think it would bring nothing but trouble for us and our kids. We need to impress upon our children that this is one secret that must not be shared with anyone who doesn't have the gift."

John turned to his children and asked them if they understood why the townspeople might be apprehensive about telepaths among them. Reading his thoughts, they all nodded their heads in agreement and then looked at each other glumly.

John Jr. went over to Ann and put his arm around her shoulders comforting her when he felt her mental distress and saw tears in her eyes. He gave her a hug and mentally told her that she wasn't alone and if she had any problems to just let him, his sister, or any of his brothers know. She tearfully looked up into his face and gave him a grateful smile.

John then told Harding about Sadie's message from *The Messenger* and why they couldn't pass this information on as coming from her without revealing how she received the message.

Harding nodded his head in agreement then laughed as he said, "You can't even say it came from you because you didn't mention it when *The Messenger* was last here."

"Well, our children know about it and they can pass the message to their children later on until eventually everyone will be aware of why we are here and who we think *The Messenger* is," John said with satisfaction.

Sarah looked thoughtful for a moment. "Honey, if our kids are telepathic why couldn't they have other gifts as well."

"What do you mean?" John said with a puzzled expression.

Mary interrupted excitedly, "She means can they lift things with their minds or teleport themselves or objects elsewhere?"

Sarah caught Mary's excitement as she nodded her head in agreement. They turned to Sadie with a questioning look who then pointed at a cup on the table. As they watched, the cup wobbled slightly then slowly rose above the table before moving toward Sadie until she snatched it from the air.

The boys looked at Sadie's performance in awe as they hadn't seen her do that before.

John picked her up and gave her a kiss on the cheek. "What else can you do, Honey?"

Sadie shrugged her shoulders as she smiled at everyone.

"I've only just begun to be able to do that. I don't know what else I can do."

John gave her a hug as he cautioned her, "Just make sure when you do any practicing that nobody other than the family is present. I can see where that little performance might scare someone else."

The boys crowded around her asking how she did that little trick? She smiled at her parents, and then asked her brothers and Alice to follow her upstairs and she would try to show them.

John looked at his wives and Harding in helpless wonderment as he shrugged his shoulders. "Well, we have taken precautions and now all we can do is hope that everything will work out. Eventually, the word is going to get out because children just can't keep a secret among themselves. We can only hope the adults don't take the news seriously."

The adults in the Bridges family continued to be in a confused state after the revelation of their children's ESP abilities. Sarah had resolved to be as helpful as possible to allow the children the opportunity to find out what their talents were and practice those abilities until they were at their peak and to only use their powers in a positive manner.

John and his other wives agreed with Sarah and they hoped as the children matured their talents would blossom. He even thought that maybe their gifts could be useful to the town sometime in the future. He and his wives discovered they also had some telepathic ability, evidently caused by their encounters with *The Messenger*, but nothing like their children's abilities.

The volcano seemed to have become dormant two months after its eruption and the Mutants appeared to have left the area either going north or south away from the ash cloud. Another bit of good news was that the *Mick* continued to flow past the town without interruption or contamination from the ash, so their water supply appeared to be safe. The volcano's adverse effects seemed limited to the enemy.

The town continued its established routine which mainly varied between work at the sawmill or the workshop and the daily hunting trips.

The twelve children, who had initially arrived with their parents at Harding, were now mostly young adults ranging in age from ten to seventeen. The three oldest young women were sixteen and seventeen years of age and were now looking towards marriage.

The three young women came to John's house early in the afternoon of a cool fall day. When he saw who was calling he thought to himself, Oh no, not again! He quickly recovered and invited them into his home while he called to his wives that they had visitors. They all knew the young women because of their almost daily interactions but Candice was more familiar with Marie, one of the young women from the North Settlement, and came over to give her a kiss on the cheek in greeting.

Honor Campbell apparently was elected as their spokeswoman and she blushed a little before beginning but seemed to gather her courage as she started talking.

"We three are now of marriageable age and want husbands. Since there are no single men our age we have decided to seek marriage into an already established family."

John looked solemnly into their anxious faces for a moment. "Honor, have you and the others discussed this marriage proposal with your families?"

Honor nodded her head. "Dad was against it last year when I was sixteen but he now realizes this is my only chance for happiness with a husband. Jan's family has finally come around as well now that she's seventeen but they want her to try for a family with only one other wife. Marie's only sixteen, but she has her family's permission to try to find a husband."

John looked over at his wives for help in this delicate matter. Sarah then asked the obvious question. "Have you women already thought about which men you would prefer for a husband?"

They all blushed again. Then Honor shyly said, "Jan and I would both like to marry into this family but we know only one can be accepted for a position and we both have a second choice. Marie would like to bid for my family."

Sarah looked at Honor and Jan closely and then with a slight smile asked, "Why our family as your first choice?"

"Why, because you're the number one family in the town. You and your sister wives seem so happy and have all been blessed with many children. Besides, John is so manly. Every girl has a crush on him." When Honor said the last part, her face suddenly blushed scarlet as John was standing right in front of her.

Sarah placed a hand over her mouth to cover her smile while John's face blushed in embarrassment, partly because he could hear both Mary and Candice giggling. With an effort, John composed himself as he tried to think of a reply that wouldn't crush their fragile egos.

"I appreciate your interest in our family but you can see that you're much younger than me or my wives. If I should accept another wife she would have to be mature in mind as well as body. If you two would wait a few years to mature, I would be happy to reconsider your request."

John then looked over at Marie who was squirming under his scrutiny. "You're going to have the same problem with the age difference with the Kit Campbell family. Most men, and especially their wives, wouldn't like a wife young enough to be their daughter." He looked at the three chastised and embarrassed young women for a few moments longer. "Why not bid for a family with a younger husband if you don't want to wait any longer. I think you would have a much better chance of getting accepted."

The young women looked at John's wives for confirmation who

slowly nodded their heads in agreement. The young women all looked disappointed but thanked John for his advice before saying their goodbyes and leaving.

After they had left, John sat down and breathed a sigh of relief. His wives sat down with him and congratulated him on his advice to them.

John nodded his head then glumly said, "Yes, it was good advice but I don't think all three will find husbands now. Maybe none of them will as there isn't that much to choose from. I bet we hear from at least one of these young women again."

The next day the three women were back asking John to make it known that they wished to join a willing family. He called a special town meeting for that evening and told the families of the desire of the three young women to become junior wives and for any family wishing to add to their family to contact him within three days.

There were no responses from the thirteen families. Apparently these young women were still too young to interest the older family members and the newlyweds were not yet interested in adding to their families. The young women came to his house at the end of three days to hear if anyone was interested.

When John told them that no family responded to their request, they looked discouraged but not surprised. Honor Campbell looked close to tears but while trying to hide her distress behind a smile, thanked him for his efforts and advice in this marriage attempt. He again advised them to wait another one or two years to see if the situation might change. Before they left, he reminded them that the first junior wives waited almost four years before the town would accept second wives.

CHAPTER 31

The three young women may have been rebuffed in their first attempt at marriage, but that didn't stop them from taking the indirect approach. In the next month John came home several times to find either Honor or Jan there talking to one or more of his wives. He asked Sarah about their sudden appearances at his house and she just said they were asking about married life, especially how multiple wives shared duties and stayed friends.

He was suspicious of their motives and asked Kit how Honor was taking her rejection from the families. Kit shrugged his shoulders as he looked into his eyes. "She told me about your advice to wait until she and the others matured more before trying again and honestly I was surprised at how well she took it. She just smiled and said there is more than one way to skin a cat."

John gave him a worried look as he asked, "What would your response have been if my family had accepted her bid?"

He gave John a wary grin. "Probably the same from you if I had accepted a bid from your daughter when she was seventeen."

John chuckled as he shook his head. "Kit, it might eventually come to that with the lack of eligible men for these young women but I'm going to hold off as long as I can. By the way, has Marie come by your house talking to your wives recently?"

Kit looked surprised at the question then smiled in understanding. "Yes she has. I was wondering what she was doing there since she had never shown such interest before. Why those minx, they're trying an end run by getting friendly with our wives first."

John nodded his head in agreement. "I wonder who the third family is there're interested in. I bet it's either Randy or George's family! In any case it appears they have a plan this time to let the families know and like them before trying again."

Kit nodded his head and looked at him with a worried expression. "I've got two more daughters that will be wanting to get married in a few years but at least there will be boys about their age by then. These three young women don't have that option unless they want to wait for the boys to grow up."

He then shook his head. "No, that's not being realistic. Their only real choice is to marry into one of the established families."

The two men looked at one another with worried expressions. John then made a decision to do something he had been avoiding doing for some time. He couldn't think of any way to avoid it any longer. He went to the Anderson house first, as Lillie had finally come around to accepting a junior wife. However, her situation was unique because Sheila had been married to Lillie's husband's twin brother.

After exchanging family news with Lillie and Sheila he asked, "Have any of the three young women interested in being junior wives come around here for friendly visits?"

They shook their heads in response to his question. "No, why are you asking?"

"You know that none of the families expressed any interest in taking them as junior wives. I think they are now trying to become friendly with the head wife of a prospective family. I would really like for you two to reconsider taking one of these women if they should ever try to reapply as a junior wife. In the meantime I'm going to ask Jenny to reconsider as well."

Lillie laughed and said, "Get real!"

As he returned home he thought that Lillie was probably right about Jenny but he still needed to try. When he entered his home, he waved at his wives as he headed for Jenny's bedroom. She met him at the doorway and invited him inside with a wary smile.

Before he could state his purpose, she interrupted, "John, you can forget about any pleas on behalf of those young women. I've got Randy and I'm not ready to share, at least not yet. Maybe I'll change my mind when I've got six children and need help around the house."

She then smiled and hugged him tightly. "I know these women don't have much to choose from but they're young and can wait a few more years."

"Well, just remember if it hadn't been for Randy you would be in the same fix as they are. By the way, have any of these women been over to pay you a social call?"

Jenny's face looked blank for a moment then she realized what he meant and slowly smiled. "Hey, that's pretty smart on their part. Both Honor and Jan have been over here asking questions from your wives and me about married life and raising a baby and asking if they could be of any help."

She winked at John and then laughed. "If we play our cards right maybe we can get some work out of these connivers."

That evening he told his wives what the young women were doing to try to ingratiate themselves into prospective families and his talk with Lillie and Jenny. He told them he didn't think either was ready to accept another wife into their families.

Sarah hugged him and said, "Don't worry, this problem will probably work itself out on its own.

The next day John decided it was about time to start his family's new house, assuming he could get his wives to agree on a floor plan. Mary was large with her pregnancy, at least as large as she had been with her previous twins at this stage. The other family members wouldn't let her do any strenuous work and most of it had to be from a sitting position. Because of this restriction Mary was starting to get cabin fever from the inactivity.

John placed the caulk board before her and asked her to work out a compromise in the new house's floor plan making sure they had ample room for future expansion. She looked up at him gratefully and then started trying various changes.

Their current floor plan was four large bedrooms downstairs with a large common room in the center and six smaller bedrooms upstairs. With Candice's mother, Joyce, along with Randy, Jenny, and their baby, the house was getting crowded. Now that the new twins were expected they needed at least two more rooms. Mary finally decided on a simple quick fix that would disrupt the family the least.

They would extend the depth of the house twenty feet which would allow two additional bedrooms downstairs and two large or four small bedrooms upstairs. They would also have to move the fireplace to the end of the house extension and would provide for a larger common area.

They would use the new cut lumber to provide siding, flooring, and new roofing for the house. The other wives approved the new floor plan and even demanded that the new siding be whitewashed to make it more striking in appearance.

The men began work on the remodeling of their house the next day by tearing out the back of the house. When the work began, other townspeople offered their help and the rubble was soon cleared away so that new construction could begin.

The work went quickly and three days later the new addition was complete except for the siding and roof. They then tore off the old roof and roofed the whole structure with new shingles. The last item was new siding for the entire house. When finished it would look like a conventional house, rather than a log home.

When the job was completed the entire town came to admire the finished product. John had even added rain gutters to divert rainwater into barrels for additional drinking water and for the women to wash their hair. This last feature was a big hit with his wives as they had started to wear their hair long again.

During this construction phase, both Honor and Jan had been over every day to help the household cope with construction. They seemed to delight in babysitting the younger children and helped Candice with the twin babies. Joyce assigned them babysitting duties when Sarah couldn't find work for them elsewhere. Jenny seemed to prefer Jan to Honor, but maybe that was because Jan made a point of being extra friendly toward her.

They both made it clear they were responsible individuals and willing to work at any assigned tasks. The children seemed to like them both as they sometimes entered into their games when time allowed.

Sadie, at almost nine years, was the only girl child in the family not a baby. She had been watching the two girls work in the household and enjoyed their company. She came over to Honor when she was taking a break and asked to sit in her lap. Honor was much taken with the precocious little girl and enjoyed her company.

Sadie looked into her eyes with a serious expression. "You're doing the right thing making friends with the children and the other moms, but Daddy still thinks you're too young for a wife. You don't look like a mommy to him yet."

Honor was at first surprised by Sadie's comments but realized that this was probably a correct assessment.

"When do you think I'll be old enough to look like a mommy?" She asked with a serious expression.

Sadie didn't answer for a few moments as she puzzled over her answer. "Maybe when you look like Jenny. Jenny and Randy both love each other so much they hardly think about anything else when they're together. My mommies love Daddy that way too so maybe when you get that way you'll look like a mommy to him."

Honor slowly smiled at Sadie and thanked her for her suggestions while thinking, how can I get him to love me if he still thinks I'm a kid?

Sadie hugged her and then said, "It's simple, don't act like a kid!" She then jumped off her lap and rejoined her brothers.

Honor sat in her seat in a state of shock. How had she known what I was thinking? She thought as she watched Sadie play with her brothers then was further dumbfounded when Sadie turned and winked at her.

When the house construction was completed the two young women continued to stop by every day to visit and offer their help. After three months of these visits the young women had gradually installed themselves into the daily lives of the family. The women of the family seemed to accept them in the role they were offering and the children accepted them in their role as a friend and sometimes babysitter.

Through Sadie they were aware of the young women's desire to become another mommy to them and seemed to watch their activities within the family with curiosity and delight. The children always seemed to have someone near the women observing their activities and reporting to the others anything unusual. Their mothers hadn't yet suspected the children had any inkling of the young women's purpose in their daily visits.

Sadie and Grace seemed to have a strong affinity for each other. As Grace got older and reached her first birthday she seemed drawn to Sadie. Candice first noticed this when Grace took her first steps, not towards her or one of the other adults, but instead toward Sadie. Sadie never baby talked to Grace but instead seemed to carry on a silent conversation with her based upon the facial expressions of both children.

Candice finally asked Sadie if she was talking to Grace silently.

She nodded her head. "Grace is really smart. She understands what you and the other people are saying but can't quite make her vocal sounds yet. Her silent voice is really strong, even the boys can hear her."

Candice smiled as her suspicions were confirmed. "What about Ralph, can you hear him too?"

Sadie frowned. "Not like Grace. They talk to each other and she says he's aware of what's going on around him but his silent voice is still weak. I prefer to talk to Grace."

Candice thought to herself, I've got to give my kids more attention. I bet I'll have them vocally talking in no time.

Candice was startled when Sadie nodded her head and smiled at her. Later that day she confided to Sarah what she had learned from Sadie about her twins.

Sarah smiled as she nodded her head. "I've always known that my Sadie was smart but apparently all our children must be geniuses."

Candice frowned in thought before speaking. "I suppose you realize we're going to have to work real hard to stay ahead of them. My Grace appears to be even smarter than Sadie and that's saying something."

Mary had another set of twins, a boy and a girl born on November 18th, year 10 N.B. of the new calendar, and was especially happy to have another girl in the family after so many boys. The proud parents agreed on Matthew for the boy and Nikki for the girl named after Mary's parents.

These twins brought the number of John's children to ten, seven boys and three girls, not including his adopted children, Randy and Jenny. Jenny brought the family news that she and Randy were expecting another child next June.

Lillie and Sheila each gave birth to twins within hours of each other. Lillie had boys and Sheila had girls born December 1st, year 10 N.B. of the new calendar. The boys were named Michael and Peter, and the girls were named Sue and Gretchen. This made Lillie two sets of twins with George, plus two children from her first marriage while it was Sheila's first children.

The Bridges clan had their hands full with so many births coming so close together. Although the Bridges family was helping the Andersons, Jenny also asked Honor and Jan if they would help with the new two sets of twins. Jenny had her hands full with supervising the care of the infants and helping Janet with the settlement's illnesses and new births.

George Anderson suddenly had two sets of twins in addition to the family's other children to care for. He was relieved when Honor and Jan agreed to help and under Jenny's instructions they soon took over their care. The young women both loved babies and enjoyed caring for the twins.

Prudence, at almost seven, was the oldest of the other children and assumed the duty as mother's helper for both mothers. She acted as their gofer and also helped take care of her younger siblings. She and Sadie were almost the same age and grew up together. So, it was not unusual for her to be in the Anderson household. The day Honor and Jan started helping out with the twins, Sadie came over and helped Prudence set up a routine helping her mothers and caring for her siblings.

When Sarah came by to check on the double set of twins, she was surprised that everything was under control except for George. He was so used to his wives taking care of him that he was lost as he watched Honor, Jan, and Prudence running the household.

Sarah put her hand on George's shoulder. "George, everything seems to be okay here. Come with me and I'll see that you get something to eat."

George looked around him almost in a daze before nodding his head and following her out of the house.

Sadie and Prudence couldn't silently communicate with each other, but Sadie could read her thoughts and could tell if she needed help. When Prudence needed help with her siblings she would read her agitation and would either come over herself or send one or more of her brothers to help her.

Lillie hoped she never again had to go through the chaotic disruption to her household caused by having two sets of twins delivered at the same time.

However, Sheila didn't seem to mind or care about the almost circus like activity surrounding the care of the two sets of twins. Her only concern was the loving care she gave her firstborn girls. At the moment they were her whole attention and except for noticing that Lillie's twins looked like their father, she concentrated on her own brood which was named after her two sisters.

Much to Mary's delight her new twins were very popular with their siblings. Their brothers seemed fascinated with the new twins especially with Nikki who always seemed to be a happy smiling baby. Both sets of her twins appeared to have lost much of her Japanese ancestry appearance.

Sadie also seemed drawn to Nikki even more so than her brothers. She would sit next to her crib and just smile at the baby for minutes at a time before moving on to other tasks. Mary assumed that Nikki was also gifted considering the attention Sadie was paying her.

Mary began to wonder why the girls seemed more powerful telepaths than their male siblings. Perhaps the boys had powers not yet developed. She made a note to herself to remind her sister wives to watch their sons for any future development of their ESP powers.

CHAPTER 32

The number of twin babies that the Bridges Clan have produced fascinated the residents of Harding. This fascination was caused in part because except for the Anderson's there had been no other twins born in Harding.

Both the Anderson and the Bridges households received more than normal interest from the other families as they came to visit and bring the mothers and babies gifts. Some townswomen even offered their help until they were assured the help already given by Honor and Jan was sufficient.

The town still posted sentries and periodically sent scouting parties out in search of any Mutants encampment within a twenty-mile radius of Harding, but they had discovered no activity since shortly after the volcanic eruption. John had made no further advancements in the town's defensive armaments since the threat from the enemy had been greatly reduced.

Instead, his efforts had turned to improving the living conditions of Harding. They had constructed a large water container at the town's center fed by a water line from the nearby *Mick*. Water from this container flowed into a basin used by the townspeople to wash their clothes. This also made the gathering of water for the individual uses of the townspeople that much easier.

John felt the town had achieved about all the advancements the people were able to do with the knowledge and materials at hand. They needed people with specific advanced knowledge and most of all they needed more young men to match with the young women coming of age. He shrugged his shoulders as he mentally placed these items on his wish list.

John decided the family needed a break from the demands of the babies and asked Honor and Jan to help Joyce baby-sit Mary's and Candice's twins while the rest of the family had an outing at the *Mick*. Mary and Candice at first were reluctant to leave their babies but after observing how well Honor and Jan took care of them under Joyce's supervision, they finally agreed to join the rest of the family.

The day was overcast, but no rain had fallen and the family was not going to let that spoil their long overdue outing. The women brought food for a picnic and while they were setting this up, the older children were the first into the water enjoying themselves in their play. The adults enjoyed watching them and soon they too shed their clothing so that they could share in the fun.

The whole family was in the water playing with the children and enjoying themselves when suddenly the wind increased in volume and *The Messenger* appeared overhead without the usual storm warning. The entity hovered over their heads for a moment then before they could react, its glow expanded to cover everyone.

The family members could see each other dimly through the bright light, with the children looking up into the light with rapt fascination including Alice who was being held by her mother, Jenny. Suddenly, John felt an increasing pressure within his mind as if it was expanding. This pressure continued for some minutes but never was so painful that it caused him to blackout.

Suddenly the pressure seemed to ease and finally ended as the light and *The Messenger* vanished. John looked around him to see the other adults removing their hands from their heads as if they too had experienced a similar sensation. The children were all smiling as if they had enjoyed the experience.

He was suddenly concerned for his wives but before he could say anything his mind received their warm reassurances followed immediately by his children's greetings and reassurance as he entered the world of telepathy. He basked in the warmth of their love as they each joined together in mutual understanding.

They eventually left the water and sat down together testing their newfound abilities with each other. Mary and Candice mentally checked on their children at home and found them in good hands and surprised to hear from them. They were curious to test their ability by reading Honor's and Jan's minds, so they tentatively searched until they both could read the women's surface thoughts but immediately disengaged when they realized they were violating their privacy.

Mary and Candice looked at each other in embarrassment then started to giggle as they realized the two women were only thinking how envious they were of them for having such pretty babies. Jenny was looking at Alice in surprise as she realized her baby already had thoughts and wants she was now able to communicate to her mother.

Sadie, who already could move objects, now raised herself above the group and started to fly slowly around them while laughing in delight at her accomplishment. Her twin, John Jr., watched her in fascination until he finally tried to match her ability.

She watched while he concentrated trying to lift himself off the ground. When it appeared that he was about to give up his efforts she entered his consciousness and showed him how she did it. He followed her lead and soon was following her high around the family while grinning at the others. It wasn't long before his other brothers were copying their siblings' abilities and were in the air playing tag with each other; however, after several near collisions John ordered them down to try other individual feats.

John had a thought that he should try teleportation. None of the other family members had tried this particular talent yet so he was curious if they had the ability. He informed Sarah what he was going to try but she smiled and pointed out his lack of clothing. John dressed quickly and then while she watched closed his eyes and concentrated on being at his front door. When he opened his eyes he was there. He looked around to see if anyone had seen him appear and when no one seemed to notice him he tried to contact Sarah.

He didn't know how to do this from a distance so he just pictured her in his mind and immediately began to hear her thoughts. He asked her to move everyone away from the picnic ground cover and when he received her confirmation that it was clear, he teleported back to them.

The family was amazed at his feat and asked how he did it. "Before I do that, I want you all to be careful that no outsiders can observe you experimenting. Also, I don't know what would happen if someone or object was in the space they were teleporting to. This needs to be checked out thoroughly before the children start experimenting."

He had everyone stand back as he pictured a nearby rock until he mentally felt its dimensions and then he pictured a nearby small tree and wished the rock to be there. He felt a mental bump just as if he had physically collided with the tree and the rock dropped down next to the target tree.

John grinned at the others. "Well, that relieves my concerns. No two objects can fill the same space. When I sent the rock to the tree it was nudged aside apparently with no ill effect to either object."

He turned to Sadie and explained how he had achieved the teleportation. She grinned in understanding and using the same rock tried to teleport it into a large tree twenty yards away achieving the same results. She then mentally picked up the stone and returned it to her hand while she considered what to do next.

John mentally urged her to use her ESP powers to hurl the stone at the white mark on another tree. They were both surprised when the stone left her hand and buried itself into the tree with a loud crack. Even better, it had hit the white mark on the tree.

Everyone looked at what Sadie had accomplished with sudden understanding. They each had the power to defend the town with their ESP abilities! John praised everyone for their efforts but again urged them to limit their ESP activities to inside their home or on outings such as today when they were alone and could practice their powers away from the townspeople.

Everyone was excited as they returned home later that day. They still hadn't fully explored the extent of their abilities but all except the babies had practiced with their ability to hurl objects as Sadie had initially demonstrated. She had even shown them they could hurl several objects at once at multiple targets; it only took more concentration.

Later that evening after putting the children to bed, the adults gathered in the common room for a discussion on what benefits their ESP abilities could bring to the town besides their ability to defend against a Mutant attack. John told the others he had some thoughts about their ability to teleport but needed to experiment more before he knew for sure that it would work.

They could move objects but they didn't know what their weight or size limits were. There were still too many unknowns about their powers so John suggested they break for the night and after more experiments with their abilities, perhaps they could come up with a plan. Later that night in bed he told Sarah his half formed thoughts about teleportation.

She smiled as he outlined his hopes. "When you're ready to experiment I'm coming with you. If you're going to risk yourself and for some reason can't return, I want to be with you."

They hugged each other as they mentally felt their love for each other surround and engulf them until they were both breathless with ecstasy. He kissed her lips and it felt like she was drawing him into her very soul. A bright light caressed his soul as they joined together in mutual bliss of mind and body. When they regained their senses they were still physically tightly joined together slowly coming down from the greatest lovemaking either had previously experienced.

Sarah softly kissed John in gratitude for their love for each other. She murmured, "I'm not letting you get away from me so where you go I'm going too!"

"Don't worry Babe, I wouldn't have it any other way," he said as he gave her a hug and then another kiss.

The next morning they were up early to do the family chores and make plans for the teleportation experiment. Mary and Candice came into the common room where Sarah was working and surprised her by both of them giving her a hug. She looked at them questioningly at first, then knew from their minds they had experienced some of what she and John had felt last night. She was expecting jealousy but instead found only shared love for their husband. She held out her arms to them and they joined together in a group hug of tenderness and acceptance.

Jenny walked in from her bedroom and found the three wives together in their hug. She hurried over and joined them until they finally broke apart with tears of happiness in their eyes. Jenny shyly smiled at Sarah as she confessed she and Randy had a similar experience once they felt her parents opening themselves to each other. It was a shared experience she didn't think was possible.

Sarah had a sudden thought, what if the children shared their parents' experiences? Their awestruck entrance downstairs almost immediately answered this question. Sadie ran to Sarah and tightly hugged her waist, looking up into her eyes and radiating her love for her mother. Then she nodded to her brothers as they followed her out to wash up for breakfast.

Sarah watched them leave with embarrassment that they had shared her most private feelings towards John but then rationalized that it was nothing to be ashamed about. They now knew how much they loved each other in the most truthful and honest way imaginable. The other women offered her their mental support and then vowed to try to block any future private explosions of emotion received from others. They would try to teach to their children this ethical block of other people's private emotions.

Later that day, John explained to the other family members what he and Sarah planned to do with long distance teleportation experiments and not to get too worried if they didn't immediately return. He entered Sarah's surface thoughts and visualized the exact location he wished for them to go then while holding her hand and with both locking this visual location firmly in their minds he wished them there.

Suddenly, they were standing before the fresh heads of Mutants blocking the *Mick* trail.

Sarah hugged him tightly. "You were right! We can go back in time to a spot we can remember."

John grinned at her then looked nervously around him. "Yes, we did it but we better leave here before any Mutants show up."

They then visualized the room they had just left with the others standing before them, and holding hands they both wished to be there. The family was startled when they suddenly reappeared but smiled when they realized the trip was successful.

Mary looked puzzled as she said, "You disappeared and then almost immediately you were back again. How could you do anything that fast?"

John then told them how they had visualized a past place, a place not exactly there anymore to test the theory that it was possible to go back in time to a place remembered and return to the time and place they left. They looked at him in awe and fear as they realized what his next planned trip must be.

CHAPTER 33

John and Sarah teleported to his Springfield, Missouri, home timed to arrive the day after his initial departure to St. Louis for his business meeting. They arrived in his kitchen where John looked at a calendar on the wall verifying the correct month and year.

"Well, let's see if we can determine what the date is."

John led the way to his bedroom where there was a bedside clock that showed the time and date. After checking the date John grinned and said, "Well, we're still batting a hundred percent."

Sarah immediately started looking through his house, curious about her husband's single life, but stopped when she realized John was watching her with a smile on his face.

"The first thing we need to do is get you some local clothing for this time period." Pointing at her deerskin dress.

She looked at him in surprise and then down at her clothing in shock. "I forgot how we must look. I must look like a witch!"

He grinned at her as she hurried to the bathroom to look at herself in the mirror. He came up behind her and placed his arms around her waist as she rubbed her cheeks with a worried expression on her face. "Babe, you look more beautiful to me now than you did when I first met you and that's saying a lot."

She looked at his face in the mirror and slowly smiled at his sincerity. "You do too but to anyone else you'll look like a hippy with that beard. Let's clean up and I'll see if there's anything of yours I can wear until I can buy some clothes of my own. There's no point in my going to my house for some because nothing will fit me now."

He was thankful that he had some shorts and shirts that he hadn't thrown away when he gained weight because they were now only slightly too big for him and would work for Sarah as well until they found the clothing they needed for the next part of their plan. It was still summer in this time period and they needed something appropriate.

John and Sarah still had their credit cards and he planned to withdraw all his cash from his checking and savings accounts. Between their credit cards and his cash they had about $80,000 to purchase what they needed before returning to Harding. But first Sarah wouldn't budge until she had a complete makeover at the mall beauty salon.

Three hours later they both left the salon looking like different people. Sarah's hair was cut in a short easy care fashion and after a facial and manicure she felt she could now face her old world. John had decided to join her in getting spruced up and had his hair razor cut and his beard trimmed short. They then went shopping for clothing to fit a middle-aged businessman and his wife.

They left the mall dressed to accomplish their next task but first they decided to eat at the best restaurant in Springfield. They hadn't eaten all day and were suddenly ravenous for prepared food. After dining on Maine Lobster, baked potato, salad, and dinner rolls with real butter, they decided to return to John's house and get some rest before tomorrow's busy day.

Although they went to bed early, they didn't get any sleep until late that night. Their new appearances were a sexual turn on for each other and they reveled in the luxury of a comfortable bed in which to make love. They finally fell into an exhausted sleep in each other arms until the rising sun awakened them.

They quickly made preparations getting ready for their trip and after a joint shower that took longer than it should have and a cold cereal breakfast they were ready. They looked at a recent picture of the MIT Campus they had gotten from a bookstore at the mall and concentrated on the main entrance to the Administration Building with their arrival timed for late April.

The transition was flawless and they soon were inside the building seeking at least two adventurous young people who had their needed qualifications. When they walked up to the receptionist she was impressed by their striking appearance. They were both close to six feet in height, slim and fit, but without the definition working with weights would give and were heavily tanned. She was drawn to him by his rugged handsome appearance but the beautiful woman at his side gave her reason to pause. They both extruded an aura of confidence and the impression that they belonged together.

John told the receptionist they would like to interview several senior students for a special position involving relocation to a foreign setting. He then gave her the specifics of the major fields of study he was interested in and asked how soon the interview could take place.

She then asked the name of his business and he gave her a business card he had prepared for this purpose with his name, address and telephone number in Springfield. In case someone should call that number he had left a message on his answering machine identifying itself as Harding Enterprises.

She gave them instructions on which halls of study and dorms where he could post his notices and she would arrange a room where he could hold the interviews the following day. After getting the interview room time and location they searched for a nearby Quick-Copy store to make the notices.

They had the notices made and posted before noon and then teleported back to Springfield where they spent the remainder of the day deciding on the best approach in interviewing the students. The following day they slept late and did some shopping before returning to the MIT campus timing their arrival shortly before the appointed time.

The interviews started at 5 P.M. and when they arrived at 4:30 P.M. there were already six students waiting for them. They immediately started the interview process at first together to hone their skills then as more students arrived they conducted separate interviews.

By the end of the session they had made appointments with eight students for final interviews the following evening at the nearby Holiday Inn. Their first interview was with a couple that planned to get married after graduation. John told them that the job was challenging and involved updating a primitive community to today's standards and had an annual salary of $40,000 with a two-year commitment required.

The couple, Joe Edwards and Denise Jacobson, seemed excited about the prospects and asked about the living conditions. When told there was no indoor plumbing and that housing would have to be constructed with the help of the other residents, they conferred together for a few minutes before asking when do they leave? Their graduation was for the following month and a pickup time and location was agreed upon.

That evening they had three more male students agreeing to their proposal and would be collected at the same time and location as the first couple. The next morning they teleported to the University of Idaho.

They arranged a similar interview process seeking majors in agricultural, wildlife, and natural resources. Using the same recruiting incentives John and Sarah acquired four more students to be picked up at about the same time as the first group from MIT. The agriculture student, Sam Williamson, suggested they bring along two crates of chicken pullets and three rolls of chicken wire to use as a starter batch for the settlement they were going to develop.

The next day John and Sarah teleported to arrive at the appointed time at the University of Idaho. They rented a school bus to pick up the students because the students needed lots of storage room for their possessions they were bringing to last for the next two years. In addition, John and Sarah had also made a few purchases that took up additional storage space. To try to avoid contaminating the future Earth with unwanted bugs they sprayed the bus thoroughly.

Once everyone was aboard John slowly drove down the street while Sarah distracted the four passengers. When John was sure no one was watching he teleported the bus to a normally empty business parking lot on a Sunday morning near the MIT pickup point. He then drove a few blocks and stopped to pick up the MIT students. After everyone was aboard John and Sarah told the students to close their eyes and pray for their safe arrival. They then jointly wished the bus to go to the Harding town center.

They had timed their arrival for early morning one day after their departure from Harding. Dawn was still two hours away and the sudden darkness had completely confused and disoriented the students. John and Sarah urged them off the bus and into their home. They quickly lit a lamp and led the group into the common room where they were soon greeted by Mary and Candice.

His wives were awakened by his mental voice when he first arrived and had only time to dress and meet the students as they entered the common room. Randy and Jenny soon joined them after being awakened by the noisy group of people from old Earth.

His other wives were giving both him and Sarah mental happy greetings for their safe return and approval of their new chic appearance but then questioned who these new people were. John held up his hands and shouted for attention. Everyone suddenly fell silent and looked at him questioningly.

"Why don't you 'all take a seat and I'll explain the situation," John said in a calmer voice.

He then told the nine students the story of how he and other residents of Harding had gotten here and his guess of what had happened to the world many years in the now past. He explained how he and his family had recently been given ESP powers and his decision to bring people from their past to help rebuild the new world.

The students looked at him with doubtful expressions until Sadie surprised them by floating down to sit cross-legged on the table. John then pointed out the Idaho students and asked them to tell where and when he had picked them up. When they told the others they had left Moscow, Idaho, only a few minutes before picking up the second group in Cambridge, Massachusetts, they were spellbound.

Joe Edwards stood up uncertainly and spoke with a cracked voice. "You're saying that our world was destroyed maybe eons ago and we have been chosen to repopulate the world and begin again?"

"Yes, except we were not given any choice in the matter, while you people can decide whether to stay or go. I had you give a commitment for two years but I was not completely honest about where you were going to bring a primitive community up to your standards. However, this is even a better goal. Just think of it! You have a chance to build a new better world without the strife and dog-eat-dog competitiveness of our old world. Give me one week here to show you what we have done with only our two hands in the past ten years before you make a decision to stay or return to your old world."

Jack looked at Denise for a moment before she nodded her head whereupon he then asked the group for a show of hands to give John his week. He and Denise immediately held up their hands and then slowly one-by-one they all raised their hands.

Sarah hugged John with delight at their success in getting them to at least consider staying. By this time the entire family had come downstairs and were greeting the new arrivals. The children were especially attracted to the strange clothing the newcomers were wearing and they in turn were fascinated with the skin garments they were wearing.

His wives were trying to be good hosts and asked them if they would like water or anything to eat before they met the rest of the townspeople.

John then explained to the new arrivals, "Most of the townspeople are unaware of my family's ESP abilities or that I planned to seek outside help. When they see the bus they will want answers to questions that I'm afraid might destroy our attempt to start over again. At first light I plan to ring the general alarm bell to call the townspeople together but first I'm going to confer with our town's founder to bring him up to date."

He pointed to his wives and suggested, "My wives will get you what you need until I'm ready to introduce you to the townspeople but until then try to get some rest because I'm thinking this is going to be a long hectic day."

John knocked on Bill Harding's door quietly hoping to not wake his neighbors. It was a few minutes before Janet came to the door with a candle lighting her way. She was still half asleep and expressed surprise to find him there so early.

"I've got something important to tell Bill that couldn't wait until morning."

Janet was at first startled by his appearance but then nodded when she saw the concern on his face and invited him into her house while she went for her husband. Harding's junior wife, Jill, lit some lamps for better light in the common room.

Harding came out of his bedroom still in the process of dressing himself, asking, "What's the problem?"

John then related to Bill and his wives the powers *The Messenger* had given him and his family and what he had decided to do to ensure that the town would survive. "I've now gotten second thoughts about what the townspeople would decide to do if they had the opportunity to return to their old world."

Harding looked at John with shock as he told his story and then with concern as he realized this revelation changed everything now that it was possible for the people to return to their past lives.

He pondered what John had told him for a few moments then put his arms around John's shoulders and gave him a hug. "I told you *The Messenger* had something in mind for you! You didn't even give a thought to returning yourself, did you?"

John looked at him in surprise. "You've got to be kidding! If I were to go back I'd lose my family. Besides, I've had the greatest time of my life here. None of my family wants to return to that world." He then gave a short laugh. "I do want some technology and people who can help us advance faster than the normal learning curve, and I especially wanted some new young men who would be available for our young women to marry when they come of age. I definitely didn't want to start the practice of taking a teenage bride because there wasn't anyone else available!"

Harding nodded his head in agreement. "Now, if we can convince our own people they should stay we should see the beginning of a new age. Let's go back to your house so that I can meet these prospective new settlers of yours."

When Harding and his family entered John's house the household suddenly became quiet as John introduced Harding as the town's founder and then his two wives and daughter.

One of the two new black men arrivals pushed forward and shook his hand and then smiled as he commented, "Sir, I'm happy to find that this isn't a mostly white settlement. I was beginning to have second thoughts about staying here."

Harding slapped him on the back. "Son, this is a mixed race settlement and we have stopped thinking of each other in colors. Take John and me; we both have wives of a different race than we are. We married them because we fell in love with them and they with us. We do have a shortage of available men so I hope you single men stay if for no other reason."

Harding turned to John and asked, "Did you tell them about the Mutants?"

With a grimace, John shook his head. "No, I was hoping to get to that later, but I guess now is a good time. When we first arrived in this world we found it populated by a race of mutated humans who attack and eat anyone outside their own tribe. We have fought several battles with these people until finally they developed a superstitious fear of us. We haven't seen any of them for about a year now. Before this stalemate we rescued another settlement to the north that had lost over half their number to the Mutants. We have lost several men and a woman to them as well and our only consolation was that they have lost ten-fold of our own losses."

He sadly shook his head as he recalled past battles and losses. "Well, that was in the past. With our new ESP powers we can defeat any force they should throw at us. Even better, since they're a superstitious lot they'll probably turn tail at the first demonstration of our powers." He looked outside and noticed that it was now light enough to start the most eventful day they had ever had in their short history. Turning to the others he smiled as he said, "Game time!"

CHAPTER 34

John walked to the workplace and rang the general alarm bell and waited for the excitement to begin when the people saw the bus parked in the town's center. Harding walked up and stood beside him as the townspeople gathered first to ogle the bus then to wait until they received an explanation.

Word passed quickly and soon everyone was gathered to hear what had to be a great story. The townspeople were asking each other what did the bus's presence here mean and the many possible answers when John held up his hand for silence.

He told them first about his and his family's new powers given to them by *The Messenger* and his discovery that he could teleport himself not only from place to place but also back in time. He let them accept that bit of news and its ramifications before he continued.

The townspeople looked at him in shock for a few moments then Jack Peterson's face broke into a smile as he shouted, "You went back to our time and returned with that bus!"

John smiled at him. "Yes, Sarah and I went back to a time just after I had left home and was stranded here. We recruited some new settlers and brought back some items we needed here."

He let this news settle in their minds before he continued. The townspeople started whooping with joy and slapping each other on their backs and hugging and kissing each other until they finally wore themselves out and turned back to John.

He looked at the townspeople with a serious expression as he addressed them. "Before I bring out the new settlers, I want you to consider what this means to each and every one of you." He put his arm around Harding's shoulder as he continued. "Bill and my family have already decided on staying. You now have the opportunity to return to your homes if you so desire but before you decide please remember what you have here and what you will lose if you should return to the old world. I have given the new settlers one week to make up their minds and you have the same time so think hard before you decide."

John gave a signal for the new arrivals to join him while the townspeople watched as the nine young men and women approached them. Honor and Jan were especially eager as they caught sight of all the handsome young men and hugged each other and giggled as they pointed to one especially handsome man in the group.

John had the MIT graduates introduce themselves first along with their major field of study followed by the graduates from the University of Idaho. Sam Williamson had a wicked sense of humor and he used it to dispel any remaining tension among the townspeople. After telling several jokes which had his audience laughing, he pointed to the bus and spoke seriously.

"John was complaining about the town's diet, so I suggested adding some white meat which we brought with us in the bus."

The townspeople immediately ran to see what the bus contained. John opened the bottom storage doors of the bus and pulled out the crates of chickens along with the chicken wire. He looked around the townspeople as he asked for volunteers to raise the chickens.

The Crandall's spoke up loudly and raised their hands excitedly. They were the oldest couple in the town and seemed ecstatic they could do something useful for the community.

Jake Crandall said with emotion plain in his voice, "We've raised chickens before and know how to take care of them."

John called him forward and slapped him on the back. He turned to the townspeople with his arm around Jake's shoulders and spoke to the crowd. "This first group is seedlings for a future crop of chickens. We'll only eat these when they get too old to lay eggs or we have too many roosters. The next offspring's are going to be our food crops. Jake here will ration out the chickens as they become available so you better make good friends with him."

Sam Williamson held up his hand for attention. "It's possible we might be able to add other species of animal life to this world but first I'll need to discover what kind of plant life is available they can use for food."

He turned to John and asked him when he and the other agricultural and wildlife experts could have a tour of the local plant and animal situation, while the MIT graduates expressed the same desire to see the town's technical advances. John called over Jacob Bell and George Anderson to show the MIT people around while he, Randy, and Jack Peterson took charge of the U of I people.

Before he joined the others on their tour, he asked Sarah to take charge of unloading the bus of the graduates' belongings and arrange for them a place to stay until they knew for sure who was going to remain. They then took the Ag graduates west along the *Mick* trail showing them the types of flora and describing the different animals they had found.

They were very interested when told there were no longer any insects. Sam Williamson started looking at the trees and foliage with a new perspective since everything growing had to be self or wind-pollinated. He also noted that there were no birds to carry seeds from place to place. He would have to be very careful what was introduced to this ecosystem as there were no natural predators other than man.

When they returned to Harding, John showed them the vegetable garden the town had started and expanded as more wild varieties were found. They were especially interested in the irrigation system they had built to service the garden. It was mid-morning when they returned to the town center and found the other new arrivals were still observing the operation of the workshop.

Jacob Bell had explained that everything was constructed from his and others' memories of actual experience or what they had learned in schools. They had used stone tools until they could forge metal objects.

Joe Edwards shook his head in wonder as he considered what they had accomplished. "You went from the stone age to steam power in ten years. I think you've done pretty good with what you knew and the materials you had to work with."

John nodded his head in agreement. "That's the main reason I've brought you here. We've hit a dead end and we need expert advice on how to continue to advance. Without adequate trained manpower we can't mine and refine the metal we need to build more elaborate machines to manufacture the things we need. I could teleport back into time and buy these items but we have limited cash resources."

He looked at them thoughtfully for a moment before speaking. "Why don't you get settled and meet back at my house later this afternoon to discuss this further. Your baggage is stacked over by my house and Sarah will tell you which family each of you will be staying with until a final decision is made on whether or not you stay in Harding."

They looked relieved to be taking a break and started walking toward John's house. After everyone had located their baggage, Sarah called their names and indicated which house they were assigned to. When only Joe Edwards, Denise Jacobson, and Sam Williamson were left, Sarah told them that they were to stay with them.

She looked at Joe and Denise with a smile on her face. "I've got the space to put you two separately or together; it's your choice."

Denise blushed scarlet then shrugged her shoulders as she smiled at Sarah. "Joe and I were going to get married as soon as we could find a preacher so I guess living together here won't be a problem."

Sarah hugged her shoulders and walked her away from the others until they were far enough away so they could speak in private. "If you want to get married, John as Mayor of Harding can marry you and Joe. However, that marriage is only legal here. Unless you and Joe have already lived together why not wait until you both have reached a decision about staying here before committing yourself."

Denise looked into Sarah's eyes with new respect and then kissed her on the cheek. She then walked up to Joe and pulled him aside. "I want a separate room at least until after we make a decision to stay then later we could get married either here or back home."

Joe slowly smiled and gave her a hug and kiss. "I was going to suggest that myself if you felt any misgivings."

The guests then followed Sarah into the house and to their assigned rooms upstairs. Sarah chuckled as she showed them their small rooms. "This is where our children's rooms are and don't be surprised if they come visiting. They are all very intelligent and curious about new things and you're at the top of their list now. In addition, Candice's mother's room is up here where she can watch over the children better."

She hesitated a moment before adding, "You should know that we're all telepaths but generally we prefer not to invade other people's privacy."

The three guests looked at each other in shock at first then Denise asked with an embarrassed expression on her face. "You can read our thoughts?"

"Yes, it's embarrassing isn't it? When we first realized we had this ability we found it embarrassed us as well and we resolved not to do it unless it was necessary. We then developed a block to not hear other family members' private thoughts and emotions. The children have a bigger problem keeping this power in check but as they get older they're understanding its logic."

Sam blurted out, "What other powers does your family have?"

Sarah shook her head slightly and frowned. "It's so new to us we really haven't explored our powers fully. So far we've found that we can read other people's minds and with our own family we can merge even our personalities. We can move or hurl objects and teleport objects or ourselves. Who knows, we may find we can do other things as we experiment."

Later that afternoon the other graduates joined the three at John's house for a discussion of possible solutions to the town's problems. They broke into two discussion groups, one technical and the other agriculture in nature.

John went from one group to the other answering questions and monitoring their progress. At the end of the day the technical discussion group had come up with some solutions, but the big hurdle they faced was Harding's small population. They needed a population of at least 1,500 people to achieve their goals.

John suggested he could try additional recruiting but that would require a permanent office on old Earth until they got the people they needed. Denise Jacobson interrupted, "I think you will need such an office in any case to find and send the needed materials back to this time so that construction could begin on the town's infrastructure. The immediate goal we have agreed upon is to provide electric power, water, and sewer to every structure. We are planning to use a combination of water and sun generation to achieve electric power and that would require materials from old Earth to accomplish these tasks."

John nodded his head then gave a hopeless sigh as he wearily sat down. "I've got enough money to begin the project but we'll need close to a million dollars to do what you suggest. Do you have any ideas on how to raise that much money?"

Joe Edwards smiled at him. "I think it will cost two million dollars before we're through, and when you add in the agriculture and wildlife supplements it may come closer to three million."

He placed his arm around Denise as they smiled at each other. "We both come from rich families and if we can convince our fathers of what we're trying to do, I'm sure we'll get the money we need."

John felt like a huge load had been lifted from his shoulders at hearing this news. "I know of one sure way to convince them and that's bringing them here!"

He and Sarah made plans to leave the following morning to return to old earth with both Joe and Denise. Sam Williamson then gave his group's suggestions, saying they had factored in the geographic location of Harding and the townspeople's recollections of the past ten years climate changes in determining the types of crops and fruit trees suitable for this location.

Sam gave John a list of the crops and fruit trees that could grow under the present conditions and another longer list if certain birds and insects were added to the environment. He said that these particular birds and insects wouldn't hurt the existing ecosystem and would be necessary for certain plants and fruits. He wanted to add other animals but had decided to test the grass for its nutrition value before proceeding any further.

John told the two groups before they started bringing any materials or agriculture products here they needed to get a commitment for funding of the project. If all went well they should get this sometime tomorrow. He then told them the townspeople had arranged a feast for them tonight so they would have a better idea of what their best meals consisted of.

After his meeting with the advisory groups he called his family together to inform them of the progress made and their plans for the future. Since he and Sarah had already made themselves presentable in the old earth style of grooming and clothing, it made sense they be the ones to return with Joe and Denise to arrange financing.

Mary and Candice chided him for his feelings of guilt but told him they expected to be included in future trips so they too might enjoy the benefits of a complete makeover. Jenny laughed as she too wanted to see what the old Earth had to offer.

Early the next morning the four joined hands and teleported to Joe's family home. They timed their arrival before Joe's father left home for work. Without knocking, Joe used his key to enter and led the others into the kitchen where his parents were eating breakfast prepared by their live-in cook. They looked up in surprise at his greetings and then rushed over to welcome their son and Denise while giving John and Sarah questioningly looks.

They were all invited for breakfast after Joe explained they had something important to discuss with them. After they finished eating, George, Joe's father, invited them into his study where they could meet in private. Joe related his and Denise's recruitment by John and Sarah and the problems experienced at the foreign location and wanted his advice on how best to achieve their goals.

George Edwards looked at John and Sarah doubtfully for a moment. "I'll need to visit the site myself before I could give any advice; how long would it take to get there?"

John chuckled. "Not long at all. But first let's all hold hands and pray for a safe trip."

He got up with the others following his lead and with all holding hands they teleported to Harding. George's mouth was open in surprise and wonder as he looked around at his surroundings.

Joe hugged his father's shoulder as he reassured him. "Dad, this place is located in what used to be Georgia and we're now several thousand years in the future from where we just left. The trip didn't take so long, did it?"

George, still a little white-faced and shaken, looked at John for an explanation. John then told him the story of how the settlement had first started and gave a short history lesson to the present time of the problems they had to overcome. He then told him of their new recruits and their recommendations that required a large capital outlay that they didn't have.

George listened to John's story without interruption until he was finished then pondered for a few minutes while looking at his son's earnest expression and his surroundings. "You can move at will between here and our time period?"

John nodded his head. "Recently my family was given this gift and other powers and I decided to use them to repopulate the world and start over; hopefully, avoiding the problems which caused the old Earth's demise."

"Who runs things here; do you?"

"I'm the Mayor, but the town council makes all the major decisions. At least they did until this happened. I made the decision to recruit others with the manpower and skills we needed."

George looked at John closely before responding. "Are you going to keep these people hostage here to fulfill your own agenda?"

John gave him a lop-sided grin. "No, everyone was given a week to make up their minds on whether to stay or return to old Earth. The town founder's family and mine have already decided to stay. I've decided to continue to recruit until the town has a strong enough base population to survive."

George suddenly held his hand out to John. "I think you're the man to get the job done and I'll make sure you get the help you need."

He then turned to Joe and Denise. "What are your plans? Do you intend to stay or return home?"

Joe looked questioningly at Denise who smiled and pointed down at her feet.

"Well, we agreed to stay two years when we were recruited even though it wasn't to a location exactly as advertised so we'll stick at least that long. Do you think you can convince Denise's father to help as well?" Joe said with a hopeful expression.

George looked at him with a gleam in his eye. "You didn't think I was going to foot the entire bill did you? I'll expect to be able to make on the spot inspections periodically with your mother so we can make sure you're all right. But, let's get back to my office so we can make the financial arrangements you need to get started on your projects."

Before they left, John told the project groups to start making a specific wish list to be filled upon his return. They then held hands and teleported back to George's office where they informed him of their immediate needs and the estimated cost of the project.

George immediately arranged an initial one million dollar line of credit for Harding Enterprise requiring the signatures of John, Joe, and Denise for each draw through John's Springfield, Missouri bank. Since he already had a base of operation in Springfield, he would run his purchases and recruitments through his old CPA Office.

After making a stop at John's bank in Springfield setting up the Harding Enterprise account, John and his two recruits teleported back to Harding where they made plans on what materials they should purchase first. After compiling a list from both groups they all boarded the bus to teleport back to old Earth. Also on this trip were Randy, Jenny, and Mary who would help teleport various members of the groups to the purchase sites.

CHAPTER 35

Upon their arrival in Springfield at John's CPA office, Sarah took Randy, Jenny, and Mary on a shopping trip for new clothing and makeovers, while the rest of the party made telephone calls arranging pickup sites for the various items they were going to purchase this trip. John was looking at the long list of plumbing items when he realized that the project needed plumbers to install much of the equipment.

He had a sudden thought. His neighbor, Gene Underwood, was a retired plumber whose wife had died recently and was now complaining he had retired too soon when he sold his business. Maybe he would be interested in starting a new project. With that thought, he called Gene and asked him to come to his office for a business proposal.

After Gene's arrival at his office John used the same recruitment proposal he had used with others about updating a primitive settlement which included bringing them inside plumbing. He showed him the items they were planning to purchase and asked if they should make any changes. Gene asked what was the water source, the size storage tank they were going to use, and how many structures were going to be served.

John pondered his questions for a moment. "Gene, the settlement is served by a small steady fresh water river for a settlement of sixty people which is expected to grow to 1,500 within a short period of time. What size of storage tank do we need?"

Gene looked at him for a moment as he rubbed his chin. "You know that a project this size is going to take at least a year to complete depending on weather conditions at the site. Who is doing the contract?"

John smiled at him as he replied. "Why you are, if you think you can handle the job."

Gene snorted then smiled with a twinkle in his eyes. "I thought so. I no longer have any heavy equipment, but that can be rented. I'll need a crew of ten men. How about recruiting men from the settlement, can they speak English?"

At John's nod, he excitedly continued with a purpose he hadn't felt since his wife died. "How soon can the supplies you ordered be at the site?"

"Well, we haven't ordered anything yet. We wanted to make sure the contractor approved of our choices before placing it. We plan on using solar energy to heat each structure's water supply instead of the usual hot water tanks. We have already determined what roof mounted units we prefer. You need to make sure we are ordering the right size and number of pipes. But before you make up your mind I want you to visit the site and see the lay of the land."

Gene grimaced. "I don't have a valid passport."

John got up from his seat and took Gene's hand. "You won't need one for this trip."

Gene blinked his eyes in disbelief as he realized he was no longer in John's office. "What did you do?" He stumbled slightly as he regained his balance and taking a deep breath he looked slowly around the town center observing its activity and the structures in place.

Placing his arm around Gene's shoulders John walked with him toward the *Mick*, explaining where they were and what they intended to do.

Gene seemed to take the news at face value and when they arrived at the stream he was all business. "I'll need some pieces of heavy equipment. How are you going to get it here?"

"I don't think I'll have any trouble. You gather the equipment and I'll arrange for it to get here. You'll also have to arrange to have fuel for their use available for transport as well. As you can see we have manpower available but you need to bring what skilled men you need. We'll arrange the financing of the rental units and construction materials and provide housing and food for you and your men. What is it going to cost us to complete the job?"

Gene thought for a few minutes as he considered the lay of the land and soil composition.

"The job might get done sooner than I expected. I'll price it at $200 per day for each of my men and a flat fee of $200,000 for myself. Since we're going to be stuck here for some time, I'd like a 25% advance and the men's salary is to be placed in their deposit accounts monthly. I think I can get by with only four men from Springfield, but that may change after I get to know your people."

John nodded his head. "I think we have a deal, but I'll check first with my backers. I'll let you know later today so if it's a go you can go ahead and make your arrangements."

Gene nodded his head as he took a last look at the settlement then John teleported them back to his office where he told Gene to wait at his desk while he consulted with his advisors. Joe and Denise nodded their acceptance after John explained to them the agreement he had worked out with Gene and then they had him sign for their first draw of $500,000 so they could start making purchases.

He then gave Gene the okay to start things from his end and told him his $50,000 advance would be given to him when he and his men were ready and to let him know when the equipment was ready to be moved to the site.

After Gene had left the office Joe brought him up to date on what they had done in his absence. They had appointments tomorrow to take delivery of items from four different locations across the country. They included equipment needed for electrical generation, plumbing, and several species of birds and insects.

He was going over the list when Sarah arrived with two gorgeous women and a much different looking Randy. If Sarah hadn't been with them he would have had a hard time recognizing them. The hairstyle they had selected for Mary emphasized her exotic Eurasian features and the tight oriental style dress she wore seemed to caress her voluptuous figure so that combined they created a package so eye catching that even other women noticed.

Jenny's appearance was also dramatically changed. Her auburn hair was done in a short style designed for easy care and with makeup sparingly but expertly applied she was a thing of beauty; especially when wearing a form fitting dress that displayed her sensual figure without revealing anything.

Randy was dressed in a smart suit and his ragged looking beard was gone. His hair was trimmed in the current style and altogether he presented the facade of a young handsome businessman.

Sarah was grinning at his openmouthed expression of surprise. "I do good work, don't I?" She whispered in his ear as she hugged him.

He noticed that the other men in the room were looking at the new arrivals with lustful expressions as well. He good naturally censured them, "Watch it boys, these are married women!"

Whereupon, Denise jabbed Joe in the ribs when she realized he was staring at the women just as hard as the other men.

John went over to Mary and had her turn around slowly so that he could get the full benefit of her transformation. He kissed her forehead as she blushed with happiness that her appearance was attractive to her husband.

"Mary, you were beautiful before but you have crossed over to world class in this outfit."

He turned to Randy and Jenny and shook his head slowly as he walked around them. He then stood back from them and suddenly grinned. "Sarah did you ever see such a handsome looking pair. They'll both have to look after each other to keep all the men and women off them."

Jenny gave Randy a hard look as she exclaimed, "I better not catch any women sniffing around him or fur will fly."

John chuckled at Randy's look of surprise and fear at Jenny's outburst then asked Sarah if she had gotten any work clothes for them as they were starting the pickups tomorrow. At her nod he told them of his plans for each of them. Each group would rent a van truck at the pickup points and after delivery in Harding they would return the trucks to the rental location. Sarah would accompany Sam and his people to retrieve the birds and insects while the rest of the family would split up to accompany each of the other three groups.

To celebrate their accomplishments the group decided to eat at one of Springfield's finest restaurants before retiring for the night at a hotel. John and his wives would return to his home and would meet the others at his office the next morning. When they arrived at his home that evening, Sarah couldn't wait to show Mary around much to John's amusement.

The women then went into the bedroom to change clothes and then model them for his approval. After they had modeled three changes of clothing he was getting bored which was not lost on his wives. When they came out of the bedroom this time they were both wearing something from Victoria's Secret that immediately got his attention and his blood racing.

Mary chuckled as she noted his sudden interest. "I told Sarah that we needed to get something for our husband to enjoy and I see we picked well."

They posed seductively before him while dancing just outside his reach until, with a smile he joined them where he was slowly disrobed. When he was nude, he started removing their clothing a piece at a time until with playful laughter his naked wives ran into the bedroom closely followed by him.

At first light the next morning he groaned as he moved sore muscles getting out of bed while Sarah and Mary laughed at his discomfort and pulled him into his large shower. At first they just let the hot water soothe their bodies but then they each started massaging one another until they got relief. When they got out of the shower his wives used towels to rub his body until he cried uncle. John then took a towel and with a playful gleam in his eyes did the same for them.

He and his wives arrived at his office a little late and found that everyone else was waiting for them. He apologized for his late arrival with a flushed face while his wives wore a satisfied expression. Each group had to leave early enough to arrange for the rental of a truck to carry their purchases with Sarah's group scheduled as the first to leave. About an hour later everyone was gone from the office en-route to their various destinations.

Later, when John's group arrived in Harding with their cargo only one group hadn't arrived but they appeared before they could unload their truck. The townspeople crowded around curiously looking at the growing pile of equipment and crates of birds and insects.

Sam and his agriculture group started releasing the birds as the townspeople watched in awe as they flew away into the nearby trees. He then gave a large container of earthworms to the gardeners with instructions to release them in the town garden. Most of the insects were bees whose hives were placed at various locations around the perimeter of Harding with instructions to the children to leave them alone unless they wanted to be stung. This instruction was necessary because they had no previous experience with insects.

Before they took the trucks back to their rental places, Sarah pulled John aside and told him about Joe and Denise's plans to get married and suggested they do it on old Earth before taking up residence here. He nodded his head then asking Sarah to join him, they walked over to where the couple was working.

John asked them to join him for a moment as he had something to discuss with them. He placed his arms around their shoulders before asking. "What kind of wedding did you want, large – small, or just your immediate family?"

Denise looked at him blankly for a moment but then it finally dawned on her that she was being asked about her immediate marriage plans. She looked over at Joe and pulled him aside while they discussed what they should do.

After about ten minutes, they came back over to them with smiles on their faces.

"I want to be married at home in my mother's beautiful flower garden with just our family and a few invited guests. We already have our marriage license, so it shouldn't take very long to get a dress and make the other arrangements," Denise excitedly blurted.

John nodded his head as he smiled at the couple.

"I can send you home now if you like to start the arrangements. When will we know when to send Joe?"

Sarah laughed. "Honey, we can send him at a predetermined date. Will a week be enough time?"

At Denise's nod, they agreed on a Saturday, September 18th for the wedding and Joe would be sent back to his home the previous Tuesday so he could make his own arrangements.

John looked at the excited couple for a moment. "Do you want a honeymoon before returning to Harding?"

They looked at one another, each blushing in embarrassment. "We would like to return here if you had a house available for our use for a working honeymoon."

Sarah gave them both a hug and told them they would make arrangements for a house for them before they returned.

Denise with tears of happiness in her eyes said, "John, would you and your family attend the wedding?"

He turned to Sarah who nodded her head. "We'll need to make arrangements for the babies in the family but that shouldn't be a problem."

He then had Denise picture in her mind the front of her home so that he could teleport her there. When he had a good lock, they found themselves in front of her home.

Sarah excitedly told the rest of the family about their invitation to Joe and Denise's wedding who then became anxious as they realized many of their family didn't have the proper clothing. They then made a decision to exclude those children who were less than seven years of age which meant the only children attending would be the first sets of twins of Sarah and Mary.

Honor and Jan agreed to help baby-sit while the family was gone, while wistfully commenting they wished they were going too. Sarah promised to bring them back something nice for helping them out.

Sadie and her three siblings were ecstatic about actually seeing old Earth. They had heard fantastic stories of their parent's old home that they now were actually going to see for themselves. They decided to arrive at old Earth two days before the wedding so they could acquire appropriate clothing for those in the family who needed them and give the younger members a chance to experience the old world.

At the end of the decision period only two older couples from the townspeople decided to return to old Earth, explaining they wanted to be near their grandchildren in their declining years. All of the graduates elected to remain for at least their two-year commitment.

John teleported each couple to their old home timed to arrive a day after their initial departure. He counseled them not to mention their experience in Harding as no one would believe them and might even think they were losing their minds.

George Randall, one of those returning, stated with a humorous grin, "Maybe so, but I can tell my grandchildren some tall tales they have never heard before."

John had the townspeople start construction on two new houses to accommodate the new recruits and construction crew which were expected to arrive soon. In the meantime he had the graduates move into one of the vacated houses while Joe started fixing up the other for his and Denise's use. John teleported him home the next day so he could begin his own wedding preparations.

Three days later John's family arrived back in Springfield where those that needed clothing could shop. While the rest of the family was busy shopping he returned to his office where he found a message from Gene who asked him to return his call.

When called, Gene replied, "John all arrangements have been made for the men and equipment and all that is needed is for someone to sign the lease agreements and take delivery of the equipment."

John replied, "I'll be over in a few minutes to take you to the various locations to complete the paperwork and I'll need to inspect the equipment and their placement to determine if I can teleport them from that location or if they needed to be moved first."

They were at the first equipment location within fifteen minutes and after completion of the paperwork John viewed the equipment's location. They were on a back lot behind a security fence away from view of the street which was perfect. He told Gene he would come back later tonight and teleport them to Harding.

They then went to the next location where the remaining equipment was located and decided he could move this equipment the same night.

After returning Gene to his home, he told him to have everyone at his office at 9 A.M. a week from next Monday for transport. He then gave him a check for his $50,000 advance and advised him to deposit it tonight.

Gene nodded his head and smiled. "I've already made arrangements for my bank to take care of my recurring bills until I return and this advance should be more than enough to cover my expenses. If there were any problems, I told them to leave a message on your answering machine; is that alright?"

"That's fine. If there's nothing else I'll meet you at the appointed time."

After shaking Gene's hand and saying good-bye, he teleported back to his office where he worked on several drafts of a recruiting advertisement he planned on putting in the newspapers starting next Monday. About two hours later his family returned with their purchases and happy stories about their experiences at the mall.

Candice was the last to enter the office and when John saw how she was dressed he could hardly believe his eyes. Sarah and Mary had performed a miracle in transforming her appearance from a tall dark pretty woman into another gorgeous creature, a match for his other two wives. He had her turn slowly around for him as she welcomed his admiration and his kiss when she finished her turn.

Lillie's appearance had been altered for the better as well. It seemed all the women in the Bridges Clan were stunning. She excitedly showed him the packages of presents she had gotten for her husband and Sheila and their children.

They dropped off the purchases at his home and then had a great meal at a local restaurant before returning home. The next morning the children, after hearing about pancakes, persuaded the others to have a leisurely breakfast at a pancake house before spending the day in Branson at an amusement park.

When they teleported to Branson the four children couldn't believe their eyes at the sights of the many rides and people dressed up in costumes. Their first ride on a roller coaster left everyone breathless, even the adults who had ridden one before.

That evening, after returning to Springfield, the children enjoyed their first eating experience in a hamburger restaurant and for dessert they had their first ice cream. Returning to John's home the family prepared the exhausted kids for bed. The three boys bunked together in the spare bedroom while Sadie and Lillie shared a large couch. John and his wives shared the queen-sized bed. Since there was no room for Randy and Jenny they stayed at a nearby motel. John told them to be ready to leave at 10 A.M. and they would all leave from that location. Everyone was tired from their long day and were soon asleep.

CHAPTER 36

They arrived at the portico of the large Colonial style home near Boston at noon with the wedding scheduled to start at 1:00. They were met at the door by a butler in formal uniform and after giving their family name, were shown into the patriarch's den. Donald Jacobson, who headed a banking empire in Massachusetts, turned from the large window he had been gazing through in deep thought when he heard the Butler announce them.

He looked at the family standing before him with a penetrating gaze. The head of the Bridges family presented an imposing figure, especially when flanked by what must be his reported three wives who were each of a different racial background. But what next drew his attention were the two young sets of twins who were watching him as closely as he had initially focused on John and his wives. The three young adults next caught his attention. Two were obviously a couple the way the attractive woman was holding the arm of the young man. The remaining woman easily matched the beauty of the other women of the family.

John broke the tense mood by introducing his family members to Mr. Jacobson. Donald shook each of the adult's hand as they were introduced but when it came time to introduce John's first-born twins, they introduced themselves mentally; followed by a similar introduction by the second set of twins.

Donald Jacobson's surprised expression soon turned to humor as he winked at Sadie who was obviously the leader of this group of children. "Very impressive indeed. John, I was told a little of what to expect but your family is none-the-less quite breathtaking, especially your charming wives."

This last comment caused his wives to blush at the unexpected complement and John to smile his own agreement. "Yes, I'm a very lucky man and you can see why I didn't even consider returning to my old life here."

"I didn't hear what your profession was, do you mind telling me?"

"Not at all, I was a CPA. When I was moved forward in time I was on my way to meet a client. Sarah and her family were caught in the same time rift and that's how we first met."

He pointed to Randy and Lillie as the rest of Sarah's family and then described how they found Jenny along the trail after the Mutants had massacred her family. Jacobson wanted to know about the current status of the Mutants since they had been so violent in the past. When John told him of the last battles and the strategy of superstition they had used against them that seemed to still be working, Jacobson nodded his head with new admiration for this unassuming man.

Jacobson shook his head slowly as he smiled. "Your whole family has ESP powers?"

"All but Lillie who was not present at the last visit by *The Messenger*. However, her children may all have some powers since Prudence, her oldest, has already demonstrated her ability."

Jacobson asked John with a serious expression on his face, "What's your take on this *Messenger*?"

Before answering, he looked at his wives and then turned back to Jacobson. "Our first experience with the entity was quite scary for all of us and painful for me. After our subsequent encounters it became clear that it was benevolent toward humans and gave us warnings of Mutants gathering to attack and once asked the Harding townspeople to save another settlement from being wiped out by the enemy."

John pointed to Candice as he related she was one of the survivors from that settlement where the Mutants killed almost half their people. "Before my family received the last visit by *The Messenger*, I had wished for a solution to the town's stalemate in technological advancement and the shortage of unmarried young men. This shortage of men was becoming a serious problem for the town."

He shook his head as if to rid his mind of these thoughts and continued, "As to the origin of *The Messenger*, my guess is that it was born from the tragedy that caused the destruction of old Earth. I believe it wants us to be the fountainhead to start over and hopefully not make the mistakes our people did before. If I were a more religious person I would think of it as an Angel sent by God to help us."

Jacobson seemed shaken by John's insight but then placed his hand on his shoulder while he shook his hand. "I can see that you're a good man and the fact that you've taken the time to arrange this wedding proves that you care for other people. If you need anything, just let me know and I'll try to get it for you. But now, I think it's time to get outside and join the wedding party as it's almost time to begin."

The bride was dressed in a beautiful white gown and the wedding went without a hitch in her mother's idyllic garden setting. After the reception and farewells, the wedding presents were placed in a pickup truck Donald Jacobson loaned them for their use in Harding. While the newlyweds were saying their farewells to everyone, John's family teleported to Harding taking the truck with them.

When John arrived later with Joe and Denise, the truck had already been driven to their new home and was being unloaded. The townspeople had gathered to welcome the newlyweds and cheered when Joe carried his bride over the threshold. They were just beginning to realize their lives were going to be changing again as improvements were going to be made in their living conditions and more settlers would begin to arrive.

John met with the town council where he outlined the proposed improvements and new settlers that were expected to arrive in the future. He suggested they also draw up plans for streets as the town would soon expand beyond its present boundaries. He recommended the present town center remain as the town's hub with all streets leading into it. He then presented the town with a manual typewriter, paper, and ledger books so that they could begin keeping records.

The council members were somewhat overwhelmed at the changes they had to assimilate but under John's leadership they began to tackle the many tasks before them. They asked for a volunteer to act as the town clerk and secretary to the council. Several townswomen volunteered for the job which was eventually filled by Jill Harding who had worked as a town clerk on old Earth.

The townspeople had finished the two new houses and were in the process of building beds, tables and chairs for the construction crew expected Monday. The council, at John's suggestion, then ordered the construction of a city hall for the town's government to operate from and to have an enclosed place to hold town meetings.

When he returned home that afternoon to the welcome of his family, he asked Candice if she would give him a massage as he was keyed up from all the decisions he had made that day. Candice's eyes lit up with happiness as she had him lie face down on his bed after first removing his shirt. She then straddled his body and began to use her strong fingers on his shoulder and back muscles until she had all the tension knots worked out and he had fallen asleep.

Candice took the draft for the recruiting advertisement John had given her to review and made some changes that she then shared with her sister wives who also made some changes until they were finally in agreement with the final draft. The notice stated they were seeking skilled individuals over 25 years of age who were seeking a change of pace and would be willing to relocate to a foreign English speaking settlement where they would have the opportunity to participate in a new beginning.

After his short nap, John reviewed the changes his wives had made to the recruiting notice and nodded his head in agreement. "I'll take this back to old Earth and arrange a mailbox through one of the private mail collection businesses - then have the notice posted in the Springfield newspaper and through its ownership chain at several of the larger newspapers across the country."

John chuckled as he visualized the volume of mail he was hoping for. "I'll probably have to make several trips back to collect the mail and bring it to Harding so that our recruiting committee can make selections for face-to-face interviews. I wonder who we can we get to serve on the committee?"

Sarah thought for a moment then smiled. "The head of every family should sit on the committee. It could be either the husband or a wife depending on their availability. That way every family has a say in the initial selection but a smaller group should make the final decision for each candidate."

"I'll run this by the council and see if they'll agree. I think the council should make the final choices but I don't foresee any problems."

John then met with the council and got their approval for the planned selection process. After relaying this news to his wives, he went back to old Earth to place the newspaper advertisements. Later, John returned for the bus and teleported forward a week to collect any mail that might have arrived from his advertisements; however, he had received so much mail he needed it boxed for him. After loading the mail aboard the bus he drove to his office to meet Gene and his construction workers.

John was killing time in his office after making arrangements with another local CPA firm to take over his business accounts when Gene arrived with his four construction workers. Gene introduced them to John who then had everyone load their belongings and equipment in the storage compartments and board the bus. The workers seemed in a festive mood as they were anticipating making some good money at this project. John teleported the bus back to Harding while Gene was talking to the workers about conditions at the construction site. He then drove a short distance and parked next to the construction equipment.

The new men were surprised and confused momentarily when Gene told everyone to get out of the bus because they had arrived at their destination even though he had already briefed them on what to expect. When they had debussed, Gene told them to check out the equipment while he and John discussed where they should start first. John then pointed out the house where the crew would be staying while they were here and they could go ahead and store their belongings before starting work.

Gene said they would need cement mix, sand, and gravel before they could pour the base for the water tower and he had already arranged for its prepackaged delivery to a vacant lot in Springfield. Before they teleported back to old Earth to retrieve the materials, John asked where he wanted it stored.

Gene pointed to a small rise northwest of town near the *Mick*. "Just put it next to that rise and we'll move it from there to where it's needed."

After John teleported this material and fuel for the equipment back to Harding, the crew began its work. John left Gene to supervise his crew while he returned home to deal with the first batch of recruit mail. After sending out word to the heads of each family to help cull the rejects from the mail, they helped him carry it from the bus to his home.

John couldn't believe the big response his ads had received. They evenly divided the mail among the families with the first cut to be for the maybes and rejects. Not surprising the rejects were about three to one of the maybes and by mid-day they had finished the first cut. After a lunch break they divided the maybes up and started over and by the end of the day they had twenty prospects they had identified for the council to review.

The next day he took this list to his old Earth office and sent letters to the prospects to begin arriving in a week's time at his office in Springfield. He then picked up his mail and returned back to Harding. The mail was only about half the volume as the first day; however, the rejects were reduced considerably and by the end of the day they had another forty prospects.

John realized then there would be no way they could construct new housing fast enough to support so large a group of people. He could bring in tents, but as he visualized a long row of tents becoming a tent city slum he realized they needed a better solution. In addition, this large volume of newcomers would overwhelm their food supply.

John finally decided to continue the selection process but would delay the new arrivals until the housing and food supply problems had been corrected. They would need additional manpower for both farming and construction of housing so those people with this background would be the first selections to arrive. He met with the council and outlined his selection plan and the delay of the majority of those selected until they had made proper arrangements for them.

The council agreed and then showed him their new city plan for future development with the major streets all leading to the town center much like a hub with spokes leading out from it. Realizing the problems that most old Earth cities had to overcome from early narrow streets, these plans involved wide boulevards for the major streets.

He told the council that the MIT group had suggested they consider building a small dam to use as a water source and for better electric generation. He suggested putting the dam downstream about five miles where the topographical features would better support a dam and lake.

Bill Harding smiled as he had a thought. "The lake can be another food source for us as well as recreation for the townspeople. I can't remember the last time I went lake fishing."

At the council's urging he met with the engineering graduates to plan what they needed to construct the recommended dam. Since this was a larger water generation project than first envisioned, they could install larger generators. This brought the cost up considerably so he consulted with Joe and Denise about its funding before they preceded any further.

The larger dam project would add another $Two million to the financing. Joe thought the project was sound, but he would need to consult with his and Denise's fathers before they proceeded.

They both agreed to be ready for the trip back to old Earth the next day. They needed to bring their financiers a progress report anyway and John could retrieve any mail on their way back.

They had gone back though the maybes and added another five people with construction and farmer skills to add to the fifteen already chosen for immediate interviews. He had originally thought to schedule the prospects to arrive six per day so that the council wouldn't be overwhelmed. However, he needed these twenty people interviewed sooner, so when they were returning from their visit with Joe and Denise's fathers, he telephoned each of the prospects to meet him at his Springfield office at 9 A.M. in two days.

He would use the bus to take this group along with any mail to Harding. They needed to be exposed to the reality of Harding for them to fully realize what they'd be doing for the rest of their lives.

Upon their return from old Earth, John was optimistic they would receive the financing for the dam and Joe and Denise's fathers seemed happy with the progress to date. They even expressed a desire to visit Harding with their wives to observe firsthand the progress they had made. However, John was sure that part of this desire to visit Harding was to ensure that their children were happy and comfortable in their new surroundings.

CHAPTER 37

John brought the twenty prospective settlers in the bus from old Earth on schedule. When they left the bus they looked around with unbelieving eyes at the busy townspeople and construction crew at work who were wearing a mixture of modern clothing and animal skins. He asked them to follow him to an area out of the way of the workmen and their noise so he could explain about the history of Harding.

When John finished telling Harding's history and its future plans, he asked if they had any questions? There was a moment of silence then a woman standing in front of the group asked, "Does everyone here have teleportation powers?"

"No, but eventually I foresee that all our children will have some form of ESP. At present only my family and I have these powers, but as my children marry these powers may eventually extend to the entire community," John replied.

Another man wanted to know what defenses were in place against the enemy. John told him about the sentries placed outside town to give them warning if any Mutants approach and informed them about the weapons they had available. He added if a new threat does occur his family's ESP abilities will be more than a match for any attack force from the enemy.

John then asked if anyone had second thoughts about immigrating to Harding and if so please step forward and he would send them back to old Earth now. There was some discussion among family members but eventually everyone decided to stay for the selection process.

John told them the review process by the town council might take several days so arrangements had been made to house them with the townspeople; however, those who have passed the final cut would eventually receive permanent housing. John then picked the first couple and had Sarah show them to where the council was meeting. He then escorted the remaining settlers around the town, showing them the new construction, their town garden, and the sawmill which was busy turning out lumber for the expected new construction demands.

John placed six people he expected to be interviewed later today in the vacant new house while he escorted the remaining people to the various homes where they would stay until the interviews were completed. The interviews went faster than expected and by the end of the day the council had finished half of the first group and had completed the interviews by the end of the second day.

Only two people were rejected because of their drug problems. The eighteen remaining settlers consisted of six married couples and six unmarried young men. Their skills were almost evenly divided between construction and farm workers which fit the community's needs perfectly. The racial mix included White, Hispanic, and Black individuals with no racial group representing a clear majority.

The following day Sam Williamson took the eight farmers northwest of Harding where he deemed the valley soil was best for crop production. He consulted with them about the best types of equipment to acquire for the crops they wanted to grow and the number of acres to put under cultivation. They decided on a medium size farm tractor that could handle a variety of implements. The farmers selected a tract of grassland at the bottom of the valley which had about 100 acres and then as the need arose they would clear adjacent land.

John teleported Sam, two other farmers, and himself back to Springfield to purchase the necessary equipment and seed. Sam also wanted to acquire some fruit trees and more worms to place in the cultivated field. After they returned to Harding with their purchases the farmers started preparing the new field for seeding.

The other new settlers were already in the process of constructing another new dwelling. Plans were to leave the walls open for wiring and include a kitchen and bathroom in all new construction. His wives had met with the senior wives of the other families on the matter of getting new bedding for everyone. They wanted double bed mattresses for every married couple and single bed mattresses for everyone else.

John slowly shook his head in exasperation. "That's going to be a lot of mattresses to bring back."

Sarah nodded her head with a patient expression on her face. "Yes dear. By our count we need sixteen double bed and thirty-seven single bed mattresses with the bedding to go with them."

John nodded his head in thought, but then replied, "Honey, why don't you and maybe two others come back with me tomorrow when I get the mail and we'll bring back what we need."

The next morning, John, Sarah, Lillie, and Sheila teleported back to Springfield and returned later to Harding with a large Van Truck filled with the requested mattresses and bedding. The women of Harding descended upon the truck, sorting through the variety of bedding, selecting what they wanted while the men carried the mattresses back to their homes. John had brought along extra mattresses and bedding which would be stored until needed.

That Saturday, the town gave a dance in honor of the new settlers and construction crew. It was a chance for the new people to become acquainted with the townspeople and make new friends. One of the purchases John had made for the townspeople was a battery powered CD player. He had brought sufficient music for several types of dancing which became an instant hit.

John noticed that the three young women who had previously come to him seeking marriage into established families were aggressively seeking dances with the new unmarried settlers. He thought, maybe that problem will soon be solved.

At the end of the evening, Mary was persuaded to sing a song that enthralled everyone before the dance ended.

The following week the council was asked to consider building a church and a schoolhouse for the children. One of the new settlers was a lay preacher who had conducted the previous Sunday services for the townspeople. John chuckled to himself as he thought; it looks like the town is really starting to grow now.

Sam Williamson wanted to introduce some dairy and beef cattle as a test case. They would graze different pastures which would have to be fenced to keep them out of the woods. John knew of two such valley pastures with water sources that had steep hillsides that would require fences only on each end. After Sam inspected the two pastures he agreed they should work perfectly.

The other farmers started building split rail fences while John and Sam teleported back to Springfield to purchase the livestock. Once in Springfield, they went to a nearby livestock auction and arranged for their purchases to be held in pens until they were ready for transport. While Sam watched over the livestock, he checked on the status of the temporary enclosures he had requested before leaving Harding. He found they were completed which meant he was able to move the animals to

Harding. Later, when the fences were completed he would move them to their respective pastures.

They brought back ten heifers and one bull calf for each of the Hereford and Holstein breeds. After the fences were completed and the livestock moved into their pastures, Sam added a salt lick to each pasture and then left them to forage on their own.

Sam suggested that John inspect the field under cultivation where he showed how they planned to divide it by the type of crops they were planting. The wheat crop would be planted within thirty days, but for now they were concentrating on vegetables they could grow all year in this climate zone.

They had already planted the fruit trees in a line running north and south so that the prevailing winds would help in cross pollination and had moved two of the bee hives to the north and south edges of the field. In order to ensure the bees had enough pollen they also planted the edges of the fields in clover.

John complimented Sam and the other farmers on their hard work when he was approached by another of the Idaho graduates about the possibility of introducing old Earth deer, elk, and game birds.

John asked, "Has any consideration been given to their impact on the local ecosystem and the fact that they would have no natural predators except man?"

Sue Gates, their wildlife management graduate, immediately made a passionate plea for their introduction. "The deer and elk would roam free searching for food and would not adversely affect any particular site. The local miniature deer shouldn't be affected as they stayed within the protective forest and the game birds would forage for different kinds of food."

John nodded his head then asked, "What about the deer and elk foraging in our garden and vegetable fields?"

Sue blushed as she realized she had overlooked that possibility. "Maybe we can fence in the field so they won't be a problem," she said hopefully.

John chuckled as he placed his arm around her shoulders.

"Don't worry, you've made your case. We'll just place the deer and elk far enough away so they won't be an immediate problem. By the time they reach us we should have electric power available for an electric fence that should keep them out of the fields."

Sue grinned as her confidence returned and asked, "How soon can we start the introductions?"

John and Sam laughed at her eagerness. "Well, first give me an idea of when you need to introduce some natural predators and what, if any, effect they would have on the local deer," John said with an earnest expression.

Sue grinned at him as she pulled some papers out of her pocket that gave him detailed information on project population growths until she got to the page with the information he had asked for. "It should be at least five years before the population is stable enough to allow any harvesting and ten years before it would be large enough to need the use of a predator such as cougars or wolves. Since the local deer keep under cover and the deer and elk would be available, I see no great threat to them from this source. Besides the Mutants will be hunting the deer and elk too and another predator may not be needed."

John chuckled and then said, "In that case, let's get your wildlife tomorrow and start releasing them."

The recruiting mail still was coming in but at a reduced rate, and the council was doing daily interviews and accepting most of the final cuts sent them by the town review board. The people accepted were given specific pickup dates a week after their acceptance; however, they would not be retrieved until the town was ready to receive them. The housing and food supply had to be adequate and they would be retrieved in the order of the skill needed.

The next skilled people to be retrieved were electricians when housing became available for them. There were now six newly constructed houses plus the homes already occupied that would require their services. The town had grown to a point that it was decided to build a bridge across the *Mick* and expand south. Clearing this area would provide the lumber needed for future construction.

The cattle seemed to be thriving and the farmers were now looking for additional pasture to move them before the present ones were overused. The deer and elk were widely dispersed to the west of Harding while the game birds were released nearby to better monitor their progress. The Prairie Chicken and Grouse mating calls were soon part of the afternoon sounds the townspeople enjoyed.

Joe and Denise's fathers, who had also agreed to arrange for the construction contract and purchase of materials, approved the financing of the dam project. John had to make plans to provide housing and food for the construction crew of about twenty men and women. The construction engineer had reviewed the site, made her surveys, and expected the final plans to be ready in a month with construction to start shortly thereafter.

Two months later Joe and Denise's parents made their first joint visit to inspect the construction projects. While Denise showed their home to Joes and her mothers, John escorted the men to the construction sites so they could observe what had been accomplished. The water tower was finished and water mains had been run through the town center with ditches starting to be dug to individual houses. The   dam project was starting to take form and in another two months should be ready to accept the generators. He then took them to the new farming operation which was now showing the results of their labors. The livestock were doing well and the first planting of vegetables would soon be ready for harvesting.

Later that afternoon they rejoined their wives who had been entertained by John's family. Joe and Denise's mothers were impressed by the size of his large family and how happy everyone was. His three wives explained how they shared household duties and how they loved all their children no matter who their birth mother was.

Marjorie Edwards was especially taken with Sadie, John's oldest daughter. Joe was her only child and she'd always wanted a daughter. Sadie knew the woman's wishful feelings for a little girl of her own and went out of her way to encourage their friendship. Janet Jacobson on the other hand had two other daughters besides Denise and had secretly wished for a son. She was almost overwhelmed by the number of little boys in the household.

They were also impressed that Candice's mother lived in the household as well. Janet Jacobson asked Joyce, "How do you get along with your son-in-law and his other wives?"

Joyce looked a little surprised at the question but then smiled as she answered, "They asked me to come live with them, I think, because they felt sorry for me being all by myself after my husband was killed. But, I love children and it was a blessing for me to be around my grandchildren and help take care of them."

Sarah heard the discussion and laughed. "Joyce is another mother to our children and we don't know what we would do without her. She doesn't meddle in the other duties of the wives and is a delight for everyone in the family."

Joyce was embarrassed by this praise. She had tried her best to fit into the family and this high praise from the head wife of the family was her validation of the effort she had made. She knew John had gone out of his way to make her stay here as pleasant as possible but the children's acceptance of her as one of the family was what was the most rewarding for her.

Janet Jacobson noticed the house didn't have indoor plumbing and asked how the family bathed as they all appeared well washed.

John answered this question with a laugh. "I hope we don't scandalize you, but we as a family all go down to a private spot on the

Mick to bathe and swim together."

Janet got the point but asked with a snicker, "You mean in the all-together?"

"Yes, but I'm not sure how much longer we can do this with all the new people arriving. I think we'll have to abide with the majority before long and start wearing swim suits."

Marjorie looked at the children for a moment before commenting. "Well, the children seem remarkably well adjusted and I don't think seeing others in the nude has harmed them a bit. In fact, the forgoing of this particular taboo seems to have strengthened their character development."

Sarah nodded her head in agreement, but added, "That, and the fact they can communicate between themselves silently. If there is a disagreement there is no hiding a grudge until it festers; but instead, it is worked out on the spot until everyone is satisfied. I have to admit my children are the happiest in Harding."

That evening Joe and Denise's parents had a quiet meal alone with their children where they caught up on their personal news both on old Earth and at Harding. Joe and Denise realized that the news from old Earth no longer held their interest that it once had. Their old friends seemed about as far away as the years separating them.

Marjorie Edwards asked, "What medical facilities do you have in Harding?"

"We have skilled nursing available which has provided excellent midwife services to the many births without any problems," Denise responded.

"However, now anybody with serious medical problems can be teleported back to old Earth for treatment. John said that so far no doctors had applied for admission to Harding but that may change at any time. We have obtained medical supplies for minor injuries and illnesses."

George Edwards was silent for a moment as he considered an idea. "I wonder if a retired doctor would be interested in such a posting," He said almost to himself.

Joe looked at his father with a smile on his face. "I don't think we need to worry about a doctor anymore now that I see that determined look."

They all laughed as they knew that once George set himself a goal he wouldn't rest until it was accomplished. George smiled self-consciously as he nodded his head in agreement.

Denise jabbed her husband in the ribs with her elbow as she half jokingly commented, "We better tell John to start building a medical clinic so that it will be ready for our new doctor."

The next day John teleported the older Edwards and Jacobsons back to old Earth. They had seemed impressed with the progress made and even more by the changes in their children. Before leaving, George Edwards told John about his plans to recruit a doctor for them and he should go ahead and build a clinic for his use.

CHAPTER 38

Upon returning from old Earth, John immediately went to Bill Harding's house to relay the good news. Harding's first wife, Janet, was ecstatic about the possibility of having a doctor in Harding. She suggested they just build a shell structure for the clinic and let the new doctor decide how it should be finished out. The town council was overjoyed about the expected doctor and authorized the construction of a clinic next to the new town hall.

The council had interviewed over 600 prospective settlers and had accepted 560, after only a little over three months time. Jill Harding as town clerk had been kept busy scheduling their retrieval dates so that there would be no conflicts. Very few of these settlers had been retrieved so far as they were only taking what skills were needed in the construction phase.

At the present rate they should reach their goal of 1,500 settlers in another six months of recruiting. Normal birth rates should bring the town's population close to 2,000 people in another five years. The town council had continued to post sentries west of the farm operation and east of the dam project on the *Mick*. John had teleported several times east on the *Mick* trailhead to look for any activity along the north/south trail but failed to find any evidence of the enemy's movements. They seemed to be staying away from this area altogether and the trail itself appeared to have reverted to a game trail.

The council initially had decided to have most of the new construction spread out from the town center east, west, and southward, making sure they would allow enough room for the lake boundaries from the new dam. They were going to have to build several sewer retention ponds far enough away from the lake and the *Mick* so as not to adversely affect their water supply.

The workshop was dismantled and moved closer to the sawmill as its former location was needed to store materials and construction equipment, with a park planned there after everything was removed.

The chicken raising experiment was successful with the result that other families wanted to raise their own flocks. It wasn't long before almost all the old families had a small chicken operation in their back yards which yielded them eggs as well as meat for their tables.

The first town meeting inside the new town hall was held six months after the start of the dam construction. All permanent residents were allowed to participate in the discussions and the advisory teams were available to answer any questions. The townspeople were anxious to hear the status of the construction projects which happily were ahead of schedule.

The major water lines were in place and most of the houses had been connected; however, before the water could be turned on they had to be connected to a sewer system which had just been started. The dam project was about fifty percent complete and the decision to bury the power lines would add some extra time to the completion date.

John brought up the question of the town earning money to pay for items brought back from old Earth. "The seed money they had been receiving would eventually run out and they needed a source of new funds."

The farmers suggested they plant extra crops for resale which received some support from the townspeople.

Sam Williamson said, "The income from this source would probably only cover the farm expenses unless they could come up with a crop that would be in demand on old Earth."

They closed the meeting with a request for the townspeople to think about this problem and offer any suggestions to the town council. Before everyone left the meeting John introduced Dr. Samuel Gates, the town's new doctor who spoke to the townspeople.

"I've met quite a few of you already during the week I've been here but I'm having an open house and I want the community to come and check out your new medical clinic. As most of you are aware Janet Harding is going to remain and will be my strong right hand in running the clinic."

Dr. Gates had retired from medical practice the previous year and welcomed the chance to continue in Harding. The idea of being a country doctor appealed to him after spending the last twenty-five years in a large city hospital. He and his wife had no children or other ties to old Earth so the move here didn't leave any emotional ties behind for them.

The two other midwives would continue to help Janet in running the clinic, but the doctor would handle future births except in the rare instances when several births would occur at the same time. The town presently had thirty pregnant women, with ten women due to deliver within a month. Dr. Gates was quite pleased with the training Janet had given her two helpers especially the midwife experience Jenny had accumulated.

The doctor and Janet worked out a schedule where either Janet or one of the two other trained women would staff the clinic each day. In an emergency they would all report for duty. So far the only emergency they had experienced was an accident at the dam construction site where two workers were injured. One worker had some cuts that were treated and was able to return to work while the other had a broken arm. Dr. Gates splinted the arm and had John send him back to old Earth for proper treatment.

The construction foreman requested John send him back as well to recruit a replacement for the one being returned for medical treatment. John returned the two men and while the foreman made some telephone calls trying to arrange a replacement, he picked up his mail. Even though they had stopped placing the recruitment advertisement he was still receiving some mail.

John checked back at his office where the foreman said, "I'm waiting on the replacement to arrive here in about two hours."

John decided to spend this time to do some shopping for his wives and children that he had forgotten on his last trip. When he returned there were two young men plus the foreman waiting on him.

The foreman said the men were twin brothers and wouldn't work apart so he had hired them both. John asked them if they were ready to leave and when they nodded he teleported them and their baggage to Harding. The sudden shift from an indoor office to an outdoor setting near the dam site caused the brothers some disorientation but they quickly recovered.

They smiled at John as one of them commented, "Boy, that's the way to travel."

John told them he would take their baggage and leave it at their dorm then wished them well while they were here. When he returned home with his packages his wives greeted him with joy but it seemed to him that they were more interested on what he brought with him. When they opened the packages they started laughing as they pulled out swimwear for everyone.

Sarah held up a one-piece suit in front of herself and commented that it was much too small. John laughed and told her it was made of spandex material and would stretch to fit her body. She and his other wives looked at him doubtfully and decided to try the suits on.

He had gotten them each three suits of white, blue, and yellow. The suits were indeed form fitting and with the built in bras they showed off the women's fabulous figures to their best advantage. Sarah and Mary each wore the white suit that went well with their tans while Candice's dark skin really set off the yellow suit she wore.

When his wives posed for him, his mouth hung open in appreciation. His wives then laughed at his lustful expression as they teased him. He finally shook his head as he made a grab at Sarah.

"I think you women are more sexy with those suits on than when you were naked."

Sarah giggled as she sat in his lap and whispered in his ear, "Yes dear, but now we meet the moral requirements of old Earth."

Candice and Mary pulled the two lovers apart and with his wives pulling him, they all retired to John's bedroom where they released their pent-up sexual tensions. Later they had John try on his swimsuit so they could give him the same ogling treatment he had given them.

After donning their clothing they resumed looking at the suits for their children. He had gotten several sizes for the boys and Sadie while getting none for the smaller children. The women were upstairs having the children try on their swimsuits when Jenny entered the house. She looked around the room and finding John alone came over and kissed him on the cheek and asked, "Where are Sarah and the other mothers?"

John caught the impish glint in her eyes and blushed. "I brought them back new swimsuits and when they modeled them for me, things got out of hand. They're upstairs with the kids trying on suits."

She smiled her understanding and then rushed upstairs to see if she could borrow one of the suits for herself.

That evening the family went to their favorite swimming hole on the *Mick* and tried out the new swimsuits. The adults had great fun with how the suits enhanced their appearance, especially the women. However, the children thought it was a pain, especially the boys and it wasn't long before they had stripped off the constricting suits.

Jenny was wearing one of the blue swimsuits Sarah had given her that seemed to enhance her natural beauty and was causing Randy considerable trouble keeping his hands off his wife. He was wearing one of John's suits that showed off his heavily muscled physique. Jenny finally took his hand and led him into the water to cool off and where the children persuaded them to join in their water sports.

This was Mary's time to spend in John's bed and that night she confided her thoughts to him silently as she snuggled her petite form closer to his body. "I'm happier and more content now than at any other time in my life."

He had his arms around her as he kissed her. "I feel that way too. I can't believe how lucky I am to have such beautiful wives and children who love me."

Their love for each other consolidated into a hot, white passionate glow as they merged their personalities until breathless, they emerged still in a tight embrace. As their passion subsided, Mary snuggled even closer into his embrace and sighed her happiness.

CHAPTER 39

John was sitting with Sadie and John Jr., his first-born twins, who were now 17 years old. They had both developed into individuals any parent would be proud of. John Jr. didn't look anything like he had at that age. His son had gotten his height early and hard work had filled out his chest and arm muscles. His brown hair and his sense of purpose and humor came from his father, while his blue eyes and large boned frame came from his Nordic mother's genes. He had been working hard at obtaining the knowledge and experience to become a leader.

Sadie also had the Nordic look of her mother and was already a beautiful woman. She too had kept busy obtaining knowledge and skills that would benefit the community. Their ESP skills had developed in the last eight years and had now surpassed their parents.

Thinking of his children's strong powers he thought of Grace who was now almost twelve. She had her mother's beautiful looks and graceful way of moving even at such a young age. However, where Candice had been dark skinned, Grace was more a soft mocha color. She was the strongest of his children in her ESP abilities and had all the abilities of her brothers and sisters.

John Jr. and Sadie had each helped move the town's excess crops to old Earth to provide cash for any needed future purchases and learned how to deal with old Earth merchants in getting the best price for their products and for what they needed to purchase.

Sam Williamson and Sue Gates from the Idaho Agriculture School were two of four people from their group who elected to settle in

Harding. Sam and Sue had since married each other and were now the proud parents of a baby girl.

Likewise, four from the MIT group elected to settle in Harding and included Joe and Denise Edwards who now had two children – both boys, who were the love of their lives.

The town had grown and was now approaching a population of 2,200. The dam project was successful and provided uninterrupted power for the town's needs and recreation for the townspeople on its lake.

Now that the townspeople had indoor plumbing and electricity in their homes they soon began craving other luxuries of life. However, due to the limited amount of funds available to the townspeople they soon began to invent ways of getting what they wanted. Some of the women were great quilters, and with the help of Sadie's bargaining skills, they were able to earn their own money to buy what they wanted.

Sam Williamson had been experimenting with a new variety of grape that flourished in Harding's climate and with the help of two new settlers who had winery skills; they attempted to make wine for resale on old Earth. The first batch had aged four years in large oak casks when they had their first taste. The local experts raved about its unique flavor so John decided to ask Joe and Denise's parents if they would be interested in marketing the wine for them.

John, Joe, and Denise had taken two cases of the wine to them for their approval and advice. The two sets of parents were ecstatic over the wine's flavor and wanted to know how much they had to sell. When told that this was only the first experimental batch of about 400 cases, they were disappointed but said they could sell everything they produced. The small volume would even serve to bring a better price for the wine.

The second year's production was slightly larger than the first year's, and according to old Earth response was an even better seller. The winery had to increase its storage capacity ten-fold to handle the increased production and the land clearing for grape production had provided much of the lumber needed in the business and house construction. The Harding bank account was now bulging with their share of the profits that promised to be the answer to their financial prayers as they were now able to start repaying the seed money.

The various farming operations now occupied almost half the town's population. The dairy and beef production was now large enough to support the townspeople's needs and had spawned the side industries of milk processing, butter production, and meat processing. The truck farming of various vegetables resulted in a canning plant to provide food for export and storage facilities for grain, both of which would be sold to old Earth.

The central square now had a bakery, medical clinic, dentist, school, and a dairy and meat outlet for the townspeople. The center of the square was now a park with a statue of William Harding, the town's founder, who had died two years ago from a massive stroke. However, before his death, he had been able to see the town take shape and prosper.

John remembered talking to him about the town's future and Harding's visualization of mankind eventually spreading across the land until they again reached the Pacific. John had served three four-year terms as the town's mayor and had decided not to run at the last election. Jack Peterson was elected and was doing a fine job.

Sadie jabbed her elbow in John's ribs, interrupting his thoughts. "Dad, that's old news! We've got Harding safely settled now. Why don't we head out there in the wilderness and start another settlement?"

John looked at his daughter in surprise, then smiled. "You've got the wanderlust, do you now? Don't you want to get a husband before we leave since there won't be any other men where we're going?"

She looked at him suspiciously. "You know about Jerry, don't you?" She said accusingly.

John nodded his head and then looked at his son questioningly. "How about you? Are you and Betty planning on getting married?"

Sadie and John Jr. looked at each other in surprise then smiled in defeat.

John looked at them for a moment. "Did you really think you could hide anything from your mothers. They've known about your lovers ever since you became serious. How about your brothers and sisters; do they want to go exploring too?"

Sadie smiled as she said, "Are you kidding? They've been brought up on stories of your adventures and are ready to experience their own. We know that you've been bored now that the town's challenge to survive is over so why not make some new experiences."

John hugged his two first born as he shook his head. "You've forgotten about your mothers. Don't you think they'd rather stay in civilization rather than fight the wilderness and the Mutants again?"

Sadie looked at him with a smug expression. "Why don't you ask them and see what they say?"

When they got back to their home, the family was waiting for them in the common room. John looked at them in surprise then looked back at Sadie accusingly.

"You kids set me up, didn't you?"

Sarah and his other wives laughed at his surprised expression. Sarah told him to sit down and they would discuss this idea of leaving the settlement. Both Candice and Mary had given birth to another set of twins who were now four and five years of age and were the youngest of his children and Jenny's youngest child was now six years old.

Sarah pointed to the children. "The kids are now old enough to travel and my sister wives and I are ready to try something new."

John had a sudden thought. "I think everyone has forgotten something. If we all leave, there won't be anyone to teleport items to and from old Earth and offer ESP protection from the Mutants."

Sarah looked proudly at her son as she offered a solution. "John Jr. has indicated that he's willing to stay behind and perform those duties."

John looked at his son questioningly as he asked, "Are you sure of this?"

"I've already discussed this move with Betty and she doesn't want to leave Harding. She's made friends here and is afraid of leaving the safety of the town, so I guess I'm the logical choice to stay if I'm going to marry her. Besides, Joyce wants to stay with me until you find a new location. She feels she's too old to walk that far but she definitely wants you to return for her."

John turned to his family with tears of happiness in his eyes. "Well, I guess you've figured it all out. It means that we will have to experience hardships again and will miss the soft living we've had these past few years. But, we now have powers that will keep us safe from the Mutants and we can still teleport back to old Earth for pampering from time to time and even back to Harding to check out John Jr. and his family."

Sarah smiled as she agreed. "Yes, I'll want to see my son and grandchildren when they arrive. However, I think we all miss the closeness we had when we were on our own, fighting for our lives. We were really alive then and not just marking time."

John asked Randy and Jenny if they wanted to join them as well.

Randy placed his arm around his wife and nodded his head. "We both decided that's where our future was and we wouldn't be happy being left behind."

"How about Lillie and her family?" He asked Sarah.

"Why don't you ask them?" She said as Lillie and her family entered the house.

George Anderson spoke for his family. "We discussed this among ourselves and finally came to the conclusion that we didn't want to remain here by ourselves. Our family ties are too close knit not to go with you. Besides it should be a big adventure for us all."

The next day John informed the town council of his decision to take his and the Anderson family out into the wilderness and establish another settlement. He wanted the council to hold a town meeting to see if any others wished to join his group.

That evening at the town meeting John explained his own wanderlust and desire to set out to establish another settlement. He explained that John Jr. would remain behind to provide ESP support for the town and then asked if any others wished to join his group. There was much discussion among the townspeople, especially those original settlers who knew of John's leadership in the defense of Harding from the enemy.

John finally held up his hand for quiet. "Why don't you all go home and discuss this among yourselves and let me know before we leave next week."

The townspeople broke up into their family groups as they headed toward their homes, still discussing the ramifications of John's decision to leave Harding. The next day Kit Campbell stopped by to see John about his plans and after several hours of discussion Kit asked to have his family included in the move.

The Campbell family was the second largest family in Harding behind the Bridges family. Kit Campbell also had three wives and seven children still in the home. His two oldest daughters, Honor and Janet, had married new settlers and had children of their own now.

Much to John's delight, Jacob Bell and his family also decided to join the group. Jacob had two wives and two children from his second wife. Jacob's previous occupation as a college Professor, teaching chemistry and geology, was instrumental in getting the town out of the Stone Age.

Sadie and John Jr. wanted to have a double wedding before they left Harding so they set the evening two days before their departure as the wedding date. Sadie's mothers had double duty now getting ready for the wedding and preparing for their departure but they seemed joyful at the prospect.

Jerry Gleason's parents were not happy about their oldest son's eminent departure into the wilderness but they realized their future daughter-in-law's ESP powers would protect him from most of the dangers they might encounter.

Betty Wilson's parents loved their future son-in-law and were relieved he was staying behind. Betty was a strong willed daughter and they thought that John Junior's strength of character was what was needed to keep her in line although Sarah secretly had her doubts.

John decided to travel light taking only some dried meat for food. They still had the packs and water containers from their initial journey from Missouri and would wear their old animal skin clothing. The other families joining them made similar plans and made their own backpacks from animal skins with slots for water containers made from wine bottles.

Each departing family placed all the items they wanted to later retrieve in a separate large container which would be stored in John's house until he returned for them.

The day the families left Harding, most of the townspeople were present to wish them well and make their final farewells. It was a heartbreaking departure for many of the townspeople as strong friendships had been forged in blood.

It was difficult for the Bridges Clan to leave two of their members behind, especially for John and Sarah as they hugged and kissed John Jr. who was remaining in Harding. Joyce, Candice's mother, received even more heart-rending goodbyes from the children even though she planned on joining them later. John Jr. promised to remain in mind contact with them daily through Grace who didn't seem to have a distance limit on her telepathy ability. If they needed him he was only a thought away.

When they left the town square, it was a long procession as the six families included forty-nine adults and children, all were the families with multiple wives. This was a larger contingent than those starting the original Harding settlement. They had also brought along several guard and hunting dogs to help them in their journey.

Grace used her unique ESP ability to determine if there were any nearby Mutants before they left Harding heading west along the *Mick*. Kit Campbell who had been John's chief scout when they were fighting the Mutants, took the lead along with his oldest son and daughter. John stopped and looked back wistfully at what they were leaving behind for a moment, before he turned and hurried to join the others.

The End and a New Beginning

ABOUT THE AUTHOR

Hugh A. Flowers retired after almost thirty years with the Federal Deposit Insurance Corporation as a bank examiner. He now spends his time reading and writing novels and short stories and traveling the world.

OTHER PUBLICATIONS BY FLOWERS

The Salvation Trilogy, Oklahoma Tomboy, and Project Inception are also books written by Hugh.

www.ingramcontent.com/pod-product-compliance
Lightning Source LLC
Chambersburg PA
CBHW051416170626
46809CB00006B/2187